Other Tor books by Andre Norton

The Crystal Gryphon
Dare To Go A-Hunting
Flight in Yiktor
Forerunner
Forerunner: The Second Venture
Gryphon's Eyrie (with A. C. Crispin)
Here Abide Monsters
House of Shadows (with Phyllis Miller)
Moon Called
Moon Mirror
The Prince Commands
Ralestone Luck
Stand and Deliver
Wheel of Stars
Wizards' Worlds

THE WITCH WORLD (editor)

Tales of the Witch World 1
Tales of the Witch World 2
Four from the Witch World

MAGIC IN ITHKAR (editor, with Robert Adams)

Magic in Ithkar 1
Magic in Ithkar 2
Magic in Ithkar 3
Magic in Ithkar 4

Other Tor books by Susan Shwartz

Heritage of Flight
Moonsinger's Friends (editor)
Silk Roads and Shadows
White Wing (writing with S. N. Lewitt
    as "Gordon Kendall")

IMPERIAL LADY

A Fantasy of Han China

=

ANDRE NORTON
AND
SUSAN SHWARTZ

TOR
fantasy

A TOM DOHERTY ASSOCIATES BOOK
NEW YORK

IMPERIAL LADY: A FANTASY OF HAN CHINA

Copyright © 1989 by Andre Norton and Susan Shwartz

A Tor Book
Published by Tom Doherty Associates, Inc.
49 West 24th Street
New York, N.Y. 10010

Cover art by Royo

ISBN: 0-812-50722-3

First edition: August 1989
First mass market printing: May 1990

Printed in the United States of America

0 9 8 7 6 5 4 3 2 1

ACKNOWLEDGMENTS

Selections of poetry that appear throughout this book are taken from more than a thousand years of Chinese verse. They have been drawn from two principal sources:

The Orchid Boat: Woman Poets of China, edited and translated by Kennoth Rexroth and Ling Chung. New York: McGraw-Hill, 1972. Selections include part of the "Lament of Hsi-chun," (110 B.C.) and the "Poem Written on a Floating Red Leaf" (ninth century A.D.) of Ts-ui-p'in. All rights reserved. Used with permission. Copyright © Harcourt Brace Jovanovich.

Translations From the Chinese, by Arthur Waley. New York: Alfred A. Knopf, 1941. Selections drawn from a T'ang dynasty poem; Wu-ti's poems on Li Fu-jen; and from "The Prisoner." All rights reserved. Used with permission.

CHAPTER

= 1 =

Vivid bronze and green against the slanting rays of the winter sun, the pheasant darted up from its cover in a flurry of snow. Just as swiftly, Lady Silver Snow raised her bow of wood and horn, released an arrow. The heavy bird dropped into the underbrush. She nodded, and one of her escort rode off to retrieve it.

"An excellent shot, most worthy lady!" cried the old trooper Ao Li, his voice as bluff as if he spoke to a recruit. "Not even the women of the Hsiung-nu . . . this one humbly begs your forgiveness. The women of the Hsiung-nu are harsh, ill-spoken, but the thrice-worthy lady . . ." His words trailed off, and his weathered face flushed with mortification.

None of the others cheered her, as they might one of their fellows. Old soldiers all, they had campaigned with her father, and now, close to the borders of their ancient enemies, the Hsiung-nu, they guarded her.

Even as Silver Snow held up an imperious hand, Ao Li flung himself from the saddle to her feet in abject shame, yes, and fear of his general who, disgraced and enfeebled though he might be, was still master in his own house.

Lady Silver Snow turned, her gloved hands so quick upon the reins of her shaggy northern pony that it almost reared. Snow cascaded from its coarse mane and pelt.

"Rise, please," she commanded, smiling at him to excuse what he believed as a grave fault. "How should I be offended?" she asked. "Your words honor my lord and father, who taught me. Have I not always heard that the women of those beyond the Purple Wall hear the language of birds and can even gather meaning from creaks of stones and wood, while the most powerful among them even hear the shadow language of the untimely dead calling from their graves?"

Her breath steamed, a pale mist against a white jade sky, and her feet, in stitched boots of heavy felt, tingled from the cold; but her cheeks burned as crimson as the blood of the fowl that Ao Li scooped up and tied to the board of his saddle, wrought according to the fashion of the Hsiung-nu, who, barbarians though they were, without a doubt were also mounted warriors beyond compare.

Even as she gravely commended the old guard's skill in tracking and appraised the plumpness of the pheasant that her bow, lighter and more supple than those of the steppes, had brought down, she blinked away tears of grief and of anger at herself. She was ungrateful. The Son of Heaven might well have executed her father's entire household for treason; for, if its head turned to evil, how could anyone ever trust the body?

Thus far, however, they lived; she and her father; lived and even, after a fashion, had been content. At times, she could even forget that they lived, existing solely upon a whim, which even a cup of heated wine could change to death.

A horncall rang out, followed by a cry, so shockingly loud that Silver Snow expected to hear the crystalline snap of icicles falling from trees. It brought Ao Li around, one age-spotted hand snatching at his swordhilt, the other pulling at his pony's reins. His mount whinnied a protest as he forced it between his general's daughter, whom he had sworn to protect with his life and soul, and this intruder.

She saw, before she felt, Ao Li's apologetic touch to her horse's harness.

"Lady," he dared to whisper.

Behind her, men strung bows and drew swords. Silver

Snow shivered, despite the warmth of her sheepskins. They had ridden out far today; had the Hsiung-nu seen them and decided to attack?

She turned to follow Ao Li's pointing finger. Though she had always thought him fearless, his scarred hand was trembling now.

Silver Snow nocked her bow with even greater speed than she had used when she brought down the pheasant. She groaned inwardly and stole a longing glance at the gleaming, curved spine of the Great Wall. It might, she thought as her heart froze and sank within her, be the last thing that she would ever see. Beyond it lay plains and freedom of a sort—as her father had no doubt discovered during his years of exile. Perhaps he should have stayed there, unfilial and ungrateful wretch though she was for daring even to harbor such a thought. For conquered and disgraced though he was, his choice of surrender rather than massacre caused the downfall of ministers in shining Ch'ang-an. He had remained with his captors for ten years as had the deplorable Li Ling, general and traitor. Like General Chang Ch'ien, who had lived among the Hsiung-nu, wed and even bred among them, yet, in time, he too had fled back to the land of the Han.

Now, riding toward her on a sweating, steaming horse, came such a messenger as she had feared for ten years. What if he came from Ch'ang-an, the capital, where the Sun of Heaven sat in glory on the Dragon Throne and voiced his edicts against those houses he perceived as traitorous? Perhaps this messenger had already delivered the scarlet cord to her father and rode now to order her also to take her own life. Did Chao Kuang's body now hang cooling on a tree, or lie contorted by poison, or bleeding from a swordcut? She would not survive him long, she vowed; and that choice was not dictated by the will of the Son of Heaven, either.

Despite the iron control in which she had early been schooled—first as a child growing up in a sad, poverty-stricken inner court, then as a girl raised by a grim, injured father—one tear streaked down her cheek, hot, but rapidly cooling. She forced herself back to a hunter's stillness as she stared out across the border between Ch'in and the steppes. Guardian of Ch'in since the reign of the First Emperor, the Great Wall curled about the land like a sleeping dragon. That ridge of stone and rammed earth rising grimly above the plain showed pale now, silvered over with fresh drifts and wind-blown gusts of the translucent snow from which, before she had died of sorrow and solitude, Lady Silver Snow's mother had named her child. Nor had the lady any living brothers. Sons of a senior wife, those all had died on the frontier, hoping to expiate their father's sin. For he had been a marquis and general who had failed the Son of Heaven's trust. Not only had he surrendered the bleeding remnants of an army of Han warriors to the barbarians, but, having done so, he had dared to remain alive.

Ao Li gestured sharply, sending the others riding out to flank her, their instant response possible because all of her pro-tectors had campaigned together since before she was born. Silver Snow glanced at the old man, then quickly away. His entire life had been governed by the code of military obe-dience. Would he really dare to order an attack upon a messen-ger from the Son of Heaven? Could she, her father's daughter, draw bow upon such a man?

She parted trembling lips and swallowed, nerving herself to order Ao Li to hold off. Then, she gasped. Her eyes were younger, quicker than those of the troop leader, despite the way that tears of thankfulness now blurred them when she perceived that the rider whose steaming horse slid and stum-bled up the track wore the shabby livery of her father's men.

She flung out a hand and touched Ao Li's, and the old man recoiled as if he had brushed a coal. "A friend," she mur-mured, and reined somewhat farther behind her escort, don-ning proper female shyness like an extra fur cloak.

The rider would have left saddle to kneel when a growl from Ao Li stopped him. Very young, the boy dared to glance up at her only for an instant. Then he had lowered his eyes to the snowy ground, offering her more the homage due an Empress or a marquis' first wife, not properly to be given the shabby and unbetrothed virago daughter of a disgraced soldier.

As winded as his horse from the speed of their coming, the messenger gasped harsh lungfuls of the thin, cold air, then coughed until Silver Snow flinched and vowed silently that that very night, she and her maid Willow must brew herbs against lung-fever. "A . . . a proclamation . . . an edict from the Son of Heaven . . ." He prostrated himself until Silver Snow could scarcely hear the words that he forced out between coughs. "Your most-honored father the general summons . . ."

"We ride!" The way Silver Snow's clear voice carried shocked her, as she turned her back on the Wall, leaving behind the bloodstained snow on which, so briefly, the trophies of her hunt had rested.

This day, Silver Snow and her guards had ridden far in search of game. Even as she pressed her horse for greater speed, she reproached herself. If a messenger from the Son of Heaven guested in her home, she, as lady there, should have been present to ensure that all was done as best as possible to honor the Emperor's man and to demonstrate that, Northerners though they might be, they served the Dragon Throne with loyal hearts.

If, however, she had remained ever dutifully at home, she thought, the official from Ch'ang-an might have had to dine off scraps. It was well that their hunt had been successful; the few aging women left in the inner courts would be able to prepare a feast that might not be too unworthy of his tasting.

Who knew, she thought with another quick jolt of alarm, what guards such a southern lord might have dispatched on his own orders? Even now such men might be watching her. She had been scanning the land about her for enemies, but now she cast down her eyes. With a guest from the capital at her father's estate, she must remember to observe all the proprieties, even this far from her home.

A watcher, she knew, might ascribe such a withdrawal to

the most decorous modesty, appropriate to an unwed maid. What words would either her Ancestors or the Book of Rites use to describe a maid who flouted proper conduct and even endangered virginity itself to ride out with a bow and hunt like a wild boy? Though the hardships of her life had made her break with customs, she knew she had much to answer for. But the Ancestors might frown at her reply, she told herself in an unusually rebellious, therefore candid, instant.

This unseen, unknown official might dare to criticize; however, thanks to her, he would eat tonight: and—what was far more to her liking—so would her father, her household, and these her outriders, whose saddles and horses' flanks all bore the bloody traces of successful hunting; that thereby the Ancestors would continue to be honored.

Those would not be so served by Silver Snow herself. As a daughter, she might not burn incense and paper images at their shrine to summon their august attention. They might only be attended by her father himself, too crippled now by years in the saddle and old wounds to ride out to hunt; but hale enough to teach his surviving child to take up the bow in his stead, to play chess, and to think and want to act in a manner that she knew full well that Master Confucius—much as she and her father venerated his *Li Chi*, or Book of Rites, and his Analects in all other ways—would not have at all approved.

Indeed, Chao Kuang's First Wife had chosen to hang herself rather than live, shamed and degraded after it was decreed that the general was general and marquis no longer. Her sons, Silver Snow's thrice-honored brothers, had ridden out to die in battle against Khujanga, *shan-yu* of the western hosts. Autumn Smoke, the second wife, and heavy with child when the news of her lord's capture and seeming defection had come from Ch'ang-an with the decree of their disgrace, had remained alive in the hope of bearing a son whose piety might, one day, redeem what the father had lost. At Silver Snow's birth, however, she had lost hope and life, and left her daughter with a name as melancholy as her own. Such a child might well have been exposed; but, through the love of her mother's old nurse, she was saved and raised; and, somehow, she throve.

When she was ten years old—past the age when a gently reared maid should be confined to the women's quarters, never to leave them until she was borne to her wedding—her father escaped the Hsiung-nu. Rumor, which traveled faster than he, credited him with the abandonment of a wife (if such as the Hsiung-nu recognized that basic human tie) and baby son, causing fears, in the shabby, chilly women's quarters, for even the restricted life that had been Silver Snow's up to that moment. How would the most noble (though, by the Emperor's decree, he was that no longer) marquis and general Chao Kuang react to the news that he had a daughter and no living sons at all?

With many head-shakings and warnings, her nurse had presented Silver Snow to him. Even now, as she recalled, it had been a heaven-sent miracle that she had not burst into frightened sobs: her father seemed more like an Ancestor come to uncertain life than a man. For all of a man's proper, vigorous semblance had fallen from him. His beard and hair, beneath a sober cap, were silvered, while the ample folds of an ancient, frayed silk robe, with its heavy, though cracking, fur collar and lining, sagged inward because of their wearer's painful thinness.

Even more painful than that loss of flesh and vigor was the limp that must have made the mad escape from the West a torture worse than any that an Emperor's officials might inflict. In full sight an ebony cane lay near to his hand, beside a silken scroll of Master Confucius' writings and the bronze burner wrought in the form of twelve mountain peaks, inlaid with precious metals and carnelian, a treasure of the house. From the burner wafted delicate trails of the piney scent of artemesia; ever afterward in Silver Snow's mind, she linked those gnarled and enduring pines with her father and his ordeals.

Even now, as Silver Snow held up one chilled hand and

breathed upon it, she recalled the warmth and fragrance from that burner. Then, it had been her one comfort as she had approached, barely moving her feet warily, one short step following another, her eyes downcast, toward the man who sat upright despite the padded cushions at his back, as if mistrustful of their softness. At that moment, as if decreed by kindly gods, sparks had flown from the brazier, and Silver Snow, her painstaking humility forgotten, looked up to meet eyes that immediately compelled her love and trust as they had the right to compel her obedience. Her father extended a hand—thin, weathered, and missing a finger—and she had run to him.

Thereafter, all thoughts of proper reticence and distance were dispatched: Silver Snow, at age ten, was to be raised as the son whom her father now lacked: to be taught to hunt, to play chess, to sing, and—the most audacious of all—to read and to write poetry.

So, they continued to live in the North, close by the Great Wall. Traditionally, there had lain their family's estates since the mist-enshrouded reigns of the Five Emperors; but traditionally, too, there also languished now other exiles, those laboring under the disgrace of a condemnation to life.

The North might be thought to be exile, but Silver Snow had always loved the severe beauty of her homeland, the vast sweep of plains, broken by the protection of the Wall and the less ancient but equally weathered shelter of her ancestral home. Now the feeble rays of late afternoon sun slanted across the Wall, awakening splendor from the ice and snow upon which her horse and those of her escort cast long violent shadows.

A greater shadow, to her way of thinking, lay upon her mind, cast by the Wall upon which she had turned her back as she hastened home to obey whatever orders the Son of Heaven, after ten years of silence, had sent them. What her father had told her of the Hsiung-nu made Silver Snow stare out across the great barrier with more curiosity than fear. She knew that beyond lay more than endless wasteland possessed by unholy savages who ate their meat raw, never bathed, and tortured civilized men. Aye, beyond the Wall lay vast spaces and open air—as well as freedom and her father's lost honor.

By the time Lady Silver Snow reached the ancient half fort, half mansion (the aged archers in its watchtower nodding as her party swept by in a cloud of snow and breath-steam), the cold was pushing her to full effort just as much as the desire to obey her father and to hear whatever news had caused this youngest of his retainers to risk death to horse and rider in such haste to summon her back. Shaking from cold and excitement, she turned the last corner—past the empty space from which, mysteriously, a jade statue had disappeared last winter, past that wall where a painting had been fading for at least two generations—to reach at last her own tiny courtyard. Here, screens and walls barred the clamor that must surely erupt afresh in the rest of the household at her return.

Her nurse seized upon Silver Snow, with hands that had the texture of a chicken's feet and the strength that apprehension lends old age, to tug her toward the innermost room where a fire, steaming water, and robes, which might be shabby but were, most assuredly, warm and scrupulously clean, awaited.

However, when the old woman would have undressed her, Silver Snow forestalled that. "Old mother, this service"—*and this speed*, she thought—"is too much for you. Where is my maid Willow?"

"She is out *there*." The woman pointed toward the courtyard. Despite a careful arrangement of faded screens, the opened door admitted a chilling draft and a glimpse of an evening sky that had turned as violet as a first concubine's spring robes.

The nurse made a sign against ill-luck. Had the old woman not been ancient, almost a grandmother to Silver Snow, she might have slapped her.

"Your mistrust is foolishness," she did contrive a faint reproof. "For ten years, ever since my father bought her, Willow has given me devoted loyalty and perfect service."

The old woman bowed—her hands laden with Silver Snow's heavy, padded, and befurred coat—and muttered something, undoubtedly the usual rumor, about Willow.

"More foolishness," said Silver Snow. "Old women's tales. Why should the girl turn against the house that saved her life?" She tested the bath with a finger. "That water looks too cold. Fetch a kettle more of hot, then leave me alone."

Unused to her nurseling's recent adoption of the manners of a grand lady, the woman bowed and fled. Her numbed fingers prickling as blood and warmth returned to them, Silver Snow fumbled with the fastenings of her robes as she padded toward her maidservant. Just outside the screen, Willow knelt, oblivious, as it seemed, to the cold. Even the meager light from the fire and the one or two lamps that burned, thriftily distant from the windy courtyard, struck ruddy splendor from Willow's long hair, the same color as the vixen with which she now seemed to chatter at in little whines and sharp barks, much as stablemen communicated with horses and children with pets of all types. A scrap of meat saved from Willow's dinner lay on the ground.

Trained as a huntress, Silver Snow knew how to stalk silently in her heavy felt boots. Fox and maidservant alike heard her though, and froze as might hunted beasts. Willow turned to face her, and fear flashed across her face, gleamed in the eerie green eyes that, as much as her reddish hair, caused the dark-haired, dark-eyed Han to condemn her as supernaturally ugly, the very semblance of one of the dreaded fox-spirits—a prejudice that Silver Snow, usually the most indulgent of mistresses, had always condemned severely.

"Younger sister, gain what news you may, but finish quickly. I have need of you." Silver Snow spoke softly and with a smile, but her voice was firm.

As if they actually could understand one another, Willow and the fox traded whines. Then the vixen barked once, sniffed the air, snapped up the meat, and ran off. Slowly, clumsily, Willow rose, her green eyes never leaving the spot where the fox vanished into the darkness. Then she limped over to attend her mistress.

"Had you not been born with a clubbed foot," Silver Snow murmured more to herself than to the girl, "would you have stayed with me, or would you have wished, just as the rumors whisper, to change your own skin and run away with your sister-in-fur?"

She thought that she had spoken too softly for anyone to hear her, but she had not reckoned on the night wind's betrayal or the preternatural keenness of Willow's hearing. The maid gently loosened Silver Snow's fingers from the fastenings of her robes. Her own hands were warm, hot even; another fault that the other servants held against her, for all knew that the blood of foxes—and of fox-spirits—is kindled to a higher degree than that of ordinary women. Such nonsense, coupled with Willow's red hair and her skill with small, wild creatures, had almost gotten her killed before Silver Snow's father purchased her. Since then, she had served the house devotedly; and, as always, Silver Snow relaxed beneath the deft, warm touch of her maid's hands.

Tears spotted the fur of Silver Snow's outer robe.

"When your father bought me to be your maid, he saved me from being killed out of hand as a fox or, later, as a slaver's cull. How shall I ever leave you—even were I unblemished and able to run with the sisters-in-fur—when I owe you my very life?" Willow asked. "Though," she added, her eyes glinting with some unspoken emotion, "it may be you who leaves me."

As quickly as her tears had flowed, they dried. Limping, Willow urged her mistress across the room. They might well have been heartbound sisters rather than mistress and maid. Willow, Silver Snow thought as she always did, simply could not be a fox-spirit, since, as all knew, fox-spirits could not love, teasing spitefully behind pretenses of caring.

"I leave you?" Silver Snow asked. She breathed deeply to subdue an awakening excitement. One must, she knew, summon *li* and *chih*—the attributes of propriety and wisdom that Master Confucius decreed were necessary if one were to attain *chung yung*, the serene and undeviating behavior that every decent person surely must wish for her own—though those proper thoughts were now difficult to heed. She must hasten to obey her father's summons, that was true; yet she could not hurry into his presence as if one were improperly lessoned in the august way of *li*.

"You might," Willow said, long lashes veiling those green eyes that seemed ever to be alive with a shadow of mischief. Were she indeed a usual inhabitant of inner courts, she should be uncomfortable at Willow's presence. Yet, from the instant that they had seen one another, they had been as sisters.

"Your most honorable father received messengers from Ch'ang-an today." Willow unfastened the heavy, divided riding skirt from around her mistress' thin body.

Silver Snow nodded, then stepped into the herb-strewn water of the bath. At least, their hunt had provided the best part of a proper feast. She must bathe and dress quickly, quickly, then hasten to the kitchens and the banqueting room to see that all was prepared with the propriety worthy of a marquis—even a degraded one.

"They brought a proclamation," Willow was continuing.

"That much I guessed," said Silver Snow. She patted the hot water on her wind-dried face as Willow proffered fragrant oils. This must indeed be a most special occasion if Willow and her old nurse had agreed to use some of the carefully hoarded perfumes from her mother's day. Refreshed and relaxed, she asked, "How do you know more?"

"From my sister," whispered Willow. Her smile betrayed white teeth, and she gave a quick motion of head and neck. For an instant, she looked very much like the beast with whom, earlier, she had entertained herself outside the chamber door. Silver Snow stood, and Willow wrapped her in a warm robe. There was no need to fear Willow, not ever. If the girl could turn rumor into a pleasantry to make her mistress smile, that but increased her merit. If she were unusually clever at making friends with animals, what of it? Such a talent was a gift.

Silver Snow herself, when riding out, was aware of small creatures that appeared to watch her curiously. In return, she was careful about what—or whom—she hunted.

"What did your sister tell you?" Silver Snow turned again, humoring Willow, as the maid combed out her long, black hair, as straight and fine in the lamplight as Willow's was red and waving. She gazed into the mirror that Willow held for her, a highly polished disk of silver, incised along the edge with wishes for good luck. This burnished moon disk was the one thing from Willow's previous life that she had brought to Silver Snow's home; rightly, she treasured it.

For a moment, the room behind her—small, shabby, but familiar and much-loved—wavered, engulfed in a brief vision of vast spaces and felt tents; there followed a rush of wind that drowned out the small, daily sounds of women working among women. Then she blinked and saw, once again, a lady of the Han with creamy skin, large, deep-set eyes the shape of almonds, brows that needed no plucking to shape them into moth wings, a tiny mouth. She shook her head, unpleasantly surprised at what she brusquely dismissed as unfitting vanity.

"We have heard"—Willow slipped the mirror once more into its protective silken bag—"that the Son of Heaven's beloved First Concubine died in childbed."

Silver Snow nodded as she dressed cautiously, fearing each time she wore the thin, ancient silk garments that she would tear them beyond any mending. Even this far to the north, the nobles had mourned that much-honored lady, who had been so brave that once, when a tiger had gotten loose, she had stepped before the Emperor until the beast could be lured again into its cage, saying to all that his life was more precious than hers, which was at his service.

"Did not the fur merchant who came last moon," Willow continued, "say that during the Son of Heaven's mourning, he returned all of his other ladies to their homes? Though all of the ministers and poets praised the depth of his mourning thus, it was a hardship for the tradespeople when the silks and furs could no longer be offered to those behind the Phoenix screens."

It is a truth, thought Silver Snow, that with no ladies to buy silk, to demand gems and embroideries and delicate foods, those supplying such would suffer. How not? But I myself am poor, she thought. What is strange about poverty? Surely a right-acting man need not suffer at heart, even though his rice bowl is near empty. Confucius had much to say about that, she knew. Did not her father's serenity, despite wounds and captivity, even in poverty and disgrace, prove the rightness of such acceptance?

"Did you know," Willow breathed slyly into an ear that Silver Snow's mirror assured her was as rosy and delicate as the rare shells from the far-off sea, "that the Son of Heaven wrote a poem about his lady before he summoned his wizards?"

A single bracelet of old white jade clicked against the lacquer chest before which Silver Snow sat. That thought brought more shivers than a winter wind. "The Emperor summoned wizards?" she breathed. "More quickly! Already I have tarried too long in obeying my father."

"Your pardon, Elder Sister," said Willow, "but I would rather err by tarrying than have you sicken in your lungs. My sister-in-fur's fifth cousin"—again, Willow smiled and flashed that uncanny impression of a beast at her mistress—"sat outside the Emperor's court in Ch'ang-an, and thus she heard him speak:

> *The sound of her silk skirt has stopped.*
> *On the marble pavement, dust grows.*
> *Her empty room is cold and still.*
> *Fallen leaves are piled against the doors.*
> > *Longing for that lovely lady,*
> *How can I bring my aching heart to rest?'"*

Silver Snow joined Willow in a heart-felt sigh. "Most beautiful," she breathed, "and so melancholy. But why did he then summon wizards?"

"To call her back." One of Willow's russet, level brows—an imperfection that no Emperor would have permitted among his ladies, but one that gave Willow a curiously trustworthy appearance—quirked, as if she had her own opinion of such wizards and such doings. "What they mumble is mostly foolishness. The Tao goes as it goes; and we, man and beast, are born and we die. Yet, the Son of Heaven is all-wise; so he summoned his wizards, who strove mightily—for men who dabble in such things. Finally, just one wizard produced a shadow . . . the merest flicker . . . against a silken hanging.

"Then the Son of Heaven wept and cried out:

> *'Is it or isn't it?*
> *I stand and look.*
> *The swish, swish of a silk skirt.*
> *How slowly she comes!'* "

"My honored father will say worse than that of me, should I delay longer," cried Silver Snow. "Are you finished with my hair, or are you not? And will you hold me here longer, you slothful girl, listening to silly news you claim to snatch from the mouths of foxes?"

Willow laughed, exposing white teeth as she threw back her head, showing her strong throat, as white as a fur blaze on a fox's chest. "Here, Elder Sister, is my most important news. After numerous tears, even more numerous verses, and more memorials than anyone would care to reckon, the Son of Heaven has agreed to choose another Illustrious Concubine, and perhaps even more than one."

Silver Snow's hand went to her throat. "But I am the child of a disgraced . . ." Then she drew a deep, shaky breath. "Oh, but what could I not do were I to become a favorite! What could I *not* do for my father? A grant of favor, his titles and honor restored, perhaps . . ." Her thoughts took wings and flew as high as the moon overhead where, surely, the lady who lived in that orb saw them and smiled. "Do you think . . ."

"I think," Willow interrupted, "that many other ladies dream such dreams tonight. However, what a mirror, mine especially, has shown you is truth. You are very fair, Elder Sister. However, the Hall of Brilliance will be filled with the fairest ladies of the Middle Kingdom. And many of them will have gems and garments that outshine you as much as your eyes outshine mine own.

"Lady," Willow continued more gravely, "the messenger arrived, the messenger spoke with your father, and you have been summoned. That is all, I tell you with all my heart, that I know to be so. Go you, to find out the rest."

Abruptly Silver Snow's eyes flashed, and though fear gripped her, she forced a laugh. "I hear and obey, at once, *Elder* Sister," she told Willow as she made for her father's study.

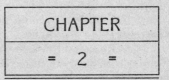

CHAPTER

= 2 =

As Silver Snow sped across the frosty courtyard she was grateful for the weight of her robes: the silk underrobe with its high, modest satin collar, falling to a hem that covered even the tips of her slippers; and the overrobe with the long sleeves that tumbled over her hands, trapping some warmth within—along with the fingers that such robes were devised to render useless. The ritualized clamor of hospitality rang in the night air. Though she herself might never see the official who had brought the Emperor's edicts to her father, she must later supervise from behind the screens the banquet her father would give later that night for their entertainment.

The stream designed to flow into a pool within her father's courtyard was stilled and frozen. Gnarled pines leaned over it to shed their dark, fragrant needles onto snow shining silver in the lamplight from her father's room. As much to guard herself from tripping over her flowing robes as to achieve the demure shuffling gait that the Book of Rites prescribed for maidens, she slowed as she climbed the slippery wooden steps. By the carved doorposts of her father's study, she paused, astonished.

The familiar and much-loved scents of pine and incense wafted out from the splendid brazier, which had been newly polished so that its silver and gold ridges and the gem inlays

17

gleamed. Usually so thrifty, her father must have ordered all twelve of the lights in the curving arms of the largest ceramic lampstand in the house to be kindled. Seated in a haze of incense and a halo of light was Chao Kuang himself. Silver Snow bowed deeply, as much out of love as from proper manners, before she glanced up.

Chao Kuang wore his finest tunic, woven and embroidered with red and blue with characters of good fortune, fastened on the right with five gold buttons. A wide vermilion belt (a privilege once granted and, unaccountably, never revoked by the Son of Heaven) was drawn atop it. His robe's long sleeves fell over her father's hands, hiding his scars and the missing finger. Though the room was warmly heated, a wide strip of sable encircled his throat, while ancient skins of the same precious fur lined his coat. There was no doubt that this splendor had been donned with care to receive an official to whom Chao Kuang would never reveal his house's poverty.

He leaned against padded cushions, holding a two-foot-long bundle of thin wooden strips on which delicate characters had been inked. That must be the Emperor's edict! Broken seals hung from it, chief of them, the signet of the Emperor himself.

Silver Snow drew a deep, shuddering breath and waited anxiously for her father to speak.

"Sit, daughter." Chao Kuang gestured toward a pillow.

Silver Snow lowered herself, settling her robes in decorous folds. Once again, she ventured to look up.

"Doubtless, you have been listening to the gossip in the women's quarters," he observed, but he was not frowning with displeasure. "Vixens' chatter, most of it; but even a fox, should it bark long enough, may once in its life utter the truth."

Had Chao Kuang heard the women's rumors about Willow? Silver Snow had asked herself so often if he had harkened to such spiteful tales that the arrow of fear once accompanying such a thought had long since lost its barbs. Was he about to examine her about that? But why would he do so at a time as important as this one? When he had purchased the maid, he had remarked only that the right-minded man tried to aid those in need, and that he had heard of a faraway province in which red hair—hard as it was to believe—was esteemed as a mark of beauty. Still, since Willow had come to live in their courtyards, Silver Snow noted, he had forbidden the hunting of foxes on their lands; he himself wore only sable or the fleece of sheep.

Chao Kuang raised the wooden strips of the Emperor's edict and, seated as she was, Silver Snow bowed before the august words until her brow touched the felted mats covering the floor.

"As you have heard, because the Emperor's Inner Courts have long been empty, the Censors have now reported to him the outcry of the people who rely upon those courts for their livelihood."

Silver Snow nodded once, and kept her head down. Her eyes, however, darted about the familiar, cozy room, and noted an unfamiliar, ancient-looking chest in one corner. An odd surge of excitement made it difficult for her to sit and listen as, in strict propriety, she should. But it had never been just strict propriety for her and her father: beyond proper behavior lay *hsin*, or sincerity, and *jen*, good will; and beyond those virtues, she knew, lay love—though, of course, a decent reserve would forever prevent either of them from giving voice to such emotion.

"Moreover—and this too is the chatter of foxes—it is said that one night the Emperor dreamed of a woman as lovely as the lady who died, and vowed that he would discover whether such beauty existed anywhere within the Middle Kingdom. Consequently, he has decreed that five hundred concubines should be chosen, and he entrusted the task to Mao Yen-shou, the Administrator of the Inner Courts." Her father paused, and Silver Snow dared to look directly at his face. His eyes were deep and shadowed with memory, the crease between them seeming to be all the deeper.

"Mao Yen-shou is a skilled artist, well able to judge beauty.

However, all that he can do is judge; for he is a eunuch, and doubtless possesses the eunuch's appetite for power. All of which he may indeed arise to in the course of this choosing and judging."

But what has this to do with me? Silver Snow wanted to ask. For the first time in her life, she was impatient with her father's measured fashion of imparting news.

Chao Kuang leaned forward and caught Silver Snow's chin in his callused fingers, raising her face so that their eyes met squarely once more. "My daughter, this ancient one may be disgraced and degraded; yet word of his young, beautiful daughter has reached the Administrator of the Inner Courts; and you have been summoned."

Silver Snow gasped. Tears stung her eyes, whether born of fear or excitement, she knew not. Out of all the maids in the Middle Kingdom, to be one of five hundred beauties selected for the Inner Courts, perhaps to become the next Brilliant Companion who would heal the heart of a grieving Emperor . . . it was beyond dreaming.

"Aye, you do well to weep, child of mine. For this means our farewell. Those ladies who enter the Inner Court—unless it pleases the Son of Heaven to dismiss them—never again see their homes. Nor, let me caution you, is their life all fine robes, sweet food, the Hall of Splendor, and an Emperor's favor. Many, indeed, never see the Son of Heaven, much less bear him a son. Yet, such as they, too, are as firmly bound within the Inner Courts as the meanest slave."

"But this insignificant wretch has been summoned," Silver Snow murmured. Her heart raced. She was beautiful. Even her father, who had the most reason of all people in the world to wish her to be humble and modest, said so. She was brave; she was true. She had only to gain the favor of the Emperor, and everything that her father had lost would be restored. For it was well known that a favorite concubine was free to advance any of her house.

"You go to exile and, though it be not open battle, to another type of risk, my daughter," said Chao Kuang. "The ladies of the Inner Courts engage, I am told, in their own wars; and their weapons are guile at the best; at the worst they spin plots, set snares, and, at length, deal even with poisons. You have been raised to much—perhaps to overmuch—freedom; you may find the life behind the walls of such courtyards as arduous as I found my own captivity. And yet . . ." Her father drew a deep sigh.

Silver Snow held her breath. It was not often that her father would speak—could bear to speak, she thought—of his ten years in captivity.

"Ever since the hour of my surrender until now, I have lived, destitute, with the bitterness of my grief aching like an unhealed wound. Even now I see in dreams the barbarians around me. That distant whole country was stiff with black ice, and I heard naught but the moaning of the bitter winter winds beneath which my hopes of return dwindled.

"And yet, my daughter, and yet, since I have returned, there have been days when it has seemed to me that my life among the Hsiung-nu was not wholly bad. What does the poet say? 'When I fell among Hsiung-nu and was taken prisoner, I pined for the land of Han. Now that I am back in the land of Han, they have turned me into Hsiung-nu . . . A Han heart and a Han tongue, set in the body of the Hsiung-nu.' My years apart were not all ill, I think now."

"When one finds himself in a foreign civilization, one adapts to foreign customs," Silver Snow adapted a maxim from the Analects. The city of Ch'ang-an would be as foreign to her as the lands and yurts of the Hsiung-nu had been to her father; but she would behave with no less honor. For all that she was a female, she was his heir.

Chao Kuang nodded warm approval. The lamplight struck sparks of light from his fur collar, shone on his vermilion sash, reflecting upward until the broad, familiar face appeared to be bathed in light.

"It may be that you too may come to 'adopt foreign customs' to such an extent that you esteem your exile. Assuredly, I shall pray to the Ancestors that you do so. My disgrace meant that I might not betroth you as befitted your station. Nevertheless, I had always meant, insofar as propriety might permit, and perhaps somewhat further, to allow you what latitude I might in a choice of husband. But alas, my child, to this summons I can allow no indulgence."

Silver Snow bowed to the mats. Had she been betrothed, she would not have been offered this dangerous blessing, this opportunity to act to retrieve her father's honor.

He gestured at the chest at the outer reaches of the firelight. "The twenty rolls of tribute silk and two hundred ounces of gold . . ."

So much? That would beggar their house! Silver Snow, who oversaw the household records as might a first wife, gasped, then flushed scarlet with shame. Her father continued as if he had not heard her outburst.

". . . are ready for presentation to Mao Yen-shou upon your arrival. You have the jewels and robes that were your mother's and my First Wife's, as well. And, there is this." Laboriously Chao Kuang rose. Obedient to his wish that his daughter not witness his infirmity, Silver Snow averted her eyes until the thump of his cane upon the mats indicated that he had reached the other mysterious carved chest that she had earlier noted.

At his gesture, she rose and approached. The lid lay back, and lamplight glittered off a splendor of jade plates and gold wire wrought into the replica of a man fully clad, even to the hood for the face, and the booted feet, in armor. Silver Snow bent close to eye the jade. Its color was that of stone precious in value, brought from across the Land of Fire and through the Jade Gate into the heart of Han. In itself, this armor was burial gear worthy of Heaven's Son—or Heaven itself.

"There is another such beneath the rolls of silk and the gold," said her father. "They were carved long ago to serve as shrouds, when our Ancestors were princes in this land. Alas, we have fallen far; and the last and greatest of our falls has been mine own. The Son of Heaven may have once heard that such a treasure lies in our possession, or he may not. Still, should you be so fortunate as to receive his favor, I charge you to present these suits of jade armor to him. He may wish to save one for himself, another for you; or he may throw them to his slaves: I care not."

But he did, Silver Snow thought. He did. The jade armor was the last great treasure of their house, and he entrusted it to her as a general might entrust a banner to the youngest of his warriors to hearten him for a test.

"Perhaps when you present this gift, he will recall the most humble, unworthy, and wretched of his servants," said Chao Kuang. His voice roughened, and he turned rapidly away.

For a long time, her father and she maintained silence. Silver Snow heard the clatter of dishes and voices raised in other courtyards in the house. The banquet in honor of the official who brought the edict—it must be under way, and her father had left it to speak with her, mere girlchild though she was. She tilted her head to listen, and he nodded.

"Indeed, I should return to my guests, but my heart is heavy within me. For, daughter, this must be our farewell. Tomorrow's dawn will see the official go from here; and you must go with him. You shall have your gifts, and your maid, and whatever escort can be contrived. And you go with my blessing—" Silver Snow dropped to her knees.

"I do not expect that life will treat you too harshly," said her father, limping back to his cushions. "For is it not written in the Analects that to be fond of learning is close to having wisdom? I know that you are fond of learning; and, in the Inner Courts, you may have opportunities to learn much that is lacking here."

Silver Snow's tears spilled over onto her sleeves, leaving round marks on the embroidered silk. "But not from you, honored father," she whispered.

To her astonishment, just as he had done when she first saw him, he held out his hand to her. With small, hasty steps, she went to him and took it; and he drew her into a close, warm embrace.

"May all our Ancestors smile upon you, my daughter," he said. "It may yet be that you shall bear a son to worship them, and our line shall not live in disgrace or die out altogether."

For a moment longer, he held her, and she smelled the camphor in which, all summer, his sables had been preserved.

"Now," he said, "I must indeed return to my guests. I congratulate you on the success of today's hunt: a good one for your last." Deliberately, as befitted a disciple of Confucius, he kept his voice even, seeking to return them both to the wholesome serenity of conduct that the Master taught.

Silver Snow withdrew from her father's embrace, blinked once, furiously, and commanded her lips not to tremble.

"I shall see you depart tomorrow," said her father. "But this shall be our true farewell. If you have time and the means, I charge you, write to me."

She bowed deeply, and listened to her father's uneven tread and the measured thump of his ebony cane as, slowly, painfully, he descended the stairs, and walked across the courtyard toward the room in which feasted the official and his officers who would, tomorrow, whisk her away from the only life that she had ever known.

The air in the room was fragrant with pine, almond, and artemisia; and the lamp shone brightly upon her as she curled into the cushions where her father had sat, weeping as she bade farewell to her home. Though excitement and splendor, she knew, might well lie ahead of her, she wept as if there were no end to tears in her whole world.

CHAPTER

= 3 =

As the daughter of a degraded noble, Silver Snow had never dwelt long on what her wedding might be like, knowing that any marriage her father would be able to arrange would not be a mating between equal ranks. Consequently, she could not complain of a limited dawn farewell upon leaving her father's home; nor that she wore, instead of the crimson and face-enshrouding headdress of the bride, serviceable sheepskins and ancient furs over her heaviest robes; nor that she was handed into a sturdy, enclosed, two-wheeled cart rather than into a chair hung with bells and bright trappings. True enough, her dowry—the tribute silk and gold stripped from her father's already impoverished holdings—was loaded into carts and onto packbeasts to make the month-long journey west and south to Ch'ang-an, the capital.

Also packed were whatever robes and ornaments she and Willow had contrived from her own and the remnants of her mother's and the First Wife's belongings. Hidden among the rolls of silk was that great treasure that Chao Kuang had entrusted to her in hope of melting the Son of Heaven's heart: the jade funeral armor far too fine for anyone but an Emperor and his consort.

Oboes, pipes, and drums were supposed to accompany marriage processions. The only music for her was the ringing

25

of harness bells from the chariot of the official who had brought the Son of Heaven's edict.

To be sure, light from lanterns and torches, such as might grace a bridal procession, bobbed and flickered about her, casting an austere glimmer on the axes and lances borne with such pride by the messenger's carriage. The steam of their breaths rose above the lantern-bearers and the soldiers, as the official, muffled to the eyebrows in fox furs (Willow's mouth twisted at the sight of those), took the place of honor in his splendid equipage.

Cloaked somewhat by the interplay of light and shadow, her father looked as wasted and wan as after his escape from the Hsiung-nu. From behind the cart's curtains, Silver Snow peered at him, desperately eager in these last few moments to record each line of his weathered face deep in her memory. She knew that, be her fortune fair or ill, she was looking upon him for the last time. That he had done her the favor of rising and dressing to see her off was precious to her. Of recent years, he usually awoke coughing in the morning. This morning, however, he was not rasping of breath, perhaps because of the potion that she had made, by Willow's teaching, yesterday. She dared now to twitch aside the curtain, and when he glanced at her, she bowed in proper leave-taking.

There was, of course, no groom, no real parade of family to accompany her, unless Silver Snow could count Willow, who sat beside her in the ox-cart, her green eyes downcast, and her nurse. Then there were the household guards whose patched uniforms and aged horses made such a poor showing alongside the uniformed half troop riding glossy mounts, with their necks proudly arching, breaths steaming in the winter dawn.

Still, custom had to be followed as far as possible, which, in this case, was not all that far. Save for Willow and the nurse, Silver Snow was the only woman in the party; and certainly the only lady of rank. She had no bevy of ladies, no elder go-between, to escort her to the capital and instruct her in the ways of the court; only a week out of Ch'ang-an, the Lady Lilac intended for the post of mentor had fallen ill on the road and had had to be left at an estate along the way. The official had almost deigned to apologize to her father for this lack of proper company, which a noble who was not in disgrace would be certain to regard as an affront. Her father, of course, did not dare to take offense. Silver Snow, while regretting the slight to her father and her house, was relieved. There would be enough strangeness in simply traveling without the need to adapt quickly to the ways of a great lady of the court.

Because Silver Snow rode in a cart, not a chair, she could not be locked from sight. Nevertheless, her father solemnly presented a key to her escort as a token of their obligation to guard her, then bowed for the last time. The official gestured imperiously to his groom, and Silver Snow, peering from behind the curtains, saw her own driver prod his oxen.

She drew a deep, shaky breath. To leave her home, her land, all she had ever known, for what might mean forgiveness for the House of Chao, or just as likely leave her sequestered within the palace women's quarters forever, a prisoner of exalted rank! It was frightening! The torchlight swam in a rainbow haze as she blinked quickly. Willow grasped her mistress' hand reassuringly.

The oxen lumbered forward, and with many a shake and many a giddy sidewise swing, the cart rolled down the familiar hill that she would never again see on the first leg of the journey to Ch'ang-an. Dawn wind cast a delicate spume of snow against her face as it brought her the last words that her father spoke before he, leaning heavily upon his stick, entered his now-daughterless house.

> *"A turn of the hill, a bend of the road and you are lost to*
> *sight;*
> *All that is left is the track on the snow where your horse's*
> *hoofs trod."*

After several nights on the road, the train of official and soldiers transporting Silver Snow toward Ch'ang-an stopped for the night in a town where they could seek more comfortable shelter in the home of a magistrate, who appeared, bowing double at the gates, in a frenzy of apology lest the thrice-honored official from Ch'ang-an find his hovel (for thus he spoke) and his First Wife's untutored efforts beneath contempt.

Silver Snow's nurse, who had been ill throughout the journey, promptly fainted; and her mistress sighed with relief as the old woman was carried within. Here, she might be tended and might rest until someone might be found to return her to her home. Her young mistress glanced at Willow, who nodded and pulled her hood farther down upon her head. How strange Willow looked! At the last halt, she had vigorously rubbed her hair with lampblack lest its ugly, ominous red hue draw comment among the ladies of the magistrate's inner courts.

"That is not necessary," Silver Snow had protested, but Willow had been silent, stubborn. Even the old nurse, from her swathings of sheepskins, had spoken (between moans and sneezes) a brief word of approbation and relief.

They were waiting for her now, judging from the hisses and giggles that she heard from outside the circle of torch- and lamplight. This far from the capital, they too must be eager for news, more eager still to see a lady who might, one day, be the most honored among all women. Straightening her furs as best she could, Silver Snow stepped down from the cart, resting her hand for the briefest of moments on the arm of a guard. Then she walked quickly toward what looked like an inviting circle of light and warmth—into a new world.

She had expected courtyards much like her own, old, shabby, and relatively bare, either of furnishings or of people. Here, however: light, colors, and smells erupted so she blinked, bewildered, glancing from elaborate hangings to wall paintings to what seemed like a veritable army of high-born ladies. Most seemed to be regarding Silver Snow with pursed lips and incredulous eyes beneath high-arched brows. Each, from First Wife to youngest concubine, wore new, intricately wrought silk garments, their full sleeves nearly brushing the matted floor. All of the robes were embroidered with flowers; and each lady wore the scent of the blossom stitched upon her robes. Now they bowed, each as befitted her own rank, until the play of color and scent made them resemble a garden in a spring breeze.

Overwhelmed by colors and scents, as well as the unfamiliar warmth of these courts, Silver Snow stepped backward—just in time to miss the ceremonious greeting of the First Wife. She recovered almost the instant thereafter, and bowed the more deeply to make amends; but, as she realized with a sinking heart, it was too late. Gossip had already begun: rustles of silk as hidden hand plucked gleaming sleeve; a gleam of moonbright cheek laid against powdered cheek; a hiss of sympathy for the slight to the First Wife; and, above all, the whispers, like the sighing of a bleak wind.

"Did you see, she *strode* into the house as if she had done no more than walk from one court to the next? She neither wept nor swooned. How robust! How very coarse."

"At least, the crone, her nurse, had to be carried in. I know that I would be prostrate, were I forced to make such a journey . . ."

"Such a *strange* appearance: no proper go-between, and only that ugly maid . . ."

"Keep her shadow away from me!" squealed one of the concubines. "I am with child; I would not have our master's son born lame."

Foolishness, Silver Snow wanted to cry as Willow shrank back into her mistress' shadow.

"Look, how the ugly wench glares at you. Do you think she heard?" A faint giggling followed that question, and the concubine and her friend flounced away.

"*I* do not think that the Emperor will even look at this one," announced an elder wife to the First Wife. "Country-bred, rough, and appallingly healthy. Who knows if she is truly a lady of the Han? You know, they say that her father married among the Hsiung-nu . . ."

"That would explain her repulsive hardiness, if she were half . . ."

"Hush!" commanded the First Wife, who approached Silver Snow with a glittering smile in which the girl could discern nothing of welcome.

Nor did the bath, more elaborate than any she had ever known, warm or refresh her. She took no pleasure in the robes in which they wrapped her, with many comments on her weathered hands, callused from bowstring and blade, and her browned face. Willow's mirror might show her to be lovely when she sat alone at home; here, however, she saw herself as she was: lacking the insipid prettiness that made each lady resemble the others as one plum resembles its companions on the branch. Where they minced and tripped, she walked; where they fluttered lashes and sleeves, she moved quickly, decisively; her brows, though finely, naturally arched, were too thick, and her mouth far too generous. Even here, she thought, chin raised and with a flash of anger, she was not ill-favored: just very different, very much a lady of the northern frontier.

As she sat among the others of the inner courtyards, spooning up a savory soup rich in spices such as her own poor kitchen could only sigh for, a sudden spasm of fear clutched her and made the soup taste flat. This was, as its master said, but a provincial house. If this passed as backward and countrified, what must the Imperial Courts be like?

Would any there accept her more willingly?

It did not matter. She had made the only choice open to her—to obey with a willing heart.

The next morning, when the whispers started again, Silver Snow learned that, despite the local magistrate's pleas, the Son of Heaven's messenger chose not to remain another day, but to press on instead. She felt only relief.

But she had not reckoned with the magistrate's First Wife.

"Sister," said the lady, according Silver Snow the tribute of equality since—who could know?—one day, she might be the beloved of an Emperor, "a thousand apologies, but I must impose on you to discuss your attendant."

The First Wife's glossy hair was scented with lilac; and lilacs glistened on her fine robes. Though she spoke of humility and apology, Silver Snow could see neither in her dress, her gait, or her speech. The girl waited courteously, feigning attention and eagerness to listen.

"The girl is ugly," said the First Wife. "Forgive this wretched one's ill-bred speech, but your maid is so ill-favored and halt. She will do you no credit in the capital."

Silver Snow cast down her eyes and murmured that Willow had long served her.

"In the North, perhaps such as she is the best that there is to choose." The First Wife shrugged a plump shoulder as if anything might be expected to happen in the barbarous North. "You are young and far from your home, younger sister. Let me advise you as should your go-between . . . but you have none, now have you?"

"She was taken ill," Silver Snow found herself explaining, feeling oddly defensive, oddly apologetic on behalf of a woman whom she did not know and who allowed infirmity to interfere with duty.

"Very well, then. I know that she would advise you to accept my offer of three lovely maids to accompany you to Ch'ang-an. *That one* can wait here until the old nurse is fit to travel, then return North, or . . ." Another comfortable, plump shrug indicated that whether or not Willow found herself well suited was of no lasting importance or concern.

"I thank you, Elder Sister"—Silver Snow bowed—"and I beg you to forgive me; but, having suffered the rigors of travel myself, I cannot bring myself to force one of your ladies—all gently reared—to endure them too. Willow is willing and strong; she suits me well."

"Indeed, she does," said the First Wife, ice in her voice and in her spine as she bowed with the merest possible inclination as Silver Snow prepared to depart.

The wind whipped at the curtains of her ox-cart, but Silver Snow could have embraced it like a sister. It was not just relief at being out of that too crowded, too hot, and too treacherous women's quarter; it was enjoyment. Silver Snow would never have imagined that she would adapt with such zest to travel—or that it would be so hard to conceal her interest and delight at each new day from her protectors, who seemed ever concerned that the hardships of the journey not overpower a lady's fragile body and spirit.

Day by day, as the land grew less and less familiar, she took increasing satisfaction in peering out from the slit that she had fashioned in the heavy curtains of her ox-cart, listening to the guttural, barely understandable words of the peasants, the arrogant demands and comments of the official and, sometimes, the tax-gatherers, also on imperial orders, who seemed to be a plague upon the land. Her sole regret was that she could not ride out herself among them as she had been accustomed (however improperly) to do at home.

It was not so much that she could not tolerate the crowded towns, or the company of her hostesses, with their constant concerns and stream of chatter about daughters, servants, concubines, and the kitchens. Not all were as frigid and hostile as the lady at her first stopover. Some were actually kind. Others pitied her; and once again, there came the buzzings, the whispers, the sleeve-pluckings. "Poor child, how weathered she is."

"She is but one among five hundred. What hope has she, with no wealth and that browned skin, of being noticed? Thus I told her; and she said that she journeyed to court at her father's will."

"They are strict in the North about obedience, if about nothing else. How mannish is her stride!"

"Let her creep back to her home. Surely, she would be

forgotten. Indeed, I think it likelier that no one will ever notice her in Ch'ang-an. When *I* saw the city . . ."

"Once, you saw it, when you were a girl of ten . . ."

"When *I* saw Ch'ang-an, let me tell you, *younger* sister . . ."

Silver Snow became adroit at feigning deafness. Never before had she imagined that words might have edges as keen as fangs or blades. The words of the ladies whom she met, kindly or ill-willing, cut deeply.

At the times when the limitations of women's quarters and women's chatter pressed her too closely or wounded her, she reminded herself of her duty to her house and its honor, and held hard to her pride that she, a woman, might serve as the means of its rebirth and the mender of its fortunes.

She realized that in Ch'ang-an she would enter just such an enclosure as those first ladies kept. Perhaps, if fate was kind, it would be a more luxurious seclusion, but seclusion nonetheless. Still, it had been her choice. Although no one dared to refuse a summons by the Son of Heaven, she was fairly certain that the kindly lady at the last house was right: should the daughter of a disgraced noble have failed to turn up, one among five hundred women, no one would have noticed; or, had someone noticed, he would not have cared. What was more, the other four hundred and ninety-nine would rejoice.

Then, her ox-cart waited, and they would be on the road again. Once more, Silver Snow would avidly peer out through the rent in the curtain, Willow beside her. Each day was an adventure. Best of all, however, were the nights when the caravan stopped along the road; nights of firelight and starlight and, overhead, the vast, wind-filled bowl of the sky.

She discovered that she was coming to welcome such nights when the packtrain, cumbersome despite the official's swift carriage and swifter impatience at delay, bypassed a town, preferring several hours more of travel and a stop on the road for the night.

If only, then, she might have ridden! Used though she was to a more active existence, she dared not suggest it to the master of their party. Already, he might have heard slighting reports of her; she dared not risk his disfavor. Even the horse that she had always considered hers was stabled at . . . the place that she must forever afterward regard as her father's house, not her home: not anymore. The hurt of that realization faded day by day, overlaid by each glimpse of a new town, or peasants, steaming with sweat as they worked on the land or the roads, though it was deep winter.

Reconciled to idleness as befitted a great lady, Silver Snow watched while camp was made, smiling at the confusion among the official's servants, approving her own guard's quick, soldierly ways as the men camped in a protective circle about her cart. Then, once the fire was kindled, her cart became a pavilion that was more comfortable than she would have imagined. She and Willow had their own fire, and, with no walls but the night, their own court, ringed at a discreet distance by her father's old soldiers.

When the wind was right, Silver Snow could hear the clicks of playing pieces, the grunts of disappointment, an occasional laugh of victory from the men's camp; she could even catch stray words of the grave, self-important speech of the official to underlings and a few scholars who had attached themselves to the procession, eager for a relatively rapid and somewhat safe trip to the capital for the all-important examinations.

She listened eagerly, warmed by the men's rough laughter, the gibes at this or that official. The names of the latter she set herself to remember with the same zeal that a young soldier polishes sword and armor. At one point, the leader of her escort train laughed and spoke slightingly of Mao Yen-shou, on whom her own fortune could rest. Not for worlds would Silver Snow have dared to violate custom by sending to ask of the man what he knew; but she was sorely tempted.

Huddled in a quilted robe, Silver Snow rubbed her hands before her night fire, waiting for Willow to return from whatever scouting mission the lame maid might have set for herself. A small bronze pot of soup steamed near the flames, and though it was no job of hers to tend it, nevertheless, she did. If only she had been a scholar, even one of the lowest rank, or perhaps simply a candidate journeying to the capital to take the arduous civil examinations, she might have sat at that larger fire to warm mind as well as body.

Her lively intelligence hungered for just such meetings, but, trapped as she was in a female body, she was reduced to tending the soup, forced to wait upon others for news to brighten a day. Her father had always addressed her as he might have spoken to a son and heir. These men, if they were of rank to notice such a fellow traveler—had she emerged directly into their company—would cast such attention on her as they might upon a stray flower, fallen from its stand in a marketplace: fair for the moment, but of no true value to serious-minded men engaged upon their business.

A chaste lady destined for the Emperor's Inner Courts, Silver Snow could appear to most of them as an item of merchandise—perhaps a roll of fine silk or a carved jade vase—to be kept safely until delivery at the Palace. When the official must speak with her, he used the elaborate, complimentary speech of the court, full of flowery compliments that meant nothing, either to him or to herself, carefully delivered from beyond the protection of the cart's curtains.

What more could she expect? Even the Lady Pan, who had lived so many years at the court and gained what renown a woman might for her upright conduct and her work on her brother's histories, claimed in her manual for court ladies a position that Silver Snow had already forfeited at home. Women, decreed Lady Pan, were formed strictly for modesty and submission, discretion and quietness. Silver Snow's longings to ride in the open air, her desire to hear, at least, the official's discourse, were highly improper, very possibly impious. She had already noted that some of the ladies who had received her, albeit reluctantly, as a guest regarded her as unfeminine because she could walk into their courts, rather than be carried within, prostrate and ill.

She knew what her father would have said—had indeed

said—because of the one time, years ago, she had broached such a subject to him. "What the Lady Pan writes is no doubt good and proper. But the lady herself is also a woman, and therefore subject to error." The gleam of humor in her father's eyes had removed any hint of rebuke from his statement.

A snatch of words floated from the official's camp. Confucius again: "Whatever acts unnaturally will come to an unnatural finish." Silver Snow shuddered and burrowed more deeply into her sheltering travel robe. For the past several nights, she knew, the guard on the packtrain had been doubled, and her own escort ringed about her more closely. That could mean a threat of bandits, peasants forced off their land for failure to pay taxes, savage in their rage; or (and this was what she hated to think upon) it might mean fear of some beast, wild or not.

Silver Snow stirred the soup again and shivered. Willow . . . her maid had carefully renewed the dye on her hair each night, always keeping to the shadows, still the ugly, barbarous rumors that Willow was more animal than human had sprung up in several houses where they had guested.

That could mean danger. A generation ago, fears of witchcraft had cost some of the Emperor's ministers their posts and others their heads—or other parts of their bodies. There would be no mercy for a lady and her father against whom toleration and shelter of a witch might be proved: even an accusation of witchcraft could be deadly, especially for a family already judged to be traitors.

Outsiders saw only a red-haired woman (or one with hair stained an unnatural black) with a limp and deemed Willow to be an unnatural creature. They did not know how loving and loyal she was, even when it came to creeping out by night in a camp full of rough, strange men. *I shall have to warn her,* thought Silver Snow, and regretted the thought. The maid would weep—her face reddening in a curious way that it had, until her green eyes looked even less seemly than usual—and swear that doubtlessly she endangered her beloved mistress by her mere presence.

Footsteps creaked against snow, stopping in the darkness outside the light cast by her fire.

"Most honored lady?"

Silver Snow stopped herself before she leapt up, gasping from surprise.

"Younger brother," she greeted Ao Li, who was at least thirty years her senior. He shifted from foot to foot, his hands behind his back, staring at the ground, as if unsure of how to begin. After a long pause, which she waited for him to break, he thrust out what he had concealed behind his back as he approached her.

"This one dared to think that the Esteemed Lady might wish to have this keepsake," he said.

It was her bow, carefully maintained, though she had not been the one to do so, and a quiver of lovingly fletched arrows.

Her eyes filled, and she opened quivering lips to thank the old soldier. Instead of vanishing, as she half expected that he might do from sheer embarrassment, Ao Li again shuffled his feet before he stood at attention, almost as if he were about to report to her father.

"The most honorable lady well knows how to use that," he nodded at the bow. Indeed she did: Ao Li had helped to teach her.

She smiled. When there came no answering smile, her own faded, to be replaced by alarm. "Does the honorable soldier think that she will have to?" she asked. "The guards . . ." She gestured at the closely picketed horses, the tight circle of protection around her wagon and her fire.

Ao Li glanced around. Despite the cold, his broad forehead was sweaty beneath the scarf that he had pulled down over it. He leaned forward, in discretion, not in insolence. "Wolves, lady," he whispered. "But not . . ."

A crackle, such as a misstep upon a twig might make, forced them to jump.

"The noble lady honors this worthless soldier," Ao Li said in a voice which sounded false. "He will depart to better guard her."

That much she could put full trust in, she thought. But what had frightened the old man so? She laid her cheek against the bow, remembering her last hunt up by the Great Wall before the messenger had summoned her to Ch'ang-an and such strange future as might now lie before her. The grip was smooth, familiar, the string, when she tested it, taut and new.

Where was Willow? If wolves were abroad, Willow was lame; she could neither run nor fight. Silver Snow almost rose to call Ao Li back and order him to seek out Willow. Yet, the maid might not want attention called to her in such a way. She forced herself to sit still, but her fists clenched within her long sleeves until the nails bit into her palms.

"The Red Brows . . . marauded hereabouts only the night before . . . three peasants . . ."

Words floated again from the official's firesite. *Not* an unnatural animal then. She need have no fears for Willow, at least not yet. But what were "Red Brows"? Perhaps bandits. In which case, Silver Snow was doubly thankful for the gift of the bow . . . assuming it was not a terrible violation of all proprieties if she used it.

Better, she thought daringly, a violation of the proprieties than of her own body. She was a general's daughter, an Emperor's concubine-to-be: no prize for bandits.

The wind shifted, overpowering the rest of the words the official was addressing to his guard, and making her shiver.

Abruptly the stars overhead no longer held the promise of freedom. Instead, the very open spaces about her seemed to threaten, rather than promise release. As a gust of wind tossed sparks from her fire high in the air, like an army beacon, Silver Snow rose and entered her wagon, where she hoped to find among her baggage that jade-handled knife she could use either to let out a bandit's life, or her own.

A scratching at the hanging of her cart made Silver Snow gasp and whirl around. The wickedly sharp little knife glinted in the firelight as she drew it, ready to her hand as the hangings parted.

Willow stood before her, her green eyes wary as a vixen's as she noted her mistress' knife.

"Lady?" she began, cautiously using one of the most formal of Silver Snow's titles.

Silver Snow flushed and laid the knife aside. She was pleased to note that her hand did not shake, either from fear or from the cold. "Come in, Willow, before the winter rules in here as it does outside."

"I rescued the soup, mistress," Willow said, lifting the pot with one rag-wrapped hand as she drew shut the cart's hangings behind her, leaving out the wind and the world beyond. As Silver Snow waited, barely schooling herself to patience, Willow made elaborate play of serving the soup, of adjusting bowls and cushions just so: all of which enabled the two of them to sit with their heads close together, bent over the bowls as if inhaling the fragrant steam.

"I am glad you returned safely," Silver Snow whispered.

Willow laughed. "It is easy to go about the camp if you are considered ugly, mistress. The men touch amulets and let me pass with a jest or two: one listens and learns much, if one ignores their harsh words." The glint in Willow's eye reminded Silver Snow that that had been a teaching that Willow had found hard to master.

"And what *does* one learn in such a way?" asked Silver Snow.

Willow pulled out a small disk, marked with glyphs and ideograms that, for all of her learning, Silver Snow could not read, besides strange pictures, symbols in what, surely, was the tongue of the beasts.

"The troopers asked me why a woman as ill-favored as I should keep such a fine thing," Willow commented, looking as if she wished to claw something. "I told them: to look behind me, and they laughed. But that is the truth: I use this to look behind me, and before and to the sides, lest not all men be what they appear."

"And you have found such?" asked Silver Snow.

Willow nodded. "Yes, Elder Sister. Some are wolves."

Wolves! That was precisely what Ao Li had tried to warn her of before their conversation was interrupted.

"What do you know," she asked Willow, "about 'Red Brows'?"

Willow's bowl did not shake in her hand, but she looked up sharply. "I could glean very little news from near the camp, Elder Sister," she said. "The brothers- and sisters-in-fur fear the soldiers' bows and lances. And they fear more the wolves. There are men in this camp who take silver, but do not requite their hire as should honest men. But . . ."

"But?" Silver Snow snapped up the word. "If they were that much afraid, they would not dare to come speak with you."

"That much is true, lady," Willow conceded. "But they are more afraid of the Red Brows, who hunt, not from hunger but for the joy of slaughter, who burn villages when they have no need of warmth, and who slaughter babes, human and animal, as if they have no thought of tomorrow. The escort soldiers, too, are afraid, I think. When I passed them, the smell of fear was on the wind . . ."

She grimaced, then sneezed. "What is worse, though many fear spies, some, I fear, *are* spies."

"Would you know them once again?"

Willow nodded.

"Very well then. Watch well."

Silver Snow produced her bow, flourishing it in delight when Willow's eyes opened in surprise. "We are not wholly unarmed," she said.

"Lady, if they know that you can shoot . . ."

"Would they prefer me to hang myself with my sash in fear of ravishment? I shall make them pay dearly for any sport they plan and slay myself before they can enjoy it. Willow, do not forget that in addition to the merchants' ware, we carry silk and gold"—*and jade, too*—"to the Son of Heaven. Our train would be a rich prize. Could you discover a trail of these bandits?" she asked.

Willow laid her hand across her felt boots, one heavily

padded to compensate for the fact that one leg was shorter than the other. "Ah, lady, had I a night to run in, I might know them again. But that leaves you unguarded, unattended . . ."

"What are you talking about?" asked Silver Snow. "I thought . . ." She gestured at Willow's lame leg, where the folds of robes hid it. Certainly Willow could not be admitting that the ugly rumors were true. Surely she spoke only of spying, as a servant aged or ill-favored might well do.

But Willow shook her head vigorously. "When your honored father purchased me from the slave-merchant, I was little more than a kitling, lost from the herbalist who had taken me in. What chance has such to survive without a master? Less than none. So I remained. Elder Sister, let me . . ."

I thought that you loved me. Now you say that if you were whole, then you would run away and leave me! The wail rose in Silver Snow's mind, and her eyes filled. Willow grasped her hand in her own callused palm, almost like a paw, and kissed it.

"I would never leave you. It is only bandits that prey upon their own and foul their nests. Beasts feel gratitude to those who feed them, warm them . . . love them," said Willow, bowing almost double. "This one is as a beast beneath your feet. Forgive me, Elder Sister, for such plain speech."

It was too great a risk . . . suppose the bandits would see Willow as a victim for quick sport and slow pain. Yet Willow's willingness to risk herself might save them all.

"Just until moonset." Though Silver Snow had the right to command, her voice rose as if she asked Willow's consent. "For was it not truly said by General Sun Tzu that 'an army without secret agents is exactly like a man without eyes or ears'?"

"Did this sage serve with your father, may the Ancestors smile upon him?" Willow asked. Dear Willow! She would never willingly share Silver Snow's lessons, try as she had to teach her.

For the maid, what counted was not the long traditions of humankind but the sights and smells of the country through which they passed, and the speech of plant and beast; for

Willow, like the women of the Hsiung-nu, was wise in the ways of the land. Wise, perhaps, and something more, something that for all the years they had been together, Silver Snow had willfully refused to see.

Silver Snow, stubborn in her innocence, had been as steadfast as Willow. What if the rumors were true, and Willow truly were a fox-spirit? *Answer your question yourself, girl,* Silver Snow thought with an asperity new to her. *What if she* were *a fox? She has given you her heart. That being the case, does aught else matter?*

For the first time, Silver Snow let herself think the unthinkable. Confucius denounced belief in fox-spirits as the rankest superstition. Well enough, then: simply say that Willow was wise; say, then, that she had powers not granted to the ordinary woman. And that she repaid love with love.

"That is man's craft; I know naught of such spies, but much of such scouting and sniffing as the beasts do. For I am my mistress' . . . servant," Willow said, her eyes gleaming with courage and wry humor. "And I shall act as my nature— and my mistress—command me."

She waited only for Silver Snow's hesitant nod before she started to leave the cart.

"Where do you go?"

"Elder Sister, to spy upon wolves."

Willow smiled enigmatically, and slipped between the enshrouding folds of the curtains of the ox-cart.

Outside the cart, Silver Snow heard yapping. She forced herself to wonder at the rashness of whatever beast ventured thus close to a camp of armed men. Pain filled those yaps, and they rose shrilly, yet she refused to go and look upon whatever cried out thus.

Finally, when the whining and barking died away, Silver Snow peered outside. On the trampled snow lay a heavy sheepskin robe . . . Willow's, thought Silver Snow. Despite her limp, the girl was hardy. She had probably discarded the robe for greater speed and agility.

Suddenly a large fox, its glossy red fur almost black in the cart's shadows, crawled from beneath their weight, then forced itself to its feet. One forepaw was badly crippled, Silver Snow noted. Had the guards set traps, or was that more than coincidence? Silver Snow held out her hand to the beast, but it darted past her, out into the night.

Bow strung, dagger ready, Silver Snow leaned against a support in her wagon, dozing, not daring wholly to sleep lest an attack come that she would not be prepared for. Where was Willow? she wondered as the night drew on.

Were this a normal night, the maid would long since have doused the fire, and performed other small tasks about her mistress' camp. Were such tasks omitted, it might be noticed. Picking up Willow's heavy sheepskin coat, Silver Snow slipped into it. Sewn for a woman taller and heavier than her mistress, Willow's coat fitted loosely over Silver Snow's own robes. She climbed outside, savoring the sweetness of the air, mingled with the ash scent of a dying fire.

For one moment she paused to admire the great arch of the heavens. Then she heard the tread of boots, and she stiffened, one hand near her dagger, the other ready to toss earth on the fire, so she and her enemy would be equally blinded. But it was a guard . . . Ao Li, to be exact. Silver Snow summoned him over and, in an imitation of Willow's voice so good that she surprised herself, she gave him whatever instructions might properly come from her "mistress."

When Ao Li hurried back to the guards, Silver Snow remained outside, straining her ears to listen. Finally, she heard an agonized yap, as if some dog—*or a fox!* she thought, stabbed by fear as though wounded with her own blade—had been kicked or slashed. Or perhaps, it was simply a wounded girl, in such extremity of anguish that her cries no longer sounded human.

A derisive shout, the impact of some missile against a chariot, and angry protests from others in the train; and whatever beast had cried out yelped again and ran . . . ran toward her.

If they have harmed Willow, I shall see their heads lopped from their bodies! Silver Snow vowed with unusual vehemence. She also swore that if Willow did not return, she would seek her.

As she leaned against the cart, she strove to appear as a serving woman through with one task yet reluctant to enter her mistress' presence where an endless round of other duties might await her. Through the clean night air, sound carried clearly. Silver Snow heard the panting of a wounded, frightened beast fleeing, desperately hoping to evade pursuit long enough to go to earth . . . fox's earth, thought Silver Snow.

Now came the rhythm of the creature's paws. One, two, three . . . drag; one, two, three . . . drag; a long pause, followed by a faint whine, almost instantly suppressed as if the beast was aware of its peril. Silver Snow forced herself to admit it: the beast had appeared when Willow vanished; the beast had a lame leg, just as Willow did; the beast had Willow's color and courage and affection. It had to be Willow!

Thus, the thing that she had fought all of these years not to believe was indeed truth: Willow was a fox. Still, Willow was also her maid, her friend; and she was in deadly danger. Silver Snow's hand went to her mouth as she willed with all her strength that Willow was not so badly wounded that her beast's senses had overpowered the human part, perhaps past her best efforts to change back.

"Willow?" she called, hardly above a whisper. Only another whimper answered her.

Silver Snow ran forward as a dark, vulpine shadow staggered forward beside the last dying coals of the cookfire. The beast flinched away as she laid her hands on its right flank. A slash ran up one paw . . . the lame one. Silver Snow hoped that that had bled clean. The wound looked painful, in this so-limited light, but not serious: more like the results of unthinking human malice than an attempt to kill. She picked up the trembling fox, which raised its good forepaw to pat her cheek. Then she bore the animal into the cart, setting it down by a pan of water, before she hurriedly draped a heavy robe around Willow's fox-shape.

She busied herself heating some of their scant, precious

supply of rice wine, another of the luxuries left from the former riches of her house. Ordinarily, such highly prized wine was reserved for the Palace, but her father had had a small store of it, and had given it to her, to warm her on the long, cold road. Wine was said to bring fever to wounds, but Willow was so cold. If she drank now, she might be the better for it.

Within the swathing of robes, the fox thrashed, first feebly, then with growing strength. Silver Snow resolutely turned away. She would not watch. The passage from fox to girl sounded even more labored, more painful, punctuated by soft barks and muffled human sobs and pleas. If only there were some help or comfort Silver Snow could offer!

Outside, the sky was paling toward dawn. Soon, the wagoners and guards would be up and moving about their tasks. Willow had work to perform to aid that departure, but, clearly, she would be unable today even to show herself abroad. For the first time, Silver Snow was glad of the curtains and the customs that kept all aloof. She pushed aside one of the shielding curtains to set, slowly and less skillfully than Willow might have, about those chores. Her impersonation apparently was successful: if anyone noted her awkwardness, he would ascribe it to those aching bones that made her limp even more pronounced.

As she reentered the cart, Silver Snow smelled the heady fumes of hot wine. Willow lay curled in uneasy sleep within the warm tumble of robe.

As Silver Snow knelt to smooth it, Willow cried out and flinched. The robe opened to expose a deeply bruised side and a badly cut foot. However, her breathing was so regular that Silver Snow thought that she had suffered no broken ribs. When Willow woke, they could see to strapping her chest. For the present, there was that foot with its angry-looking wound. As Silver Snow bathed it in the dregs of the wine, Willow cried out and jolted back to consciousness.

"Let me finish with this, younger sister," murmured Silver Snow.

"I did not risk my life only that you might nurse me," snapped the maid. "We must flee this place. The red brows of whom men speak have agents in this camp who suspect that you carry great treasure. It is only by the grace of . . ." she broke off.

Fox-spirits' sky must have many gods, thought her mistress. Had these shape-changers, indeed, a god to whom they prayed? "Well and enough that they did not attack tonight. Your guards were watchful and loyal to you. Others . . . I marked one or two. But we can expect bandits along the road: perhaps attack will come today as we go; perhaps not.

"But, Elder Sister, be warned. If we camp outside a town tonight, we must look well to ourselves. This band is strong, and very angry. Many of them are farmers thrust from their lands when they could not pay taxes to bandits of officials, who grasp all in the Emperor's name."

"Then it is wrongs which have reduced them to this," observed Silver Snow.

Willow shook her head. Her eyes were bright and angry. "One of them gave me *this*, I think, for no other reason than as I walked by, I disturbed his thoughts. Wronged, perhaps they have been, but they themselves have committed greater wrongs since then. Mistress, I tell you, we must look to ourselves lest they put hands on us! Watch for bay horses. I heard bay horses mentioned among them!"

CHAPTER

= 4 =

Silver Snow had little sleep in that last hour before dawn, when the unwieldy train creaked onto the road to Ch'ang-an. Though several times before she had slept comfortably enough in the cart, wedged with quilts and cushions against its lurching, today she did not surrender to any rest. For which of the outriders were Willow's spies? A number were mounted on bay horses. From where the cart was situated in the line of march, it was impossible for her to tell how many were, or even if Willow had indeed discovered them among the guards.

Also, her maid was listless, almost feverish, too weak for her usual sharp-tongued chaffering with their driver, which, in the past, had brought them scraps of news. Willow dozed or tossed, though she firmly refused to let Silver Snow examine her wounds again.

Thus the day was an ordeal, a test of Silver Snow's composure and *li*, or propriety. She must sit calmly in her cart, not crane her neck like an unpledged peasant maid to stare through her private peephole and make sure *her* soldiers followed closely, their bows strung taut as she had ordered the night before. Nor was she about to demand of this haughty official extra guards and reassurances that he could not, in all truth, give, even to a woman as valuable as a candidate for Imperial Concubine.

Each jolting length the cart traveled became an ordeal, each cloud shadowed a possible massing of Red Brows. The clatter of a peasant's mattock on frozen field sounded like the first swordstroke of battle. A creak of branch, or a bough snapping from a winter-killed tree, sounded attack signals to her overwrought mind. Yet Silver Snow dared not complain to the official, who would wonder at what she knew and how she had gained that knowledge. His own file of guards was large. She herself, despite her possible future rank, rode less straitly guarded.

Silver Snow kept her hands passively folded in her sleeves. Underneath her outer robe lay dagger and arrows; her bow waited for her, strung, barely concealed by spare cushions. She came tensely to full alert each time they swept past peasants trudging on the road. Who knew whether or not those figures muffled in patches of rag upon rag might not actually be scouts, swords and bows near to hand? Once again she attempted a study of each rider within her range of sight who bestrode a bay horse. Was *he* the spy? Her fingers slid back and forth across the hilt of the sharp little dagger that she had tucked within her sash.

Slowly, the day wore on, a day of drab skies, and sullen, spitting snow. Rather than shadows here and there, a general haze misted sight. As the afternoon gave way to evening, the sky began to lighten, even to assume a faint imperial vermilion tinge at the western horizon toward which they journeyed. Even the heavy cloud cover began to dissipate, allowing the limited light to send long shadows from man, from horse, from cart across the ice-bound fields.

Willow roused and pulled herself up to find her own spy place behind the driver. She drew a gasping breath that brought Silver Snow to her side. The beggars just ahead, two or three of them, one missing a leg. Armed only with the staves they needed for balance on the treacherous icy road, they squatted by its side to allow the cortege to pass, looking miserably cold. As the official's own elaborate carriage passed, they held out their cracked palms beseechingly. The carriage ground to a laborious halt at the imperious command of one of the official's outriders.

"Why do you stop?" came a cry, which carried to a distance through the icy air.

"Is charity not a virtue, lord?" The insolence of that must have rendered the official dumb, for he made no answer. Two guards dismounted and walked toward the crouching beggars, leading their horses. Their *bay* horses.

Silver Snow tensed. The order in which the caravan had stopped brought her own cart to face the beggars. Beside her, Willow hissed. Her hands clenched and unclenched as if she possessed claws in her human, as well as in her animal, guise.

Silver Snow saw those green eyes mirrored her own suspicions and mounting fear. She nodded. Willow took a deep breath to utter a sharp, yapping cry. With the craft of the fox-people, she threw her voice so that the outcry seemed to echo from behind the beggars and those guards who tossed them strings of cash.

Pure shock jolted one of the guards upright. Then Willow yapped again, and from the nearest patch of underbrush burst two foxes, who ran toward the beggars, hurling themselves against the hunched men. Even from where she was, Silver Snow could see that the animals' eyes were glazed. Their fur roughened in near panic at what Willow had commanded of them, action that violated their every protective instinct.

"Oh, the brave ones. The brave ones!" Silver Snow cried. She dragged the curtain hastily aside and leaned out of her cart to see that her own escort had formed up a wall between the cart and the clamor of the struggle.

"My friends," murmured Willow, and uttered a series of barks that, even to Silver Snow's dull human ears, sounded like praise and encouragement. The foxes looked once to the cart, gave tongue sharply, and were gone before any of the cursing men could move.

One of the beggars, he who had first been thrown off balance by the foxes' sudden onslaught, strove to lever himself up from the ground. His dirty rag of a cap was lost beneath a headscarf coming askew now . . . *to expose eyebrows dyed a vivid crimson*. Their unnatural color made his eyes gleam as if filled with fire, rather than mere greed and the lust for violence and who knew what—or whom—else.

Silver Snow drew a deep breath. Time for her to act, even though she disliked that she must still enact the defenseless woman. Throwing back her head, she screamed, impressed at the shrill note of terror that she managed to put into her outcry.

Instantly her guard acted. The archers among them formed up on the wings. Ao Li, his voice rusty from years of bellowing commands on the steppe, cried the alarm. "Beware! Bandits, spies! Spearsmen, to me!"

That brought the official's escort toward him at a run—or a gallop. Unfortunately, it also seemed that from every available patch of cover, from every ditch or from behind every tree, appeared more men in the guise of beggars, their headgear pushed back to reveal eyebrows stained like bloody gashes across their brows. Each of them had both a staff and dagger; many also possessed spears, bows, and swords. Those who came up now in answer to a shrill whistle rode bay horses.

Silver Snow had read of battles, but she had never thought to see one. This melee across ice and blood-slicked snow bore no resemblance to the orderly massings and dispersals of troops as described in the scrolls written by General Sun Tzu. Even in the cold, the smells of blood and death shocked her. This was as much worse than a hunt as a forest fire was worse than a hearthfire.

Willow retreated into a corner of the cart, huddling, head down, in her robes. Silver Snow caught her wrist.

"Hand me my arrows!" she commanded.

Her own archers, she saw, had assumed a winged formation that would catch the bandits in a lethal crossfire, if the official's escort drove them between the wings. The only problem—and it was a significant one—was that her own cart lay too close to the path of the necessary charge.

In that press, surely no one would note arrows flying from a direction from which no one would expect them to come. At least, she hoped so. She aimed carefully, trying to pick off a bandit who snarled and thrust at one of the oxen. Then the fellow was scrabbling at his eye, the crimson of blood gouting out over the scarlet of his eyebrow as he sought to pull out her arrow. She discovered suddenly that, even though her quarry might happily have killed or violated her, killing him was far different from killing a beast. Her hand shook; she missed her next shot and was speedily ashamed. Her supply of arrows was strictly limited; she needed a steady hand.

Even the official, she saw, armed with a fine sword, had entered the fight. A mounted bandit, attracted by the richness of the lord's sable robes, kicked his horse toward the official and swung savagely at him. Carefully Silver Snow aimed, but Ao Li intervened with a shrewd thrust of a spear, to bear the choking man to the ground. At his gesture, two troopers dragged the bandit away from the fight.

That captive must have been the leader. For at his taking, the others panicked as might a hill of ants stirred by a stick. They broke from the rough order in which they had fought, now charging in, cutting, slashing, and shooting with the ferocity of cornered wolves.

Willow's eyes were bright, and she yapped again, smiling when animals erupted from shadows to slash at the bandits' ankles, skillfully evading the blows of the men whom they brought down.

"They will be killed!" protested Silver Snow.

"Elder Sister, many will die willingly to protect their kits, or to avenge those already lost. They too are soldiers . . . there!" She pointed, and Silver Snow drew bow and fired at the bandit who had slashed down to cripple Ao Li's sword-arm, so that he stood weaponless.

"Get back!" shouted Silver Snow, but, of course, the old man would not. Seizing the spear of a fallen bandit in his left hand, he advanced until two of the bandits rode at him from opposite directions. Their double attack brought him down.

Silver Snow blinked furiously. Tears formed in the corners of her eyes, hotter even than her heated cheeks. For Ao Li's men, his death was a signal as potent as the capture of the bandit chief had been to his followers. The soldiers pushed ahead relentlessly, their faces grim as they deployed in a well-drilled formation that the bandits could not match, nor from which the wretches could not retreat.

"This is death country," murmured Silver Snow.

"Aye." Willow pressed closer to her mistress, offering comfort, just as a beast reassures a kit.

"No!" Silver Snow gasped. "It is not just what we see about us. Those whom we fight must have a line of retreat or they are speedily swallowed in death country."

"More from your dusty scrolls, mistress?" Willow asked.

"Yes. Sun Tzu taught that an army should never engage in death country, meaning any ground from which their enemies were unable to retreat."

Willow nodded. "So is truth spoken. Have I not seen a vixen backed up by hounds against a wall turn and fight, killing one hound and forcing the other to let her flee to her earth? We cannot let the soldiers' blind courage drive these bandits against such a wall."

She cried out once again in that strange yapping tongue, something that sounded like a string of commands. The power of fox-spirits over the friends-in-fur became manifest as the animals charged from cover, distracting soldiers and bandits alike with their sortie and their equally sudden and inexplicable retreat. Willow had no intention of permitting her friends to be forced into death country of their own.

"The bay horses," reminded Willow.

That was right. Were not some among the guards spies who deserved no better fate than that of their scarlet-browed conspirators? Creeping to another corner of her cart, Silver Snow peered out just in time to see a man wearing the livery of the escort single out a soldier to slay. She drew and shot, and Willow nodded approvingly.

"Now, that one," she pointed with a sharp-nailed finger.

"Quick, Willow! Another arrow!" A mounted bandit—one of the men who had killed Ao Li had assailed the official who had seized the reins of a riderless mount. Silver Snow nocked, drew, and shot in one smooth, practiced motion. The bandit fell, doubling over his chest from which an arrow jutted, sunk in almost to the fletching. She had not known that she possessed the strength to send an arrow that deep . . . *Ao Li, that death was for you! Do you see it? Do you approve?*

However she was not sure that he would. He had spent his life serving the father and his death serving the daughter. Still, he might not have approved a lady's taking part in a battle.

"Watch the bay horses," whispered Willow.

The soldiers were pressing forward once again. Then the official shouted, and Silver Snow nodded approvingly. He, too, had read Sun Tzu and wished to risk no more men. The bandits turned and fled, leaving their dead and wounded behind them.

Now that the battle was over, Silver Snow tried to hide her bow beneath the cushions and quilts in the cart, but she was shaking so violently that she allowed Willow to push her down into the nest meant to keep them warm. Her hands trembled, and the bow dropped from them. Runnels of sweat ran beneath her robes, but still she shivered from the cold. She pressed her hands against her burning cheeks, unaware that now she presented the very image of a delicate lady overborne by violence. Her bow—it must be hid! And she mastered herself enough to thrust it beneath a cushion.

Outside, she could hear the official's now-hoarse voice, commanding that the bandits be bound, that the ones among them who were wounded have those wounds bandaged until they could be sentenced, she was certain, to one of the more painful methods of execution. Hearing the groans and cries of wounded soldiers and wounded bandits alike, she decided that there were far too many methods of inflicting pain and death.

Her father had spent a lifetime in such actions, well learned in such methods. Yet he was not mad, not brutal with others. Truly, he was even more worthy of veneration than she, in what she now perceived to be sheltered innocence, had been capable of understanding. Perhaps she could write to tell him so. He was owed that tribute too.

Then, lamenting, a troop of men in faded garments and old leather armor marched slowly toward her. Several clearly struggled to hold themselves proudly, not out of deference, surely, for her, whom they had known since she was old enough to shoot at a mark or ride a pony. Rather, they marched to honor the man whose body they laid down before the cart.

"Ao Li." Silver Snow's eyes filled with tears. The old troop leader's face still wore a look of anger and surprise, though blood trickling from his mouth and nose turned his well-known (and to her, always kindly) features into a demon-mask. His open eyes gazed up at the darkening sky.

What would her father have done? This far away from him, she must stand in the place of Ao Li's general, for whom he had died. Drawing a deep, shuddering breath, she snatched up a veil and stepped down from the sanctuary of the ox-cart.

She knelt at the guardsman's side, put out one hand, and closed his staring eyes. "I avenged you, old friend," she murmured.

A spasm of trembling shook her. For a disgraceful moment, she thought that she might be sick. It would be a terrible, inauspicious moment for such illness. A quick, sharp pinch from Willow's hand as she aided Silver Snow back to her feet startled her, and she looked up to learn the reason for this attack.

She shut her eyes in momentary exasperation to wish, for the first time in a healthy life, that she had the power to sink into a faint whenever she chose. For only such weakness, she feared, would let her escape confronting the official, his bulky, luxurious robes now sweated and bloodstained, as he puffed and nodded a ceremonious way toward her.

Here she stood, sweaty, shaken, with her father's troops about her. She was as bare of face as a peasant wench, nor had she scrupled to look upon battles and wounds, or close a dead man's eyes. At least, she thought somewhat wildly, her bow was safely hidden beneath cushions. Quickly she flung the veil about her.

Had she not regained control of herself, she might have moaned, however, at the official's first words.

"The lady"—he bowed, as did she, even more deeply—"is a warrior of no mean prowess."

She contrived, somehow, despite the scarlet painting her cheeks, to look confused. "Ao Li"—she looked down sadly at the dead man—"was one of this worthless one's father's most faithful companions."

"Who has been worthily avenged." The official waved to two of his own guards and gave swift, welcome orders that they should help set Ao Li's body in order. Silver Snow fell to her knees.

"This one begs the most noble lord that the worthy Ao Li be returned to her father's lands, where he may lie in familiar ground," she whispered, her head down, her tears falling now that the immediate horror of the battle—and the stern composure that had let her know how best to act during it—had ebbed.

"Rise, rise," insisted the magistrate, waving one well-kept hand, stained now and blistered from his own work with sword and bow. "Let it be done as you wish, lady. But it will mean that you arrive in Ch'ang-an with fewer than your proper guard."

Silver Snow rose, this time not waiting for Willow's assistance. "What difference should that make?" she demanded, dropping formal speech and daring to look the man in his astonished black eyes. "Ao Li shall rest in his own place, fitly mourned by his sons and his friends. Compared with that, whether my guard numbers three or thirty is of no matter . . .

my most noble lord," she added, a guilty instant later after a hiss from Willow.

"You understand a soldier's loyalty well," said the official. "I heard you give the order—nay, do not wave your hand at me and look as if you would say it is not so—to let some bandits escape. I would know why."

Silver Snow looked downward in the direction of the besmirched tips of her felt boots, saw an impatient tapping of one of the official's boots, and knew that she must answer.

"Death country," she said, employing the die-away whisper that her nurse had tried to make her use whenever she replied to men. "Their leader was gone. Without him, they are a fowl from which the head has been twisted. It may jump about for a moment longer, but its death has been ordained. Yet, if one would restrain them, they might have fought as one does who knows himself already doomed. Or," she added hastily, "thus my father once said."

"And you listen to your father, even when he quotes Sun Tzu," the official said.

"It is this one's duty and her honor to listen if her father deigns to speak."

"Did he also teach you to draw a bow?" asked the official.

Silver Snow again cast down her eyes, realizing how strong a defense the conventional trappings of maidenly shyness might be. "I see that you wear a knife . . ."

Once again, she met his eyes, this time without deliberation. "I am the daughter of a marquis, however disgraced. Thus, may it please the Ancestors, I am perhaps to be concubine to the Son of Heaven. How should I then continue to exist should I be besmirched by such as those?"

"Lady, lady," interrupted the official, "though it be treason to whisper this, you will be wasted in the Palace, where there are ladies perhaps almost as lovely but far more richly adorned and skilled in the art of dissembling than you. If it were left to me . . . lady," he almost stammered in his eagerness to lay his plan before her, "I have an eldest son, a fine young man. Let me be his go-between . . ."

Silver Snow flushed again, this time with true anger. The man had forgotten not just fear but honor in his search for a proper bride for his son. Did he think that, because she was the daughter of a man judged to be a traitor, he could address her thus?

"I am promised—I and my father's honor with me—to the Palace; and to the Palace I shall go! These words do neither of us proper honor, my lord."

She turned and began to climb back into her cart.

"Lady, you shame me," the official called after her. "You are right. But, lady, a word of advice about propriety, from that same Confucius who is, no doubt, its author. When one finds himself in a foreign civilization, one adapts to foreign customs."

She turned, still angry, and countered his quotation with one of her own. "One's genuine personal nature is self-sufficient."

"But how few people can maintain that for a long time!" the official capped her statement. His own cap, one of its starched black wings almost hacked off, all but bobbed in his zeal and, Silver Snow realized, his pleasure! Thus her father had looked once, the first time she proved to be a not-unworthy opponent in chess.

"When one develops his nature most fully, he finds that the principles of fidelity and mutuality are not something apart from his nature," he quoted. "We know that is true, and we venerate the sage who first wrote it. But I say to you, lady, beware! You may not always meet men who are honorable, who study and respect the classics and the way of life they teach. And such meetings can test to breaking whether you can maintain your composure in adversity as well as you have done this day in battle. I would have been honored to have you as a daughter-in-law, an honorable and valued addition to the family and its estate. Better thus, than as an idle court ornament."

Once again, Silver Snow shook her head. "Your words shame us both, you for speaking them; I for listening."

The official nodded, understanding. "I wish I could say that I would also be glad to have you as a well-wisher at court; but I do not expect you to prosper if you will not bend."

Silver Snow bowed, folded her hands into her sleeves, and, this time, she waited for permission to withdraw. The man, his lips thinned and twisted as if he chewed on some unpalatable food, waved his hand to dismiss her to the refuge of her cart. Moments later, she could hear him shouting angrily at the soldiers.

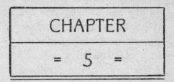

CHAPTER

= 5 =

Ahead of the cortege of chariots, carts, horses, and soldiers, some still limping from their encounter with the Red Brows bandits, towered the immense bulwark of Ch'ang-an's eastern wall. It ran in a straight, splendid line from north to the south, which marked the domain of the *Yang* and the Sun's zenith as it soared through the heavens. Silver Snow peered out at the city as her cart maneuvered for place, in company not only with her own party now, but with the thousands of others who thronged into the capital. For the first time since she had started this journey, she was thankful for the heavy curtains that enclosed her. If they left her riding in a constant twilight and prevented her from freely breathing fresh air, at least they protected her father's daughter from prying eyes as she stared—*or tried to stare*—at the wonders now rising before her.

Like the Wall that loomed near the home that Silver Snow had resigned herself never to see again, Ch'ang-an's defenses were wrought of rammed earth and bricks. But that was where the resemblance ended. The Wall at the northern border was old, mounding over in some places: a drowsy dragon covered, as it slept, by snow. Ch'ang-an's defenses, however, were veritable imperial dragons in comparison, bright with ornament, bearing armed watchmen who peered jealously over each of the three gates that pierced the thick, sloping wall.

Before Silver Snow could stop herself, she reached for the slit that she had made in the curtains of the ox-cart. She had heard much of the gates of Ch'ang-an. Each gate had three separate entrances; each entrance could admit three carts at once. She fancied that even beneath the shaking and lurching of the ox-cart, she could feel the earth tremble as so many carts and horses converged upon one place. Not just thousands of households made up Ch'ang-an, but tens of thousands. Silver Snow had never even thought of so many people, all of them crammed behind the city's immensely thick barriers. In this hour, laborers shouted and pounded on the walls; their voices reached her from a distance. Uncouth accents of men rounded up from the farthest corners of the Middle Kingdom vied with speech that she knew well.

As her fingers touched the shabby cloth, the lady behind her coughed faintly in reminder and reproof.

"Forgive me, Elder Sister," said Silver Snow, bowing her head in feigned contrition and true shame, for Lady Lilac, the go-between who had finally rejoined Silver Snow's wedding procession—such as it was—not two days outside the city, was a woman she could neither respect nor trust. She tucked her hand within her sleeves, lest the lady seize upon its callused, short-nailed appearance for yet another lecture about Silver Snow's lamentable unworthiness for life in the Palace.

At least her voice was soft and true, and her words appropriately quick and humble! Lilac nodded, a quick, barely perceptible lift of the fur-trimmed hood so bewitchingly framing a face that, though not now in its first youth, had the plump, delicate prettiness that Silver Snow knew that she lacked. Her eyebrows were plucked to mothlike delicacy, and the mouth that smiled grudgingly, as if she had nibbled on a spoiled fruit, yet did not wish to seem rude, had the round fullness of a winter plum, though its smile, like a plum too long preserved, was too sweet to be wholesome. She coughed again, as if to prove that she still suffered from the remnants of the lamentable illness that had compelled her to leave the official's party at the first suitable magistrate's estate, sick almost unto death with a cough that racked her, a fever that leached youth from her face, and shivers that made her teeth chatter in a shockingly unladylike manner. No, even if she had the strength to take this daughter of a disgraced provincial in hand, Lilac would not dream of reproving the girl whom Mao Yen-shou, the thrice-worthy Chief Eunuch, had dispatched her to guide and guard on her way to Ch'ang-an from whatever barbarous hut in which she had been kenneled. She was only desolate that she could not have tutored Silver Snow *all* the way back to Ch'ang-an; for, the Ancestors knew, the girl desperately needed training were she to be anything but a laughingstock amidst the refinement and grace of the ladies who, by right, lived within the Ninefold Gates.

Silver Snow lowered her eyes again, and suppressed a sigh. She had come all this way to see Ch'ang-an's splendid walls; and now it seemed that she would be within them, immured within the Palace itself, and would never have a chance to view them as fully as she would wish. At least, though, she no longer tried to dart a glance of amusement back at Willow. Such sharings were too dangerous for the maidservant. When Silver Snow had first been presented to Lady Lilac in the inner courts of a very grand magistrate indeed, with a great deal of bowing and sleeve-waving of the most decorous type, Lilac had seen Willow in the shadows and had recoiled with horror that, to Silver Snow's own fear, was only half exaggerated.

For once, perhaps, Silver Snow thought with an irony wholly new to her, the older woman's reaction had not been feigned. She shrank back, appalled, then turned her gesture into a delicate, dry cough, a reminder of how ill she had been. That cough, as far as Silver Snow could perceive, had been the only trace of illness about her. When she first heard it, Silver Snow had made the mistake of bowing again and, before she had been spoken to, blurting out how much of herbal lore her maid knew. Surely, she suggested, Willow could brew a tisane to ease that cough.

Lady Lilac had glared at the very idea, and Silver Snow had realized that her new go-between was one of the sort of lady who uses illness as an excuse for avoiding a task she loathed—in this case, conveying Silver Snow south to Ch'ang-an. And in an ox-cart! Beyond lamenting that propriety would not permit her to ride, Silver Snow had thought little of its disadvantages as a method of traveling. But Lady Lilac Silk had turned that very unconsciousness into yet another fault: Silver Snow should have swooned until she was presented with a carriage, its wheels wrapped in felt, its windows hung with the finest brocade (and most probably brocade far finer than any robe among her meager store of garments).

Lilac had had, of course, no intention of making the arduous journey north. She had been unable to refuse the command of the Chief Eunuch. Very well, however: it was not her fault that sickness compelled her to drop out of the cortege into the luxurious idleness of the magistrate's home where she reveled in the attention lavished upon her, as if she had been the Illustrious Concubine herself rather than, in her prime, merely a lady of the fourth rank at whom, once or twice, the Emperor had smiled.

She had glared at Willow, before, obviously, dismissing her from the ranks not just of those who mattered, but of humankind. Just as obviously, Silver Snow soon realized, her cough was as false as the smile that she produced, or the affected cries of horror with which she greeted the bow calluses across Silver Snow's right palm or any other evidence of the total unworthiness of the northern girl for the elevated station to which she was called.

Not, of course, that the Emperor would choose to dignify with his notice a girl whose family was under such a cloud, oh my no! Especially not one as plain of speech, as scant of courtesy, as mannish and as ugly as she made Silver Snow feel. Though Lilac professed never to listen to the gossip of servants or soldiers, in actual fact, she eavesdropped avidly; thus, she had heard of Silver Snow's battle with the bandits, and she professed horror that any aspirant to the imperial bed could so demean herself.

What would become of Willow if Lilac refused to let the maid accompany her mistress? Silver Snow had no illusions that this far from her father's estates, Willow could be conveyed back North: no, it would be the poison, the noose, or the slave-market for the faithful maidservant; or worse than death if her secret was discovered, try as Lilac might to pry out what made this odiously self-sufficient northern candidate for the imperial favor and her maid with the ineptly dyed hair and odious limp so very strange.

Silver Snow had tried to placate the elder woman. As might a recruit facing a vastly more experienced adversary, she had opened her arsenal, had recalled and sought to employ each of the tricks that she had seen used in the various inner courts in which she had guested on her way to Ch'ang-an, the die-away whispers, the smiles, the lowered eyes, the professions of utter and abject obedience, even the horror at dirt or cold or any kind of inconvenience. Contemptibly lazy and remiss in her duty Lilac might be, but she was no fool, to be quickly taken in by the mask Silver Snow tried to don. A country girl's native wits were no match for a court lady's skill in ruse and falsehood.

Though Silver Snow's attempts to alter her behavior warmed her go-between not at all, at least they allowed Willow to slink back into shadows, and they enabled Silver Snow to ride in the cart with her sighing, reluctant guardian in at least the semblance of peace.

It might well be, Willow had said, before retreating to a silence that the lady had condemned as sullen, that she resented the role of go-between, casting her as it did into the ranks of elder ladies, those too old to catch the Emperor's eye or bear a son to win favor and fortune for her and her family.

What, Silver Snow thought suddenly, if she had been able to offer the older woman some gift other than herbal brews? The thought came as a shock. Appalled at the very idea of bribing someone who stood in the place of an imperial representative, she tried to force the thought from her mind, but it stubbornly remained: Lilac had much to teach her, much to impart; but there was a price for such learning. The thought of bribery was abhorrent. Besides that, Silver Snow knew that nothing among her robes and ornaments would attract this lady's envy. Nor could aught be spared from her exceedingly modest baggage. Nothing, of course, except the jade armor—and that was reserved for the Son of Heaven himself.

She sighed, sounding in that moment like Lilac, and longed to sweep the curtains aside and gape like the meanest but most lighthearted peasant wench as her cart's wheels jolted into the well-worn ruts in the road that led into Ch'ang-an.

Now, as they were driving up to the great gates of Ch'ang-an, Silver Snow dared not look beyond the travel-stained curtain! It required her long moments of strict self-reproof before she was able to accept that restriction with the dignity that Confucius and her father enjoined upon her. If only Lilac's condescending chatter had provided her with the advice that she knew that she needed in a city as huge and splendid as Ch'ang-an! Had Lady Lilac been a true go-between or even simply a woman with kindness in her heart, Silver Snow could enter the Palace as fully briefed as a general who had sent out well-trained scouts. Given that kind of information, she could set about her campaign of winning first the Emperor's attention, and then his devotion.

Failing that, Silver Snow could but do her best and make the most of such information as the lady let drop.

But Lilac Silk spoke only of dear Mao Yen-shou, of the magnificence of the Son of Heaven, the splendor of the First Concubine's robes (not that she expected Silver Snow ever to reach the illustrious height that she would be clad in such), the fragrance of pavilions built of cassia wood to scent the breezes which, in the spring, made the kingfisher feathers woven into the screens shiver as if they were living clouds. She sighed over the beauty of the round temple south of the city where, every spring, the Emperor worshipped the Sun. She was like a bird with splendid plumage who repeated only what she had heard, and who sang only for those who provided her with seed . . . or gold.

The clamor of the Eastern Market rose up about them. Silver Snow had heard of that market. A bloodthirsty roar shook the curtains of the cart, and she shuddered.

"Why shiver, child?" asked Lilac. "Possibly, they execute a thief or a killer. Justice must be served."

It was fine for Lady Lilac, whose cloak was lined with sable and trimmed with fox—fox! (Willow had taken one look at it and shrunk even further into her silent wretchedness)—to ascribe Silver Snow's shudders to the cold. She had not faced bloody death, had not seen a man die, shot by an arrow from her own bow, had not wept as an old friend died in anger and pain, then avenged him, all the while in mortal fear of her own actions even more than those of the bandits.

"At least," Lilac continued, magnanimous in the face of Silver Snow's uneasiness, "you do not put yourself forward to gape at the market like a peasant. Beyond it, well, perhaps if we are discreet, no harm will be done if you glance out at the palaces as we go by. See the fine, high walls with the trees behind them. Each of those palaces has such gardens as you would not believe. How lovely they are in the spring, when the lilacs bloom!"

They drove past block after block. Used to the meandering tracks of her northern home, Lady Silver Snow found Ch'ang-an's conformity to a grid oppressive in its regularity. How could so many tens of thousands of families be forced into such narrow spaces? Indeed, the palace walls with their enameled signet tiles and their fine towers were magnificent, but how many poor crowded together in hovels this very moment so that the palace-dwellers could luxuriate in their lavish gardens?

Countryfolk were poor; Silver Snow herself was poor; but she had always had the freedom of the outside air. Now, she must surrender even that.

Glancing sideways, she could see how bright Lilac's eyes

were as the ox-cart rumbled toward the palace gate, which gaped to receive it. The sound of the gate's closing behind them was the most final noise Silver Snow had ever heard. At a sharp command, the driver stopped the oxen, and the shaking and jolting that had been a part of Silver Snow's life since leaving the North more than a month ago ceased.

This will be my home for as long as I live! Will it be prison or paradise? In either case, she knew, she must see it—immediately! Longing and fear gripped her just as Lady Lilac sighed in satisfaction. Before she could control herself, her hand—shaking, she noted, much to her shame—jerked out from her furred sleeve to the curtains. Lilac's hand shot out not a whit more slowly; and its grip was such as to leave pale crescents in the too-weathered skin of her charge's wrist.

In darkness and shadow, they sat, Silver Snow, the self-assured woman beside her, and, trying her best to simulate the cushions that wedged them into the cart, Willow, whose bright, frightened eyes flicked about her as might those of a fox caught in a snare. This Palace—it could be the greatest snare in Ch'ang-an. Or it might, Silver Snow compelled herself to remember, be the instrument of her success and her father's pardon. Before Lady Lilac could rebuke her yet again, she straightened the folds of her robes, consciously smoothed away the wariness that she knew tightened her lips and eyes into an expression as hunted as Willow's, and forced a bland, satisfied look upon her face.

Behind them, the baggage carts that carried her dowry, tribute silk and gold looted from her father's impoverished estates, clattered to a halt, but here the cries of the drivers were subdued.

Abruptly a beam of light struck Silver Snow's eyes, and a man's voice made Lady Lilac gasp in horror.

"Lady," said the official who had escorted Silver Snow from her father's house.

He deserved, at the least, thanks for his care of her; and thanks were all that she had to give, thought Silver Snow.

But, as she opened her mouth on words of gratitude, Lady Lilac shook her head.

"No!" she whispered. For the first time since her acquaintance had been forced upon Silver Snow, the horror in the woman's face was unfeigned—but not unmixed. In the sudden light, fear showed in her lips and eyes, revealing cruelly the skill with which she had applied her cosmetics only that morning and, even more cruelly, the lines and dry skin that they had been intended to conceal.

"The eunuchs will come now. Speak no word!"

Willow had frozen into the stillness of a cornered animal. Even her eyes were glazed now. Silver Snow held herself still, erect, as if she were hunting; but her breath came fast.

"Remember, lady, what I said about well-wishing."

She could not speak to thank him and dared not bow; but she shut her eyes briefly, and hoped that the official would take that for understanding and farewell.

Then the curtain dropped down again, leaving the ladies in darkness. She heard footsteps, a pause, as if men bowed deeply or saluted, and then the official's voice, commending the Illustrious Lady and her charge, the most worthy Silver Snow, to the keeping of the thrice-esteemed Mao Yen-shou.

A well-kept hand stripped the curtains from the cart, and Silver Snow sat blinking in the unfamiliar light.

CHAPTER

= 6 =

She blinked to prevent tears from rolling down the cheeks that, grudgingly, Lady Lilac had shown her how to paint just that morning *lest I disgrace her too badly by entering the Palace with cheeks as raw as those of any bumpkin wench*. In a moment her sight would clear, and she would see this wonder of a palace that henceforth was to be her home.

"Remember what I said," whispered Lilac, and her voice quivered.

"Descend, ladies," fluted a high, cultivated voice. For a moment, Silver Snow thought that other ladies had been dispatched to welcome her go-between back to her quarters and to greet her. Then the dazzle in her eyes subsided. She saw that the cart was surrounded not by ladies but by . . . they had the height and garb of men, though their robes were richer and more lavish than her father's holiday robes or the furs that the official had worn at the banquet at her home. The robes fastened as men's robes should. And, where ladies wore no headgear other than flowers or jeweled ornaments, these officials wore stiffly lacquered hats of a wondrous variety of shapes, each of which, surely, had some meaning that it would doubtless give grave offense not to know.

Used, however, as Silver Snow was to her father's soldiers,

she found the splendor of the robes, the smoothness of hair, the plumpness of belly and well-kept, grasping hands, and, above all, the lack of scars and the high, fluting voices utterly strange. These men, she knew, were eunuchs of the Palace.

Only such men—or not-men—might guard the ladies of the Inner Chambers. Incapable themselves of marriage or progeny, their loyalty was said to be directed solely toward the Emperor Yuan Ti whose new concubines they would guard with a jealousy that outdid even that of the most ambitious first wife for a younger, pregnant rival. Silver Snow's future might well depend upon their favor even more than upon the say-so of women like Lilac.

It was not their fault, she told herself, that they had suffered mutilation as children, or even as young men for the sake of the Emperor. *But for the sake of power?* a voice asked in her mind. One eunuch, whose robes were less elaborate than the others', clapped his hands, and a bevy of young women, their hair knotted forward in the style of serving girls, ran forward.

Lady Lilac tossed her head and extended her hand haughtily as she descended. Silver Snow began to slide from the cart, glancing eagerly about. The eunuch who clapped his hands could not be Mao Yen-shou; such an official as important as the Minister of Selection, the Administrator of the Inner Courts, would receive them within, if he deigned to receive a concubine as inauspicious as Silver Snow at all.

She glanced at the eunuchs, then cast down her eyes in a better-than-passable imitation of the maidenliness that she had observed in houses along the road to Ch'ang-an. But in that one glance had been a huntress' awareness; her eyes took in plum, pear, and apricot trees, their bare branches pruned into symmetrical order and leafless now, and white flower beds in which silk flowers fluttered gaily, harbingers of the real blossoms that would fill them in the spring. Incense, not the sweetness of leaves and blooms, nor the wild freshness of wind and snow, scented the courtyard. In all that vast space encircled by the palace walls, Silver Snow thought, there was not one thing that had been left to nature itself. Beyond the wilderness of sculpted trees and silken gardens rose a splendor of walls and columns, enameled and gilded, pillars stretching up from polished porches to intricately carven roofs of great pavilions.

It was toward one such pavilion that Silver Snow and Lilac were led, Willow stumping behind them.

Lilac licked her lips, dry beneath their red paint.

Why, she is frightened! Silver Snow thought. *And her fear stems, not from ignorance, as does mine, but from knowledge.* She did not need her father's scrolls filled with the wisdom of General Sun Tzu to warn her that she must be very careful. Despite all of Lilac's gushing praise of the dear, dear Administrator Mao Yen-shou, clearly he commanded fear as well as obedience.

And on him, her future rested.

Up the stairs they were led, Silver Snow careful to mince as delicately as the elder lady by her side. *Perhaps she fears that I shall tell this eunuch that she did not make the journey North.* For a moment she toyed with the idea, finding brief respite from fear in a malice that brought a flush to her cheeks in the next instant. Surely, were their positions reversed, Lilac would not hesitate to betray her. But she herself had been raised in a Confucian household; thus was not how she would wish Lilac to behave; and therefore, she herself must not do it. True propriety, not courtly artifice, silenced her.

They entered a pavilion in which incense fumes wafted in soft gray spirals and melded with the fragrance of the cassia wood of which Silver Snow thought it must be constructed. This pavilion, however, was so richly carved—its pillars inlaid with jade, its walls and cornices inlaid with precious stones, its ceilings brilliant with floral designs—that she could not see the wood itself. Up a flight of marble stairs they climbed, Silver Snow's eyes flickering from side to side at heavily robed officials and scholars. She despaired at ever understanding the faint, but significant, distinctions of color and headgear that set one rank apart from the next. The ladies—splendid in their robes and hair ornaments, their scent bags fluttering from their sashes—clustered briefly on landings, like flocks of great butterflies pausing on a single stem, before a glance from the ponderously important eunuch, who conducted Silver Snow within, sent them scurrying as fast as decorum and expensive garments would permit.

The next room was warm, unusually, unnaturally so. Rising from huge glazed jars were the trees which had blossomed and budded in the heat. Behind them, as if hidden in an embrasure or behind a door, musicians played flutes or, with a jade plectrum, plucked music from the strings and sounding board of the *p'i-pa*.

A burst of high-pitched voices greeted Silver Snow as she entered the room, but they were speaking not to her, but of politics.

"Why support one barbarian against another?" asked one eunuch. "In fact, how does one tell the difference between them?"

"Khujanga," said a second, deeper voice, with some patience, "is no fool. More than his enemy, he is willing to be guided . . ."

"Croak . . . croak . . ." several people interrupted, and laughter rose.

Her guide thumped on the polished wood floor with a staff, then walked boldly into the center of the room. Whether any of the eunuchs would even have looked at her unless her escort had been so dramatic, she neither knew or cared. She was too busy looking about. Here lounged or stood a veritable eunuchs' court, all more or less brightly clad, more or less avidly curious, save for one man, older than most, thinner than all, who sketched a greeting and slipped from the room. It had been he, she suspected, at whom the others had laughed. And yet, save that he was thinner than the others, she could see no difference among them.

The next eldest, and far the heaviest and most splendidly

dressed, stepped forward. Surely, Silver Snow thought, surely this must be the Administrator of the Inner Courts, responsible for . . . all this splendor.

But no, he was gesturing them toward the most elaborate door that Silver Snow had yet seen.

"Will this new lady be received by *him*?" asked their attendant, apprehension and awe evident in his voice. Just as evidently, he felt that this was an honor that the likes of Silver Snow did not deserve.

"Take off your outer coat," hissed Lilac, that odd, fearful quaver in her voice.

Following the elder woman's example, Silver Snow let the heavy sheepskin robes fall from her shoulders. Willow bent to retrieve them, but "leave them, girl!" ordered the eunuch, and led them farther inside the pavilion.

There, a finely carved draughts-board and a tray of delicacies lay forgotten on a low table at his side. An artist's paints and silks were neatly arranged where they might easily be picked up; and the Minister of Selection, the Son of Heaven's Administrator of the Inner Courts, Mao Yen-shou, reclined on a silk-cushioned low seat.

"Bow deeply," whispered Lilac, who had already dropped down in the first head-knocking kowtow that Silver Snow had ever actually seen performed. Quickly she imitated Lilac, but not before her quick, appraising glance had taken in this man too.

He was a veritable eunuch among eunuchs. Where the eunuchs who had met and conducted her from her cart had been plump and sleek, this man resembled a ripe plum, even to the sheen of the silken embroideries of his garments. His flesh was pale and better kept than Silver Snow's own; and his eyes, made even more narrow by cheeks as round as white melons, gleamed like jet, and flickered with intelligent speculation: the quick, appraising eye of the artist—or the courtier.

They glistened as they gazed at Silver Snow, who found herself rising from her humble posture to meet them, much as a bird stares into the eyes of a hungry serpent. He nodded once and pursed red lips, as if aware that the young woman who knelt before him was something other than the docile bud that she tried so hard to appear to be.

He extended one beautifully kept hand to a box that lay on the floor at his feet. Impossible, Silver Snow thought, that a man's hand would be that small, that well-tended, or that free of scars. Though Mao Yen-shou was an artist, not even a smudge of paint or ink defiled the white cleanliness of hands that, clearly, had never felt honest labor of any sort.

"Let us see this lady's dowry," Mao Yen-shou spoke for the first time. Silver Snow felt herself grow hot at the insult he set upon her. No welcome; no greeting. Simply "let us see your dowry." He would not even use his own soft hands, she thought, to inspect the gifts that her father had starved himself to provide.

Yet what a cultivated voice the artist had! High-pitched, beautifully modulated, it was as beyond courtesy as it was beyond ugliness: unthinkable, its accents seemed to imply, that such a voice, or its possessor, could do aught that was incorrect or unfair, or even subject to criticism by lesser mortals—such as a very young, very frightened, and very innocent young woman.

"And this lady is . . . ?" the voice asked, its self-conscious musicality pretending to conceal a yawn. *He knows my name!* Silver Snow was sure of it. Her fingers curled beneath her hanging sleeves, so much narrower, she realized now, than Lady Lilac's or those fluttering from the shoulders of the ladies who had stared and whispered as she passed. Surely even the serving girls who had helped to unload her parcels wore finer robes than she had donned for this most important meeting.

"Lady Silver Snow," replied the younger eunuch, complicit amusement in his voice, which attempted to mimic the melody of his master's speech.

"Ah yes," yawned Mao Yen-shou. "Old Chao Kuang's daughter. The traitor."

Tears of anger and humiliation welled into her eyes, and

she dropped her head, unwilling to betray her sorrow; but not before she saw the triumph in the eunuch's eyes. He had tried to goad her, and he had succeeded. She blinked furiously and determined that she would not be caught in such a snare again.

"Well, let us see if the North can provide the Son of Heaven with his due. Open the chests. Greetings, Lilac," he added as an afterthought.

Lilac rose from her own prostration and began, her voice shaken from the hauteur that had so affronted Silver Snow, to babble greetings and thanks.

"You may go. I am certain that you will be glad to see your own courtyard again . . . and what it now contains."

Lilac left the room with a speed of which Silver Snow would personally thought the woman incapable.

"You, lady. You may be seated. Fetch cushions for this . . . lady," ordered Mao Yen-shou. "And perhaps rice wine. No? No wine? Bring almond cakes too. And litchi. You must try litchi now that you have come to Ch'ang-an."

The cushions were more luxurious than any that she had ever dreamed of, much less touched. Silver Snow perforce accepted rice wine, but merely touched her lips to the rim of her bowl when it came. She shook her head at the cakes, which Mao Yen-shou ate with relish, but with never a crumb falling upon his sable collar or satined belly. At his insistence, she tasted litchi, and when she wrinkled her nose at its unfamiliar taste, Mao Yen-shou laughed uproariously, and clapped his hands for a servant to take the fruit from her.

"Take a cake instead," he ordered, and watched until, reluctantly, she did. "You are an original, lady; that let me tell you!" he said, leaning forward with a rustle of straining fabric.

If that silk splits, Silver Snow thought in fascination, *I can take my sash, go to one of those trees in the courtyard, and hang myself from the nearest branch.* She forced herself to look away.

"Most Estimable Administrator, the silk and gold appear all to be in order," said the younger eunuch.

"Splendid, splendid," approved Mao Yen-shou. He

snatched up a peach, took a quick, dripping bite from it, and then tossed it to the other. "Tell them we want more cakes, then sit with me."

"Now, little lady from the North. Well for you that your father is as obtusely honest as I thought. He has stinted you in nothing except, perhaps, the matter of dress." Mao Yen-shou gestured contemptuously at the silvery, antique brocade that Silver Snow had thought so lovely only a month ago when she found it in her mother's chests. "Most likely, after half a lifetime and a marriage on the steppes, he forgets how important such things are to ladies. But we can contrive, I tell you; we can contrive."

A plump hand went swiftly from the empty tray of sweets to a chest of gold, deft fingers gliding across the heavy, gleaming metal.

Like a fish jumping in a pool, fear leapt across the surface of Silver Snow's thoughts, then submerged. The gold and tribute silk were for the Son of Heaven; surely the Emperor's minister would not think of misappropriating them.

Mao Yen-shou laughed. "An honest child!" he commended her, and she flushed, finding that his praise made her feel more helpless and more unschooled than had his rudeness. At least that had let her use anger to protect herself. "Doubtless, where other maids learn flute and drum, old Chao Kuang insisted that his daughter study only the Analects. Come with me to the window, child, and see on what your dowry will be spent."

Having no choice, Silver Snow followed the Administrator across the room, the last almond cake that she had taken sticking to her hand. As she passed Willow, however, she let it fall into the girl's lap. Quickly, the serving girl snapped it up, and Mao Yen-shou laughed.

"I was not supposed to see that, was I, lady? But come: I shall show you something more worth looking at."

He led her to the window and pointed to the Inner Courts of which he was the master. Even in the winter, servants set out silken flowers and the women's orchestra played from a boat that floated in a lake in the center of one impossibly huge court. Individual pavilions glittered with gold and jade and polished wood; gem-bright were the joining of the paving-stones, but not as bright as the ladies who fluttered by in their gauzy jackets and skirts or long, flowing robes.

Mao Yen-shou sighed. "It has been too long since these courts rang with music and laughter. I have created beauty here, beauty as a fit setting for beauty. But the Son of Heaven rarely walks herein; too many ladies, says he. He still misses the Bright Companion." In a move as quick as it was unexpected, he turned away from the window and the beauty of the Inner Courts, and walked back into the room. Whatever Silver Snow had expected, she had not expected such an important official to be so mercurial.

"No use standing there in the draft all day, lady. Come back to your seat." To her surprise, he waited until she seated herself on the cushions. Then he picked up a brush.

"The Son of Heaven has told me that he will not have five hundred ladies paraded before the Dragon Throne. No: he has commissioned me to paint the likeness of each lady." He fell silent, and the silence continued so long that Silver Snow knew that he wanted some reply from her. She had seen a cat stalking mice more than once; was she now the mouse in some strange game?

"An honor," Silver Snow commented demurely.

The eunuch cast down his eyes in a fine imitation of her own mock-modesty, then smiled. "A heavy burden for one no longer young. So many ladies; all young; all fair. How should I favor one above the other? And yet, art is such a matter of chance. One slip of the brush, and the loveliest lady can be rendered plain; a touch of paint here, and see, the palest girl glows like a peony. And all lies within my hands to flatter or to blight. Lady, you are not in the common way. It would take a great artist to accent your good points . . ."

"And you are such a one?" she asked. Color flamed in her cheeks; surely she was not the pallid maid whom he spoke of having to beautify. "Alas," she said with some asperity, "this girl is but a poor maid, and a modest one. How should she dare to have one such as the Son of Heaven esteem her own insignificant looks as more than they are?"

She raised her eyebrows at the eunuch and saw him flush with anger. Behind her and to the side, she heard Willow shift on her knees, making ready in case her mistress should need her.

"You have remarked on how poor the North is, and spoken of my lord and father's misfortunes." Once again, iron edged her words. "We are very honest in the North, but we are poor. Too poor to give such great artists their deserts."

"But if you were to wish such artists well, lady . . ." Mao Yen-shou smiled. He was enjoying his little game, Silver Snow thought indignantly. He knew she had no money to bribe him, but he enjoyed her struggles and her embarrassment. "It is not true, as some say, that we of the Inner Courts cannot love; and we are loyal to those who wish us well. To those who do not . . ."

She thought of the official who had spoken to her of well-wishers and how he had prophesied that she was too blunt-spoken to be in a position to benefit any man by her good wishes. How true his words were.

Silver Snow's eyes blazed; and this time, she let the eunuch see it. "I have no gifts to give, and no prospects, sir," she told Mao Yen-shou. "And even if I had . . ."

"Is that your last word, lady?" asked the artist. "Bring in the other chests!" he called.

Four men staggered into the room, each pair carrying the chests that Silver Snow had last seen in her father's room, the chests that held two suits of jade armor, the gifts intended to make an old lord's peace with his Emperor.

"You say that you have no gifts, no wealth. Lady, what are these?" demanded Mao Yen-shou.

CHAPTER

= 7 =

Though Silver Snow had met poverty, betrayal, and battle without flinching, this ambush in the midst of luxury left her speechless. She opened her mouth to reply, but no sound came out. Her hands, concealed in the fraying sleeves of her robe, balled into tiny fists, then, deliberately, loosened. They were as cold as ever they had been in the long days and nights of her journey.

Slowly and with an immense settling of flesh about him, Mao Yen-shou lowered himself to his knees beside one of the chests.

"Stupid one!" he told the younger eunuch. "Am I to labor like a fieldworker? Open this at once!"

"Open the chest!" His companion clapped his hands at Willow who rose painfully, cast a despairing glance at Silver Snow, and then lifted the lid of the larger chest to expose the funeral armor of jade plates, gleaming in the light. Simple and severe in the style of a much earlier age, nevertheless, the armor had its own splendor, which fitted well in this room of high pillars and inlaid walls.

"You have no gifts to give, lady?" repeated Mao Yen-shou. He ran one hand over the faceplates of the armor, almost purring with pleasure at the jade's cold smoothness. "My servants found these . . . what do you call these trinkets . . . hidden amid your baggage."

At last, Silver Snow recovered her powers of speech. "That is an heirloom of this one's house," she said, her voice calm despite the rage and fear that made her heart feel as if it might burst through her breast. "This one's father commanded that it be presented to the Son of Heaven . . ."

"On what might be considered your wedding night? How sentimental, and how dutiful," said the eunuch. "But before you can celebrate that happy occasion, you must first win the Son of Heaven's attention. And his attention must be won through me."

"I told you," snapped Silver Snow, abandoning the careful proprieties of formal speech, "the armor is my father's gift to the Son of Heaven. I myself have no gifts to give. Can you not believe that? Look at me. Do I glitter with gems? Are my robes in the fashion of the court? We are poor in the North. But . . ."

Willow hissed, but Silver Snow was too angry to pay heed to her. "I tell you, Master Artist, had I gifts to give, I would not give them to such a one who seeks to exact them by trickery and threats."

Despite his immense bulk, Mao Yen-shou rose so quickly that Silver Snow was left kneeling on the floor. He towered over her, attempting to intimidate by his very height.

"Noble words, lady, for one who should not dare to boast. A gift, you call this; an heirloom. How if I say otherwise?"

"What else can be said?" demanded Silver Snow.

"Elder Sister," hissed Willow, "hush, I beg you!"

Willow! Silver Snow felt herself chill with concern, but not for herself. For the first time in her life, she regretted her inability to take refuge in tears or swoons, then despised herself for the weakness. She had Willow to protect! She gestured, and the maid scuttled back into the corner in which she had hidden herself. Silver Snow only hoped that Willow—with her unnaturally black hair and her limp, so grotesque in this magnificent room—would pass unnoticed; but Mao Yen-Shou was as skilled an artist as he was greedy. He could not help but notice her.

"Lady," said the eunuch, menace chill in that supple, exquisite voice of his, "do you persist in your claim that these suits of funerary armor are an heirloom?"

"My father says," Silver Snow knew that she was faltering, but fought hopelessly on, "that they have always belonged to his house and that they are fit only for a Son of Heaven and his First Wife."

"Would you swear, then, that they were never used?"

"On my Ancestors!" Silver Snow's indignant voice echoed in the room.

"Then how—Wang Lu, be you my witness to this—do you explain *these?*"

Mao Yen-shou swooped down and opened his hand beneath Silver Snow's nose.

There on his palm lay three teeth, broken and yellowed as if with age.

Silver Snow glanced up, confused at the sight of the teeth and the triumph that gleamed on the artist's florid, sweaty face.

"Lady, lady, if these suits had never been used, as you swear, how would I have found these teeth in one of them?"

Mao Yen-shou was actor, then, as well as artist; the disgust and horror on his face, the revulsion in his voice were so well-crafted that, for a mad instant, Silver Snow was all but convinced that she indeed was a violator of her Ancestors' tombs.

The incense in the air, the sight of the teeth, the sandalwood and camphor that scented the eunuch's clothing, and, above all, the sheer horror of what he implied . . . the floral patterns on the ceiling began to whirl and Silver Snow felt herself slipping sideways.

An accusation of grave-robbing, and robbing of one's own Ancestors at that: such crimes were too terrible to think of, much less to discuss. There were but two reasons to rob graves, too: greed or sorcery. And she was the daughter of a disgraced general. It would be her word against that of Mao Yen-shou and his friend. No one would believe her, should he bring charges against her of grave-robbery. She was innocent, but who would believe that? She was daughter to a man widely believed to be a traitor.

But the thought, the very thought of either crime—not to mention how hideous the punishment was likely to be for her and for her family! She reeled, then drew herself upright. She would not faint, not be sick: not here, not before this sleek enemy.

"You palmed those teeth," she told the eunuch. "Like a mountebank at a farmer's festival, you hid those teeth in your hand and would use them to force me to give you the armor. Let the world know it! I am innocent," she whispered.

"But who will believe you?" asked Mao Yen-shou. "Let a man be ever so innocent, yet, always, there is some act, some thought, that he would rather die than have revealed. Even such a simpleton as you, lady; I would wager that you cherish secrets too."

Silver Snow felt, rather than heard, the low growl. Willow! By all the Ancestors, she might be able to withstand a charge of grave-robbing—though what would become of her were such a cry even raised against her she hated to think; but a charge of sorcery, or of consorting with sorcerers? Of that, though she felt it to be no crime, she was most assuredly guilty; and the court feared sorcery as it feared little else beside pestilence or war with the Hsiung-nu. Death would be the least she could hope for, and her punishment would be a caress in comparison with Willow's.

She let her head droop, her entire body sag beneath the consciousness that she had been defeated by a thief. Worse yet, her hopes were shattered. Mao Yen-shou would take her one treasure and, because he dared not risk that she come to the Emperor's attention, when he painted her, he would use a lying brush to make her as unattractive as possible.

There was no hope now of success; no hope at all. Only her pride as a general's daughter kept her from weeping and flinging herself to the floor as Mao Yen-shou clapped hands for a servant to conduct her to temporary lodgings and for another to bring him the scroll that he had rejected as being unfit to paint upon.

She forced herself to stand passively, though she wanted to stab or to scream. She remembered the battle with the Red Brows. Then, there had been things that she could do to help herself. Now, there was nothing at all. The court, she had learned in this first, disastrous engagement, was more treacherous than any battle. But her father had survived defeat, survived and retained his dignity. Somehow, she must do the same, proving herself a worthy daughter of her line.

Months might pass, Silver Snow gathered, before Mao Yen-shou completed the portraits of five hundred ladies summoned from all over the Middle Kingdom. She had as much chance of becoming one of the Brilliant Companions of the Son of Heaven as Willow had of leaping over the walls of Ch'ang-an and racing back to the North. As artists and artisans put the finishing touches to the Sun Bright Residence where the ladies most favored by the Emperor would live, Silver Snow wondered what her own lot would be.

She could not aspire to such heights, nor perhaps even to the Residence of Increasing Reflection where the Favorite Beauties would live. Realistically, she thought that she might be placed among the lowest ranked of the concubines: the daughters of noble families. Because she preferred study to idleness, she set about learning the customs she must follow in this new and far from welcome life.

She took part in the festivals that heralded the spring plantings, eagerly seized upon any chance to improve her calligraphy, and spent many hours composing upon silk a hopeful and dutiful account to her father of her journey to the capital. When older women such as the Lady Lilac—ladies too faded to attract notice and whose lusts were, in any case, for power—called for willing hands or sweet voices, she was quick to volunteer and quicker yet to withdraw should a brow be raised at the way that the northern girl of no particular prospects, the one with the maidservant of such surpassing, horrid ugliness, put herself forward.

Such ladies seemed to sense that Silver Snow's fortunes were different and far more lowly than the prospects of the scores of Precious Pearls, Cassias, Jasmines, and Plum Fragrances who clustered like so many blossoms in the Inner Courts, thronging in the terraces and passageways that joined one pavilion to the next. Under the guise of assisting the elder ladies, they exclaimed over the rich silk hangings, the huge painted pots, the ornate inlays of gold, malachite, and turquoise that, day by day, appeared in their quarters.

How they talked! Silver Snow, raised to quiet and meditation, found that enduring the ever-present, ever-chattering crowd of young women the most onerous task of her days. Unlike her, they seemed to have no trouble adapting to the life of the courts, circumscribed, rigid, relentlessly polite even at its most hostile. She often thought that even if Mao Yen-shou painted her in his most flattering colors, she would have no chance among this garden of beauties. Each one, it seemed to her, embodied the highest praise that could be accorded a woman's beauty. For a woman to have the expression of a flower, the mouth of a bud, the soul of the moon, the posture of the willow, bones of jade and a skin of snow, the charm of an autumn lake and the heart of poetry—that would indeed be perfect!

Perfection indeed, unlike her own looks. Even the mirror held in Willow's loving hands showed a woman whose eyes could flash or soften, depending upon her mood; whose mouth was quick to laugh; and whose soul was turbulent and whose charm—assuming that anyone would credit her with possessing it—was a matter of obedience, duty, and repose, not the quicksilver grace prized at court. The official had been right; Silver Snow might have been far more content as the busy first wife of an heir to a country estate than as a court lady of little favor and many trivial chores.

Although she was forced often into the company of the

other ladies, increasingly a gulf widened between her and them. With the same unconscious knowledge that let them place their hair ornaments to best advantage, they seemed somehow to sense that Silver Snow could not expect a bright future, let alone one as Illustrious Concubine. More and more often, they avoided her. Not even the too-tall girl so absurdly named Peony Bud nor Apricot, who wept because her skin was sallow and the others teased her about it, bothered to speak to her; they preferred instead to hover on the outskirts of the bevy of more fortunate girls, clustering eagerly about those whom they felt the Emperor might be likeliest to favor. Not for any of these ladies was the type of loyalty that made her father's soldiers follow him into disgrace; they preferred to curry favor with potential favorites.

Would I be any better? Silver Snow asked herself time and again in the silence that she now had time to appreciate. She could spend time with Willow, calming the maid's alarms, assuring her that, with the jade armor in his possession, Mao Yen-shou would be too concerned to avoid scandal to bring charges of sorcery against mistress and maid. She performed whatever tasks were assigned her and spent any leisure that she had contemplating what she had to admit was the very real beauty that Mao Yen-shou had created. If only his soul had been the equal of the craft of his hands and mind!

"The portraits!" Suppressed laughs and shrieks of affected horror rang out in the courtyard where the willow trees had begun to bud. Three ladies passed the small court that had been assigned to Silver Snow; none stopped to call in at her door to invite her to come view them.

"So he has finished these paintings?" Silver Snow mused, with only Willow as an audience. She bent her head over her own brushstrokes. "Wealth and poverty, fame and obscurity: each has its time." Painstakingly she drew characters that she hoped her father would not find too unworthy. By now he must realize that she would be unlikely to achieve their fondest hopes. Let him, at least, realize that she was suitably resigned and that, as he had said, she had found some occupation in study.

She raised her brush once again, but found that her hand was shaking. After so many weeks, the mere mention that the completed portraits of the court ladies would be submitted to the Son of Heaven for his choice could reduce all her philosophy to a sham.

"Willow?" Her voice trembled too.

At once the faithful maid was at her side, her head bent as if admiring her mistress' writing.

"Willow," whispered Silver Snow, "I know that Mao Yen-shou has painted no fine portrait of me. I know how foolish it is even to dream. But if I do not see it, if I do not know for certain, I believe that I shall never sleep again."

Willow nodded. "Then go and see, Elder Sister."

"I do not dare to," Silver Snow flinched as if she faced the ridicule that had so often troubled her in dreams that she dared not admit, even to Willow. "At least, I do not think I can bear to be seen. Willow, I know that you . . ."

"Indeed, yes, little mistress. I have explored the courts, Inner and Outer, and have seen this Son of Heaven about which these fine ladies chatter like so many jealous nightingales. Which, I make bold to say, is more than any of them have, so far. A fine, upright man, I must say, though I cannot understand one such who prefers to look upon paint and silk rather than on beautiful ladies."

"Willow!" Despite Silver Snow's apprehension, Willow's irreverence made her gasp with guilty laughter.

"In all my prowlings, though, have I found a place where you might hide and view the portraits? Is that what my Elder Sister wants to know?"

Silver Snow nodded reluctantly.

Greatly daring, Willow put out a work-hardened hand, its three middle fingers all of equal length, to touch Silver Snow's trailing sleeve. It fluttered as her hand shook despite her attempts to control it. "Is this the brave lady who avenged the worthy Ao Li? Courage, Elder Sister! I have found such a place from which you may see and not be seen. It is well that the Son of Heaven will come to the Inner Courts; to bring a lady into the Outer Courts might be perilous. Come you with me, though, and you will be safe."

Silver Snow allowed herself to be tugged from her mat onto her feet. Sweeping up her long robes, she hurried after Willow through dusty ways that, she thought, not even the designer of these pavilions would remember. *You will be safe*, Willow had said, but Silver Snow doubted it.

"This way!" hissed Willow, and Silver Snow crept into a tiny passage on the third level of the Hall of Brilliance. She squeezed through it into a space the size of a small cabinet, gazed out through a peephole, and stifled a gasp.

"Mistress, I beg you, do not sneeze!" Willow whispered.

Silver Snow could only shake her head faintly. Just once in her life, she had ridden out on a sunny day in winter at noon and glanced from the sun to the snow and back into the sun. The very strength of its brilliance had made her reel in the saddle, and she had ridden thereafter with black specks before her eyes. She blinked and expected to see such specks dance before her eyes now too. Even the robes of the musicians and servants were finer than her most elaborate gowns; the robes, hats, and parasols of those officials who ran into the Son of Heaven's presence chamber and prostrated themselves before the Dragon Throne provided a vivid magnificence against which the gauzy finery of those ladies who had dared to assemble appeared like Tung Shuang-ch'eng, the fairy who, in the legends that Silver Snow had loved as a child, guards the crystal snow vase.

The ladies clustered in one corner, occupying themselves, or pretending to do so, with the placement of their sisters' ornaments, the float of a sleeve, the particular angle at which a scent bag fell from a lavishly embroidered sash. But their eyes, beneath their plucked and painted brows, kept flickering toward the ranks of the eunuchs where, in a place of pride, his companions arrayed behind him, stood Mao Yen-shou, awaiting the Emperor's pleasure, his young assistant hovering close at his plump shoulder.

Silver Snow drew a deep, shuddering breath. Finally, she permitted herself to gaze upon this Son of Heaven for whom she had journeyed so long and so fruitlessly. Despite his youth, the Emperor Yuan Ti bore himself with the dignity of a man at least of middle years. He wore his heavy robes, embroidered with five-toed dragons, negligently, as if he would much prefer the dark simplicity of a scholar's gown, and he kept his eyes resolutely averted from the bevy of ladies who watched and sighed over his every move.

"*Wan Sui!*" Silver Snow whispered dutifully. "May the Emperor live ten thousand years!"

Was it her imagination, or, in that moment, did the Son of Heaven look up as if his vision could pierce the wall behind which she had concealed herself? She flushed, and tried to hear what he was talking about.

The Emperor apparently shared the court's preoccupation with the Hsiung-nu. At least that subject intrigued him far more than the chance that, among such pictures, he might find a lady who would be to his liking. From the way he spoke and the way that the eunuchs replied, he had been discussing them all day; and, when he had perforce broken off council to come into the Inner Courts, he had brought what he clearly felt to be more pressing concerns than a new chief concubine with him.

Because none of his advisors except his eunuchs could accompany him into the Inner Courts, his eunuchs must now serve to discuss it rather than generals, treasurers, and ministers of state. Their attempts, coupled with a lack of interest that was total and a lack of information that came close, to humor their Emperor pleased neither eunuchs nor Emperor. Mao Yen-shou's shining face bore a poorly concealed petulance; several of his underlings flared their nostrils in attempts to conceal their yawns; and the Emperor himself grew impatient.

From her vantage point, Silver Snow could see the ladies

droop as they realized that they could not compete with the Son of Heaven's interest in negotiations with the Hsiung-nu. It would all be unfamiliar names and threats of violence to them, Silver Snow was sure. To her, however, the names were well known as antagonists or worthy opponents of her house. She longed to creep closer to hear the discussion that, against strict propriety, the Emperor had brought into the Inner Courts where all should be lightness, beauty, and peace. A vain, foolish custom, she told herself, and was immediately aghast at her daring to have such a thought.

The Emperor looked up dissatisfied, waving aside those eunuchs who had stood closest to him. What—or whom— was he seeking? Certainly he glanced about as if he lacked something . . . or someone. Then memory seemed to come to him. He nodded and beckoned. To the hissed amazement of the eunuchs, out walked one among their number: thinner than most; his face weathered and lined, where his brother eunuchs' cheeks glowed like plums; his eyes thoughtful, a little wry. While the splendid silks of the other eunuchs' robes seemed to rival the gowns of the ladies whom they guarded, this one wore a plain scholar's robe. He bowed himself to the floor, and when he replied to the Emperor's questions, it was in a voice deeper than properly belonged to the eunuch's kind.

"This one, the most miserable Li Ling, wishes the Son of Heaven to live ten thousand years. This abject one thanks the Son of Heaven for the summons after so long, so very long." (The eunuchs gasped with righteous outrage at that too.) "How may this one serve? What may this one speak of?"

Li Ling! Silver Snow had heard of him. Like her father, he was a general and a noble . . . or had been. Like her father, he had been unlucky, both in battle and in his choice of allies at court. But, unlike her father, Li Ling was no longer a man. Involvement with losing generals had begun the downfall that an accusation of sorcery had only hastened. And when instruments of alchemy had been discovered in his home, he had been put first to the question, then to the knife that reduced him from general, noble, and lord of a domain, to last of his line and a eunuch of the court like the once-illustrious Ssu-ma Chien, who had been similarly unlucky.

Never mind that! Silver Snow told herself. She concentrated on Li Ling's words. The disgraced courtier drew himself up, put on wisdom and his former dignity as if they were the finest of robes.

"We are a mighty nation," said the Son of Heaven. "Why do the Hsiung-nu dare to raid our borders?"

Once again, Li Ling bowed. "May this one recall to the Son of Heaven his feeble words. Ever since the hour of my surrender until now, destitute of all resources, I have sat alone with the bitterness of my grief. All day long, I see none but barbarians around me."

One of the younger eunuchs giggled, and the disgraced lord halted. The Emperor gestured quickly in aggravation for him to continue. The eunuchs opened their ranks, concealing the young fool who had had so little control as to snicker at the Son of Heaven's choice of advisor, regardless of his previous status among them.

"Skins and felt protect me from wind and rain. With mutton and whey I satisfy my hunger and slake my thirst. The whole country is still with black ice. I hear naught but the moaning of the bitter autumn blast, beneath which all vegetation has disappeared. Most Illustrious Son of Heaven"—the old eunuch looked up earnestly—"the Hsiung-nu are poor in all but valor. They hold it a virtue to wrest what they will from those whom they consider weak."

"And yet this Khujanga promises us that, should we grant him our support, he will cease to raid. Will he keep his word?"

The eunuch-lord appeared to consider. "May this one most humbly inquire what his words were?"

The Emperor flicked his fingers, and a minister passed Li Ling a bundle of wood strips. He bent, shook his head over the awkwardness of the writing, and read, "'I propose to have a frontier trade with Ch'in on a large scale, to marry a Ch'in princess, to receive annually ten thousand firkins of spirits, ten thousand pieces of assorted silk, besides all the rest as provided by previous treaties; if this is done, we will not raid the frontier.'"

Li Ling paused momentarily as a brief eddy in the group of ladies rose and died at the mention of a Ch'in princess as the bride of the Hsiung-nu ruler. "Having naught else now to stake, this most miserable and unworthy one would stake his life that the *shan-yu* will keep to such an agreement."

Silver Snow could hear angry mutterings about tribute, about barbarians, and about the Emperor's greatness of heart in hearing out an ill-fortuned dotard.

From the side of the Hall of Brilliance, someone gestured, and the Son of Heaven sighed, as if recalling himself to matters less interesting, if more pressing.

"We shall think on this and give the *shan-yu* our answer should he become the *shan-yu* in truth as he is in boast. You shall continue to advise us. Nay, you are too old for those skull-thumpings on the floor, man! But now . . . let our Administrator of the Inner Courts, Mao Yen-shou, come forward."

With a flourish of his embroidered robes, Mao Yen-shou prostrated himself before the Dragon Throne.

"Let his robes split!" whispered Willow, and Silver Snow glared her maid into silence.

So hard did her heart beat that she could not hear his words of greeting and of praise. But she saw, clearly enough, when the portraits of the ladies were unveiled. Aye, there was Precious Pearl, as lovely as her name and nature. The Son of Heaven deigned to nod. He smiled at the portrait of Cassia, shrugged at a number of others.

"You are but one of five hundred," Willow whispered. "Perhaps he will not even present your likeness at all."

Silver Snow shook her head. The Master of the Inner Courts would most certainly not ignore her, lest someone ask why but four hundred and ninety-nine ladies had been depicted. Peony Bud, Jade, Apricot—he must be showing the least attractive girls in a group. Silver Snow braced herself.

At first, she did not recognize her own portrait. Then her

hand jerked as if in instinct to cover her mouth, and she bit down to keep from crying out in anger. She had thought that she had very little vanity; that she knew that she was the equal of only a very few of the ladies who now pretended to gasp in shock at her picture. But that . . . that girl on the silk screen! Oh, it was she, all right: the darkness of the hair, the decisiveness of the tiny pursed mouth, the flash of the almond-shaped eyes. Those were all hers. No one could say that the painter had lied.

But Mao Yen-shou had painted her with her lips parted to reveal gapping teeth just the slightest bit yellowed. He had lowered her forehead, making her appear to seem stubborn, had mixed yellow with his skin tones until she looked unhealthy, and, worst of all, had painted an ugly black mole below her right eye, the unluckiest of all places for a maid to have such a blemish.

Yuan Ti shook his head in amazement.

"How was such a one ever selected for our Inner Courts?" he asked the self-assured eunuch. "Let a woman have a mole beneath her right eye, and she brings misfortune to all whom she sees."

As if sensing his master's irritation, the mynah on the elaborately wrought perch at his side fluffed out its crest and shrieked. The Emperor caressed it with a careful finger.

Mao Yen-shou flung himself spectacularly to the floor, wailing as if at his father's funeral. The maid, he said, was as crafty as she was ill-favored; she had concealed her blemish. "Let this vile one's head serve as recompense for the error!" he lamented. "The girl is as inauspicious as all her family, but I did not know that she was so homely!"

Had it not been she, Silver Snow wondered if she would not have laughed. She noted that alone of the courtiers and ladies, the elder eunuch Li Ling had not joined in condemning her portrait. He chewed upon his beardless lip, and seemed to want to turn away.

"Ill-favored and ill-fortuned," mused the Emperor. "Was her father not a traitor?"

"Let this one send the maid away!" begged Mao Yen-shou.

Li Ling flung himself down too. "This one begs the Most August! Homely the maid may be, but she is blameless and should not have such a shame put upon her. Her father has already been punished twice. This one submits most humbly that he should not receive another punishment without having deserved it."

Silver Snow stifled a sob. *Father, if only I could tell you how your old friend defends your honor and your most miserable child's!* But she knew that this scene was one that she would never describe in a letter; it was too humiliating.

Mao Yen-shou glared at the older eunuch, and looked as if he wished to do worse when the Emperor held up a hand.

"Li Ling has a point, Administrator. We cannot visit Chao Kuang with an undeserved punishment, not when he has already been cursed with . . ." He shut his eyes. "Take that picture from our sight."

"Let this one do more, Son of Heaven!" begged Mao Yen-shou. "Let that wretched girl be moved from the Inner Courts, whose harmonies she spoils and where, by chance, your eyes might light upon her, to the Cold Palace."

Silver Snow had been kind to Plum Blossom and Apricot, whose portraits had received so little attention, but not even they showed any sorrow at that sentence of exile.

The Cold Palace! It was utterly isolated. That, Silver Snow felt in her present mood, might be a blessing, but the Cold Palace was as inauspicious as it was isolated. Some of the more timorous women even whispered that it was haunted by foxes.

"It is not so bad, mistress," whispered Willow at her side, but Silver Snow had stiffened, hearing a ribald murmur from one courtier to his fellow standing two floors below her vantage point. "Perhaps the girl will hang herself. I know I would, were I a maid with a face like that!"

That snapped the control that Silver Snow had kept on herself all the weeks of her journey and all the months of her imprisonment, which would now be solitary and for the rest of her life. Knowing only that she must escape, that she must hide, she flung herself out of the passage and into a corridor that she had never seen before. Gone were the tiny, decorous steps enjoined upon fine ladies. She was no fine lady; she was but a girl so sorely insulted that she did not hear her maid's hiss of caution, nor did she realize what she had done.

The passage down which she ran was screened from the Hall of Brilliance but by a thin veiling of silk; and it was directly across from the Dragon Throne. As she ran, the outline of her form, graceful in its trailing robes, flickered across the silk for all the court—and the Son of Heaven himself—to see.

"Hold! What is that?" He half rose from his chair, one hand pressed against his heart. "My lady, whom even the wisest of my wizards could not restore to me.

> *Is it or isn't it?*
> *I stand and look.*
> *The swish, swish of a silk skirt.*
> *How swiftly she flees!*"

Tears streaming down her face, Silver Snow had fled long before the echo of the Emperor's heartbroken verse had died away.

CHAPTER

= 8 =

On the other side of the wall, sweet strains of flute and zither rang out, almost as sweet and considerably less artificial than the laughter and sighs of the ladies who drifted across the arched bridges or who, with outcries of mock fear, reclined on intricately painted boats on the lake in the central courtyard. Sunbeams slanted down into that court, though they seemed, thought Silver Snow as she gazed down at her hands, never to illuminate her own shabby courtyard in the Cold Palace.

Today, for a change, she sat not in the courtyard with its unpruned trees and its bushes that had gone to seed, but in the green and white octagonal pavilion that, even now, had not lost the chill of winter. No wonder, she thought, that this place was called the Cold Palace; but it was a cold not so much of air or water, but of the spirit.

She shut her eyes as if she were infinitely weary. Yet even in the darkness, with Willow kneeling beside her, crooning a wordless song, she found no comfort. The day's humiliations had left wounds in her heart and mind, wounds that still bled. Even now, she panted as if, once again, she had to run weeping through the palace corridors, had reached her own tiny courtyard, and flung herself down, only to find herself almost instantly assailed by servants. With courtesy distinguishable from insolence only by an observer who worked hard to make that distinction, they had invaded her room, stripping even the hangings from her bed as they packed up her few possessions and hurried them—and herself—to the Cold Palace.

Her gamble to bring her father to the Son of Heaven's attention had failed. Now, lifelong imprisonment was the punishment for losing her game.

The Cold Palace, isolated and unlucky, was a quiet, solitary world. No one called on her, except, of course, those who sought to save on tips to servants by using her for labor: an elder concubine or two who needed some tedious chore or other to be completed by someone who would not complain; a young woman whose fear, laziness, or caprice brought her to Silver Snow to remedy a mistake or shorten a lengthy task. Having little else to do, Silver Snow complied with their requests; had she refused, she might have lost the little goodwill that she might still have left. It was better to be patronized, she thought, than to be persecuted.

Such women swept in, bestowed the work upon her as if they honored her by their presence, and pressed her to complete it speedily. When it was finished, though, they came no more to the Cold Palace. It was better, she decided then, to be ignored than to be patronized.

Occasionally, Silver Snow heard their voices ring out over the wall. They called her the Shadowed One. That name that had spread throughout the Inner Courts and chilled Silver Snow even more than the usual dearth of fuel for her braziers. Even the one or two servants assigned for their misdeeds to wait upon her used that name when they spoke of her. To her and to Willow, they spoke as little as they could, and there was no way she could punish them for their insolence. Few creatures, she quickly learned, had as little influence as she who lives in disfavor among eunuchs and women.

Once or twice an occasional pitying girl with more sentimentality than intelligence might glance in upon her, then flee, as if fearing that Silver Snow's disgrace might contaminate her too. After all, birds peck at the one who is different and judged to be an outcast; the pretty, bejeweled creatures of the Inner Courts much resembled those birds. By tormenting an outcast, they hoped to prevent themselves from being made outcast too.

Silver Snow might have sunk into a quiet, despairing madness had she not had Willow with her. Loving, patient Willow, who sat with her during the twelve hours of the day and, when she could not sleep, during the watches of the nights that grew shorter and shorter as the season turned toward a summer of joy and beauty in which Silver Snow, alone among palace maidens, might not share. (She did, however, accomplish more than one woman's share of the needlework for the various festivals.) It was Willow, who gazed for long moments into her scrying mirror or cast the hexagrams time and again, trying to discern in their arrangement some scrap of good fortune.

"It is all change, Elder Sister," the maid sighed after one such session. "Change and travel."

Silver Snow threw down her brush with such force that it snapped. "But I am not destined to travel; I am immured here!" she cried. "Your yarrow stalks are as crooked as your . . . oh, Willow, forgive me!"

She covered her face with tiny hands from which the months in the Cold Palace had peeled the bow calluses and wept. To think that she would turn thus upon Willow, who had put her life in jeopardy to follow her and asked only to serve her! To think that she had lost control! How ashamed her father would be—almost as ashamed as she herself was.

After what seemed like a long, miserable hour, a soft, hesitant touch on her knee made her lift her head and see Willow crouched at her side.

"Oh, Willow," said Silver Snow, dashing her hand across eyes that she had not painted all spring long, "rather than live as such an ingrate, I should hang myself with my sash from that withered tree before I too wither."

"Mistress, hush!" cried Willow. "There is nothing," she

added with a mischievous glance, "in the hexagrams to tell me you face death."

Despite her shame at her self-pity, Silver Snow found herself laughing. "Ah, Willow, Willow," she said, "you make me realize just how true is the proverb that one does not live in vain if there is one person in all this world who totally understands one."

To her surprise, Willow flushed deeply and turned away. Lest Silver Snow embarrass the maid further, she cast about for some diversion. "I have embroidered until I have pads on my fingertips! And it does not seem as if I shall write any further today to my honored father. How can I? Even assuming that some worthy man would have the charity to deliver the messages of a maid as out of favor as myself, my father would see my distress in the clumsiness of my brushstrokes. But it seems to me that if I do not speak to someone other than you, I shall be distracted."

"Perhaps, mistress, if you turned your sorrow into poetry, it might be sorrow no longer. Write down your thoughts, mistress, and let the winds carry your words to those who have hearts and minds to hear them," suggested Willow.

"Excellent idea!" cried Silver Snow. "But what shall I write upon?" The small store of writing silk that she had must be hoarded for letters to her father, and she could hardly expect thin wooden strips to be carried away by the winds or, as Willow probably and more prosaically intended, to bob from some tree in another court.

"One moment, Elder Sister . . . ah, I have it!" Willow leapt up with a grace belying her crippled leg and darted out into the court where she seized up a leaf that had blown across the wall from some rare tree or other. "Write on this leaf, then set it free."

To her own astonishment, Silver Snow found that she was smiling. It had been months since she had even attempted verse. She settled herself more comfortably on her frayed mat and took up a fresh brush. A poem flickered into her consciousness, and she dipped her brush in the ink that glimmered on her inkstone.

How fast this water flows away! she wrote, looking at the clouded little stream that flowed past the windows of her octagonal pavilion.

> *Buried in the women's quarters,*
> *The days pass in idleness.*
> *Red leaf, I order you—*
> *Go find someone*
> *In the world of men.*

She read the verse to Willow, who clapped her hands.

"Now," she commanded, "take this leaf and set it free to find the person of whom I wrote."

"And if no one replies, Elder Sister?" asked Willow, her head cocked to one side, her eyes inquisitive.

"Why then, tomorrow, you shall hunt me out another leaf, and I shall write another poem." She found herself smiling, and the very unexpectedness of that made her dare a little laugh. Hearing it, Willow brightened.

No, thought Silver Snow. *She loves me, and I have not been a kind mistress to her.*

Silver Snow rose and watched Willow limp down the steps, dulled by neglect, of the Cold Palace. Like a beast toying with its prey, she batted the leaf up into the air. A stray gust took it, and tossed it over the crumbling wall.

The next day, Silver Snow wrote out another verse: the day after, another; and the day after that, yet another.

"If I continue writing on leaves," she told Willow, "I may just pluck the trees bare."

The maid eyed her narrowly and laughed only when she did. As the days went by, however, Silver Snow admitted how keen her disappointment was. Tossing leaves that bore messages over a broken wall—that was a child's game. It was ridiculous of her to have placed any hope at all upon it. And yet . . . and yet . . . tears stung her eyes, and she could not see clearly enough to make the next careful, exquisite brushstroke. She blinked fiercely.

Surely, on the steppes, her father must have had his lonely days when his exile galled him worse than the pain of any wound. Yet he had persevered and survived. All that was good in her, she thought, came from him; she must not disgrace his teaching by even a moment's weakness. She drew a deep, consciously steady breath and bent to draw the next character on the fresh green leaf that lay upon the crazed lacquer table before which she knelt.

"Lady, oh lady!"

So steady was her hand that she completed the stroke flawlessly before she looked up. Never before had Willow's voice lilted in precisely that way; in fact, she had always taken care to keep it low as befitted a humble maid, especially now that they were in disgrace. She heard the familiar *step/drag*— first of Willow's strong leg, then of her lame one—up the hollowed stairs to the pavilion.

But what were those other, heavier and more measured footsteps that followed the maid's?

The smile on Willow's face as she entered the pavilion that, even in summer, retained some chill from its very isolation was as bright as sunlight flashing from the mirror that the maid used to foretell. Just as quickly as a maid blows out a lamp, however, Willow shuttered her smile, hooded her eyes, and bowed slowly, painfully, and ceremonially to the floor in appropriate homage to the visitor who followed her into the pavilion.

It was the eunuch Li Ling who had spoken bravely to the Emperor of the Hsiung-nu before the entire court. In his hand, he held, as another might carry a spray of lilacs or a fan, a number of drying leaves, each of which bore the verses of lament and loneliness that she had composed and so painstakingly inscribed.

She bowed herself before him, shaking with a return of the old, childish hope. Surely he would speak first. If he did not, then she might venture a word, assuming she could find the power of speech at all.

"Seeing you, lady," said Li Ling, "this one feels as if he has asked for melons and been given fine jade."

Wondering, Silver Snow looked up. Li Ling stepped forward, his hand going out so that the leaves brushed her chin. Then, quickly, he recollected himself and drew it back.

"Those are the features of the ill-favored lady of Mao Yenshou's portrait," mused the eunuch-scholar, "and yet, how different! Your complexion is like almonds, not like mud; and your brow and chin do not protrude like a soldier's. As for the mole—surely that was our worthy Administrator's invention."

Aware that her cheeks were flushing so that her skin resembled not an almond but a peony, Silver Snow looked down.

"Yes, yes, I am well aware that my behavior is unpardonable, but I pray that you will pardon it for the sake of my old friend, your most estimable father. I had heard that his last child had come to court, and it grieved me to know that you were unhappy and alone."

Silver Snow felt the corners of her mouth ache from the unfamiliar wideness of her smile. She cocked her head to one side, looking at the leaves that Li Ling held.

"Is this writing yours? The brushstrokes are very fine."

She shook her head and gestured as if to decry her own ability.

"And the verses too? I have never seen them before. You composed them upon the leaves, then simply blew them into the air, to fly where they would? Is that it, lady?"

Silver Snow nodded, then realized that a nod was hardly sufficient courtesy to a friend of her father, an advisor to the Son of Heaven, and the only person, save Willow, to come to her in her exile with no thought but to cheer her. She rose, ceremoniously begged that he seat himself, and ordered Willow to heat the last of the rice wine that she had brought with her from the North.

"Willow threw the leaves over the wall," said Silver Snow.

"And that is Willow?" asked the eunuch-scholar. He stared at her with the same keen interest that he had taken in Silver Snow's own appearance and her writing: glanced at her hair, which gleamed with russet highlights in the summer sunshine, then dropped his speculative, narrow-eyed gaze to Willow's hands and the curious way in which the middle three fingers of each hand were of equal length.

"Very interesting," he said calmly. "Your maid. Is she from—" he paused, then spoke the name of a region of the Middle Kingdom so obscure that Silver Snow remembered hearing it pronounced but once or twice.

Willow, entering with the hot wine, heard him and froze on the threshold, the delicate winecups and flask trembling on the tray that she bore.

"Well, girl, are you?"

Willow dropped to her knees awkwardly, favoring her lame leg. "Yes," she whispered. Her hands trembled as she set out the wine on the low table.

"Then I take it that you are an herbalist? I too have interests in that direction . . . and in alchemy." He flashed mistress and maid a quick, warning look.

Alchemy. Some men said that the study revealed secrets of the Tao that otherwise would be locked away from humankind; others, more fearful and more numerous, held that those secrets were, indeed, proscribed to man. From the study of alchemy to accusations of witchcraft, Silver Snow thought, was but a tiny step, no more than a lady in a new gown and shoes might take crossing a high-arched bridge.

"Be honest with me, as I have been honest with you," said Li Ling. "Lady, you are my old companion's youngest child. I mean you only well in your solitude. As for my . . . studies"— he paused delicately—"they, along with music, calligraphy, and poetry"—he bowed at her, a subtle compliment to her verse—"are compensations for what I have lost. I have no heir nor am likely to now. What else can they do but kill me?"

"Mao Yen-shou threatened me with the penalty for grave-robbing." The words, still painful after all of these months, slipped out with a speed and bitterness that made Silver Snow gasp, wishing that she unsay them. This man—impossible to think of him as one of the posturing, flabby effeminates who surrounded Mao Yen-shou!—his lordly manner and his keen wit drew the entire sorry tale from her before he had finished his first cup of wine, though, in courtesy, she truly should have waited until he had refreshed himself before she spoke.

When the tale was finished, Silver Snow sat quietly. For the first time in months, the tension that had knotted in her belly and tightened her spine after the Administrator of the Inner Court's theft of the jade armor dissipated. Telling Ling Li had brought its own healing, just as lancing a boil relieved pain and swelling.

"You are indeed your father's child," said the old alchemist. "It was not just alchemy for which I was punished. I was your father's advocate as well as his friend. Do you know, I was there when he was captured? Ah, that was a mighty battle. We would have pursued the Hsiung-nu, but I had no support to follow. Your father set out the crossbowmen. Their aim was so deadly that even the *shan-yu* himself was forced to dismount and fight on foot. And the Hsiung-nu, without their horses, are but half alive.

"As I said, we followed. Perhaps we were immodest, maddened by the thought of victory. Your father pursued the Hsiung-nu into a narrow valley, determined to wipe them out. That was when they rolled rocks down to block the valley. Thus, your father was trapped within with his men; I without.

"First, your father's men ran out of arrows. In their haste to escape the valley, they abandoned their supply carts . . . a fatal error. Soon they were brought to fighting with axles torn from the carts, with short swords; very quickly, their numbers were reduced. Even had your father been minded to flee, he could not have done so.

"Once the sun went down, your father took desperate measures. He ordered his men to put away the banners and the flags that they had marched behind with such pride. He burned the treasure that the army carried, ordered his troops to disperse, and himself set off with ten men. Two of those died before he surrendered himself to the Hsiung-nu to save the lives of the other eight—and, lady, you would not fear death in the Middle Kingdom had you but seen death as the Hsiung-nu deal it. The bows, the whistling arrows, the knives, cunningly . . . no!

"Your father surrendered to save his troops. And yet, of all those brave soldiers, only four hundred ever escaped.

"I returned to Ch'ang-an, of course, to resign my commission and confess my failure to save my friend, who, I wanted to assure the Son of Heaven, had acquitted himself with courage and dignity. However, I found myself plunged from defeat into scandal and intrigue. Your father's name and Ancestors were blackened as traitors. I pleaded; all the spirits of my own house know how I pleaded. The fact," he added with a glance at her, "that you are alive for me to repeat this story is proof of how well I pled. Yet, when the great fears of witchcraft arose, as they do every few years, my defense of a man who now rode with the Hsiung-nu was remembered; and my name and manhood paid the forfeit of my loyalty.

"After such a life, lady, can you truly fear that I would ever mean harm to you and yours?"

Silver Snow shook her head, moved past speech.

"Then let me be your friend. You are in exile from your home. I, too, am in a kind of exile; I miss the honor that once I had. That unfortunate day of the presentation of the pictures, when the Son of Heaven summoned me, was the first time for many sorrowful years. Your father would want you to study, and there is much that I can teach. Will you accept me as a friend?"

Her eyes bright with admiration at the story of her father's valor, Silver Snow did not answer for a moment. For a few precious moments, Li Ling's story had freed Silver Snow from the confinement of the Cold Palace, released her from the constraints of the Inner Courts, set her free to wander, in her imagination, the lands that she had gazed at for all of her girlhood. There too the freedom that she sought was walled away from her. Though her father had had the freedom of the steppes, yet he too had not been free. She sighed deeply.

Sorrow and disappointment flickered on Li Ling's face, and he began to rise.

She held out a hand, daring to restrain him. If he left, she would never again have company, and, once again, she would retreat into the hateful cocoon of the Shadowed One. She would rather die than do that—or would she? Li Ling had not. Her father had not.

Neither would she.

She raised her eyes and realized that she had kept the scholar waiting too long for his answer. Both of them were prisoners, suffering shame and loneliness. She would not start this new friendship with more hurt. She smiled, nodded, and poured him some more rice wine.

"Wonderful!" cried Li Ling. "Your lessons—and yours too, little changeling—will begin immediately." And this time his smile included Willow.

Αll that summer, laughter and music, not leaves inscribed with grieving verse, floated over the wall of the Cold Palace as Silver Snow, Willow, and Li Ling—three exiles from what might well have been rich, satisfying lives— shared their talents and memories.

"The most estimable Li Ling has deigned to seek this unworthy one out," wrote Silver Snow, her brushstrokes sure and delicate, "and has taught her many things. He presents his duty to you and humbly asks that this one remember him to you . . ."

She could write with a tranquil heart to her father now and, thanks to Li Ling, be certain of the delivery of her letter. In fact, she could almost smile when she looked back at the torments of rebellion and regret that she had suffered during her entry to the Inner Courts and her banishment to the Cold Palace. The court, which she had hoped would be the instrument of her freedom and her father's pardon, had turned out to be a snare; the Cold Palace, which had seemed like worse exile to her than the western frontier might have been for that absurd Lady Lilac, now brought her quiet, learning, even peace and freedom of a sort.

True, her physical being was restricted to the pavilions, and they were no better kept, no warmer, than they had been the previous winter. They were, however, no worse than the courtyards of her lost northern home; and now they contained a treasure that meant more to her than any warmth of brazier or luxury of gem and screen. Above them, her mind ranged afar, as if she finally had crossed the Purple Barrier and now rode free upon grassland and steppe.

If she had little treasure of silk and none at all of jade, she had the vast resources of Li Ling's mind. At first, he had confined his lessons to such subjects as he thought might interest a lady of fine breeding: music, calligraphy, verse, botany, and herbs—though, in the study of herbs, Willow far outstripped her and rapidly became even Li Ling's superior. Hers was the greater kinship with nature; hers was the sharper eye; and hers, Silver Snow realized now, must have been the greater suffering in the first days that they had been immured here.

This new joy and freedom, she knew, would cease one day. Li Ling was far older than she and, quite possibly, enfeebled by campaigns, wounds, and the punishment wreaked upon him for his loyalty. One day, he would die, and she would be left to her own resources. By then, however, she would be older. She could hope that the scandal surrounding her and the picture that had so slandered her might have been forgotten and that she would be allowed somewhat more liberty to move within the Inner Courts. Perhaps then, she might find and befriend someone just as Li Ling had befriended her.

". . . this one cannot honor her esteemed father enough for the lessons in patience and setting correct values upon things that he has been good enough to teach. Although this one had no choice but to obey the Son of Heaven's edict, she now esteems the order and dignity of her father's home and the wisdom of his teachings beyond jade. She will be content to recall them and to attempt obediently to live by them for the rest of her insignificant life . . ."

Early in the autumn of the second year of Silver Snow's life in the Cold Palace, she sat in the well-swept courtyard, watching the gold leaves and the pine needles rustle on their branches. The smells recalled her homeland; the breath of the wind, even after it had spent itself crossing the many walls of the Palace, brought her a hint of motion, of freedom. In the grasslands, she knew, the wind would blow long silver swathes in the grass as if it moved over the sea rather than over green growing things.

Li Ling entered with a step more rapid than was his wont. Silver Snow bowed. Before she had half risen from her obeisance, Li Ling had interrupted her greeting.

"Where is Willow?" he asked. "Tell her to fetch her yarrow stalks and cast the hexagrams."

"Is there change in the wind?" Silver Snow asked with a quiet smile. That too was a sign of her growth, she thought. A year ago, she might have been all flame and anticipation to hear it, and all apprehension lest it harm her. Now, she could look forward to change with curiosity, set it at its proper value, then leave it behind: it would probably be none of her concern.

"Change?" demanded Li Ling. His weary, wise eyes gleamed, and he was more animated than Silver Snow had ever seen him. "The merest maid—and I do not mean your Willow, either—could know that change is in the wind, a wind that blows across the grassland, bringing us news from the West and, possibly, a new alliance."

A swish of robes, an uneven step, and an awkward bow heralded Willow. Hastily she knelt—"careful, child!" cried Li Ling and leaned forward to ease her descent. Out came the yarrow stalks, and as she had not done for months, she cast and scanned the stalks to see what hexagram they formed.

"Change," mused Silver Snow. "Travel. Willow, the last time you showed me these same hexagrams . . . yes, she did, Li Ling, and I scolded her. Tell me, most worthy teacher, does this mean that you shall soon be taken from us, to travel once again to the West?"

It was too early, a childish, rebellious voice in her heart lamented, to lose the man who had been friend, teacher, and surrogate father. Yet, if he was to journey once again to the West, it could only be because the Son of Heaven had restored him to full favor. If that was indeed true, Silver Snow would rejoice. And how much worthier was that second thought than the selfish, timid first one!

Li Ling smiled and shook his head. "This one's traveling days are done, little lady. It is the Hsiung-nu who are the great travelers, as you know. The *shan-yu* Khujanga—you remember his name?"

"My father was his prisoner," said Silver Snow. "And you once said before the Son of Heaven that Khujanga, if he won his battles for supremacy in the West, would seek an alliance with the Middle Kingdom. Is it he who rides to Ch'ang-an, then?"

To her surprise, Li Ling laughed, but there was sadness in his laughter. "So you oversaw the court that day, did you, lady? *Your* doing, one supposes," he shot that comment at Willow, who flushed. "You discovered a bolthole for your mistress and, from it, she heard herself reviled."

"Yet I also saw and heard you!" Silver Snow retorted.

"You know," mused Li Ling, "all that evening, the Son of Heaven swore that he had seen the shadow of his lost lady, running down the corridor. Despite the bevies of Jasmines and Precious Pearls and whatever their sentimental names are whom he possesses, the Son of Heaven is a quiet man who forms deep attachments and grieves cruelly when they are lost or, as he thinks, betrayed. Then, his punishments are all the more severe for his disappointment. Such, I know now, was indeed the case when he sentenced me and let me sit idle in the Inner Chambers. I do not think that he has forgotten his lost love. Still, it is ironic: the shadow that he saw was you . . ."

Li Ling's voice trailed off as he entered a reverie. Despite herself, Silver Snow drummed fingers upon the mat.

"Does this *shan-yu* Khujanga come then to Ch'ang-an? I had thought he was quite old."

"And so he is, child," Li Ling agreed. "Old, seamed with scars, and worn out with battles. He would die if he rode this far from his grasslands now. But he has won his battles and now seeks his alliance."

"Why?" demanded Silver Snow. "The Wall protects us from the Hsiung-nu. Beyond it, however, what restrains them from faring where they will? Barbarians they may be, but they may ride free."

For the first time since she had met him, Li Ling almost preened himself. "I have never been more relieved to have my advice disregarded. Years ago, when I rode the grasslands myself, Khujanga used to ask me about the Middle Kingdom. And I told him, 'Your whole horde scarcely equals the population of a couple of prefectures, but the secret of your strength lies in your independence of Ch'in for all your real necessities. I notice an increasing fondness for Ch'in luxuries. Reflect that one-fifth of the Chinese wealth would suffice to buy your people completely. Silks and satins are not half so well suited as felts to the rough life you lead, nor are the perishable delicacies of Ch'in so wholesome as your kumiss and cheese.'

"But Khujanga continues to cherish his silks and his luxuries, and to regard Ch'in as the mother of wise life. That is why he will send a son to court as hostage for his continued friendship with Ch'in."

"And in return?"

"Ah, lady, if you overheard the court when I spoke to the Son of Heaven about the alliance that Khujanga would have, then you know what he hopes for—silks and gold, and a princess of Ch'in as his bride to seal the alliance."

As the man who advised the *shan-yu* to seek alliance, Li Ling was much in favor these days, a fact that he accepted with faint irony. Nevertheless, as shortly thereafter as friends might consider at all polite, Li Ling left her. Silver Snow sat, the tip of a brush tapping against her lip. In the days before Mao Yen-shou's caricature had disgraced her, Silver Snow had seen the pretty, pallid princesses. Which of them would be selected to make the trip west to marry the elderly *shan-yu*? How could such a girl survive, a girl who wept over a pet bird's death as if it were a worse tragedy than defeat in battle, a girl who required a bevy of maids merely to dress her in the morning?

Such a girl might well go mad even before she set off with the Hsiung-nu. Once again, Silver Snow tapped her lower lip with the brush. *My father and Li Ling have told me, if not a great deal about the West, more than such a maid is likely to know. Perhaps . . . perhaps I might be able to speak with her, console her.*

Envy flashed through Silver Snow so hotly that her hand, holding the brush, trembled. *At least that girl will be free!* She shut her eyes, the better to savor her sudden vision of a land she had never seen: the grasslands—tough green stalks waving in the summer the way that wind streaks patterns on a pond; horses pounding over the land, the grass brushing their flanks; the cold of winter with wind howling, building its fury across thousands of *li;* or the heat baking the grit and pebbles of the innermost desert.

Soon whispers pierced even Silver Snow's solitude. Precious Pearl, she heard, had received a higher order of rank from the Son of Heaven; soon she might even become Illustrious Consort, or one of several. That was the only news of the court itself; the rest was concerned with the Hsiung-nu.

The ladies—yes, and some of the men and eunuchs too—of the court took positive pleasure in terrifying one another with stories of the Hsiung-nu. Those stories grew more and more common immediately after Mao Yen-shou announced that none of the princesses could be spared as a barbarian's bride. Instead, the Son of Heaven would "adopt" one of the other ladies from the five hundred who had entered the Palace over a year ago. Royal she would be, but "daughter," not consort; and she would not have long to enjoy the luxury of a princess of the Han.

Naturally, Silver Snow had not actually heard the corrupt, sleek eunuch make his announcement. She could imagine the bribes flowing into his well-kept hands as lady after lady begged not to be the one selected. Which lady would be chosen?

Mao Yen-shou must be enjoying himself, she thought, as

the rumors grew more and more lurid. The Inner Courts boiled as might an anthill into which a warrior maliciously thrust a spear. The Hsiung-nu ate only raw meat; the Hsiung-nu ate only roots and meat pressed between their bodies and the saddles of their horses; the Hsiung-nu never dismounted from their horses; they scarcely looked human.

As gossip shrilled upward toward terror, Silver Snow dared the risk of venturing from exile if only to calm the most terrified (and poverty-stricken) of the lesser concubines, from whom the selection most probably would be made.

"If the Hsiung-nu eat but raw meat, why does the most worthy minister Li Ling speak of great brass cauldrons? If they never leave their horses, how is it that the Hsiung-nu at court walk among us like men?"

The whispers and fears spread like blight across the gardens in the Inner Courts, and high summer rose and waned without the sighs of beauty that those gardens had exacted in other years.

Did they look like beasts?

Willow, of course, had contrived to see one or two. Sullen or proud she called them, anxious not to be disgraced in this unfamiliar city and even more unfamiliar splendor; but they were indeed men, not beasts. Though the Emperor's Hall of Brightness was, to her, a site of remembered humiliation, Silver Snow thought that soon she must contrive to enter it, to hide once again behind a screen and see these strangers for herself.

CHAPTER

= 10 =

For many, many days Li Ling did not visit her. It must be affairs of state, Silver Snow thought at first. Even in her isolation, Silver Snow had heard how the *shan-yu*'s youngest son would remain at court, hostage for the Hsiung-nu's good behavior in case their honor failed them. Once again, as had been done when, years ago, Khujanga came to power, Ch'in ruler and Hsiung-nu drank wine and horse's blood out of a cup carved out of the skull of Modun, who had been enemy to *shan-yu* and Son of Heaven both.

She had heard whispers of the splended gifts that the Hsiung-nu had brought to Ch'ang-an—a hundred highland-bred horses, a string of camels, and fine sable and fox skins. (Willow winced even at the mention of them.) She had also heard about the gifts prepared against the return of the Hsiung-nu to the grasslands: lacquer and silk and fine bronze mirrors. Only the gift of a princess to be the *shan-yu*'s bride was yet lacking.

Silver Snow had just begun to reproach herself for some slight to the wise old eunuch when he appeared in the gateway of the Cold Palace. The instant he was safely within and might not be observed, his face altered from the masklike formality that a minister in his position found safe and politic to

112

wear at court. Now he gazed at her with a mixture of regret and humor.

The past year had taught Silver Snow to wait with, at least, the appearance of unconcern. Thus, she met his eyes with a serene brow and raised eyebrows.

"Events have finally conspired against Mao Yen-shou!" Li Ling exploded, laughing. "No sooner had he left for Lo-Yang than the Son of Heaven reached a decision about the Hsiung-nu's desire for a princess as a bride for the *shan-yu*. Once again, the Son of Heaven has shown himself more interested in speed and ease of choice than in lovely ladies. He has declared that he will use Mao Yen-shou's pictures to determine which lady among the five hundred may best be spared."

"And you think I may be selected?"

Silver Snow's composure suddenly abandoned her.

It was logical that she be selected. She had seen the lying portrait that the Administrator had painted of her; it was, by far, the ugliest. The Emperor had acceded to her exile to this Cold Palace; he would be glad to be rid of her. And she, O heavens, she would be delighted to escape the prison that the Inner Courts had become.

She could mark one major obstacle, however. Although Mao Yen-shou might be glad to be rid of her, he would hardly want her to come to the Son of Heaven's attention at all. True enough, he possessed the jade armor, but Silver Snow possessed knowledge of what he was: liar and thief, willing to threaten a young woman with charges of grave-robbing in order to secure her house's last treasure. No, Mao Yen-shou had chosen a disastrous time to travel to Lo-Yang.

Li Ling knew that for Silver Snow, the Cold Palace was a worse fate than exile to the West, and he wished her well. Could he really contrive to have her selected? Her face flushed and her eyes filled with tears, not of fear, save of the over-whelming and unfamiliar, but of excitement. To be free once again! To ride free! To see finally the grasslands and the lands over which her father had ridden!

Lines from an old poem echoed in her mind:

The yellow sagebrush of the border,
The bare branches and dry leaves,
Desert battlefields, white bones
Scarred with swords and arrows,
Wind, frost, piercing cold,
Cold springs and summers . . .

She shivered, overcome with a feeling that she was appalled to admit was longing.

"I cannot believe," she began almost whimsically, "that Mao Yen-shou would do me such a good turn."

Then she saw the sorrow on the old man's face. "In the normal way of things, most revered teacher," she assured him, "and in the run of time, it would have been you who left me. In the grasslands, there are horses, and where there are horses, there may perhaps be messengers to carry letters, if one who is called a queen sends them. And besides, I have not yet been selected."

The eunuch shook his head, smiling. "Yet, like you, I think that you will be. Especially if it can be contrived that the worthy Mao Yen-shou can be summoned elsewhere."

He glanced aside at Willow. "And you, child?"

Willow bowed, expressing in the dip of her head her complete willingness to follow Silver Snow wherever she walked or rode. Among the Hsiung-nu, Silver Snow recalled, there were some women who possessed powers more than those granted to normal beings. Perhaps Willow, crippled leg or not, might not be as out of place among them as she was in the Inner Courts of Ch'ang-an where the only things for which a woman might gain notice were physical beauty and grace.

Once again, Li Ling sat in the Cold Palace, drinking rice wine in a rare celebration. Now, he had roused from his usual, disciplined quiet as he described how Mao Yen-shou's chief assistant had brought out the portraits, bowed, and had to be hauled upright, so much weight had he gained in the past year.

"And then the Son of Heaven looked through the pictures, rapidly, as if he well knew what he wished to see. When he came to your picture, 'That one!' he waved at it. 'And may she bring the Hsiung-nu luck, with her black mole.'"

"Do you know," Li Ling added, "you might just do that too?"

"She will," whispered Willow.

Silver Snow darted a quick glance at her. For a moment, Willow had gone utterly pale, and her eyes stared not at her friend and mistress but through them. Then she shivered and seemed to wake from whatever trance she had entered.

"What did you say, Willow?" Li Ling pressed her gently.

"I, noble lord?" asked Willow. "How should I speak before I am invited to? I said nothing."

"The Hsiung-nu believe that you may be auspicious," Li Ling explained.

Their—what must Silver Snow call them?—priests?—though, surely, the Hsiung-nu could have nothing that civilized—had sacrificed a sheep, scrutinized its scapular bones, and decreed that the Lady Silver Snow, beloved "daughter" of the Emperor, was an auspicious choice of wife for Khujanga, *shan-yu* of the hordes.

In her new status as cherished child of the Son of Heaven, Silver Snow was not suffered to remain in the Cold Palace. Servants, as obsequious now in their eagerness to please as they had previously been arrogant, moved her few belongings and brought new, rich clothing and lavish screens into the vast, well-lit chamber to which she had been assigned. It might, she thought, be the last time that she ever lived beneath a fixed roof, for they said that the Hsiung-nu hated such confinement, living in felt tents that could be taken down and put up as they moved from winter quarters to summer pastures.

To her amusement, visitors came to bow to her like a flock of butterflies about a particularly splendid flower. She was in favor; and they constructed their lives upon serving whoever was in favor. Besides, she suspected, they wanted to study her and perhaps to gloat if she showed signs of terror or flinching.

"It is like the weak," Willow remarked sardonically, after the flock had fluttered itself out of the courtyard, "ever to savor the misfortunes of their betters."

"Hush, Willow." Silver Snow had forced herself not even to smile at that sally, though she had to admit that it was true.

Even Lady Lilac—whom Silver Snow knew had disliked her and whom she hoped had forgotten her (and far, far better thus!)—came, weeping over her former charge, trying to gain her confidence.

"Lady," the girl broke in on one of her more overwrought laments, "you know how vulgarly hardy I am, how ill-suited to the Inner Courts. My father lived quite well among the Hsiung-nu as a prisoner, and so, I think, can I. I shall be the precious consort of the *shan-yu* himself; I cannot think that *they* will mistreat me."

That tiny barb, she thought later, might be unworthy of her, but it had been quite irresistible.

As the day when Silver Snow must leave the Inner Courts, step into the specially built traveling chariot, and ride out from one of the western gates of Ch'ang-an, drew closer, she found herself regarding the journey as an adventure. Not so, however, the ladies who had been ordered to attend her. (To Lilac's immense relief, she was not among them.) Already, they wailed as if they went to their own funerals.

Would they survive the journey? Although the *Hsiung-yu* prince who would conduct his father's bride to the grasslands had vowed that they would be turned back at the border, would he keep his word? Time and again they wept over those questions, despite Silver Snow's assurances that she would ride on alone with the Hsiung-nu and whatever ladies they had brought to meet her. She would, after all, have Willow at her back. (As always, the ladies pursed their painted lips when she mentioned her club-footed maid.) She could not think of such a journey, such a total alteration of the fabric of her life, without her faithful Willow.

Finally the day came when Silver Snow sat dressed in robes so rich and so heavy that she hardly dared to move, awaiting her summons to the throne room. In that same room where she had once spied upon her own disgrace, Silver Snow must, in her role as dutiful child to the Son of Heaven, bid farewell to her "father" whom she had journeyed from the North to see, but had never met.

She glanced into the mirror that Willow held for her.

"Ah, that eunuch, that Mao Yen-shou, will burst from sheer mortification, Elder Sister!" The maid smiled, and her teeth were very white and sharp. "How is it that he could not prevent this meeting?"

"Li Ling may have been stripped of his armies," Silver Snow replied, "but he is still a far better general than the Master of the Inner Courts."

"Ah, lady, the instant that the Son of Heaven sees you, he will know that you are not the homely creature of that fat thief's portrait."

"Perhaps the artist thinks that the Emperor will not look beyond the painting to the woman. After all, the headdress that I shall be wearing is very heavy."

"Then it is for you to *make* him look!" stated Willow.

"For what purpose, child? I leave Ch'ang-an as I left my father's house: never to return."

"For revenge!" Willow almost spat.

But Silver Snow shook her head. "I have no need of revenge," she said.

"You shall have it!" Willow cried. "The Son of Heaven will fear that you are too plain for even the Hsiung-nu to accept as a bride. Let him just look upon you, and behold what he will see!"

Once again, Willow offered the mirror to Silver Snow. In

it, she saw several kinds of truth. One such truth was her own beauty. Another was her own nature; she was the daughter of a soldier, raised hardily in the North. Such a one could not easily forgo vengeance, no matter what sort of wise sayings she might mouth.

"Yet," she admitted, "I would like to clear my father's name, even though, by my adoption and marriage"—she shivered, despite the weight of silk that pressed down upon her—"he gains great face. It is not the same, however."

Willow shrugged, clearly and silently expressing her impatience with such fine distinctions. Then, just as she bent with infinite delicacy to straighten Silver Snow's headdress, the summons came. Surrounded by ladies and a guard of honor, Silver Snow was borne away to the throne room.

Slowly, impressively, Silver Snow entered. Suddenly her knees felt like ice thrown into boiling water; she thought that her bones might spin, melt, and cast her down. Her headdress was so heavy that, perforce, she kept her head down for fear of breaking her neck if not of being thought overly bold. And, thanks to the fringe of her headdress, strands of pearls swinging and chiming sweetly against her brow, Silver Snow kept her eyelids lowered too, like a proper modest maid and not a woman come to do battle for her house and for her future.

She accomplished her entry into the hall in which she had been so cruelly humiliated and sank into the ceremonial prostration as she had been drilled. A sigh went up at what the court seemed to regard as her grace. But her breath came rapidly, and she knew that she was trembling. Even the kingfisher feathers that adorned her glossy hair quivered.

She had wanted a good look at the Emperor, but now that she was but a glance away, she kept her eyes fixed on the floor, overcome by simultaneous feelings of awe and rage. This man, this thin, pale man with his scholar's hands, was the Son of Heaven, the heir to Ch'in Shih Huang-di who had set a border to the Middle Kingdom and appointed laws for all things. He was practically a god on earth. Yet this man was the man who had humiliated her, banished her, outraged her father's friend, and all but killed her father for his too-austere loyalty. She was afraid to look upon him; she was too angry to look upon him. Let the Ancestors look upon her with forgiveness: he was too weak for the role he played.

She turned her attention to the Hsiung-nu, the beardless barbarians among whom she must live or die. A child dressed so richly that his gear reminded her of a horse's caparison stood surrounded by guards. The boy's flattish face and bold stance made her sure that the child was the hostage that the Emperor had demanded that the Hsiung-nu produce in return for a treaty. Would he deal any better with the luxurious imprisonment of the Palace than had she?

He looked up at her, laughing as a child does when it sees a bright toy. Before Silver Snow thought, she greeted him in the tongue that her father and his men had taught her, and he all but jumped in amazement.

Nearby him, his face somewhat averted as if he participated in this ceremony only with the greatest reluctance, was a man of the Hsiung-nu, whose sable-trimmed robes marked him out as one of importance, perhaps even a prince. Hearing his own uncouth speech in the mouth of a Ch'in lady, he glanced up, jolted out of his rigid stance of attention. Then his eyes glazed the way they do when a man looks at a horse, but decides that he does not wish to buy it. Quickly he looked away and, once again, became like a statue, and not a breathing man.

So these were Hsiung-nu, she thought. They were hardly the brutes about which the ladies of the Inner Courts had terrified themselves into frenzies. Take away their ornaments and their furs, dress them in a soldier's worn garb, and they would look remarkably like her father's guardsmen.

But the Son of Heaven was speaking; it was not for the likes of her to fall into daydreams just at the moment for which she had waited. The very thought brought a blush to her face.

"What exquisite modesty," mused the Emperor. "It is a woman's greatest ornament. Look up, daughter."

To disobey the express word of the Son of Heaven was treason or worse. Having no choice, Silver Snow looked up and, in the next instant, shrank back as the Emperor gasped.

"Again, it is my lady, my lost favorite!"

To Silver Snow's amazement and the muttered horror of the court, the Son of Heaven did not use the "we" of propriety, and he spoke to her as if the two of them were the only people in the splendid, crowded room.

"Child, you have my dear lady's look, her walk, her very aspect!" the Emperor told Silver Snow. In that instant, the distinctions between Emperor and woman fell; they were left facing one another, a grieving man and the woman whom he had grievously injured.

"Why did no one tell me?" demanded the Son of Heaven.

He had spoken to no one in particular; no one, therefore, would dare to take upon himself the responsibility of framing an answer: no one, save for Silver Snow.

"Most dreaded Son of Heaven," said Silver Snow, "this one begs your forgiveness for the insolence, but she suggests most humbly that you ask Mao Yen-shou."

As she spoke, her voice rose from the die-away murmur in which she had been drilled to a strong, echoing voice. From the corner of her eye, she saw the Hsiung-nu turn, drawn by the power in her voice. One of them, the most richly dressed except for the hostage, set his lips and glowered in what Silver Snow realized was approval.

"Rest assured: that we shall do," said the Emperor. Once again, his words and voice *were* those of the Son of Heaven, not the scholar so ill-suited for the Dragon Throne. "But before we bring Mao Yen-shou before us, lady, I ask it again. *I* ask it. How was I not told that you are the image of my dear, lost lady?"

"Most Sacred Majesty," began Silver Snow, but the Emperor held up a hand.

"No," he said, his voice so soft and warm that Silver Snow knew that he spoke through her to a familiar, most beloved ghost. "Would *she* call me that? Speak, my dear child, and do not fear."

Silver Snow sank once again on her knees, grateful for the cool solidity of the floor. She had come to the irrevocable choice now: lie to the Emperor, which was almost blasphemy; or denounce the very powerful master of the Inner Courts, which might be deadly. As much as any battlefield might be, this was death country, and she had no choice but to attack.

The knowledge restored her courage and her composure. "Mao Yen-shou did not wish for you to see me," she spoke calmly, as if she discussed history with Li Ling. "When I came to court, Majesty . . ." he held up a hand, but he was smiling.

"When I arrived, the Administrator . . . suggested that your favor might lie in his hands and brush, which could be inspired by a suitable gift. But I had no gifts . . . save one; and that gift was reserved for you."

The Son of Heaven smiled at her, a smile that seemed to inquire where that gift was and to reassure her that she herself was the finest gift that he could ask.

"Most Sacred, I mean, my lord, my father's lands are poor; we have lived desolate for years under the affliction of your disfavor. Even the dowry that I brought to Ch'ang-an was more than my father might easily spare, but he provided that with a willing, obedient heart. And he provided more besides.

"My lord, our house had one great, remaining treasure— two suits of jade armor worthy, despite our own unworthiness to possess such treasures, for an Emperor and his First Lady to be buried in. These he entrusted to me, and he commanded me that, should I win your favor, the . . ." She was scarlet, as if she had dipped her hand in scalding water. ". . . first night . . ." Silver Snow shook her head, and finished quickly. "He told me to give them to you as a token of his obedience."

A commotion, quickly stifled at the door, told her that Mao Yen-shou had sought to leave the hall and been restrained.

"The girl lies!" he cried, and his finely trained, high voice rang out to the rafters.

"Do I?" demanded Silver Snow, who turned so that she could see both him and the Emperor whose face had darkened with anger. Disheveled by his struggle for escape, he seemed fatter and less formidable than the man who had terrorized a tired girl from the North who had a father and a maidservant to protect. "Then call this a lie too: you took the jade armor and, when I protested, you showed me old teeth that you had dropped into the chest that held them. And you said that if I protested, you would accuse me of grave-robbing, and bring my father's house to less than naught!"

She turned back to the Emperor. "I beg you," she cried, "seek for that armor and then judge between us as we deserve. This one is wretched, weak, and would rather die than live longer in the icy shadow of your displeasure."

The Emperor waved, and footsteps backed down the hall, headed, no doubt, for wherever Mao Yen-shou sequestered his greatest treasures. Only then did Silver Snow have time to invent fears for herself. What if Mao Yen-shou had sold or broken up the armor? He could not have sold it; for who would buy such a treasure? And its worth lay not so much in the jade or the gold but in its workmanship and antiquity; thus, he would not have broken it up, either. The guards would have to find it.

Even though her reason told her clearly that that was the truth, her teeth chattered, and she wanted very much to weep with fear. Yet, this was death country, and she had laid her plans, launched her attack, and, like a general—like her father himself—she must abide by the wisdom of her battle plan, whether it brought her to victory or to disaster.

She heard footsteps echoing toward the hall. The guards must be returning! She refused to look at them, concentrating instead on the sounds about her. How slow, how labored were their steps! Surely, they walked as if they bore something heavy . . . something like two suits of jade armor?

How she hoped so!

The guards strode up the hall, dropped what they bore on the floor, and bowed abjectly. Now Silver Snow forced herself to look at what they bore: she knew those chests! From them Mao Yen-shou had lifted the jade armors and claimed them for his own.

The Son of Heaven gestured impatiently. *Well*, his agitated hand motion revealed, *open, open them*.

The peaceful, mellow green of fine jade and the splendor of gold winked out of the chest at them.

"I trusted you!" the Son of Heaven shouted at Mao Yen-shou, who prostrated himself, his face on the floor. "I trusted you, and you painted me this lie of a likeness, this slander of a portrait of a lady worthy to be Illustrious Companion. Had you not treasure enough already? Was I not a generous master?"

Mao Yen-shou's face went so red that Silver Snow feared, for a single, unselfish moment, that he might collapse right then and there. Almost, she could pity him. His mouth opened and closed; the folds of flesh at his throat, enclosed by the high collar of his rich silk robe, shook, but no words came out.

"Take him away." The Emperor waved his hand, his voice bored. "I want his head to adorn the western gate by sundown."

This time, Mao Yen-shou did find voice enough only for a sharp, wordless cry of protest before the guardsmen dragged him past his former companions (who drew their robes aside from the contamination that he now represented with a rapid hiss of satin) and out toward his death.

For a moment everyone in the hall stood transfixed, staring at the door. Then the eyes flickered back to Silver Snow.

"This one begs the Son of Heaven to accept her father's worthless gift for the sake of the love and loyalty that he has borne the Son of Heaven all of his life." There! The words, the ones that she had journeyed all the way to Ch'ang-an to say, were finally out.

The Son of Heaven rose from the Dragon Throne to the

accompaniment of gasps of amazement. Slowly, deliberately, he walked over to the jade armor and ran one finely kept hand over the smooth, cool jade.

"We accept the gift," he announced. "And we thank Chao Kuang, whom we restore to all of his old titles and honors. Once again, let him be marquis and general. The scribes shall record it, and an edict shall be sent to Chao Kuang."

Silver Snow laid her brow against the cool floor so quickly that the kingfisher feathers fluttered in her hair and the pearls rang against one another. Tears heated her eyes, and what felt like a knife transfixed her at the center of her chest; but she did not care.

If I die in the next moment, she told herself, *I have lived long enough. I have my victory, and, my father, you have your honor back.*

To her astonishment, a gentle hand touched her hair.

"Rise, lady," whispered the Emperor. "I have my burial armor, it seems. But, who is the lady to wear its companion through forever? You, perhaps?"

"Dread Emperor," whispered Silver Snow, "I am pledged to the *shan-yu*. What am I beside the sanctity of your word?"

The Emperor gestured to the Hsiung-nu party. Not at all to Silver Snow's surprise, the young, richly dressed barbarian strode up, bowing tardily and with an awkwardness that was astounding, considering that the young man must have spent his entire life in the saddle. He was muscular, stocky, though not as portly as a Ch'in prince would be, and about as tall as the Son of Heaven himself.

"Prince Vughturoi," called the Son of Heaven, and his voice was very crisp. "Let us discuss the bargain that we have made. This is not the princess whom we promised to your father. Another lady will be provided as a bride. Will you and your companions accept that lady?"

The young Hsiung-nu ambassador jerked his head at Emperor Yuan Ti; then turned back to his fellow ambassadors and the shamans who stood in attendance on them.

The eldest of them stepped forward.

"Emperor," he said bluntly, "we will not."

CHAPTER

= 11 =

"We are well content with this lady as a bride for our *shan-yu*," said the old barbarian. "She is very fair, and our *kam-quams*, those who speak to spirits, tell us that she is most auspicious."

"I cannot let her go," the Emperor whispered, more to himself than either to Silver Snow or to the Hsiung-nu. "My lost lady . . . the rustle of a skirt as she walks down the hall. I have lost this lady, dreamed her, and found her. Shall I see her for the first time, only to lose her again?"

The Hsiung-nu muttered among themselves, and the crowds of courtiers and ladies in the hall parted, as if they expected the Hsiung-nu to draw bows in that very instant. Such ripples and eddies in the groups enabled Silver Snow to see Li Ling for the first time since she had entered the hall. To her astonishment (and no little horror), he winked at her.

Then she turned her attention back upon the Hsiung-nu. She could understand, however haltingly, their speech.

"He seeks to take this lady from us and give us some lesser woman, perhaps with a squint or a mole," said the man called Vughturoi. "Yet we are not prisoners in this city of stone tents. Shall we permit it?"

"Indeed not," said the eldest of the ambassadors. "Surely if this is the lady promised to the *shan-yu*, it is an auspicious sign.

125

Behold her beauty: were the Emperor of the Middle Kingdom not afraid of us, or did he not favor us above all others, would he part with such a treasure to buy peace at our hands?"

Vughturoi snorted something about gilded birds and the impossibility of keeping a peace treaty, given . . . But he was immediately hushed.

Silver Snow found herself looking once again at Li Ling, who had edged adroitly into a position where the Emperor was certain to see him and demand his counsel. He raised a brow at her. *Do you wish to stay?* he seemed to ask.

If she did not want to leave Ch'ang-an, she might well stay; stay and adorn the Inner Courts as the most illustrious of Illustrious Companions in centuries, perhaps, with a palace full of women to fawn upon her. She could avenge every slight ever dealt her; she could beg to bring her father to court, enrich him, favor Li Ling . . .

Or she could be true to her birth and her upbringing, and could keep her word, which lay in the Emperor's promise to send her to the frontier. She had the example of her father, who kept faith during the ten years of his exile among the very Hsiung-nu to whom she would be dispatched, and thereafter, when he was condemned as a traitor. She had the example of Li Ling, who continued to serve, though he lost reputation, family, and manhood thereby, but who served because he had vowed to do no other.

Before her stood the Son of Heaven himself, a quiet, moody man who seemed to want her to remain with him. Silver Snow thought that she had made her last throw, but now she saw that yet another throw remained in the game.

She considered it. What if she remained? What would happen to the peace that the Son of Heaven and these Hsiung-nu had just forged? It would be shattered, of course. How long would any such agreement with barbarians last? That was a question she knew that she had to ask. But if she went out to the plains, perhaps it might last for years.

They are not barbarians! she remembered her father's words.

Well then, what of the men of Ch'in? How long might she expect the Son of Heaven's favor to last, especially were she to become the cause of a war? He was shifting, changeable, unlike the Hsiung-nu who now confronted him.

"Let us give you another princess, and we will offer you more gold, more jade and silk . . ." The eagerness in the Son of Heaven's voice cut deeply.

"Offer us another princess," said the Hsiung-nu, "and we shall offer you war!"

The Emperor turned to her, the look of a man whom fate had driven to his limits. "What would you, lady?" he asked, and it was almost pleading.

"This one begs His Most Sacred Majesty to consider the health of the Middle Kingdom, which is our Mother," she whispered. Tears gushed into her eyes, as she spoke to condemn herself to exile. "This one is nothing beside that."

"We will give you her weight in gold and pearls!" cried the Son of Heaven, and desperation quivered in his voice.

The Hsiung-nu folded arms across their chests and did not bother to speak. Slowly, the Son of Heaven sank back onto the Dragon Throne. He gestured halfheartedly, and Li Ling was at his side, whispering as the Hsiung-nu grumbled among themselves. Silver Snow knew that the eunuch was trying to convince the Emperor that no woman was worth a war.

"But how will she live out there, among barbarians?" She heard the question, not of an Emperor, but of an anguished man who wished to accord her a protection that she had never known before. She did not know whether to laugh or to rage. Having the right to do neither in the Emperor's presence, she kept her face expressionless as Li Ling assured the Son of Heaven of her strength, her vitality, her knowledge of the language and some customs of the Hsiung-nu.

"I had forgotten," came the Son of Heaven's words, pitched just loudly enough that she could hear them. "This lady speaks the tongue of the Hsiung-nu, and writes, do you say? She writes to her father?"

Li Ling bowed his assent.

"Then, she shall write you too, and I shall read those letters; that much, at the very least, I shall have of her!" the Son of Heaven concluded. "I shall read her letters to her father, and his to her. Thus let it be done," commanded the Emperor.

Li Ling bowed and left the hall. Silver Snow stood alone, facing the Son of Heaven, terribly conscious of the Hsiung-nu who still observed her as if she were a horse that, after spirited bargaining, they had contrived to buy. Or to steal. The old man bowed and left the hall, and the Emperor Yuan Ti assured the Hsiung-nu that Silver Snow could leave whenever they were prepared.

"The lady," the young man called Vughturoi gave her title a small, wry stress, "must travel rapidly and with a minimum of companions. She may have her own traveling carriage and a donkey. If she proves able to ride, we may also provide her with a horse."

For a moment Silver Snow knew anger and embarrassment: did these Hsiung-nu think that she was such a paltry creature that they would not sully the back of one of their horses to carry her? Or did they simply think that she was soft? Despising them, she decided at that moment, could harm her; she must win their respect. Thus, when the information was relayed to her, she nodded.

"I will need no companions beside Willow," she said. "I came to Ch'ang-an with her, and I will not be parted from her now. That way, I shall require no court ladies, which, I am certain, will reassure all of them."

She could imagine Lilac accompanying her on this journey, and her ears ached with even the thought of that much weeping and whining.

"That is as well," said Vughturoi. "The grasslands in winter are no place for sheltered ladies." Silver Snow did not think that she had imagined the disdain in his voice for such soft, frail creatures. "I shall send riders ahead to summon wives and daughters of our horde to greet and serve the princess."

Vughturoi raised his head and kept his eyes fixed on a point behind Silver Snow's shoulder. For the first time Silver Snow quailed inwardly as she wondered what those wives and daughters would make of her. Would they be kinswomen of the *shan-yu*, forced to yield precedence to a woman of the Middle Kingdom, which had been their enemy for as long as they could remember? For that matter, what of this guide of hers, this Vughturoi? He was said to be a son of the old man who would be—she suppressed a shiver—her husband. Was his mother still alive? What would such a woman do, if the *shan-yu* required her to call a young woman of Ch'in "elder sister"?

Silver Snow had suffered enough from the spite of the concubines in the Inner Courts to fear that. It was said that the women of the grasslands had much more freedom. Would that freedom of theirs be license to abuse the stranger in their midst?

"I am well content," she ventured to say to the Hsiung-nu prince. No die-away voice, no overly polite "this one": those were manners she would leave in Ch'ang-an, like baggage abandoned along the line of march. She would, she thought, be abandoning a great deal more—and she doubted that she would regret it.

Silver Snow gazed about the hall that she knew she would never see again. What was more, she knew that she did not care.

"When will we depart?" she asked.

"It is summer now," Vughturoi replied, although he gave the impression that he did her a great favor by speaking with her directly. "We have the journey from here to the Wall. But from there to our grasslands where my father the *shan-yu* holds court is another three months. It would be well to finish our journey before the worst of the winter storms."

Silver Snow contrived to look unconcerned. A slight cough behind her, which she identified as coming from Li Ling, told her that she was holding her own. *Keep your own counsel; never show weakness before these people*, she warned herself. *You must ever be on guard.*

Her father had lived thus among them; so too would she.

"Lady," whispered Yuan Ti. Silver Snow ventured to meet the Son of Heaven's eyes, which glistened with more than interest in her journey. "Will you truly do this thing?"

It was her last chance, she thought. If, truly, she did not desire this journey, she had only to say so, and he would keep her in the Inner Courts, or, better yet, by his side. That was a fate that any lady in Ch'in would envy. Yet, if he did so, he would throw away a treaty and involve the Middle Kingdom in war once again, war such as had swept her father and Li Ling almost into ruin. No woman was worth that; and no man, be he general, prince, or Son of Heaven, ought to decide otherwise.

Yuan Ti was a man of strange decisions and passions, Silver Snow decided. At one moment, he wanted to banish her; in the next, he would incite a war to keep her. He turned on his advisors like Mao Yen-shou, then rewarded those whom he had turned on—like her father.

Silver Snow glanced at the rigid, unyielding Hsiung-nu. She rather thought that she would take her chances among them.

"This one, as always, is obedient to your commands," she told the Emperor. "But if she were permitted her own will, she would act as would best serve the Son of Heaven, who has done her the unutterable honor to make her a princess of Ch'in, the Middle Kingdom, and her father. To this one's weak mind, desolate as she is to admit it, she might serve best as the *shan-yu's* first wife."

She bowed herself at the Emperor's feet in farewell just as, long ago, she had bowed before her own father.

The Son of Heaven clapped his hands. "You shall be sent to the Wall with all that befits your rank, lady: an imperial chariot, a mounted escort, musicians to enliven your journey, and whatever servants you require. You may bring companions, should you wish. We reserve only the worthy Li Ling, and we charge you to write to him and to your father, that we may profit from your observations."

The court murmured approval of his words. Then Yuan Ti stepped forward. "As for me, lady," he said, his voice all but trembling, "once you leave, I shall issue an edict of mourning. The court will fast and wear white robes, as it did"—he drew a deep breath—"the last time that I lost you. And, once you leave Ch'in through the Jade Gate in the West, I decree that it shall ever afterward be called the Gate of Tears."

Wearied of this courtliness in a language of which he was but an imperfect master, the Hsiung-nu prince stepped forward. "How soon can the princess be ready to depart? We would pass through this Gate of Tears of yours before the frosts."

Once again Silver Snow glanced up at the Son of Heaven, whose eyes mutely urged delay. Then she looked over at Li Ling, who shook his head, almost imperceptibly. She did him—and herself—no favor by delaying, he clearly thought. Every day that she remained would be a temptation for the Son of Heaven to withdraw his consent to her going and embroil Ch'in in war.

The Hsiung-nu, she understood, were restless, able always to lash up their felt tents and to journey to new pastures. Speed might be the most auspicious beginning of her new life among them. She nodded at Li Ling.

"Behold: already, the princess is a dutiful wife to the *shanyu*. As soon as the princess' chariot is made ready," Li Ling stepped forward and spoke in the Hsiung-nu's tongue, "she will depart."

Seated in the lavishly equipped imperial chariot, Silver Snow could not help but contrast her previous "wedding journey" with the one she now took. Then, shabbily dressed, she had climbed into an ox-cart, her few belongings rolled into it or strapped on pack animals. There had been fewer than ten tens of torches and no musicians, no sounds at all save the clicking and ringing harness of the mounts of her escort and the official in whose train she rode, the least and loneliest. So she had ridden to the bright heart of the Middle Kingdom, the Inner Courts of Ch'ang-an, and had thought never to leave.

Now she went journeying once again. No, she thought. That was not true. The Hsiung-nu were nomads. Henceforward, her life would be one long journey, and never again would she be confined within the walls of a city or a palace— or within any walls at all.

There was no loving, grieving father to say farewell to Silver Snow this time, but Li Ling stood by to oversee the preparations. For the first time that Silver Snow could remember, he had dressed in the full magnificence of silks and sables available to a ranking eunuch, as if to do her honor. It was hard to recognize in the ornately robed official the same friend and teacher who had called, the night before, wearing a worn scholar's robe, and had presented gifts that, homely as they were, Silver Snow and Willow both esteemed more than furs, jades, or silk. For Silver Snow, he had strips of wood and treated silk, a supply of fine brushes, and a new inkstone. For Willow, he had pouches of dried herbs at which she sniffed and nodded, eyes bright.

He locked her into the chariot, as one must always lock a bride, and presented the key to Vughturoi, who received it as something strange and not wholly welcome. Then, at a gesture, musicians struck up a tune that managed simultaneously to suggest both cheers and wailing.

They puffed, piped, and drummed as her chariot rolled out of the confines of the Palace. Behind her came her companions, behind them an immense baggage train. Packed amid the silks, the gold, the precious spices was a treasure older than them all: the burial armor fashioned fit for an Empress. The Son of Heaven had sent it with her, since she would not stay to use it. Though the sun had risen, torchbearers ran beside it, and outside the yawning gates, she could see a crowd of people, waiting to witness her passing, guarded by soldiers both of Ch'in and the Hsiung-nu.

No sooner than the palace gates closed behind her, she knew that Yuan Ti would keep his vow and plunge the court into the deepest mourning for the lady whom first his indifference, then his oath, had taken from him. She suspected that many in her party—the ladies who had been detailed to accompany her to the Wall—felt that they too risked death in traveling that far from Ch'ang-an and the Son of Heaven. She almost thought that she could hear their weeping; certainly Willow had commented scathingly on fine ladies who used herbs and cosmetics to mask their terror and their tears.

Neither the Emperor nor the ladies who were her unwilling companions could know that Silver Snow regarded her journey as escape from prison.

The wedding procession, if one could call it that, wound through the city and out through the Western Gate.

Willow hissed a curse, and Silver Snow roused from the reverie in which she rode with her eyes turned ever to the West.

"Why such heavy words?" she asked her maid in mild reproof. "In fact, why curse at all?"

Willow simply pointed.

Leering from a spike on the Western Gate, the head of Mao Yen-shou was planted, the last witness in the city to her departure.

Was *this* a spectacle such as he would have admired? She hardly thought so.

Silver Snow shivered, then turned her gaze back to the West. Already her eyes and mind were fixed on what might lie ahead of her. High above the rumble of horsemen and the clamor of the Ch'in musicians rose the bamboo flutes of the Hsiung-nu, plaintive, free, and more than a trifle wild.

CHAPTER

= 12 =

As Silver Snow traveled north and west toward the meeting with her future lord and people, she journeyed through summer into autumn. Behind her, she left a mourning court; but she herself did not lament as her train of guards, ladies, musicians, servants, and Hsiung-nu wound slowly toward the grasslands. Gradually the grass withered, and the scrub that covered the ground turned orange, then bronze, just as Silver Snow remembered it from her earliest childhood. She could not help but compare this journey with her last. When she had left her father's house for Ch'ang-an, she and Willow had counted themselves lucky to have clean, unpatched quilts and adequate food. A fire was a luxury.

Now, she traveled in an imperial chariot that made the one in which her former escort had traveled seem as shabby and clumsy as an ox-cart. She wore robes of quilted silk and (when there was need) a cape and hood lined with satin and wrought of fur so soft and deep that her hands sank into it. Should she express the desire to stop for an hour or a day along the line of march, she was instantly heeded and surrounded with every tender attention. Did the lady require rice wine or litchi—or the presence of her maid or a flute-player?

So many questions; so many tiny, wearisome decisions; and so many calls upon her attention to praise, to mediate, or to chastise just when she wanted to look out at the land, which, day by day, assumed the familiar aspect of her beloved northlands! She might just as well be immured at court, she thought, because her ladies insisted on behaving as if they had not left the Palace. She would be relieved, she realized, to see the last of them.

Viewing the Hsiung-nu, supposedly her future subjects, brought her more satisfaction. Though gasps and squeaks from her ladies (when they were not weeping or exclaiming in fear at what was unfamiliar—as nearly everything was) greeted her actions, she questioned her guards, both the men of Ch'in and of the plains. Each day, her command of her new people's language grew better. She also insisted on riding out, at least for a brief time, every day. At first, she had perforce to ride the disgraceful donkey that the Hsiung-nu had deemed fit for a sheltered princess. Later, as they saw that she neither wobbled in her saddle nor complained, she was raised to the dignity of a horse; the grunts and brief words she overheard from the Hsiung-nu in her train convinced her that her riding, if nothing else, met with their approval.

Day by day, the weather grew steadily cooler, and the wind that swept down from the great bowl of Heaven to ruffle the fur of her cloak and hood became fiercer and dryer. In it, she could smell drying grass and the bruised, hardy plants of the North.

They had had music from sundown late into the night. Flutes and zithers had played, and her maids had sung. Willow passed wine and sweetmeats about on delicate plates; and, for once, no one had grimaced or recoiled from her. Seated in her tent, basking in the light of many lamps, Silver Snow, her maids, and her companions had drawn together, the music linking them in a unity that was the warmer, the finer for the wind blowing outside and the fact that it had not long to last.

Finally, as the lamps burned lower, casting shadows on the tent's taut walls, Silver Snow had let herself be coaxed into singing.

"This is a song of the North," she explained, and then she had sung, the wind outside and the drums within fit counterpoint for her sweet, reedy voice.

Abruptly one of the ladies gasped, hand to mouth. Roused from a trance of music-making, Silver Snow started and broke off her song.

"Forgive this wretched, foolish one, Imperial Lady," wept the woman. "But outside, outside, I saw a shadow, and . . . oh, it frightened me!"

That had ended the night's music. Silver Snow had had much ado to prevent that lady's cries and tears from spreading like fire across dried-out brush. When she could spare time to look up, the shadow of which the woman had spoken was gone, assuming that it—one particular shadow among the shadow-dance that played on the tent's walls—had ever been there.

Shortly afterward, she had dismissed all of her other attendants, laid aside her heavy garments, and sighed in the peace and solitude.

"Good hunting, Elder Sister," whispered Willow as the girl sank down on a pallet at the foot of Silver Snow's own bed-place.

In the light of the one tiny jade lamp that had been left to be extinguished, she rose upon one elbow to study her maid. Willow's eyes glowed green, reflecting the lamplight, filled with the desire to run free and to hunt. Perhaps she wanted to roam free forever, Silver Snow thought with a pang.

Then Willow blinked, and her eyes were only those of a young woman's—tired and red-rimmed from the touch of wind and dust.

"No," whispered the maid. "I do not speak for myself, but for you. This is a royal hunt on which we go; you hunt out a future for yourself, and I—I follow at your heels."

Then she smiled, showing white teeth that were incongruously, delicately perfect in such an undistinguished face.

The next day, they spotted the Yellow River, the huge, unruly dragon of a river that swept across Ch'in, bringing life to the lands—or disastrous floods. They would follow the river even farther north, to the rocky pass where Yellow River met the Purple Barrier of the Great Wall, where Ch'in ended and the grasslands of the Hsiung-nu began.

For now, the river was quiescent, a strong, wide, rippling thing that extended from where they rode to the horizon.

A flicker of motion on its nearer bank drew Silver Snow's attention, as, apparently, it drew the attention of the Hsiung-nu, who nodded among themselves, and reached for bows and quivers.

"Riverbirds," whispered Willow, coming up beside her mistress' horse on the donkey that sweated and sidled but, nevertheless, bore her. "Did I not tell you, lady, that we would have good hunting?"

"Quick, Willow, ride back and fetch my bow," Silver Snow ordered. Unworthy, unseemly it might be to boast, but she would like to bring down at least one of those waterfowl before the Hsiung-nu, especially before that taciturn Prince Vughturoi. They should see that their new queen could provide food as well as eat it, and that she could ably defend herself.

Besides, some omen-making part of her mind recalled that she had been hunting wildfowl the day that the summons had come from the Palace. To shoot down another bird today would be an auspicious event.

Willow laughed mischievously, handed over the bundle that she had strapped to her saddle, and rode away. Silver Snow unrolled it: there lay a quiver of arrows and the bow that Silver Snow had borne in the North and with which she had slain the bandits during her journey to the capital. Silver Snow tested the string, nodded at its faint, sweet twang, and ignored the Hsiung-nu, who, for once, were startled into grins at the sight of the Imperial Lady, bow in hand.

A fox's bark yapped from the riverbank, panicking the waterfowl and sending them crying and flapping into the air. The Hsiung-nu drew as one, and Silver Snow drew with them, firing once, then again, almost as rapidly as they.

Birds fell, some upon the land, some splashing into the shallows; and the Hsiung-nu rode forward to retrieve them. Their shouts of triumph rose, then changed. Quickly Prince Vughturoi rode back from the riverbank and gestured, as if begging—as much as Hsiung-nu ever could beg—permission to approach her. Draped before him on his saddle were two plump fowl. One had been felled with two arrows, so close together that their feathers touched. The second had been a clean kill—one arrow, shot neatly through the bird's neck.

"Lady," he said, pointing to the bird that had been killed with two arrows. He looked puzzled, so puzzled that, clearly, he gave no thought to the possibility that Silver Snow might flinch at the presence of blood and death, "This arrow I know. It is of the fletching common in the grasslands. But this arrow—and this one, a fine shot, too—I do not know at all. Is there a marksman among the soldiers of Ch'in who ride among us?"

Silver Snow reached out one tiny hand to touch the arrow. Its fletching was indeed familiar, the work of her father's bowyer. She reached into her quiver, and brought out the arrow's mate. Then she smiled and, very quickly, glanced away.

Finally they reached the pass where great river and Great Wall met. Strangely enough, in this sheltered place, the winds were fainter, warmer, and the grass still was green. Because the Hsiung-nu for whom Prince Vughturoi had sent had not yet arrived, soldiers and servants pitched tents and unpacked for what might prove to be a long stay.

Silver Snow dismounted without aid. After days in the saddle, she had regained all of the hardiness that she had feared that her time in the Palace might have cost her. Nevertheless, she thought, as she straightened her cloak, the land here was fair, if bleak. She would use the respite to write to her fathers, she thought, with a wry smile, all three of them: Chao Kuang, who had begotten her; Li Ling, his friend, who had saved her from despair and had taught her; and Yuan Ti, the Son of Heaven, who had adopted her to toss her away, yet who had, in the end, grieved over his decision. That was her obligation; it was also her pleasure. Thanks to Li Ling, she even had silk fit for the task.

She was not, however, to have uninterrupted tranquillity for the task. The instant that Silver Snow's tent was pitched and that her ladies were free to come to her, they broke out in tears and wails of grief and fear.

Silver Snow sighed. Willow winced. The Hsiung-nu and Ch'in soldiers, not faced with the need for self-control, grimaced and grinned. Silver Snow bent over the most distraught of the ladies.

"What troubles you?" she crooned in the voice that they all swore was as sweet as litchi. (When they had called her the Shadowed One, however, they had condemned that very same voice as reedy and shrill; best not think of that.) "You are not ill; we shall rest here; and soon you shall return to your home."

The mention of home made the wailing break out afresh. That was it, then. The Hsiung-nu ladies had not yet arrived, and now this flock of affrighted palace ladies feared that they never would. In that case, perforce, it would be their obligation to accompany Silver Snow to the court of the Hsiung-nu, from which, they were sure, there could be no return.

"I shall die!" shrieked one woman.

"Did you see the grass?" another lamented. "Green, ever green, like the tombs of exiles, watered with tears."

"We will never see our homes again!"

"They will carry us off to the West, and we will never again see the Palace, or a garden, or my little courtyard with the golden carp in the pool. And they will make us eat our meat raw!"

Had their fear not been so real, and so likely to drive them into a frenzy, Silver Snow might have found it comical. But she was tired and apprehensive herself, and she wanted only to rest and compose her thoughts before she wrote out an account of her days for the men whom she revered most in all the world.

"This is my work, Elder Sister." Blessed Willow burrowed into her baggage for the herbs that Li Ling had given her, hastened to the fire, and began to steep a soothing decoction. Her eyes met her mistress', and Silver Snow nodded.

At least what few trees remained were stunted, flimsy things that would not hold the weight of a lady who sought to avoid worse by hanging herself with her silken sash. "We are too close to the river here, too close to the rocks," she murmured. She would have to have the guard doubled around the ladies' quarters until they turned back toward Ch'ang-an.

She emerged from her tent, thankful, at least, that their terror forestalled her ladies from criticizing her going out among armed men without proper supervision. Seeking the captain of her guard, she found him in attendance on Prince Vughturoi, who pointed west and gestured, but who broke off at her approach. Silver Snow nodded to him, then explained her wishes.

The guard captain abased himself, then ran off to do her bidding. The prince, however, held his ground and regarded her with that expressionless stare of his. "There is no illness?" he asked.

"None, save fear," she declared. "I seek to prevent the fear driving some fragile soul mad."

She glanced out in the direction toward which the prince had been gazing. "Our people approach," he deigned to tell her.

How keen his sight must be! She could see nothing except, yes, surely, that was it, a puff of dust, of less size against the immensity of the land and sky than a gnat. She sighed. Uncouth the women of the Hsiung-nu might be, but, at least, they would be used to the land.

"I shall be glad when they arrive," Silver Snow ventured to say. For the first time, the prince smiled, the merest quirk of one side of his mouth. Silver Snow withdrew, feeling that she had won a major victory.

She returned to her tent, where a more ignominious and

far louder battle raged, and did her best to calm her over-wrought ladies. Long into the night she and Willow labored; it was only when they had put the last of the gulping, shivering ladies to bed and hidden any knife that they might find that she and Willow had time quietly to drink some warmed rice wine themselves, eat but a morsel or two, and, finally, try to sleep.

Still, the ladies' wailing had plucked at Silver Snow's nerves to such an extent that she slept but shallowly. Her sleep was full of dreams of horses and blowing dust, a weird whistling sound, and blood dripping onto the land while, somewhere in the distance, came loud, cruel laughter. She woke, sweating, and breathed quiet thanks into the shaking hands that she held cupped before her lips.

Then she sat up, as stiff as if she had undertaken a day's ride after a year's inaction. The fire had burnt itself out; she might summon a servant to rekindle it, or do so herself, if she wanted to wake Willow, who slept deeply and enviably, with only a twitch, from time to time, to show that she indeed lived. Even if she kindled a fire, she would probably only wake the most distraught of the ladies, who also slept within her quarters.

The tent should have been dark, but moonlight shone into it, letting Silver Snow see her warm robe wadded at the foot of her pallet, her sleeping maid—and the small, hunched shadow-figure that darted from the tent toward the river.

Quickly Silver Snow rose and whipped her robe, then her cloak, about her. She thrust her feet into fur-lined boots, seized up her bow, and set out after the shadow.

Behind her Willow muttered, sleepy, but rapidly coming alert and alarmed. However, Silver Snow could not stay to reassure her. With a huntress' care, Silver Snow stalked the figure whose shadow she had seen. Her feet in their furred boots made no sound, even on the crisp ground scrub; and soon she had reached the too-green grass that her ladies had chosen to see as a sign of ill-omen.

She was nearing the figure. It was all silver-gray in the moonlight, but Silver Snow recognized the embroideries on the gown that straggled from the woman's shoulders, trailing after her on the grass. It was the lady who had feared that she would be made to eat raw meat. Silver Snow stifled a groan. Of all of her women, that one was the most sensitive. Let a pet bird be injured, and she was in tears; let a friend be ill, and she too took to bed.

What had caused her to walk in her sleep? Silver Snow raised her hands to clap them sharply together, thus waking the woman into sense. Then, she thought better of it. Who knew to what strange realms her spirit might have fled, or what might happen if she were waked thus unceremoniously?

She quickened her pace to catch the woman and turn her before she reached the river. That was when Silver Snow heard the whimpering. "Winds across the plains . . . no rest . . . no peace . . . no friends. I shall die, and none will remain to mark my grave or set up a tablet in my memory . . . misery, misery . . . to be cursed so far from my home."

To be cursed? Silver Snow stopped and drew a deep breath. As if she herself were a creature of the wilds, she sniffed at the air. It was sweet and untainted; from whence came this muttering of curses and exile?

Silver Snow felt her robe catch in the ground scrub. She freed it with a tearing sound, and hurried more quickly after the endangered lady. The long skirt caught again, and again, until she was tempted to shed it and run after the lady in her undergown. Above her, the sky seemed suddenly to whirl, and she flung out a hand to protect herself. The ground was twirling and shaking; there was no anchorage, no stability anywhere . . . she herself would fall into the river that rippled so steadily and deeply ahead and be carried away, beyond anyone's ken . . .

Then a cold nose touched the hand she had flung out, and metal rattled against it.

Silver Snow gasped and looked down at the fox that nuzzled her fingers. Larger than most it was, with a particularly lush coat. It walked with a peculiar limp, and, in its mouth, it bore an amulet dangling from a chain.

"I cannot reach her," she gasped, still giddy from whatever force had all but hurled her to the ground. The fox pressed its pointed muzzle into her hand, releasing the amulet into her palm.

As Silver Snow looped the cord of the amulet about her neck, the fox ran on ahead. As it had with Silver Snow's, it nuzzled the dreaming lady's fingers, then took them delicately in its mouth and began, ever so gently and patiently, to tug her away from the river, and back toward Silver Snow.

With one last furious tug, she freed her garments. A moment later—though it would have been too late for the sleep-walker whom the fox now guided—she had the woman by the arm and was steering her toward the tent, when a shadow fell across her path, moonlight glinting from the sharp blade that it held.

Silver Snow gasped and stopped. The fox melted into the nightshadows, and Vughturoi sheathed his blade.

"Is such night walking a custom of Ch'in?" he asked, with no amusement at all in his deep voice.

She was a princess of Ch'in, she was queen of the hordes, and she was her father's daughter: she had the power to order him away. She did not know why she answered with the absolute truth.

"I dreamed ill," she said, looking down, suddenly aware that she wore a thin gown and a quilted robe, and that her hair tumbled about her face and down her back. Even if the moonlight silvered over her flush, this was no time for maiden modesty.

"When I woke," said Silver Snow, "I saw that Jade Butterfly here had left my tent. She was walking in her sleep, crying about a curse that she feared so that she would drown herself lest she yield to it. *We* do not curse thus in Ch'in," she added angrily. "It is a strong tongue that can frame that sort of curse."

"Aye," muttered Vughturoi, as if he had bitten down on a

rotten fruit. "A strong tongue indeed. Shall I see you back to your tent, lady?"

Silver Snow shook her head. "What if this one wakes and sees you? Then we shall have more tears and frenzy. I thank you, Prince, but no." The sooner she returned to her tent, the sooner Willow might return to her true form. She thought she could hear her maid in fox-guise even now, yapping as she prowled—with a lame leg, yet!—about the outskirts of the camp thrice.

Vughturoi blended back into the shadows with a skill that set at naught her own small knowledge of trail lore. Silver Snow dragged Jade Butterfly back toward the tent and the safety of her own sleeping mats.

It was a long time until she could sleep, and when, finally, her eyes closed, the last things that she saw were Willow's bright, wary eyes and a rigid shadow mounting guard outside the tent.

By noon of the next day, the Hsiung-nu caravan arrived.

"It is as well, lady," Willow remarked. "The novelty will distract your companions, and we shall be gone before this sleeping Butterfly of yours can awake and claim she was possessed by a fox."

Silver Snow nodded and waved Willow into her usual, shadowed place. She herself was fascinated by the approaching troop. Leather-armored riders bore the reflexive and bone-reinforced bows of the hordes; musicians who raised weird instruments to bray music like nothing that she had ever heard before; two ladies, who seemed to be taller and broader than half of the Ch'in guardsmen; carts; an immense herd of pack animals and remounts; and the chariot that was clearly intended for Silver Snow.

That especially fascinated her, for it was drawn, not by horses nor by oxen, but by camels, the first that she had ever seen, two smooth-striding, swaying beasts that bore the double humps on their backs with the same unconcern as they pulled the chariot. The whole of the arriving escort shrieked and yelped as they approached Vughturoi, and rode in a circle just beyond the shadow of the Wall.

Above all else, it was the sight of the camels that made so very plain to Silver Snow that she had reached to the place where Ch'in met the wilderness. She drew a deep breath of fear, wonder, and—yes—delight, and turned toward her ladies. Abstracted, she handed a packet of letters, painstakingly calligraphed upon silk, to the chief of them, commended herself to the Son of Heaven and—as if in a dream—by rote to whomever else the lady considered proper, then bid the rest of her short-term companions farewell. She would never see them again, and that contented her well. It surprised her that they seemed to feel otherwise about her. They clustered about and declaimed, some in tears, the sorrow of parting.

Their tears are more than ritual, more than what is due to the Son of Heaven's favor. Yet, I was ever the Shadowed One, she thought, bemused. *When and why did they come to love me?*

"It is three months' journey to where my father the *shan-yu* holds winter court," Vughturoi remarked as Silver Snow mounted and prepared to ride out beyond the Wall and the only country she had ever dreamed of knowing.

"Indeed?" She raised brows that had not lost their delicacy, even if she no longer bothered to pluck and pencil them to the proper moth-wing shape. Where she rode, there would be none to care for such things, in any case. "That being the case, lord Prince, had we not better start immediately?"

They rode up to the Wall, and her Ch'in guards presented their tokens. The gate that the Son of Heaven had decreed must henceforward be called the Gate of Tears groaned open. Despite herself, Silver Snow glanced back once at the confusion as her camp beside the Yellow River was dismantled. She was disconcerted by how very little she cared for the bustle of plots and activity that she was leaving behind. She raised hand in farewell, and a wail of grief went up from those ladies who had assembled to see her go. She winced as she touched heels to her horse's flanks.

As Silver Snow crossed through the gate, her horse's

hooves rasped against the grit and scant scrub of the true desert, deposited here by the wind. Thus, she rode out into the lands of the Hsiung-nu, and the wind, laden with dust and sand, buffeted her scarf-protected face.

CHAPTER

= 13 =

Day after day, they traversed a land in which no tree, stream, rock, nor hill appeared to separate one day's travel from another. Then, one morning, the sight of ten rocks crumbling, perhaps once the site of some ancient outpost, came as a surprise. The sight of this ruin, its stonework tumbled, was a major event—for Silver Snow, that was. The Hsiung-nu simply shrugged as they rode on.

"The sky," growled one close enough for her to hear, "is all the roof that the Hsiung-nu need."

She herself was concerned. If such ruin existed this close to the Wall (for they had turned slightly south and could still sight that barrier now and then), would the Middle Kingdom not grow overly dependent upon the Hsiung-nu for protection? She had not believed what Li Ling had told her: that smug officials at court were wont to assure the Emperor: that the Wall was more a defense for the barbarians against the Middle Kingdom.

Certainly it was folly for Ch'in to rely always upon the Wall to keep out invasion, to rely too much upon the goodwill of such horsemen. Was that a vain thing, too? *I myself am a weapon in my nation's hands*, Silver Snow told herself when the wind lashed tears from her eyes to freeze on the edges of the scarf against her cheeks.

The air grew cold and dry, then colder and dryer yet. Snow covered the dead grasses. Some days, the sky itself turned pale, and the sun gleamed in it like silver cash, providing light but no warmth. To Silver Snow's astonishment, despite the cold and the wind, the tough, stocky horses, each bearing its owner's mark, became more and more shaggy, even thrived, while the camels strode on through the waste, sublimely indifferent to everything save their burdens, their handlers, and their sullen dispositions.

At first, the days' journeys tired Silver Snow so sorely that at night all she wanted to do was creep into her fur blankets and sleep, perhaps without even bothering to eat. There was so much that no one at court understood about the Hsiung-nu, so much that she had not fully comprehended from her father's stories, now made clear! Their hatred of walls and restraint, their curious dress, with its shorter tunics and trousers rather than proper robes, even their diet, heavy in meat and fats, were not signs of savagery but simply ways they embraced in order to live in this land. Here, under the vast bowl of the sky, which resounded, day after day, with windsongs more poignant and memorable than those of any voice or bamboo flute, those ways made sense. They possessed a particular rhythm, even a grace, that Silver Snow knew that she would one day come to appreciate.

Gradually, however, the result of the training she had had in her father's house was regained. Used to the sweet smells of the Inner Courts, at first she found the pungency of the Hsiung-nu's dung fires to be eye-watering and intolerable. Then she became inured to the smell and smoke, and, finally, she did not notice either. She had been healthy before; now she became hardy, flesh and sinew fining down to form a creature that, if she were less consciously elegant than the vision in pearls and kingfisher feathers who had charmed the Son of Heaven, was nevertheless beautiful and perfectly suited to thrive in her new home.

"Do I look," she asked Willow once, "precisely now as Mao Yen-shou painted me—thin, weathered, and mannish?"

Willow laughed. "Lady, you lack a black mole, while Mao Yen-shou lacks a head. There is no point even in speaking of him."

The Hsiung-nu who earlier had inspected them and had shaken heads, especially so the women, began, if not to approve, to assume that the women from Ch'in could endure a day's travel without lamenting, fainting, or growing ill. Silver Snow wondered if they were disappointed. Their leader, Prince Vughturoi, rarely spoke. Was he angry, perhaps, that some girl-princess of Ch'in had been sent out to supplant his mother? She tried to cause no trouble and knew that she had succeeded in that; but still he kept away from her.

Then she noticed something else. Even though Willow was lame, mounted, she was as hardy as the rest of the troop. Nor, because of her blood, did the cold afflict her as harshly. And, where the Hsiung-nu had been inclined to think Silver Snow too frail, too alien for the journey to Khujanga the *shan-yu*'s court, they greeted Willow with what could pass for grudging respect. As Li Ling had said, some women of the Hsiung-nu were said to have powers more than mortal. Gradually, Willow's herb-lore let her gain face among a people who, if they were wild and harsh, were also open and free. It was even the source of some half-heard, partially understood jests.

"You need a strong tongue to withstand one of her herb drenches," joked a rider who had come to Willow for a potion.

"Aye, and will that very strong tongue . . ."

At that moment, however, the Lord Vughturoi had appeared from behind a tent, and the men had dispersed like whipped curs. The prince had simply glared and stalked on his way.

Gradually, once again, Silver Snow and Willow found themselves able to see the nightly camps as opportunities for more than a little food and sleep. Shielded from the wind that, it was said, the white tiger blew from the far west, all the way across steppe and plain, by a sturdy tent of silk, felt, and leather, Willow sorted her herbs, and Silver Snow tried either to write or to play her lute.

One night was so cold that the ink froze on its stone, and, perforce, she must lay aside her latest letter to her father. Instead, she warmed her fingers at their tiny brazier and picked up her lute, strumming idly upon it. After a time, her strumming modulated into a very old song that she had heard her maids at home sing. They had not known that she was present, and once they had seen her, they had broken off at once.

The song dealt with, she supposed, the emotions of another lady such as she, married to a ruler of the hordes.

> *"My people have married me*
> *In a far corner of Earth:*
> *Sent me away to a strange land,*
> *To the king of the . . ."*

"Mistress!" hissed Willow, more shape of the lips than sound.

Silver Snow's fingers struck a discord. "This lute is not in tune," she excused herself. With her eyes, she followed Willow's pointing finger. Clearly limned against the rippling wall of their tent was the shadow that they had seen there before.

Why does he not come in? she asked herself. *I am wed to his father, the* shan-yu; *we are as kin, then; and it is no impropriety.*

Yet, he did not. If he chose to remain outside in the wind, the dark, and the cold, that was his choice; and grave impropriety on her part to seek to sway him from it.

Once again, she picked up the lute.

> *"A tent is my house,*
> *Of felt are my walls;*
> *Raw flesh my food . . ."*

Both she and Willow broke off to laugh. It was true that since they had come into the West, they had eaten mutton nearly every night, and that that was a meat little favored in Ch'ang-an. However, the mutton had always been seethed ir the huge bronze cauldron borne each day by the most reliable of the camels.

"Probably, lady, the fool of a poet who wrote that song never journeyed farther west than to the west gate of Ch'ang-an," Willow observed, her voice wry.

"Aye, so I think too."

"How does it end?" Willow asked.

Silver Snow, recalling how the song went, wished she had chosen any song but that. The shadow lingering outside to hear her music could not like what he would hear. Nevertheless, to refuse to sing might reveal her awareness of the eavesdropper. Sighing, she picked up the lute for the last time.

> *Always thinking of my own country,*
> *My heart sad within.*
> *Would I were a yellow stork*
> *And could fly to my old home!"*

Decisively, Silver Snow covered the lute and laid it aside. Raising her voice that it might reach her audience, she said, "No yellow stork could survive in the northlands in which I myself was born. A pretty song, but sad and nonsensical. I shall not sing it again."

The next morning, as Silver Snow emerged gasping into the cold and brushed away the flakes of snow already clinging to the lavish fur trim of her hood, she knew that the Lord Vughturoi's eyes were upon her, but she feigned unconcern as she walked to her horse.

That song had been nonsense. The next evening, Silver Snow asked the Hsiung-nu women to join her too. She waited until the shadow again revealed itself upon the wall of her tent and sang another, which more closely captured the strange beauty of the frozen waste.

> *"The north winds coil the earth, the pale grasses break;*
> *The tartar sky in the eighth month is made of flying snow . . ."*

Then she broke off her song. "Do you hear that?" she demanded.

One of the Hsiung-nu women, Bronze Mirror, nodded indulgently at Sable, the other. Both were women of some standing among the Hsiung-nu: Bronze Mirror with one son grown; Sable, who was too young by far to be a widow with children (as she was), but who derived her standing from her brother Basich, who stood high in Prince Vughturoi's favor.

Their opinions, as Silver Snow knew all too well from her days in Ch'ang-an, would spread like fire, to the rest of the Hsiung-nu. Perhaps this young little Ch'in princess had not collapsed during the trip west and north, but she had her fancies, her weaknesses.

"It is the wind, lady, roaring across the plain," Bronze Mirror reassured her.

Silver Snow might have blushed and let the subject drop had she not, at that moment, seen Willow. She crouched at the sealed tent flap, almost as if she sought to outwait some prey, and her eyes gleamed feral and green the way that they did whenever she scented danger.

"The breath of the white tiger," she whispered.

What of it? Silver Snow knew that the sigil of the West was the white tiger; the wind could well be called its breath. Once again rose the sound that had caused her to break off her music. Involuntarily she glanced at the tent wall. The shadow that she had come to expect there had also stiffened. Then it disappeared.

"That is not the mere breath of the white tiger," Silver Snow stated flatly. "That is an animal out there. Perhaps *a* white tiger, perhaps something else," she added, more for bravado than because she believed it to be true. She had heard that white tigers and snow leopards were among the dangers to be found in the West: and suddenly, terrifyingly, she suspected that such a beast now stalked their camp, perhaps came sniffing about her very tent.

Aside from the wind and the sound of whatever prowled

and stalked outside, the tent grew suddenly, ominously still. Silver Snow glanced over at Willow, who had stiffened, her red hair glowing in the light from the brazier. Her green eyes seemed to glaze over, as if she listened to something that her mistress could not hear.

Gradually sounds insinuated themselves into that silence: what seemed almost like a purr of feral satisfaction and the rhythm of a huge heart pounding.

Willow's lips pulled back from her teeth. Had she been in beast form, she would have growled. The Hsiung-nu women, almost shy for the first time since Silver Snow had met them, hung back, not in fear, but in awe. Then their eagerness for a fight—and possibly their fear of the Lord Vughturoi and his father—awoke.

Careful not to make a sound, she reached for her fur cloak, donned it, and caught up bow and arrow. Sable and Bronze Mirror drew out sharp daggers. Willow, however, had none. When Sable would have tossed her a knife from her soft, supple riding boot, the maid nodded thanks, but refused.

"This is the only weapon I need," she explained, and drew out her mirror, curiously incised with strange symbols, the one she had borne as long as Silver Snow had known her.

When a horse screamed in mortal fear and agony, Silver Snow realized that her worst fears must be true. Other horses screamed in panic. Now men, too, shouted an alarm as they raced to seize arms and guard the camp against the intruder.

"We cannot wait here for our fate to come upon us," she said, shaping her lips without sound lest she draw their enemy upon them. "Not while we are armed and able to defend ourselves."

Either Bronze Mirror or Sable could have restrained her with one hard hand. However, before they protested or tried to stop her, Silver Snow slipped outside, and Willow followed.

Overhead shone the moon, incredibly vast and close-seeming in this land where no houses, walls, or trees might hide it from view. Starlight, obscured at times by gusts of fine snow, bloomed in the night sky and glanced off the mirror that Willow held up.

"Elder Sister," the maid whispered, "I think that this is another such sending as troubled Jade Butterfly when we parted."

"Aimed at me, do you think?" Silver Snow nodded to herself. Jade Butterfly had been no more a menace than her namesake, but she, with her brideprice and her rank, might well have enemies with whom she had yet to reckon and of whom, she now realized, Bronze Mirror and Sable might not dare to speak.

Perhaps they will trust me if I can prove my strength, thought Silver Snow. Fine archer though she knew that she was, going on foot and armed only with a bow against a tiger was not a test that she would have chosen. She chose an arrow with care and nocked her bow.

Just as Willow's mirror flashed a warning, Silver Snow heard the coughing grunt of a beast poised to spring. The light flashed once more, and the leap went awry.

She whirled, drew, shot, and was rewarded with an anguished yowl. She had wounded the creature, then, but not slain it, she realized. And a wounded beast was ever the deadlier. Paws padded against the ground. She shot again.

"Behind me!" cried a man, as his horse pounded toward her. She heard the whine of his bow and of several others. The beast shrieked and thrashed, at one point rolling so close to Silver Snow that she could feel its hot breath, rank with blood. She saw the starlight gleam on its teeth and claws, which seemed to flicker with a phosphorescence of their own. Unholy, accursed! Something shrilled in her mind, and she could not restrain a scream.

Then the beast toppled, kicked once or twice, and, finally, lay still.

The warrior leapt from his horse, raked one glance over Silver Snow and her maid to assure himself that they were unhurt, and turned to their quarry.

"Bring fire!" he called.

Silver Snow pressed in closer. She too wanted to see the beast that she had helped to slay. Torches wavered and guttered, the wind all but blowing their flame sideways in the cold. In their fitful red light, Silver Snow saw a white tiger. It was immense, with massive paws and jaws upon which a bloody froth was now freezing. Even now, its green eyes glowed, then went out, like emeralds shattered by a hammer blow. Had Silver Snow imagined the light she had seen? No! Flickers still clung to claws and teeth, flickers that faded and died in glittering death throes of their own as the beast's body twitched and cooled.

Carrying one of the Hsiung-nu's long, deadly spears, Vughturoi walked toward the tiger and prodded it from a distance. When the beast did not move, he edged in closer and bent over its body, his hand going out to count the arrows that feathered it.

"Another excellent shot, lady," he said to Silver Snow. "Though you might recall that it is my head that will fall should I fail to bring you unharmed to the *shan-yu*."

Silver Snow knew that she had earned the rebuke for her rashness, but she held her ground. Among the Hsiung-nu, she would gain more face from stubbornness than from retreat, she thought.

Vughturoi investigated more closely. "Two fine shots," he commented, not at all surprised that she had not withdrawn.

"Very well," he shouted to the cluster of hunters. "Finish tending the horses and go to your rest, all of you! We will carry this tiger with us—if our own beasts will bear it—until our next stopping point, where we can skin it. And you, lady," he added in a softer voice, "may present it to my father as a sign of your prowess. It will be interesting to see the flurry that that will cause in the *shan-yu*'s tents."

Now he sounded, not displeased, but speculative, as if Silver Snow were a gamepiece that a particularly canny player had moved with surpassing skill. She did not understand him in that mood, not at all, nor did she trust it. She returned to her tent and tried to compose herself for sleep.

The next morning, when men came to load the tiger's body upon the least restive of their packbeasts, they found only the blackened stains of its blood, which even now the snow was covering over, and the charred shafts of the arrows that had slain it. But the beast itself had vanished.

They finished breaking camp in silence and moved on with what was great haste, even among the Hsiung-nu.

CHAPTER

= 14 =

Silver Snow chose to use her chariot for entrance to the main camp of the Hsiung-nu. Though that decision might make them regard her as weak, she wanted the advantage that a few minutes of study, behind the chariot's protective curtains, would give her.

"It is custom," said Willow, "for a bride to arrive in a carriage or litter. Besides," she added practically, "should snow fall, you will not ruin your brocades."

"Foolish one," replied Silver Snow, as she pushed away the mirror that Willow held out for her, "what will the Hsiung-nu care about fine silks?"

"They were eager enough to accept those that the Son of Heaven sent to this *shan-yu*, and they will be glad, I make no doubt, of those that you bring in your dowry. These are simple, robust people. Let them see you shine out like the sun and the moon, and they will respect you the more."

Willow held out Silver Snow's finest cloak, a magnificent thing of soft brown sable, under which she wore the red robe of a bride. When the call came, she left her tent, gathering her robes about her with more care than she had shown at any other time during the months of their journey to the court of the *shan-yu*. Behind her, Sable and Bronze Mirror gasped in wonder and admiration.

"She is worthy," said one of them, with a fondness in her voice that made Silver Snow arch delicate eyebrows in astonishment as she eavesdropped, "to be called Heavenly Majesty. Indeed, she looks not like a woman at all, but like a creature from the sky."

The other chuckled, a ribald laugh that was returned by Sable, Silver Snow decided.

"Surely, no," the deeper voice belonged to Bronze Mirror. "Would you lay rude hands upon a piece of jade? The *shan-yu*'s sons are full-grown, and his daughters have sons of their own. He will cherish this little lady as an ornament for his tent, not his bed-place, being far beyond such sport."

"A pity. When her beauty fades, a son would give her more arrows for her bow than she now has. And she is a lady who well understands the use of . . . well, weapons."

Why, thought Silver Snow, *they wish me well! Would that all in the camp to which I am about to fare do so as well!*

"Aye, indeed. But the Heavenly Majesty wanes. A day may come . . ."

"Hush!"

Silver Snow was not at all surprised to see Vughturoi ride up and give the order to start on the very last leg of their journey to the court of his father. She was, however, surprised to see that he had donned fresh leathers and furs and that, round his neck, hung the key with which Li Ling had ceremoniously locked Silver Snow into her chariot upon her departure from Ch'ang-an and then had presented to Vughturoi in token of his authority to guard her.

He grinned as he rode by her chariot, practically under the noses of the camels that were swaying and groaning their way to their ungainly feet. "Courage, lady!" he called in an undertone as he made the key swing on its heavy chain. "How much worse can it be to enter my father's tents than to slay the white tiger?"

That was a question to which Silver Snow would have given all that she possessed or might hope to possess for an auspicious answer.

* * *

The pale winter sun was high overhead when the first riders from the *shan-yu*'s court met Silver Snow's caravan, a cavalcade of shaggy horses and men who were wrapped in felts and furs and who bore the bows and long spears of the horde. They rode straight at the caravan as if, at any moment, they might level their spears or nock arrow to bow, and charge.

Silver Snow peered out from the curtains of her chariot. Her guards were worse, she thought, than no protection at all, for they signaled all too clearly, "Here is she whom you seek."

"Do you want your bow, Elder Sister?" asked Willow.

Silver Snow touched Willow's hand gently. Though a bow had served her well in many a battle, it was her wits that must serve her now. "Even if I needed it, it would serve no use."

She watched Lord Vughturoi ride out toward the newcomers, admiring his skill with horses, a mastery so deep that it was unconscious. Those from the camp were a very different type of man than Vughturoi and his companions, whom, Silver Snow guessed, must have been among the younger and more adaptable of the Hsiung-nu for the *shan-yu* to risk sending them to Ch'ang-an at all. These riders were not all older men, by no means, but they seemed somehow rougher, wilder, lacking the refinements of Ch'in culture that Silver Snow had occasionally noted in her escort. Though, like Vughturoi, they were sparsely bearded, many of these men bore facial scars from the custom that many of the Hsiung-nu still observed of slashing their faces when mourning a friend, a kinsman, or a leader.

Had the men been any people other than Hsiung-nu, Silver Snow knew that they would have made much of dismounting, of sitting together and sharing food before discussing their business. Such a meeting might well have lasted the entire day. However, she did not expect that the Hsiung-nu would so much as stir from horseback, and she was right. A trick of the wind brought their voices toward her, and she strained to listen.

"A good journey, and a better one back," Vughturoi commented to an older man who clapped him about the shoulders. Again the wind blew, and Silver Snow caught only half of his next speech ". . . not as bad as I expected, and, in fact, well enough. I see that Sandilik the *kam-quam*, is among you. We have had . . ."

Again, a gust of the treacherous, frustrating wind blew away the words Silver Snow listened for as if her life might depend upon them. *Kam-quam*, she knew, meant a male shaman; and, yes, such a one rode among them, with his spirit drum and his robes trimmed with bones and the skins of snakes, here in this land where no such creatures ever hissed and coiled. Vughturoi's voice had not sounded that strained and anxious even on the night they stalked the white tiger.

She waited for him to bring up what, she knew, must be the questions that he had suppressed.

"How is . . . those gashes look fresh, Kursik."

"His Heavenly Majesty survived your absence," replied the man called Kursik. "He is well, and sent us to seek you."

"The Sun be praised!" Vughturoi's voice roughed. "But still, you bear scars that look fresh."

"My brother, Prince. Erlik take him, but, for all that, he *was* my brother."

"He followed *my* esteemed brother Tadiqan, did he not?"

"Aye, and that was what undid him. Tadiqan has new arrows, ones that whistle. They say," the newcomer dropped his voice, and Silver Snow strained to hear him, "that they are bespelled, never to miss the mark. Now he has made a new law for those that follow him. When he fires a whistling arrow, all must fire after him. Well, there was a small thing, a claim of a stolen bride, I think, and Tadiqan fired one of his arrows. At my brother. Am I to require bloodprice from a prince or all of the men who dog his heels?"

Vughtoroi reached out and clapped Kursik on the shoulder. "You may require it of me when I have unpacked. Ch'in, praise Tangr and the Sun, is still rich and eager to share its wealth with us, lest we overrun them. But I must deliver my father's new bride."

"That too," said Kursik. "Tadiqan and his mother have said that no spoiled child of the Inner Courts shall displace Strong Tongue for long, and that when His Heavenly Majesty . . ."

"Enough!" Vughturoi's hand tightened on his spear, then released, as if he longed to hurl it at an enemy but did not dare. "My father lives, and I have returned. It is by no means certain that Tadiqan will be the first of Khujanga's sons to find his husk. His mother is well named. But should *I* live to become *shan-yu*, let her beware that she does not poison herself and her son with that tongue!"

Perhaps Sable, the more friendly and more malleable of the two Hsiung-nu ladies, might tell her more. After all, it was she who had told her of the *shan-yu*'s sons, how, of ten strong men, all but three had died: two elder and the youngest, the child who was left hostage in the Middle Kingdom.

Silver Snow let the curtains drop. "Fetch Sable," she whispered to Willow. So Strong Tongue was not a phrase of ill-wishing, inauspicious words that could turn Prince Vughturoi's face grim in an instant, but an actual person: the *shan-yu*'s eldest wife and mother of a prince who clearly expected to inherit. Those two obviously held some power, or else Vughturoi would not have been dispatched to Ch'ang-an when his father was old enough for people to expect him to die. His sullenness had been fear, for himself and an old man whom he clearly revered, and perhaps even for a young woman who journeyed into more danger than she could possibly expect.

Sable rode up. At Silver Snow's invitation, she leapt with what seemed astonishing ease from horseback into the chariot just as Prince Vughturoi gave the command to ride.

The narrow eyes of the Hsiung-nu noblewoman widened and shone as Silver Snow greeted her with all the elegance that she might have used for a Brilliant Companion, then moved on to the pleasantries suitable between equals before they attended to any serious matter that might be discussed. Clearly she was impatient to get to the core of whatever Silver

Snow had to say; just as clearly, she forced herself to allow her new queen to take the lead.

Finally—less time than would have been proper in Ch'ang-an but more time than either woman wanted to squander on preliminaries—Silver Snow leaned forward and saw Sable's eyes brighten. Finally, an end to waiting!

"Tell me of our people," invited Silver Snow.

Sable was glad to expand upon the strength of the royal clan, the majesty of the *shan-yu* who ruled it, the wealth of its tents and herds, and the prowess of its warriors, among them Basich, her brother, and his hero, the Prince Vughturoi. Basich, Silver Snow learned, had children but no wives; Vughturoi had had a household, but "ill fortune struck, and his elder wife died in childbed," Sable spoke dispassionately, in the even tones of one for whom such misfortunes were part of everyday life. "Then his younger wife fell from her horse when it stumbled. He was glad, this one thinks, to obey His Heavenly Majesty's command to travel past the Purple Walls to fetch . . ." she trailed off, in a kind of embarrassment that surprised both herself and Silver Snow, who had not been aware that Hsiung-nu could blush.

"Who is Strong Tongue?" Silver Snow asked. For the first time in all her travels, she saw one of the Hsiung-nu flinch.

Her eyes grew round, almost distending from their shallow sockets. "She is like your handmaid, only more. Strong Tongue is a woman of power who knows all about the birth or death of a man or woman and whose voice is strong, like unto the voice of gods. When she fares from her yurt, all cover their faces and abase themselves in fear of her power."

Or, thought Silver Snow, *in fear of her son's whistling arrows*.

"She is no friend to me, then," she concluded, and saw Sable relax a little. Now, at least, she would be able to say, should Strong Tongue question her, that she had told Silver Snow, the interloper from Ch'in, nothing except that Strong Tongue had power.

She spoke gently, easily to Sable. *Let her see that I have no fear*, she thought. Then, just as swirls of dust up ahead heralded the approach of more riders from the *shan-yu*'s camp, she released the Hsiung-nu woman to remount her horse, lest she be seen sitting at ease with Strong Tongue's enemy.

Silver Snow shivered and tucked both hands into her voluminous sleeves. "More than ever, Willow," she said, "I am glad that you are with me. The day on which my father gave you to me is thrice auspicious."

Willow reached out, greatly daring, to pat her mistress' arm. "It will be all right. My head upon it; you shall come to no harm, little mistress."

At that moment, the Hsiung-nu's camp guards reached the caravan, surrounded it, and, with blood-chilling shrieks of welcome, escorted it into the camp of the *shan-yu*, the ancient husband whom Silver now had journeyed so far to meet.

Riders flowed about the wagons and chariot of Silver Snow's caravan, bringing it down a narrow aisle which was guarded by bowmen and over which loomed figures hacked into rocks and set up along the line of march. From where had they borne such stones, and why? Silver Snow wondered. She glanced at them, then glanced aside at the nakedness of the male and female figures, their private parts embarrassingly plain to be seen.

She had expected a camp. What, finally, her train paused in front of was just as much a court as any assortment of pavilions and gardens in Ch'ang-an, though it was as different from the capital as she herself might be from the robust, brawling women who tended the huge cauldrons that steamed outside many of the felt yurts.

Vughturoi gestured, and Silver Snow's driver stopped the chariot in front of the largest and most splendid of the tents. Actually, if a palace could be wrought of silk, leather, and felt, with occasional struts of rare, precious wood, the *shan-yu*'s tent was such a place. Despite the cold, its flaps gaped open, and fires burned within, their smoke rising through holes in the roof. So heavy and so firmly pitched was the tent that its walls scarcely rippled at gusts of wind that might have bowled over lesser structures.

Carpets of wool and silk, brought either from Ch'in or taken from the cities even farther west, in the land of the *Hu*, or Persia, lay scattered in and out of the tent, piled one upon another in shining layers. Farther inside, Silver Snow could make out plump brocaded cushions, the sleek gleam of lacquered chests, and ordered heaps of furs and silks. She had expected stark necessity. What she saw now had a splendor that might be barbaric but was also curiously attractive.

To Silver Snow's astonishment, Vughturoi dismounted and, with a flourish, applied the key that he wore to Silver Snow's chariot, though, since it was of Hsiung-nu design, possessed nothing that even resembled a lock. Silver Snow stepped down on ground that felt pebbled, unfamiliar beneath her feet. How odd it seemed now that she would be traveling no farther, at least until spring, she thought; and knew that for nomad thinking.

An elderly man shuffled forward, awkward with age as well as with the gait of a man who had, lifelong, ridden more often than he had walked. Beneath swathing furs, he wore a robe of Ch'in, embroidered with dragons and trimmed with vermilion. It hung on him in such a way as to suggest that once he had been a far heavier, more muscular man. Though he too wore the soft-soled boots of a rider, his were so lavishly fur-trimmed and embroidered that it was clear that he had not set foot to stirrup in many a day. The thin, scraggly beard common to males of his race was white from extreme age. Though his eyes were sunk deep in the wrinkles formed by gazing for too many years at the trackless horizon of the steppes, they were wise, cunning, and even a little humorous.

With great effort, he bent to touch Vughturoi's head, from which the young man had swept his fur cap. "As you can see, my son, the Sun has not yet claimed me," he said. "Rise."

"At your command, Most Heavenly Majesty," Vughturoi

answered, Then, his voice choking, he added, "It is most good to see you . . . Father."

"There, now, and so it is for an old man to see you too." The *shan-yu* patted his son's arm, then turned to Silver Snow, who went immediately to her knees, Willow pulling her robes into order and away from possible contamination from straw, dust, or dung.

"My bride," said the *shan-yu*, laboriously edging forward to take Silver Snow's chin in his hand and raise it with the eagerness of a child examining a new kite in the spring. "She is more fair than aught else I have seen from the Middle Kingdom," he declared. "Child, I bid you welcome. You shall be chief among my consorts, and I name you the queen who brings peace to the Hsiung-nu. For it is peace that you have brought. Henceforward, I decree that my cousin Yuan Ti has no need to defend his Wall. From the Great River to Dunhuang, I myself shall order my sons to maintain it."

Silver Snow blinked. As quickly as she could, she must write that news to Li Ling and to her father, together with what she thought best to do. Yet, to do that, she must observe, must spend time within these tents. That, of course, would be easy enough; henceforward, they were to be her home.

"Tents have been prepared for you and . . . you have brought ladies? Those sent to you were adequate?" asked Khujanga the *shan-yu* as if he truly cared what became of her. "They shall unpack . . . ah, I see a lute! Do you play?"

She nodded and cast down her eyes, grateful for one thing: that her Hsiung-nu ladies had assured her that this man, old enough to be her father's father, was past bed-sport.

"I am glad. I favor the music of the Middle Kingdom and much else that that ancient, rich land has given us. Your name and family, child?" Abruptly he shot that question at her, and Silver Snow realized that, kindly though he was, he was still every shrunken inch the ruler.

"Before the Son of Heaven raised me up, I was Silver Snow of the house of Chao; he who begot me was Chao Kuang, marquis and general—"

"And long-time dweller in my tents." The *shan-yu* nodded. "But come in, come in and eat with us, drink with us, meet those over whom you will rule."

Silver Snow followed the *shan-yu* into his palacelike tent and allowed herself to be seated next to a brazier, elaborately wrought of bronze trimmed with jade, malachite, and lapis lazuli. Scented smoke coiled up from it, masking the ever-present odors of dung, sweat, beasts, and cooking meat. She was handed a delicate cup that contained a coarse dark brew at which she sipped and concealed her reaction to its taste. That it was warm and made her tingle sufficed.

From outside came the shriek of a whistle, followed by the buzz of a flight of arrows, then a *chunk* as they went home in . . . in what? Silver Snow remembered the words of Kursik, who had met her train on the way to the *shan-yu*'s camp. That must have been one of Prince Tadiqan's whistling arrows. The Ancestors send that it had found its mark only in a post, not in a human heart.

When a squat, bandy-legged man, his face gashed, his sheepskins and furs grimy, stalked into the tent, brandishing a bow, Silver Snow knew that she had guessed aright. This must be the eldest prince, son of Strong Tongue, master of many men and horses. And if he succeeded his father as *shan-yu*, tribal custom decreed that he would become her husband in turn. Judging from the way his dark eyes raked her, he would most definitely be her husband in far more than name. She controlled herself before she could recoil, a movement that most probably would have tumbled her from her cushions onto the scattered carpets.

Unfortunately, as she composed herself, with one foot she knocked over a plate, and the meat that it contained rolled into the fire. Only a quick grab by one of the other women saved her knife from going after it.

That, Silver Snow thought, was nothing too bad compared with what might have occurred.

Instantly she was proved wrong. The tent grew silent, the Hsiung-nu very still . . . too still. In that quiet, the pad-pad of heavy, booted feet was all too loud, all too reminiscent of the beat of a huge, hostile heart. Many of the Hsiung-nu sighed and turned their heads away, they, who prided themselves on their very fearlessness.

Silver Snow, seeing no cause for silence or fear, looked up, expecting speedily to see a slave or servant who might clean up what she had dropped.

Instead, she felt a sudden gust of wind as the tent flap was hurled open. The fire sparked and swirled upward toward the vent in the ceiling. A huge bulk loomed on the threshold of the tent. Even as Silver Snow watched, it resolved into the figure of an enormous woman, one hand thrust out in accusation.

"The hearthfire is polluted!" The woman's voice rose up in reprimand and lamentation. It was deeper than any woman's voice that Silver Snow had ever heard, and it had about it an odd, growling rasp. "Douse it, that I may purify the hearth to warm this ignorant, frail creature whom those weaklings beyond the Wall have sent here to supplant me."

An immense and immensely powerful woman pushed her way through the clustering Hsiung-nu. At her approach, they laid aside mutton and mare's milk to watch her. Many bowed. Resembling Prince Tadiqan, by whom she took up a defensive stance, she was broad and squat. Like the shaman who Silver Snow had seen on the road, she wore a robe trimmed with feathers, strips of fur, and snakeskins. Also like him, she bore a spirit drum, its drumhead taut with a skin too delicate to belong to horse or sheep or camel or aught else . . . until Silver Snow looked down at her own hand and wrist, where they emerged from her sleeves, and surmised the fate of one, at least, among the Ch'in prisoners or the children whom they had had.

This then was Strong Tongue. Her sister-wife—and, by every readable sign, her enemy.

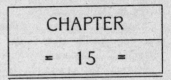

With a speed astonishing in one who was lame, Willow edged out from behind Silver Snow and knelt between her and Strong Tongue, by the fire's edge. As if to obey Strong Tongue's imperious demand that she be allowed through to purify the hearth, she carried implements for tending a fire. Her long hair gleamed russet in the light of the polluted fire, then darkened as she extinguished the blaze.

"Get away, girl!" snarled Strong Tongue. "What do you women of Ch'in know about that which is of Tangr, of the gods?"

She raised a foot, massive in heavy stitched leather and felt, as if to spurn Willow with her foot. Silver Snow stepped forward quickly, her jaw set, one hand flashing out to clasp her maid's shoulder and support her. Like an animal dodging a blow, Willow twisted to one side. As she moved, her silver mirror rolled from safekeeping in the bag that Willow ever kept tucked into the breast of her robes. It clattered and rang with the sweetness of fine metal. As it glinted up at Strong Tongue, the characters incised upon it glowed.

"Stand off, slave," commanded Strong Tongue. "Lest I curse you and that whey-faced weakling who holds your leash."

"My mistress did not know; does not know," hissed

Willow. Silver Snow had not thought that her maid had learned so much of the Hsiung-nu's speech. "But I do." She pitched her voice with a curious little hissing whine and met the older woman's eyes. *A fox, facing off against a wild sow, each well aware of the other's will to fight, should there be need*, Silver Snow thought.

"Willow, get back!" Silver Snow ordered, fear for her maid making her whisper more harsh than any she had ever before used with the girl.

Willow grabbed after her mirror before Strong Tongue could spurn at it or someone else could snatch it away. Then she looked up at her mistress. In the half light of the *shan-yu's* great tent, her skin seemed very pale, her eyes huge and lustrous. Her long hair, freed of its coils, billowed and crackled about her, its reddish glints seeming to send up sparks that held the light in the way that amber, rubbed by silk, attracts and clings to it.

Do not challenge this woman! Silver Snow wished at her maid. Sun Tzu might not have written thus in his *Art of War*, but it was only common sense not to go up against a strong foe in that foe's own territory. As if Willow understood her mind, she looked aside from Strong Tongue, and the tension that crackled between the two of them subsided. There would be no battle between them: at least, not this day.

Silver Snow glanced quickly about the great tent, past where Strong Tongue postured in righteous indignation and made great play of dispatching follower after follower for this packet of herbs or this image, or that other flute, while her son Tadiqan stood behind his mother, arms crossed on his chest, bandy legs splayed. Behind them clustered what seemed to be hundreds of Hsiung-nu, all watching.

Silver Snow spotted Bronze Mirror and Sable, whose hand covered her mouth. None spoke to her or made those slight shifts back and forth, the faint nods and subtle gestures that can indicate support. Bronze Mirror and Sable might respect and even like Silver Snow, but they had lived all their lives in a camp of which Strong Tongue was mistress and shaman; the other Hsiung-nu knew nothing of Silver Snow, save that the Emperor of Ch'in had dispatched her as a bride to their ancient *shan-yu*. For all they knew, she might be just as weak, as vain, and as ignorant as Strong Tongue clearly hoped that she was. She had yet to prove herself, and right now she must distract Strong Tongue. For, if her memory was as strong as her tongue, Willow was in grave danger.

She spared one foolish, self-indulgent second to wish that she indeed had been able to lay the skin of the white "tiger" that she and Prince Vughturoi had slain before *shan-yu* Khujanga's feet, in token of her prowess. Then Silver Snow met Strong Tongue's eyes.

"I had no desire to scorn the customs of the Hsiung-nu," she declared firmly. "After all, they are my people too; their weal is my well-being; their fate, my fate. I pray you, if I have offended powers in this land, tell me how best to make it right."

To Silver Snow's surprise, Strong Tongue did not glare. Instead, she held Silver Snow's eyes the way—as Li Ling had once told her—that the hooded snake of Hind, when it rises to hunt, holds the eyes of a bird, forcing the wretched creature to wait until the snake can strike it. The woman's tiny, deep-set eyes seemed to expand, a point of greenish flame kindling in their depths. She drew a deep breath, gusty like the purr of a tiger . . . a white tiger. Again the thud-thud of a heartbeat resounded. Surely that pounding filled the tent, Silver Snow thought. It nearly deafened her, but none of the Hsiung-nu seemed to notice it.

The night that the white tiger stalked the camp, Sable and Bronze Mirror had not noticed that same sound. It was almost as if the Hsiung-nu were immune to it.

Had *she* sent the white tiger to slay the unknown but hated Ch'in princess who would displace her or to terrify her into witlessness or a dishonorable, treaty-breaking flight back to her home? That now seemed likely. Perhaps Willow could find out more.

Willow. From whatever obscurity Willow had limped off

to, now she hissed, recalling Silver Snow's attention, reassuring her that she had an ally. Light flashed over Silver Snow, and she drew herself upright. Even thus, she lacked several inches of Strong Tongue's height; and she was barely half the elder woman's weight.

The ancient *shan-yu* seemed to shake himself, as if rousing from a long dream. "Spoken with courage and propriety!" he announced, smiling upon . . . *his new toy*, thought Silver Snow. *I am like the jade vase or the silk robe, not to be kept locked away, but to be displayed and admired as a sign of his wealth and power.* For this one moment, however, she was glad of it.

"Strong Tongue is mother of Tadiqan, my eldest son," the *shan-yu* continued.

"And heir," whispered Strong Tongue, though her lord paid that comment no heed.

"She knows the language of birds and has the learning to understand the sound of stones, the creaking of doors and hinges, and the talk of the dead in their graves. There is no better teacher among the women of the Hsiung-nu. Strong Tongue, I charge you, when you have purified the hearth, instruct your elder sister in the ways of the Hsiung-nu, that she may make us gain even more face than we have by her mere presence."

Elder sister! Silver Snow suppressed a groan of dismay. Any hope that she might ever have had to conciliate such a woman had just vanished the way that smoke drifts up through gaps in the tent into the trackless air.

"I would be humbly grateful for such instruction," Silver Snow compelled herself to say, and won another smile from her new lord. Standing at his shoulder, Prince Vughturoi barely nodded, but Silver Snow felt herself approved, even protected for the moment. It was a protection granted her for her courage, she knew.

Then she glanced at Strong Tongue, who had circled the hearth with powders and discolored, cracked scapular bones. She grimaced, as if unconvinced—as well she might be. As she busied herself, she moved not just with the gravity of a shaman about a vital rite but with the same self-righteous importance that Silver Snow had noted in the eunuchs of the Inner Courts: each movement made with ostentatious precision as if to ridicule the possibility that her enemy might ever learn them. Catching Silver Snow's eye, she snorted with highly elaborate disdain, and bent to adjust the placement of a bone. Her massive breasts and haunches seemed to bob with the weight of her own righteousness and her consciousness of her worth.

Silver Snow had seen men and women like her in the Palace, those who delighted in others' mistakes, who pointed them out loudly in the presence of superiors, and who never forgot them, nor let anyone else do so. She herself found the vindictiveness of such behavior gravely improper. After all, Confucius had taught that one should do nothing that one would not wish to have done to oneself—and Silver Snow, who lamented each of her mistakes as if it cost lives, would sorrow when they were cast up to her.

Nevertheless it was she who was the stranger here, she who must prove herself. These lands, as she had known from childhood, were harsh. Perhaps constant reproofs and reminders of past errors made the difference between survival and death. Well, even though Strong Tongue definitely had no interest in insuring Silver Snow's survival, she would make certain that such harm would be as difficult to accomplish as possible. *I will not fail*, Silver Snow told herself. *I will use her hostility to harden myself, to become more and more fit to live in this place.*

Still, she knew that Strong Tongue would not be content until Silver Snow failed, failed and died.

Thus, I must be ever watchful, she told herself. From the way that the *shan-yu* Khujanga beamed at both of his senior wives, she knew that he thought that his mere command would guarantee their friendship. That assurance taught her much, both about his former strength and about how badly his mind was fading. A leader sure enough of his power to issue such commands would surely have noted the hostility between his former chief wife and the newcomer who had supplanted her. After all, what was the Ch'in character for "trouble"? Two women under one roof . . . or, in this case, in one tent.

Then a new fear struck her. Was Khujanga fading because of simple old age, or something more? She would have to take great care of him herself lest she speedily become a widow.

Silver Snow studied the woman she knew as unfriend, but who had been set her as sister wife and teacher. A long tiger's claw hung among the amulets at her muscular neck, and the knife that she wore seemed to be well honed. Of all of the Hsiung-nu in the *shan-yu*'s tent, only she and her son wore dress that was totally bare of any Ch'in bravery of silk, embroidery, or jade. Considering that Tadiqan seemed to be the leader of those opposed to peace with the Middle Kingdom, that was but logical.

As she held Strong Tongue's gaze, she became aware that Tadiqan also stared back. Where his mother's gaze was hostile, vindictive, however, Tadiqan's was openly lustful. Silver Snow felt as if, right now, she would trade half of her dowry for a hot bath.

"You wish to learn?" demanded Strong Tongue. "Then your lessons may begin now. Kneel down and place your hand upon my spirit drum."

How trivial a thing that demand seemed to be. Kneel, touch the drum, assist this woman to purify the hearth. Strong Tongue's eyes had darkened again so that they seemed all pupil, and, at their centers, that greenish point of flame was forming, intensifying, would soon dart out and . . .

Elder sister, no! A cry seemed to explode in Silver Snow's ears, and she rocked back on her heels. For a moment her mind and Willow's mind were twinned. Her hearing and her sense of smell were as sharp as those of a fox that had retreated to her earth to protect her kits. Though the scents of dung fire, sweat, and food threatened to overwhelm them, Silver Snow perceived what her maid did, as Willow projected to her mistress the smells of fear, of rage, and—from Strong Tongue—a great satisfaction. She heard the rustlings and whispers of the

Hsiung-nu, the half-stifled protest as she watched as her hand went out, poised, to touch Strong Tongue's drum . . .

Skin reaching to touch drumhead . . . Scrape off the smoke and fat, and the drumhead's leather—it looked like her skin. Silver Snow recoiled.

"Afraid?" jeered the woman.

Silver Snow shook her head and knew that that was a lie. "How would I presume to touch the tools of a shaman?" she asked. "That is a thing of power."

Tadiqan laughed. "How powerful, you do not know," he said. "That drum was the result of a great hunt . . ."

And the beast that they hunted, Silver Snow thought, almost paralyzed, *ran on two legs, gasping, sobbing in Hsiung-nu and in the tongue of the Middle Kingdom, beseeching the Fire, the Sky, or the Ancestors to preserve him, or, at least, to grant him a clean, sudden death.*

There would have been no whistling arrows to bring down such a one mercifully, sacrificed to provide a covering for Strong Tongue's spirit drum. *Do I look upon the remains of some kin of mine?* thought Silver Snow. After the disgrace of his defeat and captivity, her father had sheltered among the Hsiung-nu, had wed, had sired a child whom he had perforce to abandon when he fled back to the Middle Kingdom.

Strong Tongue reached out, as if to force Silver Snow's fingers down to the drum, but the younger woman was quicker.

"Do what you must to purify the hearth," she commanded, all desire to mend her quarrel with Strong Tongue gone. "I shall not sully it again."

"We shall see," muttered Strong Tongue.

She beat upon the drum, kindled her fire, and hurled her incense, none producing the scents that were spicy, clean, or sweet, those that Silver Snow recalled from home. These odors were wilder, muskier. The drum beat faster, and Tadiqan took a step forward, laying his hands upon his mother's shoulders as if to give her strength. He smiled at Silver Snow, and the healing gashes on his face made his expression a demon's mask. He did not want her just for pleasure, then, but for power; as if, in wishing to violate her, he somehow sought to ravish all of the land from which she came.

Silver Snow could hear the drumbeats resonate in the air and underfoot as Strong Tongue chanted, as she leaned closer over the ashes in the hearth, and labored to kindle flame.

His fact taut with disgust and apprehension, Vughturoi bent toward his father and eased him down onto a pile of soft furs. The old man did not seem to share the disquiet that filled the great central tent; instead, he smiled with what looked like benign pleasure at the sight of his wives, the new chief consort and the old, seated beside his hearth, tending his fire.

Abruptly fire rose where no fire had been before, and a beam of white light blinked out and was instantly gone. The beat of that vile little drum ceased, and Silver Snow found herself able to breathe normally.

A muffled cry rose, and Silver Snow whirled to see Willow sink onto her knees in a shadowed corner. Her eyes were deeply shadowed, and she seemed to be about to swoon, but she thrust her mirror into the bosom of her robe before wrapping arms about herself as if she were so cold that never again might she be warmed. Faintly, as if from a great distance, Silver Snow "heard" her maid's voice in her head. *How should I let my mistress, my pretty little elder sister, be welcomed to a hearthfire kindled by . . . by that!*

Willow crumpled to one side, and Sable and Bronze Mirror leapt to her aid.

"What is it, child?" asked the *shan-yu*.

"We . . . my maid and I . . . are not used to so many people after such a long journey, Heavenly Majesty," she ventured.

"Say 'husband,'" urged Khujanga, as one might encourage a child to swallow food.

Silver Snow cast down her eyes with an artistic imitation of shyness, learned from observing some of the more successful concubines, and repeated the word, winning a smile. *By my Ancestors, he is weak, feeble. How does he hold these men's loyalties?*

This was the man who had defeated her father and Li Ling? *This* was the man who had made a goblet out of the skull of Modun, enemy to the Empire as well as to his own hordes? This wizened, smiling man, with his wives and his many sons, two of whom glared at one another at this very moment? There must be more to him than Silver Snow perceived. There *must* be, or she faced a fate that she did not even wish to think about.

"We need air, perhaps," Silver Snow said, playing for time.

"I had not thought that you would wish or have the strength to move about so soon after your arrival," said the *shan-yu* indulgently, "but, then, I expected no one so fair either. Should you wish to see . . . it is mean, humble, nothing at all, but the Hsiung-nu have wintered here since before my grandfather was a lad."

Smiling, he gestured, and a woman opened the flap of the great tent. The gust of cold wind that plucked at tent, furs, rugs, and the newly kindled fire was doubly sweet after the tension of quarrel and ritual that—every bit as much as the ever-present smells of fuel, sweat, leather, and seethed meat— had fouled the air.

"Yurts have been prepared that are your own, lady. And now, I shall show you your home," the *shan-yu* said.

"Heavenly Majesty, should you—" began Tadiqan.

"My eldest son," said Khujanga. "Let me remind you for the last time. I fought Modun. Side by side with my kinsman the Emperor, I fought Modun and his Yueh-chih. I have ridden our plains since my mother foaled me. When I cannot withstand the kiss of the wind, it will be time to dig my grave-pit. But until then, I rule here, and I decide what I shall do.

"Attend me!" he commanded, but to Vughturoi, not to Tadiqan. Silver Snow drew her robes about her and left the dusky yurt before she could see Strong Tongue's face.

In the days that followed, Silver Snow learned more of the temper of the people over whom Fate, the lords of the land,

and her own faithfulness had set her. None walked when he could ride, and the women were just as fierce as the men, just as skilled with the deadly, matchless bows of the grassland riders.

In the lavish yurts that the *shan-yu* had ordained as her own, Silver Snow set up her own tiny court. In the days and weeks that followed, she learned much. She had expected stark simplicity, such as she had known in her own home; she had been prepared for actual hardship. What she found, instead, was a curious combination of rigor and luxury. She might dwell in a tent of felt and leather, but it was warmer, by far, than the Cold Palace of her disgrace in Ch'ang-an. She had furs and rugs and silken hangings that a Brilliant Companion might envy, the deference due to the *shan-yu*'s chief consort and a woman who had been adopted by the Son of Heaven. True, the tea that Bronze Mirror and Sable brewed from blocks that seemed to be as hard as jade and as old as the nearly forgotten Shang was strong, bitter, and black, but it put heat into her in cold mornings as she rose from her quilts of sable and marten.

By far the best thing about her new life was that she was no longer confined within a court and expected to regard that as desirable. She had the horse that she had ridden to the winter quarters of the horde and an endless supply of mares and geldings for remounts, should she require them; and the horizon itself was the extent of her boundaries.

The *shan-yu*, she realized very quickly, had wanted only a princess to seal his treaty with Emperor Yuan Ti and to gain face among the tribes. When he realized that the bride that fate had brought him was no mean rider or archer, however, he showed the delight of a man who received his first great-grandson in his arms. Indeed, Silver Snow thought, he treated her like a favorite grandchild, not a wife, in all but precedence among the women of the Hsiung-nu.

She was his nightingale, skilled in singing and talk of the court. That she was no fragile creature, but one able to savor the life of the Hsiung-nu increased her value in his sight. On those evenings during which she did not sing to Khujanga in the privacy of her yurt—Willow nearby to replenish supplies of hot wine, or the mare's milk that the *shan-yu*, despite his admiration for all things Ch'in, evidently preferred—she listened to his tales of the grasslands and the steppes, the long rides far to the west, where, he told her, rose the Roof of the World; the wild raids for sheep and horses and, occasionally, wives; the battles with the other tribes.

On such occasions, the age that filmed his eyes and occasionally restricted his awareness of what went on in his camp to what lay immediately at his feet fell from him, and he was young again, strong again:

"And, lady, when Edika, my father, died, my mother contrived that I, of all the princes that he sired, should approach the body first. Thus, by right, I became *shan-yu*, but those sons of Erlik fought me for it tooth and nail. Yet, I prevailed, through the will of the Heavenly Majesty; that, and my bow and the strength of my men's arms. And still, I rule, and shall do so for many years more."

Then he would laugh. From laughter, he would pass to coughing, and from coughing to thirst. Silver Snow would be quick to pass him the skin of mare's milk or to coax him prettily to drink the brews into which Willow had carefully sprinkled doses of healing herbs: herbs to strengthen the heart and keep clear the lungs. As he sipped, once again, Silver Snow would sing.

Once, he brought a son to hear her or to amuse her with tales of a hunt or battle. Prince Vughturoi came, but, after that one time, never again. Later on, Silver Snow found herself searching for the shadow that had stalked, keeping guard, outside her tent during her journey hither. That discovery angered her, and she turned her attention back to pleasing her lord and preparing the letter that she hoped, somehow, to send to her father.

"Ah, he had a son here, did Chao Kuang. Did you know that, lady?" asked the Hsiung-nu chief one night.

Silver Snow glanced down into the tiny, delicate cup that

she held. Her cheeks suddenly flamed, and her hands grew cold. "Thus I had heard, Most Heav—"

"Ah, what did I command you to call me, child?" Khujanga raised a gnarled, scarred fingertip and shook it indulgently at her.

Each day he gains strength, and his mind clears. Each day is a victory, she thought, but knew that time was her enemy. Nevertheless, as a general does with troops who know themselves to be outnumbered, she summoned confidence. Willow knew much of herbs and had learned much more of medicine and alchemy in Ch'ang-an; she might well preserve the *shan-yu* for years.

"Husband!" Silver Snow corrected herself with the demure smile that she knew Khujanga liked. "Thus, as I said, I had heard, and would willingly pay my duty to an elder brother."

"He was weak, sickly, my wife said, and he knew it. When his mother died, he knew that he speedily would be a burden to someone else. Thus, one day, he rode out, away from the host. Whether his horse fell upon him, or he simply rode away from the clan, we never knew. But it was in a season of great sickness. I myself think that he chose thus to die that other and fitter youths might eat their fill, and I honor him."

And thus Strong Tongue lets you believe, thought Silver Snow sorrowfully. *You honor him, yet you see him—or what I fear may have been him—on that vile little drum of hers. Should I ever truly be the queen that they hail me as, I shall have that thing buried . . . and perhaps her alongside it.*

That evening, she saw the shadow flicker upon the outer wall of her yurt; and if her laugh rang the more musically, and her song the sweeter, she did not know it. Nor did Willow make her any the wiser. As the days of winter wore by, Silver Snow grew more and more amazed at the changes in her maid. Because of Willow's lameness, Silver Snow had always thought of her as a more sickly creature than herself. Now, however, in the manner of a canny beast who has evaded one trap—albeit at some cost to herself—Willow thrived. Her hair grew thicker, longer, and more lustrous, and her skin became less sallow.

Where does she go? thought Silver Snow. For the endless herds of horses and sheep made no outcry; no child announced her presence; and no hunter swore to have a new fox cap by spring. Yet, at dawn, Willow was always asleep upon her pallet at the foot of Silver Snow's own bed-place, her fingers twitching, her eyes moving beneath flat lids, as if, deep in dreams, she hunted, wild and free. Thus far, Willow had not confided in her, and Silver Snow forebore to press her.

Silver Snow had completed yet another letter. Perhaps when a thaw came, some bold riders might deign to journey east, there to give her message, most carefully painted upon the finest silk, to the nearest outpost of Ch'in's army for transport back into the Middle Kingdom. She felt certain that this letter would encourage Li Ling and her father; in it, she spoke of the *shan-yu*'s renewed offer to defend the Middle Kingdom's borders.

And perhaps, one day, such riders might even dash up to her yurt, bearing a message in reply.

With a high heart, she went to the great tent of Khujanga, saluted him, and took the pile of cushions close to him that her rank—and his fondness for his latest treasure—demanded that she enjoy.

To her surprise, however, Prince Vughturoi was missing from the assembly. She was wondering how she might find out why he was not present when Khujanga spoke.

"My younger son has ridden forth with those of his men that have a mind to look in and, perhaps, study the flocks of the Yueh-chih." That sly observation from the *shan-yu* drew a laugh from his assembled tribesmen.

A journey across the plains in the full of winter? That was not bravery, thought Silver Snow, but folly—and Vughturoi was anything but a fool. Then she saw the complacent smile of Strong Tongue and realized that it was not folly, either, but policy. The shaman's policy. Put into the old man's thoughts the notion that the once-rebellious Yueh-chih must be observed, and Vughturoi, who was an obedient son, would fare out to do so. Then, once he was far from the camp . . . well, many sicknesses stalked the plains in the winter, and the *shan-yu* was old. Let him die, when Vughturoi was gone; and who was there among the Hsiung-nu with a strong enough following to oppose her plans, which called for her own son Tadiqan to seize power, the old *shan-yu*'s possessions . . . and his wives.

Silver Snow shivered at that line of reasoning, and drew her robes more closely around her despite the warmth of the great yurt. Her thoughts made her feel as if a thick outer coat had been ripped from arms and shoulders, leaving her to shiver unprotected in the winds that swept from the Roof of the World east to the Wall itself. *Surely*, she told herself, *Khujanga is in good health; he might yet last for years, or at least for long enough* . . .

"Today is a day of feasting," the *shan-yu* told Silver Snow. "My son Vughturoi's notions"—he shook his head in fond amusement at that younger son—"are well known; he holds with me on the Middle Kingdom. Always, however, Tadiqan has pulled against the traces. Today, though; today, he agrees that we should work with Ch'in against our enemies. Perhaps, if we did that, the men of the Han would no longer need to dwell in those drafty fortresses and could rove free in their homes, just as we do now."

Silver Snow almost gasped in horror. Who had put *that* idea into Khujanga's head? It was diabolically clever: precisely what Li Ling feared that the Emperor might agree to. Let the forts be emptied; let Tadiqan have the run of the garrisons and the manning of them; and Hsiung-nu "protection" could rapidly become invasion. *Ch'ang-an must know of this!* she thought.

"Drink, my father!" cried Tadiqan. The men who followed him cheered as the eldest prince strode toward his father with the graceless stride of one who spent more time in the saddle than on foot. In his hands shone a cup wrought of silver and of some yellowed substance . . . ivory, perhaps? From the yell of triumph and bloodlust that went up at the sight of that cup, however, Silver Snow knew what it was: the very goblet that had been fashioned from the skull of Modun of the Yueh-chih, last of the enemies of both Khujanga and Yuan Ti. A curdled, pinkish liquid sloshed in its bowl—mare's milk and blood.

The *shan-yu* heaved himself up to his feet, snatched up the cup, and drained it. "Ahhhh!" he cried, and tossed it back to his son. A few drops scattered over the priceless furs and carpets.

"Thus to all enemies of the Hsiung-nu!" he shouted, to cheers that seemed to ripple the fabric of the yurts as much as the winter gales.

"To all enemies of the Hsiung-nu!" repeated his eldest son. "I myself shall hew off their heads and make their skulls into cups!"

Screaming rose to a feverish pitch, intensified by the *beat-beat-beat* of what Silver Snow identified with loathing as Strong Tongue's spirit drum.

"That is," Tadiqan said, turning his face toward Silver Snow so that she might read his lips, "all but one of them."

If I do not flee, I will be sick, she thought, then admonished herself fiercely. *You will stay, and you will not be sick, and tonight, you will not rest before you write an account of this to your father, Li Ling, and the Son of Heaven.*

The letter that she had previously drafted and painstakingly written must be discarded.

But how should she get it to them? That was a question for which she had no answer. Nor had she one when, finally, her eyes burning, she sought her bed-furs, nor that dawn, nor the days after, days that steadily lengthened as the time drew toward a frigid spring.

Finally Silver Snow saw only one way to solve her problems. The *shan-yu* indulged her; let him give her a messenger to carry her letter to her father, his old captive/guest.

"Or," Willow hinted at her shoulder, with her usual skill at fathoming Silver Snow's thoughts, "Sable's brother might ride out for you. Since his wife died, he has been most devoted to his sister, who now cares for his children."

Silver Snow nodded. Sable's brother Basich—young, dashing (for one of the Hsiung-nu), and rash almost to madness—might indeed carry a letter for her. Moreover, he was as loyal to Vughturoi (or so she thought) as his sister was to Silver Snow. Yet, it might be best after all if she asked the *shanyu*, who prided himself on being an indulgent husband to her. Throwing on her most colorful garments, since the old man's weary eyes brightened at the sight of finery, she beckoned to Willow, picked up her carefully sealed silk packet, and hastened toward the great tent.

"Hold!" came a shout, accompanied by raucous, ribald hoots and hoof beats.

That was Tadiqan's voice.

So, is he dead, that old man who was kind to me? Silver Snow thought, while panic shrilled in heart and nerves. *And does Tadiqan give himself the powers of the* shan-yu *so soon, so soon after his father's body cools? I have avenged my father and honored my oaths; before I let him despoil me, I shall hang myself with my sash.*

Willow tugged at her sleeve, as if eager to get her into some safekeeping before the hunters came. "You go, Willow," hissed Silver Snow. The less that any kin of Strong Tongue saw of Willow, the better. "*You* go."

Willow, however, stood her ground, and Silver Snow bit her lip in dismay. Inspiration seized her, though, and she thrust the letter into Willow's cold, strong hands.

"You *must* go. Take this letter to Sable and tell her that Basich must carry it, and ride unseen!"

At her best pace, half run, half limp, Willow retreated toward Sable's tent, and Silver Snow had perforce to stiffen her knees lest relief make her unable to stand proudly as Strong Tongue's son rode at her in arrogant, terrifying parade.

The horses pounded forward. Still Silver Snow held her ground. Then, with a shriek that Silver Snow thought must surely shatter ice, Tadiqan fired a whistling arrow; his men's arrows buzzed and whined in her ears as the troop of them thundered past her on either side.

Silver Snow stood, while people emerged cautiously from their yurts to discover who, this time, Tadiqan and his men had slain. Only shock, which had frozen her, kept her upright; the instant that the joints of her knees melted, she feared that she would fall.

Tadiqan rode toward her, and Silver Snow forced herself to open her eyes. His eyes, as they raked over her, felt as intrusive as hands fondling her against her will.

"For the first time," he told her, his voice a feral purr, "my mother has been wrong. You have courage, at the very least. I like that, lady. Remember what I have said. I like that very much."

CHAPTER

= 16 =

The rest of the winter was a time of waiting: waiting for spring; waiting for Sable's brother Basich to ride with a few chosen friends back into camp and for Sable to report that her letter had been delivered to the garrison; waiting for Prince Vughturoi to return; or for Strong Tongue to show her hand. To Silver Snow's amazement, even her time of immurement in the Palace now proved to be useful: she knew well how to wait, even unto despair.

The frozen grasses had begun to thaw by the time Prince Vughturoi returned, riding back from the camps of the Yueh-chih. He entered the great tent, prostrated himself as was fitting before his father, then rose eagerly at the invitation to sit beside him and feast.

Silver Snow had bent over her handiwork, aware that his eyes had gone straight to her, had approved the fact that she sat calmly among them, accepting and—to all appearances—accepted. The warmth she felt had nothing to do with the heat of the tent, a thing of close-packed bodies and warmth bound together by layers upon layers of felt. If anyone among the Hsiung-nu was a link between her past and her present, it was Prince Vughturoi, who saw her resplendent in Ch'ang-an, refused to accept another princess in her stead, and, even now, did not disdain her. Together, they had driven off the white tiger.

The presence of one warrior—or of one warlord and the warriors whom he led—should not have made her feel so much safer as this Hsiung-nu prince's sudden appearance did. Yet she might now have a shield lifted between her and her enemies, or a warm cloak laid over her shoulders during the howling climax of a winter storm.

After that first, relieved glance, however, she kept her gaze relentlessly down, allowing the *shan-yu* some privacy to speak with his son, though how private such speech could be before a tentful of keen-eared Hsiung-nu was highly questionable.

"How fare Modun's former children, my son?" Khujanga asked.

"They follow us," he told the *shan-yu*, "as the lamb follows the ewe. Do you but command, and they shall obey."

"That is well," said the old man, his eyes brighter than they had been for many a day. Some of that had to be due to Vughturoi's triumphant return, without the loss of a single man. However, much was also due to the care that Silver Snow and Willow took of him. The fevers that swept over the camp at the thaw, frequently taking with them the spirits of those who were eldest, youngest, or most sickly, had swept around him. He scarcely coughed, even at dawn, his slaves told Willow, and each day he rode out with great zest.

All around a cheer went up, a cheer rapidly silenced as the robust secondary wives of the *shan-yu*, wielding heavy copper meathooks, drew mutton from the great cauldrons, then passed around the skins of mare's milk. The Hsiung-nu ate rapidly and hugely, as if they never knew from whence their next meal might come or whether someone might attack them while they feasted. Gradually, however, as the edge wore off their hunger, and the mare's milk was passed again and again, men lay back, belching and groaning in satisfaction. Now that the all-important business of eating was done, gradually they began again to speak.

"So, *brother*," said Tadiqan, "the Yueh-chih follow like

lambs. Does this seem right for kin of ours, to obey thus, following like sheep when Ch'in commands?"

Vughturoi leaned back, but his eyes were wary. "I had not heard, Elder Brother, that the Yueh-chih obeyed the Middle Kingdom or anyone but the beloved of Heaven, our father the *shan-yu* who defeated them in honest battle. So long as they obey *us*, that seems well to me. I have heard, however, that there are others, who do not obey the royal clan of the *shan-yu*, whose will is—is it not, my father?—that there shall be peace with Ch'in. The Fu Yu and the Jo-Chiang, it is said, speak of raids against the Middle Kingdom, despite our father's ban. Most Heavenly . . ."

At Khujanga's gesture of impatience with his elaborate title, Vughturoi grinned. Silver Snow was surprised at how much younger and less formidable he looked. ". . . my father, come spring, permit me to ride with my warriors and teach them proper obedience!"

His enthusiasm was contagious. All around the tent, warriors grinned and shouted, pledging support.

Silver Snow suppressed a frown. Impressed with the Middle Kingdom Vughturoi might be, but in some things, he was all Hsiung-nu. She could but hope that he would fight only when attempts to subdue the Fu Yu by argument or show of strength had failed. Not so the others, however.

"Nay, brother," cried Tadiqan. "You have had your mission to the other clans. Let *me* and mine go against the Fu Yu, at least, now! I swear that we shall return before the time comes to break camp and move to the summer pastures."

A flicker of the light drew Silver Snow's attention to Strong Tongue. Though the woman set her face almost instantly in a grin of triumph, Silver Snow would have taken oath that, for at least a moment, the shaman had been shocked and displeased by her son's impulsive demand. He had been caught up in the excitement for a good fight, more than in any struggle for power over the royal clan.

A faint pounding rang through the tent, then died away, as if Strong Tongue tapped restively upon that damnable spirit drum of hers, then laid it aside and was quiet. She bent over her son's shoulder then and muttered urgently, raising a hand when he hissed back. Finally, however, she smiled, showing strong white teeth, and sank back in her place, nodding. The look of satisfaction returned, and she sat serenely, like a beast that has fed well and now will sleep until it wakes to feast again.

Not so the rest of the Hsiung-nu, however. Khujanga's delighted acquiescence set off cheers and demands for more and more drink until, finally, the noise and heat became intolerable and Silver Snow sought leave to withdraw. She was aware of Strong Tongue's now-scornful gaze as she left. Probably the elder woman thought her too weak to endure a Hsiung-nu celebration; that is, if she did not resent the fastidiousness that made her draw her skirts aside from the warriors who sprawled, unconscious from drink, on the rich, grease-stained rugs.

Stout and gleaming with oil and with every bit of copper and gold that she owned, Strong Tongue would probably try to usurp Silver Snow's seat by the *shan-yu*, too. But, were Silver Snow's suspicions true, if Tadiqan were gone from the camp, she would try no other evil. That fact that she was required to restrain herself from some of her intrigues might well have accounted for her displeasure.

That was not, Silver Snow learned later, to be quite the case. True it was, the next day, all went round the camp quietly, for Hsiung-nu, as if Strong Tongue's spirit drum banged in their heads. Venturing out for a ride, Silver Snow noted how many men—restive after a winter's inaction, or chafing, perhaps, that Vughturoi had not selected them to ride with him to spy out the Yueh-chih's flocks—now followed Tadiqan. Even some of the younger prince's own retainers trailed after them. Clearly they longed to be chosen to visit the Fu Yu or Jo-Chiang and awe them into submission.

Action. Tadiqan knew one thing, at least, besides whistling arrows and the forces of arms and fear. He knew that his people required constant movement, a constant promise of battle. Unlike the race of the Han, the Hsiung-nu were too young a tribe to relish the fruits of peace.

Silver Snow had a map, however crude, of the grasslands, provided her by Li Ling. She must, she thought, find out where precisely those tribes ranged and somehow get the news back to Ch'ang-an.

Strong Tongue sauntered from her own tenthold to stand, arms akimbo, before the great tent of the *shan-yu*.

"She acts as if she, not the old man, rules this camp," Willow muttered. "Make her understand otherwise, Elder Sister."

So much, Silver Snow thought wryly, for her earlier musings on the love of the people of the Han for peace. She, however, was a warrior's daughter on a mission for the Son of Heaven; she dared bow to no barbarian, even if that refusal meant war. Besides, the armies of the Middle Kingdom were many and strong; the Middle Kingdom knew that peace might be bought at a greater price than silks or jade.

Thus it was, when Strong Tongue caught Silver Snow's eye for the customary battle of looks between them, Silver Snow held her gaze. More than that, she greeted the older woman with the salutation that senior wife used to junior, and waited until Strong Tongue responded accordingly and withdrew. To her horror, as she stared at the woman's broad, retreating back, Silver Snow found herself shaking even from so paltry a test of strength.

All that day and the next, Silver Snow wondered what form Strong Tongue's vengeance might take. She checked her horse's legs; she sniffed her food; she waited, in the *shan-yu*'s feasting tent, for an attack in words. No such attack came. Strong Tongue, without her son, seemed to be only half the fighter that she was when he was present.

Yet, because it was Tadiqan whom the *shan-yu* had entrusted with the leaderhip of this new mission, Tadiqan who might lead what could prove to be a new war, the talk was all

of Tadiqan and his prowess. Prince Vughturoi seemed to be
forgotten. Much to Silver Snow's surprise, he appeared to be
content that this was so. She became aware that, each evening, Vughturoi was seated farther and farther from his father.
Whenever he attempted to speak with him, some distraction
intervened, some clamor of Strong Tongue's, some disagee-
ment between Vughturoi's warriors; while the proud, touchy
elders who clustered still around the *shan-yu* regarded Silver
Snow as an old man's toy, and paid homage to Strong Tongue
as shaman.

These older men began to speak of war in the spring, plan
for it, hope for it. Silver Snow listened with rising apprehension as the old men worked themselves into a frenzy of anticipation. Beyond a certain point, she feared, there was no
recalling them to such sanity as the more warlike Hsiung-nu
ever possessed. Besides, she seemed to recall edicts, treaties
with Ch'in, that forbade such wars in the grasslands.

If only Sable's brother Basich would return! If only Silver
Snow knew for certain that her message had been delivered!
She clenched her fists within the concealment of her silken
sleeves. Just let the letter arrive; to hope for a letter in return
was to ask for far too much.

Vughturoi's keen eyes studied the other Hsiung-nu too.
He must remember those treaties, Silver Snow thought. He
must. Why, then, did he choose to enflame his fellow tribesmen? To test to see who his partisans were? To gauge his father's support? Or—Silver Snow snatched at this thought—
did he seek to oust Tadiqan from the camp just as he had been
ousted earlier that year? He watched his elder brother like a
fox, poised to hunt its prey.

"I spoke but of an embassy," Vughturoi said, at length. "Is
it not true, Heavenly Majesty," he finally asked, raising his
voice to be heard from his seat that was now so far from his
father, "that your treaty with your cousin in Ch'ang-an forbids
such a combat?"

First the stalk; then the pounce. Vughturoi had *not* forgotten the treaties. Then his suggestion of riding forth to the Fu

Yu was a suggestion not of war but of embassy; that Tadiqan snatched it up might do him no favor in his father's eyes.

Silver Snow glanced about the tent, and her heart sank. Clever Vughturoi might be, but he was not adept in statescraft. His suggestion had escaped him, much as fire, spilled from a firepot in a dry summer, flames up over the grassland and threatens to devour all that is in its path. Much as his father might favor him, he could not go against the will of his people if it were strongly expressed.

"What do we care about the swirls of a foolish brush on wood or silk?" came the shouted reply from an elder warrior near the front of the tent. "Such are easily burnt or forgotten! We care about herds and swords, bows, and speedy obedience to our commands!"

"I have seen the armies of Ch'in," Vughturoi flung back. "And I say that I would not willingly go up against them."

"We have seen their soldiers," snapped Strong Tongue, taking a shaman's freedom to intrude in the affairs of war. "When the arrows pierce them, they bleed like other men, though, perhaps, more weakly. Alive, and in our camps, they do the work of slaves."

She stroked her spirit drum, as if reminding the assembly that one, at least, of the half Ch'in had done other service to the Hsiung-nu, long after his untimely death. Silver Snow controlled a shudder, then pursed her lips in revulsion. She must pretend to ignore Strong Tongue's spite.

"True that may be," said Vughturoi. "But surely it is also true that those who cannot lay aside their weapons shall in the end be consumed by them."

Why, Vughturoi had lifted those words from Confucius' Spring and Autumn Analects, Silver Snow realized. Perhaps he had even heard them from her or from Li Ling. She had not known just how impressed the prince had been with Ch'in during his stay. No, he was no savage child of a savage race, but a thinking man to whom, he hoped, his father would listen.

"What coward made that noise?" came a raucous yell, accompanied by some comment about lazy camels and dung, bawled out too fast and too slurred by drink for Silver Snow fully to understand, even had she wished to.

The shout of coward shattered the control that Vughturoi had maintained, the careful veneer of Han civilization.

"Coward?" screamed Vughturoi. In that moment, he was all Hsiung-nu. "Coward? Let me show you who is a coward!" He launched himself forward, knife out, his face contorted into a mask of rage.

Although the Hsiung-nu cheered his energy, they separated prince and warrior before blood could stain the cushions and carpets, and Khujanga shouted for order. "Obey your own words!" he snapped at his younger son, and turned his attention away from him for the rest of the evening. Silver Snow cast one glance at Vughturoi as he sat glowering by the fire, too proud to withdraw, then bent her energies to entertaining the *shan-yu* and softening his mood. She was very much afraid that she had but indifferent success.

And in the days that followed, the breach between the *shan-yu* and his younger son appeared to widen.

Remembering her own time out of favor in Ch'ang-an, Silver Snow could recognize the skill and subtlety of Strong Tongue's latest gambit: isolate the young prince, make certain that he was angered and placed in bad situations, then spread and nurture doubts about him. Vughturoi's response came that evening. As Khujanga sat in Silver Snow's tent, listening to a song of the North, Vughturoi appeared. He bowed to his father, head to earth, though, usually, the *shan-yu* insisted that sons and warriors who were high in his favor omit the full prostration. Then he nodded to Silver Snow and, at a gesture from his father, sat down.

Permission that may have been; nevertheless, Vughturoi sat very near to the tent's opening, as if uncertain of his welcome. He accepted rice wine, but spoke not a word. He was simply there, as a minister who favored an unpopular cause might do at the Son of Heaven's court: saying nothing; simply maintaining his presence and that of his cause.

Silver Snow's fingers flickered upon her sewing, and never had her voice risen so sweetly, her wit sparkled like firelight upon rock crystal. Khujanga shook his head in doting admiration at this stranger-wife of his. "I will admit it; some among my own retainers think me a fool, as they whisper all men are fools who take a young wife. They think me a double fool for listening to her songs and stories. You have seen Ch'in, though. What do you think, son?"

He had spoken to his out-of-favor son! Silver Snow's fingers tightened on her handiwork for one moment, and she glanced at Vughturoi, who leaned forward deferentially. His square face was flushed, and light flickered in his eyes.

"The day that the beloved of heaven is a fool, the plains will become mountains," Vughturoi began cautiously. "I have been in Ch'in, as you say. I can say that the lady's stories are true." Khujanga raised a white, skeptical brow.

"But," Vughturoi added, "they are too modest."

He glanced quickly at Silver Snow, then away.

"The people of the Han are a great people," said the prince.

"As are we, my son. And we are a freer people, besides."

Vughturoi bowed, head to rugs.

"As indeed we are, Heavenly Majesty. But the Middle Kingdom has as many folk as the desert has pebbles. It is very old and, in its ages, it has enriched itself. One pestilence or one harsh winter will not wipe out a clan and threaten the weal of all. They have abundance; and in their abundance, they can afford to create wonders, to hold treasures, and to protect them beyond the power of our yurts and horses."

Resolutely Silver Snow kept her eyes fixed upon her work, glad that it kept her from twining her fingers or plaiting her sleeves with them. Both were unsightly gestures that broke the serene facade that she attempted to show the *shan-yu*. She must mean rest, peace, and grace for him, so he would seek her out, and, thus, her influence would grow. As father and son spoke together, the days' estrangement gone from voice and manner, she turned her eyes back to her other work, the finely crafted bag that she was stitching. Though her knowledge violated modesty, she well knew that she was one of the wonders of the Han to which Vughturoi had referred.

One or two more evenings' work, she thought, and this scent bag would be completed. This scent bag. Abruptly she dropped the intricately wrought piece of fur and stitchwork into her lap and stared at it. Always in Ch'ang-an, ladies made scent bags as a way of passing the time, of adorning themselves, and—occasionally—of making gifts to men whom they admired.

Why had she crafted this scent bag of brocades, sables, and heavy silken knotwork? She had more delicate fabrics and feathers aplenty in her chests; she might well have created something more dainty for her own use. She remembered the herbs that Willow had ready to be selected for such uses— how many of those would be strong enough to serve in this place of over-strong odors—horse sweat, boiling mutton, and unwashed and greasy bodies? Yet not all of Willow's herbs were prized for their scent. Others possessed the power to stanch blood, to ward off illness, to avert ill-wishing.

I too might use such powers, she protested to herself, though she knew that she tried to deceive herself.

Her cheeks flamed again, and she tried to turn the talk to spring and the gardens that she recalled. She was aware that she was chattering just as inanely as any of the Peach Blossoms, Jade Butterflies, or Apricots who thronged the Inner Courts. Shortly afterward, the *shan-yu* rose to depart. Silver Snow glanced away, as he struggled to his feet, just as she had done for her own father. Yet, the *shan-yu* accepted the arm of his son and walked out leaning on him. Silver Snow was greatly relieved and heartened, and not solely for the dreams of peace that she cherished between Hsiung-nu and Han.

She followed them out and peered beyond the flaps of her tent. For a few paces more, father leaned upon son, as if glad of the younger man's support and nearness. Then, as two horsemen rode toward them, the *shan-yu* abruptly disengaged his arm from his son's and walked forward to greet them. Silver Snow could see from the stiffness of his back the effort that Khujanga made not to totter. Vughturoi stared after his father, then melted into the shadows.

So, he was no longer in disgrace with his father, yet Khujanga seemed to prefer that the tribe think that he was. Silver Snow knit her brows, then knit them more thoroughly as the memories of scandalized, high-pitched voices warning her not to wrinkle her brow dinned in her head. *Why* would Khujanga not announce his reconciliation with his youngest son?

She could think of only one reason: that in appearing to draw away from Vughturoi, the *shan-yu* was actually protecting him.

Like it or not, a bond existed between Silver Snow and Vughturoi, and had done so ever since Ch'ang-an, when she had fought to clear her father's name and her own, and won his grudging approval. That bond had strengthened on the journey west, with each new travail.

Silver Snow knew well that she understood little of men. There had been no other women of her own rank in her home; along the road and in the Cold Palace, she had been isolated from the subtle manipulations by which one thrived in the Inner Courts, the tyrannies and savage, but tiny, humiliations that one used to cast down other women; the flatteries and games that one used to exalt those men by whose favor one rapidly learned to live.

Silver Snow had never seen men thus. For her, there were men like her father and Li Ling: to be venerated and obeyed as elders and teachers; there were men like the Son of Heaven and the *shan-yu*, leaders who had the power of life, death, or—worst of all—disgrace; and there were officials, eunuchs, warriors, who owed allegiance to the first two classes, and whose opinion of her depended upon their masters'. However, of young men—with a sudden, painful clarity, she thought of the eldest son to which, long ago, an official had offered to betroth her—over whom a woman might sigh or laugh, she had no knowledge.

Never had the women in the Inner Courts or in the houses in which she had stayed during her trip to Ch'ang-an seemed more alien and unsympathetic to her than when they spoke of men and what they delicately called spring musings, everlasting longings, mortal yearnings, or a lot of other names: all flowery, and—to her, brought up as she had been in poverty and duty—all foolish.

Yet she had made a scent bag that fused the art of Ch'in and the wealth of the grasslands, and she knew now that, with every stitch she had taken, she had thought of the prince who had been her first defender among the Hsiung-nu; the prince who had stood outside her tent to listen to her songs and who now spoke in veiled terms of his father's chief wife, calling her a wonder.

She was a wedded lady, though no wife; she was a queen; and she was the embodiment of the Son of Heaven's peace with the Hsiung-nu. Should she abandon that to disgrace herself and giggle like a flighty maid? For that matter, did she dare?

"Here!" she cried to Willow. "Take this thing and pack it away. I am ashamed at how sloppily I have wrought it."

"As you command, Elder Sister," Willow said, a smile hovering on too-red lips.

"Do not *dare* to smile!" Silver Snow commanded.

"Indeed not," Willow agreed. "Forgive this one, if her elder sister thought that she smiled at what she terms poor needlework. Yet, the furs are fine and might perhaps be put to another use. I"—at least, she dropped that aggravating, abject courtesy, which was worse than any smile—"shall pack this in the black chest."

She did so, then knelt to her mistress. "By your leave," she said, "the night"—she sniffed at the air, her eyes bright, her head turning constantly toward the opening of the tent—"will be fresh and sweet tonight, if still cold, and I should like to rove. Who knows what I may hear about . . ."

"Oh, go!" Silver Snow cried. "But see that you meet no handsome male fox as you range free in your desire to scent the spring wind. I should not like to have to explain why a litter of fox kits sleeps by the fire in my tent."

She clapped both hands to the treacherous mouth that had uttered such impropriety. Willow, however, laughed sharply, almost a fox's bark, and vanished behind a heavy hanging. Shortly afterward came a scrabbling at the tent wall, and Silver Snow knew that she was alone.

Much against her will, Silver Snow rushed over to the black chest, flung it open, and pulled out the scent bag. Wrapping herself in her furs, she cradled it in her arms, watching the moon through the vent of her yurt, until her eyes closed.

Scrabbling at the wall of Silver Snow's yurt brought her halfway out of a deep, almost a drugged sleep, but the effort was too great. Silver Snow moaned and sank back down, burrowing deeper into the furs. When she again woke, it was to a smell of something charred. She sniffed, then glanced with sudden anxiety at the brazier. No, the fire was not just banked; it was dead and must be rekindled. That had ever been Willow's task.

Silver Snow tugged her robes about her and grimaced with aggravation as she discovered that she had clung, all night long, to the scent bag that she had wrought. Where *was* Willow? Out all night; and now that the sun was shining she chose to lie sprawling upon her pallet. All of the Hsiung-nu had, doubtless, been up before dawn.

Well, she would just go and wake Elder Sister Willow, and then she would speak . . . In this determined mood, she walked toward her maid. The smell of charring intensified.

When Silver Snow looked down, she saw that a long swathe of Willow's luxuriant, reddish hair was burned away, as if someone had cast a flaming torch at her. Now the girl slept on her side, curled in protectively about herself, her too-short leg drawn up as that of a stork, standing in the water.

"Willow?" Silver Snow whispered. "Willow!" She knelt

and shook the maid, who came awake with one blink of her greenish eyes. They filled with the morning light, then kindled into such humor and energy that Silver Snow rocked back upon her heels.

"What happened, child?" said Silver Snow, all her anger gone. She brushed at Willow's long hair. Reddish hair might be considered a grave blemish in Ch'in, but there was no denying that the lustrous, thick mane that glinted under Silver Snow's searching fingers had a unique beauty, much like a fine pelt. To see it marred was a sadness that Silver Snow had not expected.

To her astonishment, Willow laughed. "Ah, such running about as I had! Air and earth are stirring, Elder Sister, and we danced all night, the brothers in fur and I. A foolish ewe ran, thinking that we sought her lamb. Soon the entire flock was in a panic, and men came on horseback. Thus, we fled, they to the grasslands, I into the camp, where *she*"—a saucy lift of Willow's chin toward Strong Tongue's domain told Silver Snow whom she meant— "sat up and muttered over old cantrips. I nudged at her tent flap with my muzzle, hoping to spy out some matter of use.

"She is quick, Elder Sister, for all that she has the bulk of a prize ram. Before I could vanish into the shadows, she rose, snapped her fingers, and flung—ho, fire of some sort!—at me, and I yelped and ran off."

"You must trim your hair, lest she see it burnt and know," warned Silver Snow.

As Willow bent to the task, Silver Snow turned to make up the fire afresh.

"I should do that, Elder Sister," said the maid. "It is not fitting that you do my work."

"Can I dance with the wind and gather news for myself?" asked Silver Snow. Then, as Willow shook her head, "Well then? What did you learn in the tent of Strong Tongue?"

"That she is well pleased with your . . . the prince's disgrace," said Willow. "Yet not as pleased as she might be; because her own son's warlike ways take him from home.

Indirectly, we have done the old man a favor by keeping Strong Tongue's son from his side. How much would you wager . . ."

Silver Snow shook her head. "Not a single cash," she said.

Vughturoi might well be in disgrace for his unwillingness to fight when his father's treaty forbade; but he was here, and Tadiqan was not. As far as Silver Snow was concerned, that was all to the good. If Tadiqan were to inherit, he must be the first of Khujanga's sons to view his father's body. To do so, he must first return to the clan. Thus, if Strong Tongue had any plans for speeding the old *shan-yu*'s departure to the eternal grasslands, she would not, for the sake of her own power as well as that of her son, put them into action as long as Tadiqan rode among the Fu Yu. Let but Tadiqan return, however, and *Vughturoi* depart . . . in that case, Silver Snow must look to herself and to the husband who was her only protection.

Outside her yurt rose commotion unlike anything she had yet heard in the Hsiung-nu's camp. She finished dressing, and stepped outside. Overhead, the sky had gone from the pallor of winter and the gray of the recent storms to the blue of lapis or turquoise. The wind that swept down across it smelled wild and sweet, somehow newly scoured and fresh. It tugged at Silver Snow's robes as it did at the manes of the horses that men rode up and down the aisles and ranks of the great camp as they cried for more and more haste. Even the moans and grunts of the camels picketed on the camp's edge sounded less glum than usual.

Children scampered, perilously close to the horses' hooves, and women shouted cheerfully. Already one of the yurts on the perimeter vanished into a flurry of heavy cloths and a frame that was rapidly stored in a nearby cart. Bronze Mirror and Sable ran up, laughing and smiling.

"It is time to break camp, lady!" Sable said. "We shall help you and your maid to pack. Will you ride or go in your chariot?"

Silver Snow blinked once again. So, after a winter here, it was finally time to head for the spring and summer pastures.

"Ah," cried Bronze Mirror, "after a winter spent in camp, the very yurts seem like walled cities. To ride free again, following the herds—that is how Hsiung-nu should live!"

Her exultation swept Silver Snow up, and she hastened back inside to dress for riding and to pack her things.

Willow had laid the scent bag out on the folds of her sleeping furs. Without a word, Silver Snow replaced it in the black chest and gently shut the lid.

Shortly afterward, her yurt came down. She bent toward the hearthfire.

"Leave it, lady," came a voice from above her.

She turned and saw Prince Vughturoi, mounted on his favorite horse. Steady and sturdy, it tossed its heavy mane in its eagerness to be off. He whistled shrilly, and one of his warriors led up Silver Snow's own white horse.

"They make the prince the shepherd of the little queen," Silver Snow heard an older man say in an undertone, and winced at the guttural laughter that followed it.

"Well, if he has no stomach for a fight, best he herd the flocks. Or one ewe lamb."

She marked which men spoke, noting that they were of the party of elder warriors who jeered at close ties with Ch'in, but who would never gainsay the *shan-yu*. These too must be considered enemies, or perhaps simply unfriends.

She gestured at the fire, fearful that chance sparks might spread a wall of flame across the grasslands.

"The ground is yet too damp for us to worry that a fire might spread beyond control. We leave the hearthfires burning, lady," Prince Vughturoi told her. With his usual control, he ignored the words that had been spoken loudly enough to reach his ears. "It is a custom of the Hsiung-nu. When we break camp, we leave the hearthfires burning as a sign that, come next winter, we shall return. Because it is spring, and the ground is wet—well, wet for this land—we need not fear that the fires will spread, as they would if we dared this in high summer. When we ride out, we shall turn around at the highest point during the day's travel. If the fires are still burning, it means good fortune."

Silver Snow mounted, then turned to survey what had been a thriving, crowded camp and what now was merely a collection of rutted ground, scattered fire, and baggage, rapidly stowed on restive animals. The *shan-yu* emerged from his tent, last of all of them to be taken down, climbed laboriously ahorse, and smiled to see the youngest of his wives awaiting the order to ride forth. Wagon after wagon rumbled by, Strong Tongue very much in the vanguard, driving a wagon that Silver Snow would have thought required the services of at least five drovers. She glared to see Silver Snow mounted and unafraid; in turn, Silver Snow smiled.

After a season of confinement, it would be good to travel again, she thought, and knew not whether that was Hsiung-nu thinking or the desire of her own heart. The wind whipped around her, bringing tears to her eyes. She bent her body, lessening her resistance to the wind, hearing in its howl a voice luring her onward, promising her wonders, change, excitement, and, above all, the freedom of the Hsiung-nu.

As if the longing to escape from the confinement of the winter camp had abruptly built up past their power to control, the Hsiung-nu warriors shrieked as the *shan-yu* gave the signal to his horsemen. Horses raced past swaying, sullen camels and the wagons with their lumbering draft animals and out into the plains that were their true home.

All that day they rode, dismounting only for the briefest intervals and greatest needs, taking food on horseback, conferring on horseback, and riding back and forth along the great, cumbersome train of wagons, herds, and families. The air was very clear. It would be easy for a tracker and rider like Tadiqan to find his people in their summer pastures, pity though that was. Though Silver Snow was certain that they had ridden for miles, the scale of land and sky here was so vast that, when she turned in her wooden saddle, they seemed to have come no space at all from the camp.

"Try now to spot the fire, lady," came Vughturoi's voice. He sounded almost amused at her surprise.

Silver Snow narrowed her eyes and gazed back at the camp. Fire . . . there had stood her tents, and there the *shanyu*'s. Plumes of smoke rose from what had been their hearths, and tiny flames still wound merrily upward.

That was a fine omen, she had been told. Then her eyes strayed to her husband, who was almost invisible in his swaddlings of fur and felt. *Let it be so*, she prayed, but she did not know with what power she pleaded.

CHAPTER

= 17 =

Day yielded to day as the tribe drew closer and closer to spring pastures. The huge flocks of sheep thrived, and as the days grew warmer, the shaggy horses lost patches from their heavy coats. Even the swaying Bactrian camels pulled their loads without savaging their handlers; their doubled humps, which had sunk during the winter, a sign of dearth and hunger in the land, began to rise once again as the grasslands grew brighter and they neared spring pastures.

Spring pastures were many days' rides, a vast distance even as the Hsiung-nu counted it. But a day's ride was no regimented matter of up at dawn and so much land covered, regardless of time or cost to beasts and riders. Nor did the Hsiung-nu travel every day; they might pause in one specially suitable place, a site known for generations, where the water or the hunting was especially good.

It was no easy life, riding or driving a wagon or flocks across grasslands that seemed to stretch on to the very edges of the world. When the wind blew and the sun shone on the trappings of the riders, the red trimmings of garments, the shining, fat-smeared faces of children who were once again growing plump, and the bronze of the huge cauldrons that were lashed to the camels' pack saddles, it was a good life, exhausting, absorbing, and richly colored. Compared with the pastel, static life of the Son of Heaven's Inner Courts—well, Silver Snow could not begin to compare the two. If the air here seared her lungs with its coldness or the violence of the wind, at least there was enough of it for her to breathe.

Absorbed in this new life, she had even stopped longing for her northern home, with its faded dreams and its cautious poverty, except when, under her husband's benign, nodding supervision, she dispatched letters by one or two Hsiung-nu warriors who relished the exploit of a mere two or three weeks' dash to a frontier outpost of the Han, where he would test the truce long enough to convince the garrison to accept and forward the carefully sealed silk strips that bore the honors of a princess of Ch'ang-an and a queen of the Hsiung-nu. Some of the older officers, she suspected, might even remember her father and Li Ling; and might pass on the letters out of ancient loyalties.

Two things remained to disquiet her: Vughturoi spoke to her shortly, if at all, as if he enacted the role of a disgraced man abasing himself before a queen; and Sable's brother Basich had not returned from delivering the urgent, secret letter that she had entrusted to him. She feared that it had fallen into her enemy's hands. Of all her letters, that one held the most power to help her or cast her down.

However, Silver Snow's life was busy, too busy for cares that might prove, in the end, to be illusions. When the sun shone brightly, and the air quivered in the throat, wilder and even more sweet than the strange wine that, some travelers said, the people of Turfan brewed out of grapes instead of rice, she could even manage to forget such worries in the exhilaration of what lay around her.

Of all of the things that Silver Snow had never expected, this abundant, exuberant life was foremost. Each day brought her new sights and sounds that occupied her fully. Each night brought the stars close, and, when the camp finally settled itself, the grasslands were so quiet that each stamp of a hoof, each cry of a child, each gust of wind could receive its full tribute of attention and concern. By nights, Willow would dash out and bring in reports of movement in the land: the Yueh-chih toward the west, the Fu Yu northward, on a course toward spring grazing that paralleled their own.

Tadiqan still rode among the Fu Yu, Silver Snow thought. His absence added to her contentment. "The spirits send that he wander lost," Willow muttered once when, weary from the anguish of the change, she lay panting on her robes in the grayness before dawn. Silver Snow had wiped her brow, covered her, and bid her hush before she sought her own sleeping furs and silks; yet she had to admit to herself that she would be well satisfied if Strong Tongue's brutal son never found his way back to his mother's tenthold.

She had no such luck, however. The next day, a whistling shriek, followed by the buzz of a flight of arrows that skewered a fat sheep and a whoop of triumph, heralded Tadiqan and his men, triumphant from their dealings with the Fu Yu. That night, the *shan-yu* held a bigger feast than usual, and his eldest son reclined at his right hand, his mother beaming at the prince's shoulder, leaning over him to whisper counsel.

That night, the *shan-yu* appeared to be more feeble than Silver Snow had ever seen him.

"Willow!" hissed the girl, much against her custom, which kept her maid well out of the sight of Strong Tongue and her son. "In the chest that Li Ling gave you. Fetch the cordial in the jade bottle." She pointed with her chin at the *shan-yu*, who leaned upon Tadiqan's arm even more heavily than he had leaned, on that much happier evening, upon Vughturoi's. Why, he was actually drooping, near to collapse.

"Fetch it or foxglove . . . quickly!" she whispered, and Willow fled, to reappear with a jade tray, a tiny flask, and two tiny white jade cups brimful of an elixir that smelled strong and sweet. Silver Snow herself rose and took one of the cups to her husband. Because she saw no alternative, she offered the other to Tadiqan, who glanced at his mother, then spurned it with an impatient gesture.

"You drink it, lady," said the elder prince, as if this might be some test.

As she had been schooled, Silver Snow demurred politely. From the corner of her eye, she saw Strong Tongue gesture imperatively at her son.

"I said, drink it!" snapped Tadiqan.

"Forgive this foolish one her folly, prince of warriors," Silver Snow said in her softest, most rippling voice. She had hard work translating the formal apologies demanded by the language of her birth into the much more rugged tongue of the Hsiung-nu. "She but meant to let you benefit from the properties of this drink, which contains naught but healthful herbs and wine." She raised the cup as if to pledge him and drained it; the *shan-yu* copied her, even to the care with which he replaced the fine jade upon the little tray.

"My son, you must not snap at my senior wife in such a way," chided the *shan-yu*. There was more resonance in his voice, and blood rose in his withered cheeks. Imperiously he pointed to the carpet at Silver Snow's feet. As Tadiqan abased himself before Silver Snow, the old chieftain beamed equally at his young wife and his huge, glowering son.

Bemused by Tadiqan's sudden attack, Silver Snow plaited the fabric of her sleeve. Just as a spell of finding and success lay on Tadiqan's arrows, a spell of homecoming seemed to bind him to Strong Tongue.

Did such a spell now bind Khujanga to his son? And did spells even stronger and more sinister bind him to Strong Tongue?

If so, then perhaps the cordial had weakened them. At least, it would be wonderful to think so, much as Silver Snow doubted it. Shortly thereafter, Strong Tongue beckoned to her son, and the *shan-yu* turned to speak to some of the older warriors.

A shadow at Silver Snow's shoulder made her whip around with a speed no doubt facilitated by the elixir that she had drunk.

"Do you wonder, lady, how my elder brother returned home?" Her astonishment that Vughturoi would speak to her after so long a silence drew her out of her haze. She murmured something about "powers of Erlik."

"Now you speak like a true daughter of the grasslands." The younger prince smiled. "It is said . . ." he dropped his voice, "that in this, as in much else, my brother has the aid of his dam. But it is said, and more truthfully, that we of the Hsiung-nu know our way across the plains that are home to us as a city-dweller knows the way across the small prison that he calls his house. We do not go astray, nor do our arrows."

Was that warning or encouragement? Silver Snow could not tell. One thing she knew, however: the powers of the Hsiung-nu were not the beneficent healing magics that Willow, taming her fox nature, had learned, nor yet were they the scholarly powers of Li Ling. Those skills were somewhat familiar to her, and the ones adept in them meant her well. These magics, however, were as deadly as they were unpredictable; and the most skillful of their adepts was her deadly enemy.

As soon as it was prudent or possible, Silver Snow withdrew.

When she returned to her tent, Willow eyed her narrowly.

"I thought you might have run free," Silver Snow told her maid, surprised that her words came out almost as an accusation.

With surprising mildness, the lame girl shook her head and bent to the task of undressing her mistress. As she helped Silver Snow to unbind her long hair, she laid a narrow hand on her brow.

"You seem fevered, Elder Sister. May I brew you a potion? I still have willow twigs, to ease headache and reduce fever," Willow offered.

"No!" Silver Snow snapped, then flushed. "No," she repeated more gently. "It was the heat in the great tent. I simply need to rest."

"So?" Willow raised her level brows without further comment. Only she pulled her mirror from its usual hiding place and showed Silver Snow the taut, pale face of the woman pictured therein.

"It was too hot," Silver Snow said again. "And Strong Tongue strewed some of her noisome herbs upon the fire. Did you not smell them? Then you must be nose-blind. Just let me sleep." Even to her own ears, her voice sounded sullen. Willow assisted Silver Snow to lie down. Much to her surprise, the maid did not slip from the tent, to change shape and dance the night away with the brothers-in-fur. Even as Silver Snow heard yapping, Willow went to the flap of the tent and paused there, and the yapping faded into the distance . . . and into the mists of a troubled, haunted sleep.

The mists swirled about her, then solidified. Once again, she stood at the opening of the *shan-yu's* great tent. She felt very much alone, very cold. Vughturoi . . . Willow . . . Sable . . . Bronze Mirror . . . where were all of her friends and advocates? As she opened her lips to call for them, the wind blew her words away.

Once again, the mist swirled. Now she saw her father, younger and not nearly as halt, moving with a stealth that was totally alien to her knowledge of him, creeping toward the horse herds, seizing a sturdy beast with sound wind, and fleeing as far as he might, sleeping in the saddle, just as the Hsiung-nu themselves did.

But he had abandoned a son, a young son. As clearly as if he lay swathed beside her, Silver Snow saw the boy, saw his puzzled, sad eyes. Even as she watched, he shrugged, as if dismissing the loss of a father, the betrayal of a whole life. What must it have been like, Silver Snow wondered as she slept, to have trusted and respected . . . a captured enemy? What would it have been like then to lose him?

She whimpered in her sleep. Pounding throughout the dream until it overpowered even the grief she shared with that stranger-lad came the beat of a spirit drum, summoning her, summoning both of them to where their enemy waited with a sharp knife and a cruel laugh.

Silver Snow woke screaming, and it required all of Willow's skill to soothe her.

She was tired all the next day, far weaker than her wont. Strong Tongue looked sleek and satisfied, like a Hsiung-nu child fed on fatty mutton to the bursting point . . . at least, she looked satisfied until Khujanga spied Silver Snow drooping in the saddle, ordered that her chariot be brought, and himself escorted her to it with tender concern.

"She does not bear; she does not tend flocks or beat felt; she neither hunts nor cooks," Sable reported that Strong Tongue snorted . . . well out of the *shan-yu*'s earshot. "Such fear for a useless, jeweled weakling."

Children clung to Sable—Basich's children as well as her own. "Let them ride with me," Silver Snow asked, and the children whooped with delight.

Children's pleasure; a day's respite—that much she could give to Sable, who had ever been true to her. Her brother's return, however—that she could not promise. Not even Willow could bring her news of Basich; the brothers-in-fur were silent, too silent, on the subject.

A night's rest restored her, and the next day Silver Snow called for her bow. The whoops of approbation from Vughturoi's men convinced her that she acted prudently in doing thus. She killed several wildfowl before the hunting party turned back.

Willow rode forward to take Silver Snow's kill from her before anyone else might intervene. Her eyes met her mistress' with perfect understanding.

"Pluck them and draw them, Willow," ordered Silver Snow. "Perhaps Sable and Bronze Mirror would aid you. Tonight, husband"—for the first time, she used the title without having to be coaxed—"this one most humbly begs that you will eat in her tents."

Once again, the warriors cheered this sign of closeness between *shan-yu* and his queen. Nor was Tadiqan present to glower. To Silver Snow's astonishment, it was Vughturoi who did that.

And, that night, the *shan-yu*'s almost childlike greed as he ate a delicately spiced dish of his youngest, fairest wife's hunting and cookery won back any favor that one day's illness might possibly have cost her.

After that, by the *shan-yu*'s will, however, they must return to the great tent, where they were greeted with loud, ribald cheers. Before the noisy, nightly gathering in the *shan-yu*'s tent broke up, the old man had decreed a great hunt, which his loyal son Vughturoi would lead.

Was Silver Snow the only person in the tent who heard the sharp snap of broken bone as Tadiqán tightened his fist on the joint of meat that he held?

"Let us take the little queen who brings peace to the Hsiung-nu!" shouted a warrior, boisterous with too much mare's milk. "Let her also be named the queen who brings game to our bows!"

That brought a yell of approval, at which Strong Tongue glared. Vughturoi turned instantly away, and Silver Snow went scarlet, relieved that her flush would go unnoticed in the shadow and the firelight. The smoke that rose through the ceiling vents made her chest tight, and she put up one hand to press her heart. It was no role of lady nor queen to have her name and titles shouted out into her lord's tent; she was as much ashamed as she was anything else. Would the *shan-yu* be angry and turn on her as quickly as he had smiled?

But no, Khujanga smiled. Leaning forward, he patted her hand just as Li Ling had often done. "I cannot spare you, little Queen," he told her. Though his breath was strong with mare's milk, it came with more regularity and force than it had for weeks. Even as Silver Snow watched, he looked at the cup of mare's milk that he held—the goblet formed of the skull of his enemy—then grimaced, and laid it aside. Silver Snow's smile was unfeigned.

"Good hunting, Elder Sister!" Willow said, after she had undressed her mistress, by way of good-night greeting. She stretched indecorously, with a suppleness that accorded ill with her lame leg. "And clever thinking."

Silver Snow raised herself on one elbow. "Which hunt, Willow mine," she asked. "And which thoughts?"

"It was clever to hunt and to succeed, more clever yet to cook for the old man," Willow said. "That cup of his," she grimaced. "It is not well to drink from something so bound up with cruelty." She limped over to the small chest that was hers, opened it, and brought out her carefully hoarded bags of herbs and simples, many of them the parting gift of Li Ling.

Silver Snow glanced at her maid. Willow scowled at her and shook her head, as if astonished at how slow her mistress was at grasping what, for Willow, seemed to be essentials. Then Silver Snow shivered, though her bedrobes were very warm and closely swathed about her. Her very upbringing—which had instilled reverence for father, Son of Heaven, all of those who were rightfully set in authority over her—made her almost unable to comprehend that Willow, brought up in the amoral worlds of slave markets, furtive sorceries, and shape-changing, found self-evident.

Today, Vughturoi had ridden with the hunt, within easy call of the *shan-yu*. Today, the *shan-yu* had not eaten Strong Tongue's cooking, and he was the stronger for it.

Would the shaman deliberately use her crafts against her own husband and the leader of her tribe? There were, Silver Snow knew, herbs that could give a canny, unscrupulous person power over the man who ate them. A quick, unpleasant vision of Strong Tongue oppressed Silver Snow's consciousness. She had only to think of the haughtiness in the older woman's tiny eyes to know that she was quite capable of drugging Khujanga into agreement with her will. Until Silver Snow herself had appeared and had supplanted one enchantment with another, more primal, magic—and Khujanga had fought, weakening himself further.

Strong Tongue would have to know that too, Silver Snow thought.

Perhaps she does. Perhaps she wearies of the struggle, came a voice within Silver Snow's thoughts. Strong Tongue, balked of the power for which she had schemed so very long, was neither a pleasant nor a patient foe. Vughturoi had ridden with the host, and Tadiqan had been absent. Had matters been otherwise, Silver Snow realized, she might well have been a widow now . . . a widow who was forced to become a wife. Why, even at this moment, she might be forced to lie beside . . .

Appalled by her new, and darkest, suspicion, she gagged, but waved Willow away when the maid crouched by her head.

"Put your head down," ordered the maid, in a voice Silver Snow could not think of refusing. "Now, breathe deeply. I feared that the truth might affect you thus."

Silver Snow took deep, steady breaths until the dizziness and sickness faded. She pulled her robes up about her shoulders, grateful for the way that they eased her body of the cold sweat that seemed to sheath it.

"The *shan-yu* is stronger tonight," she stated. "If, after just one meal, he was stronger . . ."

"Why then, Elder Sister, we . . . *you* . . . must cook for him from now on. Cosset him as if he were your only grandson, and suffering from a flux. I shall ensure that not only will his food be worth the tasting, but that it shall contain nothing more that will harm him."

"And if Strong Tongue charges us with sorcery?" asked Silver Snow.

"Then," hissed Willow, "let her look to her own. Ahhh, Elder Sister, could I but slip into her tent, I would wager that I should find such things that would earn her speedy and painful death!"

Thereafter, Silver Snow and her maid cooked for the *shan-yu*. Intrigued by the delicate dishes and subtle spices, he beamed upon his wife and her handmaid and ate heartily. Nor did Silver Snow think that it was her imagination that, in the days that followed, he walked more steadily, spoke without the quaver that had entered his voice in recent weeks, especially after meals, and was even able to mount unassisted. In this new flush of health, his heart warmed once again to Vughturoi, who seemed content, each evening, to sit and watch his father, whose eyes were fixed—as Silver Snow was well aware—upon her.

She played and sang, all too well aware that now she played for her life. For the first time, she found herself echoing the wish of Sable and Bronze Mirror that she bear a son. Had the *shan-yu* been a younger man, she thought, there would have been no question. By now, almost certainly, she would have been carrying a child. Yet, had the *shan-yu* been a younger man, he—and she—would not be in this danger from Strong Tongue.

One night, much afraid, Silver Snow sorted through Willow's chests of simples. The *shan-yu* was ancient; yet, it was true, old men had wed and begotten (or had acknowledged fatherhood) thousands of times. Silver Snow fingered herbs that aided conception, that strengthened the body, that dulled the will. Perhaps the *shan-yu* could be slightly drugged, then enticed . . . and she would have her heir, her safety.

For as long as Strong Tongue and Tadiqan let him live! It was no strange thing for a child of the grasslands to die during his first three years; though, should he survive them, thereafter it might take a flight of arrows to kill him. The birth of a boychild postponed nothing. And then there was the matter of conceiving such a child. An older woman, more experienced or less scrupulous, might use such methods to secure the heir that she needed. How could Silver Snow, who had never known a man, implement a plan that required the wiles and skills of an accomplished courtesan?

If it were not the shan-yu *who must be the father* . . .

She shook her head, and though only the firelight was present to witness went scarlet with shame that she had entertained such a thought even for a moment. That thought led not just to death but to dishonor. Carefully Silver Snow laid the herbs aside and locked the chest in which they were stored. She bent to check her bowstring and judged it sound. Then she opened another chest and burrowed into it until she found the knife that she sought and hid it on her person.

She vowed to herself that she would never stir without it.

* * *

"Lady," Willow woke her in the gray chill before dawn. The maid's face was pale and drawn, her russet hair leached of all color in the half light, and her lame leg dragged more than it usually did.

Silver Snow let her fingers loosen from the jade hilt of the dagger that she kept beneath her pallet. "You have been running all night," she accused, smiling, though she tried to make her voice sound severe. "I suppose that that means that you will be worthless all day today. Strong Tongue will say that you should be beaten."

Willow's characteristic hiss of irritation silenced her mistress. "This one has proved her worth time and time again. And never more than now. Look you, elder sister, at what my kin-in-fur have brought me."

Awkwardly she crouched beside Silver Snow and dangled a thing that she held where her mistress could see it.

"What is that foul thing?" Silver Snow cried, and flung up a hand to ward off Willow's trophy. "Do they bring you carrion now? I never knew that fox and kite were kin before."

"*Look* you." Willow's voice was softer but more inexorable than Silver Snow had ever known it to be. Some of Strong Tongue's power of command seemed to lie beneath it: in this moment, Willow was shaman, not serving maid.

Silver Snow looked. What Willow held appeared to be a tangle of leather straps, much chewed and fouled with old, dried blood. For a moment, her hand trembled, then she disciplined it to such stillness that she might have been a statue.

"It looks like harness leathers," Silver Snow mused. "But . . . there is a medallion there, still fastened to the strap. Wait!" she breathed. "This is a bridle, and that medallion, those cheekpieces . . ."

The design incised on the bronze was unmistakable: a squat, fat woman, or goddess, or some such creature. She had last seen that piece of harness on one of Basich's horses.

Silver Snow sat up, her sleeping furs dropping to her waist. "Where got you this?" she demanded.

She pushed past it, snatched up her robes where Willow

had laid them at the foot of her bed, and began to dress before Willow could assist her.

"The brothers-in-fur waited," Willow said, "until the white tiger fed, then brought this hither."

Silver Snow remembered a cold, clear night, its silence broken only by frightened breathing, the occasional footstep, and the thumping of a huge, hostile heart that she had heard when the white tiger stalked her tent and as she stalked the white tiger. Basich had not been as fortunate. Sable would wail; and how was Silver Snow to comfort her? How could she demand redress? Did she even have proof that Sable's brother was dead?

And what became of your letter, or of some reply? came the quiet, fearsome voice that constantly chided Silver Snow for choosing the personal over the political. Angrily she shook her head. This was not Ch'in; this was the grasslands—and state-craft was as much a matter of personal ties as it was of law or custom.

"Did they . . ." her voice faltered. "Did your kin on the plains discover any traces of the man, as well as his horse?"

Willow shook her head, but her eyes under their level brows were mournful. Seeing how Silver Snow's eyes followed her grisly prize, she wrapped it in a square of silk and hid it from sight in the chest where she stored instruments for divining. Did Silver Snow imagine it, or did Willow's hand linger on the chest after she closed it?

"He might have lived, might yet have sacrificed his horse and escaped." Neither she nor Willow could put much faith in that, however. The grasslands were immeasurably broad. A man who might be wounded, who would be weary and mortally afraid of the white tiger, a man, above all else, who had ridden lifelong, how should such a man in Basich's case ever find the tribe again?

"Perhaps," Willow said slowly. "Perhaps."

"Willow, you should warn your kin to watch for him." Silver Snow glanced quickly at her maid. She seemed grieved by Basich's disappearance.

Willow smiled. "They know to watch for me, and they will ward him; I have told them that he was kind to me. Believe me, Elder Sister, they hate and fear the white tiger just as we do. Let us learn who sends it against us, and we shall speedily see a hunt even greater than those of this *shan-yu* of yours!"

CHAPTER

= 18 =

Spring yielded to summer on the grasslands, which grew greener and more lush; ewes dropped their lambs, and the flocks prospered; the great herds of horses grew sleek once again, and even the camels thrived, their doubled humps ever swelling, a sign of ample food and water. The Hsiung-nu rode as pleased hearts and minds across the immensity of the plains that stretched out so far below the impossibly huge, impossibly distant horizon where shadowy mountains reared up until their snow-crested peaks were indistinguishable from the clouds that clustered there, but nowhere else in the sky.

Against such vastness, even a clan the size of the royal clan with its huge herds seemed no more than a trail of ants, following its leader across a piece of jade. Silver Snow's eyes became accustomed to the sun and to the vastness of the land; she could barely remember the times when an ordinary day's ride had left her exhausted and sore. Day after day, the Hsiung-nu rode, but they drew no closer to the mountains where, by now, snow was melting from the living ice and flowing down to the fields, making them green and rich.

They *were* like ants, Silver Snow thought, walking across not a piece of jade, but across a drum. The game was to pass by in silence, lest the drum rumble and expose them to discovery. All that spring and well into summer, she had the sensation that she had had years ago in the North before a storm: the sky might be clear and the winds mild, but hints of thunder flickered along her nerves the way that the grass bent before the breath of the wind.

Spring was fair, summer fairer still. Very often the warriors rode out to tend the herds, leaving the tents themselves in the charge of the oldest men and the women. Yet, if Vughturoi was absent, so too was Tadiqan. That was a fair trade, and the way that the *shan-yu* Khujanga had welcomed his younger son made it fairer still in Silver Snow's eyes. Always, she took care to keep her eyes down, a contrast to the Hsiung-nu women, who looked where and at whom they would, and even to her earlier behavior, before she realized why she had wrought a scent bag of fine Hsiung-nu sables and elegant Ch'in perfumes, now buried far beneath her heaviest robes.

For hours at a time, Silver Snow might ride, work, and live in contentment, to be jolted back to awareness of jeopardy by a glower or an accusation of neglect from Strong Tongue, who had many adherents among the elder women who ruled the great tents. Still, if Strong Tongue had her partisans, so did Silver Snow, and she was happy when she realized that their number waxed day after day.

She had all but forgotten that she had never received a reply to that first message she had sent out in such urgency and fear with Basich. Gradually she came to accept that if Basich had not perished under the claws and fangs of the white tiger, he must have died of exposure and the letter been lost. That acceptance helped her to comfort Sable, who boasted of her hardihood, that she could not grieve over what was fated to be, yet who mourned all the more passionately for her inability to lament publicly. Quite often Willow sat with her, easing her grief by her silent calm, in the fashion that wild beasts tend one another by their presence alone.

Was Silver Snow alone in perceiving summer to be a time of calm between storms that rose like the brief, ferocious rain squalls that pounded down from the heights? Such storms brought water to the fields, and thus were welcome; yet, if the fields were dry, such storms also brought lightning and the threat of fires that the wind would drive howling across the grasslands, as hungry, free, and violent as the Hsiung-nu themselves, but disastrously more fleet.

For the first time, Silver Snow truly understood how sacred fire was to the Hsiung-nu. In the winter, fire had to be guarded because it cooked their meals and warmed their yurts; in the summer, it must be restrained lest it devour them. Silver Snow heard tales of the Hu far to the west, who thought of fire as a demon. Barbarians they might be, but understanding the Hsiung-nu's fear of flame in the grasslands, she could sympathize with their belief.

Still, Khujanga thrived. Strong Tongue's full hostility seemed to have subsided, yet Silver Snow retained that sensation of a drumhead about to sound out the cadence of a huge pulse, or of a beast—say, a white tiger—crouching to await its tiny prey's first unwary movement.

Sunlight more richly golden and opulent than the *lung*, or dragon, embroidery on an Emperor's robes slanted down on the royal clan's camp. It thrust its gleaming talons into the *shan-yu*'s great tent, drawing new splendor from the tumble of rugs and cushions within, and reducing the hearthfire, smoldering imprisoned in its brazier, to seem like no more than a few sullen sparks. Because the day had been so fair, Silver Snow had commanded some of her women to drag rugs and cushions to the flap of the tent, that she and the *shan-yu* might gaze out over the land as they waited for the evening meal.

Voices raised from within the great tent told her that Willow had entered, to take over Silver Snow's share of the cooking and, just incidentally, to ensure that Strong Tongue had no opportunity to add harmful herbs and leaves to the meal. From behind the tent came the faint piping of a bamboo flute, played, no doubt, by some child free, just for the moment, from the tasks that children on the grasslands learned to perform almost as soon as they could walk or ride. The wind caught up the song, and it blended, poignant, bittersweet, with the strings of Silver Snow's lute, and her soft, high voice.

The old *shan-yu* smiled. For the moment, Silver Snow's heart was high within her. The old man beside her was called husband, not father; yet, in easing these past months, was she not performing obedient service, as befitted a woman raised in the reverend traditions of Confucius?

The wind blew a descant to her song and brought her the smells of her new home: pungent horses, the dust of the plains, and the tantalizing scents of cooking meat, seasoned with condiments that came from her own supplies.

Then Strong Tongue tramped out of the tent, discreetly trailed by Willow. Silver Snow's brief moment of satisfaction faded. Instinctively she glanced around. No, Vughturoi rode out to inspect the horse herds and count the foals: that was a shame. Still, he might return tonight, and if not tonight, then tomorrow: he was a free man and could come and go as he chose. Yet, Silver Snow could find some ease in knowing that, only that dawn, Tadiqan too had ridden out with a troop of his followers, declaring his intention once again to overawe the Fu Yu.

The melancholy song of the flute faded, to be replaced by the far-less-sonorous reproof of the musician's mother, angry at the child's idleness. Silver Snow finished her song. Khujanga's gap-toothed grin and laughter encouraged her to begin another, this time a merry drinking song that she had heard in Ch'ang-an. She ignored Strong Tongue's sigh of aggravation and the too-obvious *tap-tap-tap* of her booted foot.

Even as Silver Snow sang, however, that tapping occupied more and more of her consciousness. She dared not glance over to see whether or not Strong Tongue had brought out her spirit drum with its hateful skin cover, but surely that tapping bore some of the same insistent cadence of the drum, set to pulse in rhythm with a beating heart.

Hoofbeats broke her fascination with the sound and ended her song. She glanced at Khujanga, the *shan-yu*, who would surely know what horsemen might be expected to return to camp this night. He tensed, clearly mustering strength to rise and seize a spear. Then he grimaced.

"Who would ride the grasslands alone?" muttered the *shan-yu*.

Now that Silver Snow turned all her concentration to the task, she found much in the sound of those hoofbeats to disquiet her. As the *shan-yu*'s more experienced ears had told him, only one man rode toward the camp; the rhythm of the hoofbeats indicated that his mount was in some distress, a severe failing, given the care that the Hsiung-nu took of their favorite horses.

"Brother!" Keen-eyed from a lifetime gazing into the distance, Sable broke the silence that she had maintained and raced forward, her braids and leather garments flapping. Willow lurched to her feet, took a halting step forward, then stopped. Never before had Silver Snow seen such misery, such hatred of her lameness on the girl's face.

Sable reached the foundering horse just as several of the old warriors did. Seizing its bridle, she tugged it toward the tent and the *shan-yu*, who now stood, grasping a spear. Silver Snow's own hand strayed from her lute to her knife. She too turned to watch and gasped as she got her first good look at Basich.

The once-robust warrior was much changed. Clawmarks scored one side of his face, drawing it into scars, and he had one arm strapped against his chest. Silver Snow swallowed against sickness as she noted that the crippled arm ended in a tangle of stained bandages that looked too small to be a full hand.

As Basich spotted her, he jerked his arm free of its strappings as if to hail her. That gesture drained him, and he sagged in the saddle, to tumble off into his sister's sturdy, waiting arms. Silver Snow leapt forward, followed by Willow. Sable sobbed once, then swallowed her tears.

"Who did this?" she demanded of her half-conscious brother, shaking him before Willow could catch her hands and restrain her. "Who?"

Willow crushed herbs beneath Basich's nose, and he gasped and choked. "White tiger . . ." he whispered. "I fled

. . . wandered until I found . . ." He gasped, a sound that ended with an ominous rattle.

Will he live, do you think? Silver Snow looked at Willow, trusting the maid to understand her thought and hoping that she might reassure her. Willow shrugged almost imperceptibly and bent to unwrap the bandages that confined Basich's hand. If the man had lived this long after the white tiger's onslaught, the wounds must not have festered, notoriously foul though the bites of great cats were. But he was still weak, especially for one of the Hsiung-nu, whose endurance was legendary. If Basich could rest, if a fever did not strike him, and his will to live held, then he might indeed survive.

"Ask who did this to him," she whispered urgently to Willow. The maid headed back toward Basich, her limp making her long, dark shadow dance almost threateningly across the land. Seeing it, several of the Hsiung-nu stepped back, and Strong Tongue's drum throbbed out, a brief rumbling of thunder before the storm strikes.

"They . . . cast me out," he rasped.

"They tortured him," Willow mouthed at Silver Snow, then bent over the warrior who lay against his sister's shoulder. "Who cast you out?"

"The Fu Yu," he moaned, then fell silent, his head lolling to one side. Sable let out the wail that she had suppressed throughout all of the weeks that she did not know whether her brother lived or died.

"He is not dead," Willow told her. "Not yet, and perhaps not for many years."

And he may have saved all of our lives, Silver Snow thought. She watched as Willow and Sable attempted to make Basich more comfortable. When they tried to lift him, to move him toward Sable's tents, however, he resisted, content for the moment to stare out at the camp and the familiar faces, sights that he obviously had abandoned all hope of ever seeing again. So, the Fu Yu had succored him, then cast him out. And the Fu Yu were the tribe about which Tadiqan had expressed such concern. She stood toying with the seals of the letter tube until her husband's voice made her jump up in guilty surprise.

"It is not a call to war," complained the *shan-yu*. "Let us call for a feast. Basich, whom we mourned as dead, has come back to us, and my elder son will avenge upon the miserable Fu Yu every injury that he has received. Perhaps I shall demand the skull of their leader and make it into a goblet, as I did with the skull of that Yueh-chih traitor. It is not every day that one of my children returns from the other world. Let us drink to him!" He drank—out of that terrible skull cup, Silver Snow noted with distaste. Then he ended his speech in a spasm of coughing, and Silver Snow darted forward to support him.

"This is not yet my funeral feast," Khujanga grumbled at her as she urged him back toward the comfortable rugs and curtains. Yet satisfaction at Silver Snow's pretty show of concern underlay his grumbles, and he seemed pleased to lean more heavily upon his young wife than he did upon his long spear. The skull cup lay untended outside until Strong Tongue sent a child to take charge of it.

Shadows like the strokes of a master calligrapher's brush fell across the grasslands, tingeing their green with evening by the time that Willow pronounced herself satisfied with Basich's condition and Silver Snow could persuade Khujanga to take a little more of the dwindling supply of restoratives that she had brought with her from Ch'ang-an. They were doubly precious now: who could tell whether a letter requesting more of the elixirs or the herbs from which Willow might possibly be able to compound them would ever reach its destination, or whether she could believe that a reply to such an appeal, would fall into her hands, rather than the jaws of the white tiger?

There would be time, Silver Snow hoped, to concern herself with her future fortunes: for now, for this moment, those whom she guarded and who guarded her were safe; she herself was safe; and Strong Tongue, her son sent away at the *shan-*

yu's orders, was held at bay. She sat glowering, tending the glowing fire whose sanctity, she clearly appeared to feel, would be polluted if Silver Snow or Willow dared even to approach it. Or was it simply the envy of a woman supplanted by a younger wife, whom she was now determined to outcook and excel in all other ways?

Silver Snow shook her head and pursed her lips; though, when Khujanga pressed her to speak her sad thoughts, she smiled and turned the subject. Had she the strength, she knew, she should call for music and sing. A melancholy as terrible in its way as the dreams that she had had possessed her. Today she was safe; this hour she might sing for a lord who was as benevolent to her as she dared expect: but what of tomorrow? She dared not even confide her fears either to her lord, whom they might agitate fatally, or to his younger son, who might consider them disloyal or a sign of weakness. Even to admit them might make her vulnerable to worse assaults than she already had endured.

Though the light outside the *shan-yu*'s tent was fading toward nightfall, the heat of the day had not yet subsided. Only the day before, Khujanga had spoken of breaking camp and riding toward the highest summer pastures in the foothills of the Heavenly Mountains where the streams, fed as they were by the ice of the highest peaks, never failed, even in the hottest weather.

The constant arrival of more and more Hsiung-nu—who reined their horses sharply in, then leapt down—cast up clouds of dust that danced in the light of the fire and the sunset at the far-off western horizon. What lay there? she wondered. Not even the Hsiung-nu, great travelers that they were, could say for certain.

She coughed, restrained an urge to tear at the high-throated closing of her silken gown and jacket, and forced her hands to rest in her lap. Surely the dust would cast Khujanga into spasms of coughing? But no, after a life spent on the grasslands, the *shan-yu* was inured; he only wheezed slightly, his slits of eyes closed, his head falling forward onto his chest in what looked like the easy slumbers of an old man.

Old men dozed in the warmth, she thought, while it fell to others, as well it should, to labor to tend them. Who tended her father now? she wondered. Lands, wealth, and honor he had once again; but no obedient daughter to kneel near to hand, to provide him with every comfort including the strong support of a son-in-law and the joy of sturdy grandsons to honor the Ancestors and plump, pretty grandchildren who would form alliances with other ancient lines.

For a moment, the *shan-yu*, though he meant her nothing but good, seemed to be one with all of the other Hsiung-nu. They were all aliens, savages, and she was stranded among them in this endless ocean of dust and grass.

She was young, lovely, yet she had been given more as daughter than as bride to a withered barbarian, given in trade, though custom and courtesy called it a marriage; she would never have children, and when the heat in her blood finally cooled, when its pulsing finally slowed, she would die alone, unhonored. She could feel that pulse now. Already it was growing slower, and soon it might stop, and she would gasp and die, of the loneliness and dust, if of nothing else. All of the old songs had been right; the life of a man or woman of Han among the grasslands was arid, bitter, and short.

Only that slowing throb broke the silence of her despair. She had known sorrow as absolute only once before. *And then*, she thought, *then I wrote out my sadness on a leaf, and Willow hurled it over the wall. And that one thing, that insignificant little leaf, brought me friendship such as I had never known.*

Perhaps such a joy could come out of this sorrow too. The throbbing subsided, then ceased; but the silence was welcome this time. Out of sorrow might come satisfaction. Silver Snow thought of the words of the Master, Confucius, of her months in the Cold Palace, and of the far worse fates that Li Ling and her father had endured for years without complaining. By her own exile, she brought them wealth and honor; and she brought even more to Ch'in. After all, was she not hailed as the queen who brought peace to the Hsiung-nu? Whether or not they wanted such peace, the Middle Kingdom did. Weighed against that, what was her one small life? Obedience had been her duty lifelong; she was privileged that her obedience could bring her land, her race, and her loved ones such a rich gift.

The thought made her able to smile once again as she glanced over at her husband, who snatched sleep when he might, as any proven warrior knew was only prudent. His cup—a plain one of incised bronze—had fallen from his hand. Carefully Silver Snow reached across him and set it upright, then turned back to regard Willow, as she sat with Sable beside Basich, her head lowered as befitted a modest maid of Ch'in, if not these Hsiung-nu, and offered him food and drink. Now that, Silver Snow thought, as Basich laughed and tried to trick Willow into looking up, was an interesting sight. Basich had young children, lacked neither horses nor power within the clan, and obviously did not despise Willow for being lame and ill-favored . . . if indeed she was. Here, so far away from Ch'ang-an and the Bright Court's inflexible pronouncements about beauty, Willow's burnished hair and level brows had a kind of comeliness all their own.

Ah, so he had won a smile from the maid, Silver Snow observed. To think she had taunted Willow about fox kits. Well, to all creatures there was a season; perhaps she did wrong to keep the maid so closely tied to her. It might be auspicious should a marriage be arranged. *I should ask Vughturoi.* The thought flickered into Silver Snow's consciousness and out again so quickly that she barely had time to flush.

Even as she watched, Basich too seemed to relax upon the rug that Willow had dragged out to him, resting as did his lord before the promised feast that, even now, Strong Tongue was supervising.

How hot the cookfires were! Silver Snow forced herself not to gasp and reached for her own cup. Even the fermented sourness of mare's milk would cool her throat and dissolve what felt like a thick layer of dust that coated it. She could almost feel the liquid trickling down her parched throat.

"Nay, little one! Do not drink that!"

The harsh crack of that order came so quickly that Silver Snow's hand jerked. Almost immediately thereafter, the *shan-yu* flung himself at her, the impact of his body, which was still wiry from a lifetime in the saddle, knocking the goblet from her hand and hurling her back against her cushions and carpets with him above her as if they were, in flesh as in oath, truly man and wife.

The cup rolled on the carpets, light striking silver and the yellowed hue of old bone. Bone? That was not her cup at all, then, but the skull cup that she detested so much that she would not look at it, much less drink from it. How had the cups been exchanged . . . and why?

The *shan-yu* thrust himself upright again, the skin from which the mare's milk had been poured dangling half empty from his hand. Even as Silver Snow gasped and sought to raise herself, he reeled and caught himself with one gnarled hand, snatching at one of the struts that supported the tent. The skin gurgled as he struggled to regain his balance, and the firelight cast a brazen light upon him. Half of his face seemed to blaze; the other half lay in shadow and appeared to sag, as if it were formed of wax onto which some careless artisan had spilled boiling water. The brazier's smoldering embers seemed to have kindled in his eyes: tiny demons danced and glared fearsomely in their depths.

With his free hand, Khujanga reached out and smoothed Silver Snow's hair, disordered from her fall. "I shall guard thee, little one," he whispered, and his words were slurred.

The skin of mare's milk sloshing in his hand, he lurched toward the cookfire and poured the mare's milk into its flames, which flickered up in eerie, shimmering colors. Then, with a hiss, the fire died. All about, women shrieked in outrage at the ruin of good food and the pollution of the sacred flame. Something acrid, with the scent of bitter almonds, blended with the small of burnt food, ash, and meat. Silver Snow bent her head to sniff at the stain on her cushions from the spilled mare's milk. The same bitter almond scent was there. Willow, with her fox-keen senses and her lifelong training in herbs, would have sensed it immediately; the *shan-yu*, with a hunter's sense of smell, had also known, even had he not noticed the exchange of cups.

The mare's milk had been poisoned. Carefully Silver Snow wiped her fingers on a cloth and tossed the cloth away lest she touch it once more.

As Strong Tongue had done on Silver Snow's very first appearance in the *shan-yu*'s tent, she hastened toward the contaminated fire. Her callused fingers alternately curled and unclenched on the sallow hide that covered her spirit drum, which throbbed as if she held a beating human heart. She gestured imperiously at the women who clustered by the hearth, as dismayed as Hsiung-nu women ever got, and they cowered before her, afraid—just as she had planned—of a woman of whom it was said that she knew the speech of grass and rocks and the very dead themselves.

"Throw that trash out!" she commanded in a whisper. Among people who were famous for never wasting a thing, her order created shock—and instant obedience. The meat must be poisoned: why else discard it if it were only burnt or smeared with ashes? Then she turned to the *shan-yu*, who had mastered his failing body and now drew himself up to confront her.

"You are ill, husband," began Strong Tongue, that tongue of hers harnessed all to wifely support, then lashing free to accuse, "That little viper in silks has bewitched you, poisoned your mind so that now you pollute the sacred flame . . ."

"It is not my mind that is poisoned," Khujanga's voice was still slurred, and though he tried to shout until the veins bulged in his temples, what emerged was a strangling rasp. "It was *this!*"

Even as Silver Snow leapt to her feet, one hand reaching for her tiny jade-hilted dagger, determined to run to the *shan-*

yu's side, he hurled the skin that had held mare's milk at Strong Tongue. She stepped neatly aside, lest she be splashed by even a stray drop of what that skin had held, more proof, if any more were needed, that she had known what it held.

"You tried to kill my wife," he whispered. "Kill her, and kill . . ."

"Aye, and slay you too, dotard, as one clubs on the head a beast that eats more than it is worth. Your sun has set; it is time to let the power pass to younger, braver men. Like Tadi-qan, whose blood has not turned to milk because some spoiled child smiles and sings through her pointed nose!"

You hear that! Silver Snow wanted to cry; but there was no one about to obey her. All of the women had fled at Strong Tongue's command. The old men, like Khujanga himself, had been napping, and only now were the warriors riding in.

"I shall have you trampled by a herd of horses!" he vowed at the eldest wife.

"You?" She laughed, seemingly well content. "You will be lying beneath your gravemound!"

Once again, her fingers moved on her spirit drum, beating out a rhythm so fast that not even a young, vital man's heart could withstand it for long. Though Khujanga clawed with one hand at his throat, his face purpled, and he gagged as if he had swallowed his tongue, hurled himself at her across the sodden firepit as he had done at Silver Snow only instants before.

The drum flew from her hand; but she stood firm above the *shan-yu*, who lay face down, his scanty beard fouled with ashes and spittle.

Despite the heat of the evening, Silver Snow shuddered and turned over the old man with hands that felt as if she had bathed them for half a day in an ice-fed stream. His body felt as light as a dead cricket, and already his eyes were dull, glazed with the dust that had filled them as he fell.

He had been dead before he had hit the ground.

Dead, thought Silver Snow. And with him died her immunity, as poor a thing as it was, to Strong Tongue and her pernicious son, who would rule if Strong Tongue could summon him from wherever he rode among the flocks of the royal clan.

"Vughturoi," Silver Snow murmured. "I must summon him." Who could she send to find him? She turned, her eyes seeking out Willow, who hastened toward her with a terrible ungainliness that threatened to overturn her at each step.

"Call for your champion, but he will come too late," Strong Tongue assured her. Though she carefully avoided turning her back to Silver Snow, she stooped with a kind of monumental assurance to retrieve her spirit drum from the tangle of rugs against which it had rolled.

Silver Snow could imagine its voice, throbbing out over the still air, summoning back Tadiqan to claim the title, flocks, and power of the *shan-yu* . . . and Silver Snow herself. Bile flooded her mouth, and she feared she would collapse on her knees by the hearth and profane it further by retching until she was empty. Still, she was younger, fleeter than Strong Tongue.

Drawing her knife, she flung herself toward the drum and stabbed into its taut drumhead, which parted with a sigh like someone's last breath. *Forgive me*, she thought, though she did not know to whom she appealed. Perhaps she but released a spirit who had struggled in torment during all of these years since Strong Tongue had used human flesh to give her spirit drum a voice.

Silver Snow panted as she rose to her feet to confront Strong Tongue. Afraid—certainly she knew fear, perhaps fear even greater than what she had endured when she waited for the bandits to attack on the road to Ch'ang-an or when she slipped out from her tent to stalk the white tiger. Yet she also knew a sort of relief. With Khujanga dead, the woman was now openly to be counted as her enemy. Silver Snow held her dagger at the ready.

Strong Tongue simply folded her arms across her massive

bosom and laughed. With insolent slowness, she thrust one hand into her robe and pulled out a tattered, bloodstained roll of silk bearing bore seals that Silver Snow recognized.

"The quarry of the white tiger's hunt," jeered the shaman.

"Give me that!" demanded Silver Snow. She leapt forward to score Strong Tongue's hand and snatch the precious letter, which brought news and counsel from Ch'in. Her dagger drew a thin, bloody line down the older woman's hand, but, in the next moment, a shove sent her reeling across the tent to sprawl onto a pile of cushions.

Strong Tongue followed her and stood above her. "Lie like that and wait till Tadiqan comes. And while you wait, think on this!"

She tore open the letter's bindings, which should have been opened with respect, and dangled the silk with its exquisitely clear brushstrokes before Silver Snow.

"What does it tell you, girl? To coo over the *savages*"—she spat out the word—"until we are as weak as you of the Middle Kingdom and can be overrun? Does it tell you to beware of the Fu Yu, who will be as my son's strong right hand to push you back beyond your foolish wall, then topple it on your head? And not just the Fu Yu. He who should have ruled the Yueh-chih rides with them and at my son's command will raise an army! He has sworn to have Vughturoi's skull as a cup, in vengeance for the ill-use of his father, and until he can obtain the skull of your Emperor!"

"Give me that!" Silver Snow launched herself once again at Strong Tongue, and once again the woman flung her down.

"Do not try your strength with me!" cried the shaman. She snapped her fingers, and a slave brought her the skull cup that had contained what Silver Snow might—should her life turn as bitter as Strong Tongue hoped—wish that she had drunk. The shaman wiped the cup on a square of leather, then set it on Khujanga's seat, above where Silver Snow had fallen. "Lie there and prepare to welcome my son and your new lord . . . daughter!"

Contemptuously she turned her back on the smaller woman and walked toward a fire that still burned brightly. Her path took her close beside the body of the *shan-yu*, and her robes flicked across his face. Laughing, she hurled the letter from Ch'in into the flames.

CHAPTER

= 19 =

"Elder Sister, Elder Sister!" Willow flung herself down beside Silver Snow. "Are you hurt?"

"Never mind that!" Silver Snow gasped. All the menace that Strong Tongue had loaded into that single word *daughter* restored her to herself in a way that no compassion, no tenderness, might have. Once again, she and Willow crouched in a shabby wagon, afraid of the bandits who bore the mark of the crimson eyebrows, afraid but determined to die rather than to be violated. Once again, she faced down a corrupt eunuch before the Son of Heaven.

She had been hailed as the queen who brought peace to the Hsiung-nu. What did it matter if the *shan-yu* to whom she was wed lay dead? She was still queen of the Hsiung-nu, and by all that she valued, she would have her say in who would be her next lord.

"Vughturoi," she ordered Willow. "We have to fetch him."

The first prince to return and to view his father's body would inherit his title: that was the law. So, it would be a race, Silver Snow knew, between Strong Tongue's powers and whatever magic that Willow might summon. Or any fortune that she herself might merit.

To her surprise, Willow did not creep into a corner and enter the agonizing spasms of the change from maid to fox.

233

Instead, she lurched past a crowd of Hsiung-nu, matching shove with shove, staggering but somehow managing to stay upright, until she stood shaking in the twilight. A chattering, yapping sound came from her lips and was answered from all sides. For a moment longer, Willow stood so. Then she dropped to her knees and with one outstretched, shaking hand smoothed the fur of the huge fox that had emerged, seemingly from nowhere, at her feet. It—no, he—nuzzled her hand, barked once more, then vanished into the night.

Then, slowly, Willow started down the slight slope on which the great tent had been pitched toward where Basich lay. Roused by the shouts and the uproar in the great tent, he had seized his own weapons and now hurried, as best he might, limping, as Willow did, upslope toward her. He seized her by one arm, and ushered her, protesting, back into the tent.

Silver Snow went over to the body of the old *shan-yu*. She herself had tried earlier to turn him over, and succeeded but partially; now his eyes stared up at the roof of the tent, and his arms were flung wide. He was an old man; he had been a good man in his way, and a friend to Ch'in; and he had been kind to her. It was neither proper nor dutiful to let him lie there asprawl, lacking the dignity of mourning and attendance. She knelt and held her hand over the glazed eyes from which all cunning and all humor had fled forever until they stayed shut after she took her hand away. Then, with a corner of her sleeve, she wiped the grime and dried spittle from his face, tried to array the sparse beard on his chin, and to ease the dreadful, contorted expression on his face.

Then it was that a drum began its insistent *pound . . . pound . . . pound*. Strong Tongue had wasted no time in repairing that damnable spirit drum of hers.

And whose was the skin that she used this time? Silver Snow shuddered.

Always before, Khujanga had risen to her defense when she was in danger. Any hope that she might have had that he had but swooned was fully dead now. Her eyes filmed over, and tears fell onto her hands as they worked, straightening out the twisted limbs, easing the *shan-yu*'s body into a posture that was more seemly.

Drops of blood sank into the dusty carpet beside him. Silver Snow let out a tiny scream as Basich dropped down beside her. Raw scores on his face showed that he mourned his dead leader according to the custom of the Hsiung-nu, who drew their knives and gashed their cheeks to display their grief. They wept, not with tears, but with blood.

"Permit me, lady." His voice was husky, and he averted his face as he stooped, picked up Khujanga's body, and bore it to the rugs before his usual seat where he laid the old man out in state. He glanced upon the grisly cup and grimaced.

Silver Snow drew up a cushion at the dead *shan-yu*'s side, just as she had often done when he was alive. She felt no fear, no abhorrence of the dead.

"She"—he gestured with his chin at Willow—"says that she has done what she might to fetch my prince. I too shall ride . . ."

"Ride?" Silver Snow asked. "You can barely walk!"

His blood-smeared face gleamed with sorrow and a kind of cold pride. "You forget, lady. I am Hsiung-nu, and we ride almost before we walk. My mare's back is better than a bed to me. I shall fetch back the prince to ward us." He let out a wordless shout, and staggered from the tent.

Silver Snow's women came and crouched down beside her. Ringing them were the oldest men of the tribe, those too old to fight. The younger warriors, those who had not ridden out with Vughturoi or Tadiqan, watched, their eyes avid, curious. All bore bleeding gashes across their cheeks; all carried blades or bows; and all had their private allegiances—whether to the *shan-yu* who was dead, to the elder prince, or to Vughturoi, Silver Snow forced herself not to guess.

What if I ordered, "Kill me that witch?" she thought.

As clearly as if she knelt at her father's feet, his face floated into her thoughts. She must not give orders that would not be immediately obeyed—or that she could not herself enforce.

She was but queen to a dead *shan-yu*, and she bore no child; the time to obey her would be the time when the Hsiung-nu could determine whether she would have the power with their new ruler that she had enjoyed with the old.

Yet, Strong Tongue tried to poison me. She as much as admitted it to . . . my husband.

No one but Khujanga had seen it, however. And, like it or not, Strong Tongue was the familiar power; she was the tribe's shaman, and they feared her. No, they would not storm her tent and kill her . . . would they?

She had lived long enough among the Hsiung-nu to judge that the attempt was worth trying. Vughturoi, the sweet, treacherous thought crept into her mind, Vughturoi would expect her to defend herself as she had ever done.

"The best man among you," Silver Snow said calmly, "brings me Strong Tongue's head."

It was no man but a boy who rose, his face alight. Ducking an awkward but profound bow at Silver Snow, he seized a spear and raced from the great tent to the place where, Silver Snow knew, Strong Tongue had ordered her own quarters pitched.

She heard his scream in the same moment that a flare of light, like oil poured on a fire at midnight, burst up with a roar and a stench of burning flesh. Two more boys leapt up, rage warring with terror on their faces, but Silver Snow held up her hand.

"No," she whispered. "I will hazard no more of you."

As she had in the Cold Palace, Silver Snow sat and waited as the night wore on, as the drum beats from Strong Tongue's tent grew louder and more insistent. Chanting rose, then subsided, to rise more hoarsely. The Hsiung-nu watched, as motionless as Khujanga, but far less calm.

And Silver Snow knelt there, deprived even of the comfort of Willow's presence. At some time during the night, she had disappeared. At this very moment, was a fox with a limp pushing through the grasses toward the Hsiung-nu prince? Perhaps he might hear it, might reach casually for the spear or the bow of which he had such deadly mastery . . . "No!" Silver Snow wrapped arms about herself and rocked back and forth as if she keened in grief over her husband's body. Sable rose and brought a fur-trimmed cloak. Summer night though it was, Silver Snow was grateful for the cloak's warmth.

She glanced up at the Hsiung-nu woman who had been first among her people to approach Silver Snow with warmth rather than deference and curiosity. Tonight, she might suffer for that loyalty. It all depended on who won a double race: a summons by magic and a mad ride back to the tents of the royal clan. Even though Tadiqan had ridden among the Fu Yu, he might well have been on his way back; and the herds that Vughturoi inspected ranged over vast areas of grassland.

Darkness waned to gray, and all of the fires in the tents died. Gradually, the drumbeats and chants that had risen from Strong Tongue's tent faded into silence. At dawn, Willow returned, walking very slowly as if her lame leg hurt even more than usual. With infinite care, she settled herself behind her mistress. When Silver Snow turned to greet her, she answered only with a sigh and a wan smile of gratitude for a proffered cushion.

Dawn brightened into a clear morning. The sun as it climbed toward zenith shone almost white; the day would be hot. It might be, Silver Snow thought, as she knelt beside the rigid body of her dead lord, that neither prince would arrive in time to view his father's body, which would not keep for long in the heat. Already the sunken features were discoloring; soon the body would swell. Silver Snow sniffed, but could smell nothing beyond ashes, sweat, and tension.

She allowed her furred cloak to slip from her shoulders. Willow, as if grateful for a task that was easy to perform, folded it and laid it aside.

A shadow blocked the sunlight at the entrance to the tent. Slowly, ponderously, Strong Tongue walked through the crowd of staring Hsiung-nu as if they did not exist, stopping only when she stood before the body of the *shan-yu*. A murmuring arose behind her, and the men and women in the tent appeared to divide as long stalks of grass bent in different courses before the high wind that heralds a vicious storm. Already some of the warriors eyed one another speculatively, wondering on whose side they would fight should Tadiqan and Vughturoi come to blows.

Not deigning to look either at her late lord or at Silver Snow, Strong Tongue knelt too. Bound by a common anxiety, they waited. From time to time, water was brought, and they sipped it. Beyond that, there were no white robes, no hired mourners, no elaborate preparations, yet. The warriors gashed their faces, the women waited. The next *shan-yu* would give whatever orders would be needed.

Hoofbeats rang out, and half the people in the tent surged to their feet. Silver Snow balled her hands into fists and drove her nails into her palms. The colors of the rugs and hangings spun and blurred, and the folds and billows of the tent seemed to heave up and down, threatening to send her toppling onto her face. Even Strong Tongue, despite that weathered skin of hers, turned gray with apprehension.

But it was one of the boys who hurled himself from the back of his horse into the tent, where he flung himself down— with superb tact, Silver Snow could not help but observe—at a distance precisely between her and her enemy.

"They come, great ladies!" he gasped, his voice cracking with the attempt to sound like a man, though his weapons and the open cuts on his face were his only signs yet of manhood.

"They, child?" Silver Snow asked.

"Which one comes, boy?" demanded Strong Tongue at the same moment.

"Both princes, mighty queens." The boy glanced from woman to woman, abased himself to both of them indiscriminately, and fled, evidently preferring the threat of actual war to proximity between two silently warring queens.

"I shall greet the new *shan-yu*," declared Strong Tongue, who surged to her feet as if she had not a doubt in the world that Tadiqan her son would arrive first.

How can I bear to watch this race? Silver Snow demanded of herself.

How do I dare not to? She answered herself a moment later, and thought hard of her father's last battle with the Hsiung-nu. She too would face her fate without flinching, even if it was to fling herself upon the mercy of her sharp little blade. She rose, straightened a back that had gone stiff from a night and a day spent watching beside the dead *shan-yu*, and walked outside with conscious grace.

Three riders, not two, raced toward the camp. From the east, rode Tadiqan, bow strung at his back, his usual troop trying desperately to catch up to him. At the sight of her son, Strong Tongue stiffened. Her stern face seemed to catch the light of the sun, and she raised her spirit drum, patched, Silver Snow noted, with a strip of darker hide. Quickly she beat out an insistent, imperious rhythm on the drum, and the pace of Tadiqan's horse quickened. Even from where she stood, Silver Snow could see how low the beast's head drooped. It stumbled, but a fast, brutal move by its rider forced it to continue.

Silver Snow glanced at Willow, who nodded and slipped away. A fox, or a number of foxes might frighten that troop of horsemen—or serve as easy, casual prey, should they be too slow in going to ground. Then she turned to look at the rider from the west. It was Vughturoi; had he been twice the distance away, even then Silver Snow thought that she would have recognized him. He was accompanied by only one rider, who lay, rather than sat, in the saddle, his arms flung about his mount's shaggy neck lest he fall.

"Brother," whispered Sable from where she stood behind Silver Snow.

Vughturoi was lighter than Tadiqan, less of a burden for his horse to bear; and the animal seemed to be fresher. Silver Snow's eyes filled with tears, and she blinked to dispel them. When she opened her eyes again, she saw Tadiqan's horse swerve, then stumble. With superb, brutal skill, the prince controlled it and forced it to a pace that was half gallop, half stagger. Again it swerved, as if to avoid something—a fox, perhaps?—in its path, and again it fell. This time, Tadiqan's skill availed only to let him roll free of the falling horse. He came up running, a sport at which the Hsiung-nu, who were master horsemen, were totally unskilled.

Silver Snow let out a laugh of relief.

"Think you so, *daughter*?" Strong Tongue snapped at her. "My son may be no runner, but he is an archer unmatched among the Hsiung-nu."

Indeed, Tadiqan had strung his bow, was reaching for an arrow; and Silver Snow remembered. Tadiqan had in his quiver some wondrous arrows that shrieked and whistled as they flew. That sound was the command for all of his men to draw and shoot at their master's target. Should he aim at Vughturoi or his horse, the younger prince was doomed.

"Get down!" Silver Snow's control broke, and she screamed that. Now it was Strong Tongue's turn to laugh scornfully, then fall silent as she watched.

A whistle broke that silence, and Silver Snow pressed one hand to her mouth. With the other, she edged her dagger free of its sheath. A cheer rose from Vughturoi's friends in the camp as their prince made his horse curvet sharply, missing the deadly flight of arrows that followed his half-brother's shot. That dodge was a fortunate one, Silver Snow thought. How could he continue to evade arrows as swift and as lethally aimed? He could not, especially not at the pace that he was traveling. He must either dismount or hide; and then Tadiqan would reach the tents first.

Strong Tongue muttered something, and beat a new rhythm on her deadly little drum. The Hsiung-nu gasped in horror and fear, and Silver Snow followed their appalled gazes. A wall of flame, the fear of every grasslander, had sprung up between the camp and Prince Vughturoi. It danced and crackled; about it, the air seemed to be thicker, curdled from the heat of the blaze.

Vughturoi's horse screamed and reared, panicked, as were all of its kind, by its nearness to fire.

"That fire will burn out of control, sweep across the plains, and wipe out the herds. Even the few beasts that will survive will starve," Silver Snow shouted at Strong Tongue. "How can you doom the very people whom you want your son to rule?"

Strong Tongue turned to sneer at Silver Snow without ceasing the deadly, insistent rhythm of drumbeats. "Fool," she said. "That is not real fire, nor will it burn out of my control. It will cease when a living creature touches it. Of course," she added, "that creature will speedily cease to walk among the living; but we cannot be greedy, now, can we?"

Whatever creature touched that blaze would douse it, and Vughturoi rode in the lead. He would touch the flame and die! Silver Snow lifted up her long skirts and prepared to run down the slope toward the fire, but a fox with glossy fur and a slight limp ran between her and her chosen path, then took that path itself.

Willow, get back! At least Silver Snow preserved enough judgment not to shriek that, though, at the time, she thought that a shriek of rage and despair would assuage her better than a silver cup of icy water at high noon.

A deep, man's voice echoed that cry: Basich, from his precarious seat on horseback. Even as he saw his lord gallop closer and closer to what appeared to be a wall of true fire, he flogged his horse into one last burst of energy that outstripped that of Prince Vughturoi's flagging mount and cut across his path. Rather than ride him down, the prince swerved, and Basich drove his horse ever closer and closer toward the wall of fire.

His horse screamed and fought him as they neared the flame. Surely he would not ride the poor beast into the flames, Silver Snow hoped. At the last moment, when it looked as if man and beast would be consumed in the high wall of flames, Basich flung himself from his horse's back into the fire.

He had time to scream once. The fire rose, then burnt down to nothing, leaving not even a path of charred grass to show where it had passed. His horse ran free, in a wide, wild circle across the plain.

Forsaking the stoic silence that was Hsiung-nu custom, Sable let out a wail of grief. Her knees buckled, and she fell.

"Quick, take her away!" commanded Silver Snow and was obeyed quickly, as queens are obeyed. There would be no marriage arranged now between Willow and Basich; no man to provide for a widowed sister's children; and a warrior's children left orphaned. *I shall take them under my protection*, thought Silver Snow, and knew that thought for one of hope.

In the next instant, she shuddered. What if, even now, Tadiqan shot one of those deadly, screaming arrows of his and struck his younger brother in the back? A shriek of greeting, almost indistinguishable from terror, rose, and Vughturoi's own guard rode into sight, chasing after the master who had so far outstripped them. Let Tadiqan fire now, and, if he lived, he would rule only over a clan stripped of its warriors.

He cast his bow down and trudged, head lowered, toward the tents. Twice he almost fell as beasts erupted from hiding in the tall grass to nip at his legs, then flee before he could kick at them or draw weapon.

Up the incline on which the *shan-yu*'s great tent was pitched rode Vughturoi. At the sight of him, Silver Snow's knees threatened to go unstrung, as had poor Sable's, but she forced herself to keep her head high, though her long hair tumbled down her back and had not been combed for a day and a night.

She turned and walked back to her place beside the dead *shan-yu*. Let Vughturoi find her at his father's side, as was fitting: Khujanga had been a great ruler and should not be left to lie unaccompanied. Her lips and hands were shaking, and her breath came too fast. She told herself that what she felt was gratitude at her delivery, either from death at her own hand or from degradation at Tadiqan's more lustful ones.

A murmur of greeting, rather than the usual exuberance of

the Hsiung-nu, and the thunder of hundreds of hoofbeats and footsteps heralded Vughturoi's approach. Covered with dust and travel stains, he walked toward his father's body, drew his knife, and slashed his cheeks in Hsiung-nu grief. Then he prostrated himself before Khujanga one last time.

When he rose, tears had partially washed away the blood that he had shed. Silver Snow had not known that Hsiung-nu could weep. His wearied eyes met Silver Snow's briefly and seemed to warm at the sight of her. Immediately she flushed, then went cold. Once again the rugs and hangings seemed to melt into one another, a too-bright, almost-sickening blur of gaudy hues. She flung out a hand to save herself from falling.

"Tend to your lady," Vughturoi commanded, and Silver Snow felt herself enfolded in a familiar, affectionate embrace: Willow! The maid helped her to rise, and steadied her. Silver Snow wanted only to sleep now, then, perhaps, to wash before she faced what she knew she must now see. Yet clamor outside the tent made her steel herself for what would come next.

"My brother, that laggard, has arrived," Prince Vughturoi, now the *shan-yu*, observed. "Let him and his mother approach."

He turned toward the *shan-yu*'s throne and saw the skull cup resting atop it. "Someone take that thing away and house it safely!" he commanded, and sat down in the seat that was now rightfully his.

When two of his guard hesitated, clearly afraid of what mischief Strong Tongue and her son might yet work, Vughturoi clapped his hands. "Bring them before us!" For the first time he spoke as befitted a ruler, and his warriors hastened to force a path down which Strong Tongue and her son could walk until they faced him.

"Well?" demanded Vughturoi.

Tadiqan flung up his chin, clearly prepared to fight to the death his younger brother's claim upon his father's power, until Strong Tongue held up a hand.

"What is it you would have?" she spoke with her old authority as shaman.

"Obedience," said the *shan-yu*. He pointed to the carpet on which the shaman stood.

Whispers went up, whispers that Silver Snow could hear, urging him to dispatch his brother and his treacherous dam. In that moment, she too was sorely tempted to speak for Strong Tongue's death.

"Let His Sacred Majesty think of how much trouble would be spared," came one whisper, louder than most, from an elder warrior who had long served Khujanga.

"Aye," muttered Vughturoi. "Yet we have no proof, and our brother's warriors are too many to be angered or driven away, lest we lose half of our fighting force."

Again he gestured at the carpets. "Down!" he commanded. "Or our command shall be what it should be, not what it must. To kneel before your *shan-yu* is a small price to pay for your lives!"

Once again Tadiqan made as if to balk. Once he prostrated himself before his brother, the thing was done, inevitable: any rebellion thereafter would be impiety as well as treason. But Strong Tongue's hand on his arm forced him first to kneel, then to go to his belly, just as the shaman did.

"Better by far to kill a snake than warm it at your hearth," murmured Willow. "Come, Elder Sister, and let me care for you."

Abruptly that suggestion sounded like the most wonderful thing that Silver Snow had ever heard. Even as Vughturoi gave orders for the hearthfires to be rekindled and funeral preparations to be put in hand for his father, she and her maid slipped from the great tent to her own place.

She had bathed, eaten sparingly, and waited, Willow attending her, combing the dust and snarls from her hair until it hung loose down her back like floss-silk. Then she had scented Silver Snow as if for her wedding, and wrapped her in delicate silks that were the hues of peach and apricot. The girl had ever been sparing of words, but tonight her mute patience cut Silver Snow as sharply as Vughturoi's blade had slashed his face in mourning. Tactfully she sought some way of drawing confidences from her maid, and found none. Thus, she borrowed a tactic from the Hsiung-nu and spoke plainly.

"Sable grieves," she said flatly. "I thought, earlier today, that the two of you might well have become sisters in truth, that I would have spoken with my lord . . ."

But now they both are dead, the old lord who wed me; the young one who might have welcomed you.

Willow shook her head with weary patience. "It was a dream, no more, like the fumes in a fourth cup of wine, Elder Sister. I allowed myself to dream: no more but that."

"Why should it have been no more?" asked Silver Snow. "And why can it not still be, with ano—"

"Why can it not still be?" cried Willow, interrupting her mistress for the first time in all the years that they had been together. "Can you look at me, look at the leg that would have meant my death had your father not pitied me, and truly ask that?"

Silver Snow shut her eyes, shaking her head in sorrow. "I see only Willow, who is as my sister. And the Hsiung-nu go mounted. There is no lameness when one rides."

"Elder Sister," Willow spoke very softly but with utter sternness. "Do you truly think that I would risk bringing into the world a child as blighted as I myself? Do you truly think I could bear to see such a child cast out to die or used as I was? Being weak, I dreamed for a space; and I have paid. Let be."

Silver Snow reached out, took her maid's hand, and sat thus, silently, as if the two of them scouted by means only of their ears. From time to time she heard a shout of acclaim rise in the great tent. The shouting died away, the feasting with it as the Hsiung-nu sought their own tents, weary after the death-watch and the race of the princes to their father's side. Still she waited, but Vughturoi did not come.

What would she do if he did not come to her? Nothing in her training had equipped her to seek him out boldly in his own quarters, to confront him with the boldness of Hsiung-nu women. No: she was a lady of Ch'in as well as a queen of the Hsiung-nu; as a lady of Ch'in, she would wait to be summoned or to be visited.

The light slanting into her tent waned, and then it was night. The energy that had sustained her began to fade, and she thought of seeking her bed. Stubbornly, however, she waited. After what seemed to be an eternal period of time, she smiled at a sudden remembrance. Perhaps she would not have to wait or seek out her new lord if he hesitated to claim what was his.

"Bring my lute," Silver Snow ordered Willow. Putting aside her own melancholy, Willow rose quickly. Silver Snow smiled at the maid's look of delighted, complicit craft.

How many years ago it seemed that she had mourned in disgrace during her exile to the Cold Palace and had written a song upon leaves that, cast upon the wind, brought her a friend and a new hope. Once again that song must serve. Smiling a little wistfully, Silver Snow plucked the strings of her lute and sang:

> *"How fast the water flows away!*
> *Buried in the women's quarters,*
> *The days pass in idleness.*
> *Red leaf, I order you—*
> *Go find someone*
> *In the world of men."*

Ah! There were the footsteps outside her tent, just as she had heard them almost every night of her long wedding journey to the domain of the Hsiung-nu. This night, however, they did not cease outside her tent, but came boldly into its entrance . . . and waited.

"Lady?" Vughturoi might be *shan-yu* now, but his voice questioned rather than demanded.

Silver Snow walked toward the entrance of the tent.

"This one," she began, "begs the *shan-yu* to enter; His Sacred Majesty has no need to question where he may command."

As Vughturoi entered the tent, she dropped into the prostration that was his due.

"No, lady!" he ordered. "You were queen before ever I was master here. Rise!"

Stubbornly, disobediently, Silver Snow kept her face pressed against the jewel-bright rugs of her domain, gifts from this man's father, until she felt rough hands upon her shoulders, drawing her upright, standing her upon her feet once more.

"May this one offer you wine?" she murmured.

"Look at me, lady," Vughturoi ordered.

Thus commanded, of course, she had no choice but to obey. She looked up, meeting his eyes, and felt that same shock of warmth, almost of homecoming that she had known—and suffered shame therefrom—once or twice before when she looked upon him.

"You," he pointed at Willow. "Out!"

Willow limped out, turning to smile almost impudently at her mistress; and then Silver Snow was quite alone with the prince whom she had summoned to rule over the Hsiung-nu and to be her chosen lord.

"I was riding among our herds," said the *shan-yu*, "when a fox yapped at my horse and would not flee. Such is not the nature of the fox kind. Yet I remembered that such a beast had helped us fight the white tiger, and I turned my path aside to join it. Shortly thereafter, I met Basich . . . my . . . my friend." Vughturoi's voice almost broke.

Before she knew it, Silver Snow held out her hands to him, offering a comfort that she had not realized that even a warrior lord of the Hsiung-nu might need. He dropped his hands from her shoulders to catch hers.

"He told me of my father's death, and that you had . . . you had sent for me. So I came, obedient," he added with a wry grin that made him wince in protest against the pain of his slashed face, "to the queen who brings peace to the Hsiung-nu. Once again you have done so."

"I have done nothing," said Silver Snow, "save my duty, I hope."

He was looking at her, frankly admiring the way that the thin, pale silks clung in this heat to the delicate curves of her body. She shivered, sought for composure, but failed to achieve it. Had she had a heavy overgarment to catch up and throw about herself, even in this heat, she would have done so.

"You are all silence and obedience," blurted the *shan-yu*, "and you look as if one gust of wind would carry you back to the Sky which, surely, must have created someone like you. Yet I have seen you confront an Emperor, rescue a lady, and hunt the white tiger. You do not appear to be strong: you bow; you obey; you bend everywhere . . . and nowhere at all. And you summoned me to your side."

"The people," said Silver Snow. "Your people, who are now mine . . . need a strong ruler."

"Just now, too, you summoned me with your music as if it were a spell. But you would not speak to me before my father's body, before my people. Lady, was there, could there be another reason why you called for me?" His words tripped over one another as if he hoped that her answer might be "yes." His hands tightened, then released, careful of the fragility of the hands within his grasp.

This, Silver Snow knew, was the time for the pretty speeches about spring longings over which the concubines in Ch'ang-an had sighed and giggled. Those speeches seemed to belong to a vanished, long-ago world; she was as incapable of making them as she was of breaking a wild horse. Silently she turned and went to the chest in which, months ago, she had hidden the scent bag that she had worked in silks and fine, soft sable pelts. She walked back over toward Vughturoi, offering him the bag as it rested across her outstretched palms.

He clasped it and the hands that held it in his own scarred

fingers. "Remember, I saw such tokens in Ch'ang-an," he told her.

She cast down her eyes and waited.

"Basich," Vughturoi said suddenly, with what Silver Snow privately thought was supreme irrelevance. "He leaves his sister with no protector, his children and hers with no provider. I shall take Sable into my tents as a lesser wife."

His words, Silver Snow decided, were not irrelevant after all; but they were supremely unwelcome.

She must have grimaced in distaste because laughter rumbled in Vughturoi's voice. "Sable will wait, if she wants a son from me, though. For I shall put no other woman before my queen, who shall ever be my chief wife and bear my eldest son. Do you understand me, lady?"

She nodded, trembling as if with cold, though she felt most wonderfully warmed and comforted. Vughturoi's eager gaze no longer seemed so frightening. Though it held a knowledge she lacked, she knew that that would not be for long.

"Then say it!" he commanded.

Why did he not simply embrace her and have done with it? Silver Snow thought. The answer was not as simple: though his own people's law gave him the right to claim her, he chose to respect her, to wait until she chose to yield. He would not want to wait too long, she sensed. Yet it was hard, hard, to know how to give herself.

For a long moment she stared at Vughturoi. Certainly he was not Han, nor was he simply Hsiung-nu: he was himself. That thought carried her over the moment of her surrender.

Silver Snow smiled. "I think," she spoke carefully, considering every word, "that we have always understood one another reasonably well."

Vughturoi stepped forward and raised a hand to touch her chin, turning her face up to look into it. He was grieved, wearier by far than she, Silver Snow realized suddenly. She could give him the assurance that, clearly, he sought from her, and let him rest in comfort, or she could continue to play the modest, die-away games of the ladies of Ch'ang-an: she, who had forced herself to courage by remembering that she was queen of the Hsiung-nu.

She smiled and saw his grief and confusion turn to a kind of elation. Boldly now, she met his eyes. Where he was concerned, she was done forever with downcast looks. Gladness swept over her and she shivered the way she did when the wind brushed the grasslands, turning the long blades silver in the spring.

"The *shan-yu* Khujanga," she told her new lord, "was more father than mate to me. I shall miss him. But I had no husband, and I had no son. Now, however . . ."

"Now you shall have both," promised Vughturoi, and drew her against him, holding her close. His arms were very strong, yet she knew that if she wished to break away from him, at least for now, he would grant her freedom. For a time, perhaps; but not forever. And it was not her wish to escape his hold, which was not that of a stranger or an outlander. Vughturoi had been her first advocate, the first of the Hsiung-nu to prefer her to any other princess and a caravan of silks and gems. He had been her first friend, her protector on the long, long journey West.

And she had made the scent bag for him. Greatly daring, Silver Snow glanced up. Vughturoi was looking at her again, as he had the night that she had run from the tents, wearing only nightrobes, her hair loose. The silks she wore now felt too hot, yet their caress made her flush and shiver with a kind of secret delight. It was a shared secret, she realized from the glow in Vughturoi's eyes. Because it abashed her to watch him any longer, she let herself lean against the man who claimed her for his wife, listening to the beat of a heart that, unlike the throb of Strong Tongue's drum, did not threaten her but promised instead strength and abiding loyalty for all the days to come . . . days that they would share.

CHAPTER

= 20 =

Surrounded by her ladies and her guards, the queen who brings peace to the Hsiung-nu sat by the *shan-yu's* empty chair and awaited his return. That, thought Silver Snow, was one way of thinking of it. But there was another way, one that she far preferred: exiled far from her home, she had made another home for herself; and now she sat among men and women who had become her friends, awaiting the return of her husband Vughturoi.

Summer had passed too rapidly, like amber beads on a silken strand; she only wished now that she could have preserved them as amber preserves the seed or the insect or the bubble of air trapped within it. Only now were the grasslands turning crimson with the approach of autumn, but that summer, the first of her true marriage, seemed to have assumed a kind of memorability: like the ancient doings of the Emperor or her father's tales. Always before, Silver Snow had felt herself to be like the northland's snows for which she had been named: silent, still, and passive; content to wait, to obey. And above all, to be cold, so very cold that not all of the wine or the furs in the world could warm her into glowing life.

She thought now that she had been a beautiful statue, nothing more, until Vughturoi had set his hand upon her. His touch, his smile, had overpowered that coldness, that mannered shyness. The vital, glowing creature who now awaited her husband's return and whom, daily, she saw in Willow's mirror was as far from the frosts of winter as she could be, though she bore a wintry name. Recently, however, that was not all that she was thought to bear.

Silver Snow smiled gently upon her maid Willow, where she sat beside Sable, plump and sweating in the rich embroideries that befitted even a minor wife of the *shan-yu*. Both women nodded and whispered together, and Willow approached with a fan. Such great friends they were, united first by service to her, then by sorrow, and now by their assurance that their mistress and elder sister bore beneath her heart a child who would unite both of their peoples.

Only today, Willow had cast the yarrow stalks and promised her that the child would be a boy, a son to secure her line, her power over her people and the *shan-yu*, if she needed additional power over him. Silver Snow had never considered what it would be like to know that she carried a child. She had expected to feel fear or wild excitement, not this serene certainty. Who would have thought that one would learn such joy of a husband, let alone such a husband?

Of course, she would have conceived quickly by Vughturoi: how not? Despite how crowded the *shan-yu*'s great tent was, Silver Snow shut her eyes, remembering her husband's quick ardor, his care of her, and his strength. She had spent half of the summer's days, she thought, dazzled by the nights. She could set a proper value on the hushed giggles and whispers of the concubines in the Imperial Court: they were as green rice compared with the harvest, the harvest that she now bore.

As the mother of a son—of a prince—she need never defer to anyone in the grasslands. Except, of course, her lord; and she had learned rapidly that she pleased him best, obeyed him most faithfully, by being herself. Downcast eyes and bows made him irritable, uneasy, eager to leave the constraints of her tent for the free air of the grasslands.

But if she rode out or tended the sick, played her music or

laughed with the bright-eyed Hsiung-nu children, he would come to her side whenever he could. Once again she played and sang almost every night before a *shan-yu*, but this time her songs were happy. Though such speech came hard to him, Vughturoi had made her understand: he did not want a silk-robed puppet but the courageous lady who had worn pearls and kingfisher feathers before the Son of Heaven to accuse a thief, the lady who had fought the white tiger and won him his throne. And, much to her surprise, she had wanted him. It was a mating unlike the marriages that she had seen, in what seemed now to be another life, on her journey to Ch'ang-an, marriages made by ladies who had pitied her and considered themselves people to be envied. She was content. Or she should have been.

I miss my husband, Silver Snow admitted. It was one thing to call him Vughturoi in the dark privacy of the nights, but she blushed to speak it, even in her thoughts, during the daylight. She had had that thought every day since he had ridden out toward the Han fort on the border of the grasslands. He had wanted, he told her, to speak with the garrison's commander—who was actually, Silver Snow had learned from Li Ling, the son of an officer who had served with her father and had survived the long march back after the general had surrendered—about a proposal that his father had dictated to Silver Snow shortly before his death, a renewal of his suggestion that the Hsiung-nu defend all under heaven from Dunhuang east to the Yellow River.

Silver Snow remembered the last, private reply to that proposal that she had received; she thought that she could hear Li Ling's very tones in it: "It is now over a century since the Great Wall was rebuilt by Wu Ti. It is not by any means a mere mud rampart. Up hill and down, it follows the natural configuration of the ground, is honeycombed with secret passages, and bristles with fortified points. Is all this vast labor to be allowed to go to rack and ruin?"

To Khujanga, however, the Son of Heaven had replied courteously enough that the Great Wall had been built to keep the Empire in, not to shut the peoples of the west out. Yet, Khujanga had not let the matter drop; and neither would his son. His sons, Silver Snow recalled. Strangely enough, Tadiqan had liked that proposal.

Perhaps Li Ling's refusal had been inspired. After all, what if Tadiqan had become *shan-yu?* Certainly he had prostrated himself before his younger brother and vowed obedience. Yet he made no secret of his detestation of the Middle Kingdom and his desire to plunder it. And his oath to his brother had not stopped him from maintaining his usual retinue of warriors and a circle of older men who were easily made disgruntled as they suspected that, under Vughturoi's rule, power might pass from them to younger men and to the *shan-yu*'s outland wife, whom, they saw, Vughturoi intended to treat as consort rather than a mark of Ch'in favor and a charming toy.

Despite such malcontents, Vughturoi had also sent out scouts, he had said, to keep an eye on the Fu Yu, who were quiescent, watching him in this first season of his rule. Nor had the heir of the Yueh-chih yet tried to fulfill his vow of having Vughturoi's skull as the bowl of a goblet. Still, that left Silver Snow at least nominally responsible for the camp and herds; just bearing those responsibilities respectably strained every resource of patience, tact, and craft that she had possessed, and a few that she hadn't known herself to own.

One morning, however, she had fainted; and the women of the camp had narrowed eyes (Silver Snow would privately have sworn that their eyes could narrow no more) at her speculatively and had gone into serious conclave with Sable. Thereafter, her lot had been somewhat less difficult, at least with some of them and with their men. Others, however . . . she could lie in an unmarked tomb and those others would still resent her presence in their lands.

No, it was not a good time for Vughturoi to have left, even though he had no choice, or so he told his people. However, there was, Silver Snow knew, another reason why Vughturoi had ridden toward that fortress, a little journey that would last

from full moon to full moon and to the dark of the moon thereafter: to bring back the letters from Li Ling or her father, or
even from the Son of Heaven. She had written them after
Khujanga's death, informing them that she had followed the
custom of the Hsiung-nu and married his successor, praying
their forgiveness for having done so without beseeching their
consent. There had simply been no time for it. Vughturoi had
to claim his father's place, and when he claimed her, she had
had no thought of naysaying him.

I shall have to write them again, she thought. How horrified
the court would be! She thought, however, that Li Ling would
understand. And her father? Well he had known that when
she departed for Ch'ang-an, theirs had been a final parting.
She blinked at the dust motes that danced in the slanting sunbeams and turned the carpets to rubies set in gold and copper
and mused on auspicious names for a first son and prince.

Against a task as important as that, Strong Tongue's hostility seemed no more than heat lightning on the horizon.
Without her son—and, oh, how she could understand Strong
Tongue's instincts to protect her own flesh and blood now—
the shaman seemed shrunken, subdued. At the same time that
her husband had ridden out, Tadiqan had decided to ride off
on the ever-present need to inspect and number the herds. He
had, of course, begged leave of her; but his "begging," as they
both knew, was the merest formality. Silver Snow could not
have stopped him had she wished. She could, however, send
with him men who were loyal to Vughturoi and who would
escort him most vigilantly: and so she did. She hoped that she
had done all aright.

When Vughturoi returned to his tents . . . oh, should she
tell him as soon as he returned, or should she wait until they
were alone? Silver Snow's soft, anticipatory laugh drew a
nostalgic smile from Sable and speculative, hopeful looks from
many of the Hsiung-nu. She met their gazes blandly.

She would order the Yueh-chih skull goblet to be hidden,
she decided; it was not a thing that a mother-to-be needed to
look upon. Perhaps she would tell Strong Tongue to hide

away her spirit drum too, that is, if she could not coax Vughturoi to do so. And, if Tadiqan or Strong Tongue said aught to unsettle her . . . just let them! she thought, smiling. She had come into her power now.

What sounded like thunder at the horizon brought her up from her seat, one hand at the small of her back, the other flashing to her lips. *See what comes,* she mouthed to her women; and Sable, who, by rights, should have had maids of her own to do her bidding, leapt up and ran to the opening of the tent.

"It is our lord!" she cried even as the shrieks and hoofbeats of Hsiung-nu greeting assaulted their ears. Silver Snow flushed and flung out a hand that Willow, greatly daring, leaned forward to take.

"Elder Sister, a bearing woman must not rise so quickly!" she warned. Nevertheless she aided Silver Snow to hasten to the door of the tent.

Dear Willow! If she sorrowed for the loss of Basich and what she might have had with him, no one would have known it from the tenderness with which she guarded Silver Snow from hazard.

"Here, Elder Sister, lean on me," she said, even as Silver Snow laughed and pretended to push her aside. It was not that she was sickly, but that, as queen, she must move with dignity, she informed her maid who managed—just barely—not to give the short, barking laugh that sounded so like a fox.

Like a dance of war, the Hsiung-nu, partnered by their horses, raced into the camp. How fast they rode and how beautifully! Let the people in Ch'ang-an see the Hsiung-nu ride, no matter how ferociously they fought; just let them see that; and they would no longer call their neighbors to the west barbarians, Silver Snow thought.

Vughturoi swung down from his horse, his eyes seeking out Silver Snow and warming with satisfaction at the sight of her: his wife, standing before his tent, helping to ward his people.

She bowed deeply. Then, when no strong hands pressed

her shoulders urging her to rise, she glanced up. Vughturoi was watching her carefully, and in his hand were letters: a bundle of wooden strips from her father, thrifty as ever; two sealed rolls of silk from the court.

The rigid courtesies to which she had been raised forbade her, in this moment, to speak until the *shan-yu* spoke to her; never had she come closer to violating its prohibitions. Then Vughturoi's hands were on her shoulders, and "Wife," his deep voice rumbled in her ears.

"Welcome, oh thrice welcome," she whispered, little more than shaping her lips soundlessly about the words before she bowed again and greeted him properly. He watched her speculatively, as if gauging her strength, then held out the rolls and wooden strips much as he might hand a stripling a sword.

"Be my brave lady," he ordered more brusquely than he had ever spoken with her, and gestured at her to open her letters. Right out here? Before she had attended to the needs of her husband and his warriors or heard their news? Bowing before the tube that held the letter from the Son of Heaven, she broke it open and began to read.

In the next moment, the world slid sideways. Only Willow's strong hands held her up. As they released her, she reeled. The sunlight was too bright; the colors that had gladdened her eyes moments ago now seemed to be garish, alien— and who were all of these strangers? None of them, save Willow, were from the Middle Kingdom. None of them would understand.

Yuan Ti, the Son of Heaven, was dead.

Once again she forced herself to glance down at the silk message with its hateful, fateful ideograms. There they were, unmistakable: the characters of the Son of Heaven's name and the symbol for death. Numb, she read a few more columns. As she expected, she was instructed to follow the customs of the Hsiung-nu and marry Khujanga's successor.

The letter jolted and danced before her. She was moving, she realized; Vughturoi was guiding her to her tent, Willow beside him, scolding to herself like an enraged fox or a woman of the Hsiung-nu at the stupidity that exposed a woman who bore a child to such a shock.

That is not how I wished him to learn of his son, she thought at her maid. Despite the heat, Silver Snow was trembling violently. Gratefully she accepted the robe that Vughturoi draped over her shoulders and watched as Willow brought out cups. What right did her tent have to look so peaceful, so much as it always did when the Son of Heaven was dead? All this time: how could it have happened and she not known? She could all but hear the laments of ritual mourning, the artistic frenzies of grief that some of the court ladies must have performed. Odd: she could not remember their names; and, at one time, the favor of this so-important, glittering creature or that had been so vital to her well-being. She suspected, however, that some members of the court might mourn sincerely. Her letter from Li Ling no doubt contained expressions of a grief as heart-felt as it was proper, and her father, no doubt, would mourn as a general and a man restored to favor should mourn his ruler. She must try to model herself upon their examples.

By now, the Son of Heaven's tomb must be near completion, laden with statues of horses, camels, a court wrought in terra cotta and precious metals with as much skill as the finest artisans of Ch'ang-an could summon. Perhaps he lay already in his coffin of many layers, rich with paint and gems.

Did he wear the suit of jade armor that had been her father's gift? Silver Snow spared a thought for the other suit, the lady's burial armor, that she had brought with her to the grasslands with the treasures that were her dowry and the Son of Heaven's too-tardy love gift. The thought made her blink back tears.

Customs warred in her spinning head. She reached for the jade hilt of her tiny knife and drew it to slash her clothing. She must have white robes; she must fast; she must seclude herself and give Yuan Ti, her adoptive father, proper respects. Already she was behind-hand in proper observances. The knife shook in her hand as she thought on that term. Proper observances . . . seeing his father stretched out dead before him, Vughturoi had gashed his face, mourning with blood, not tears. And now, Silver Snow was a woman of the Hsiung-nu.

Trembling, she raised her knife, and Vughturoi dashed it from her hands.

"You are a bearing woman," he shouted at her, "and I command you that you will not fast, you will not harm yourself! You, Willow! See that you guard your lady, from herself, if need be. If you do not, you shall answer to me."

He had never shouted at her before, never shown her the fury that Ch'in fears attributed to the Hsiung-nu. Though she had been too stunned to weep as she read the news of the Son of Heaven's death, Vughturoi's angry words drew tears from her, and she sank limply onto the nearest pile of cushions, weeping like a weakling of the Inner Courts of the Palace.

Her husband was at her feet in an instant, holding her hands, drawing her wholly into his arms, cajoling her in low, soothing tones *as if she were a mare in foal*, Silver Snow thought with a horrible pang of inappropriate mirth. The Hsiung-nu were gentle with their horses; despite a summer's proof to the contrary, she had not suspected that that gentleness might extend to her, too.

"I did not want you to cut yourself, or to grieve so that you harmed our child," he told her. Had that been fear that she had seen in his eyes, then? Once scolded, the women whom she had known in Ch'ang-an, that garden of Lilacs and Peonies and Peach Blossoms, would have languished and sulked, demanded gifts of jewels or furs before they turned brighter faces to their lords; but that was not Silver Snow's way. It would baffle and frustrate Vughturoi, not control him (which was not her goal) or comfort him.

"I had hoped," she told him, "to have told you about our son at a more auspicious moment."

She would ask Willow to cast the yarrow stalks and, above all else, she would even write to Li Ling and ask him to consult a Taoist sorcerer about this child's future. He must not share the sorrow of the Son of Heaven's death.

"Whatever the moment," Vughturoi said, with a grass-lander's indifference to the propriety of finding auspicious moments, "he is welcome. An heir for the Hsiung-nu!" His exultation all but stirred the silk and felt panels of her tent's walls. Then he dropped his voice again and held her closely.

"Do not weep, lady," he murmured. "Is it that I forbade you to mourn? Mourn you shall, if you must; but you must not hurt yourself or our son. You must eat, and walk in the fresh air; and above all, you must not cut yourself. You are too fair. Leave that for men like me. Promise me that, lady."

She nodded, unable to resist. Docile as a child, she drank what Willow offered her, then let the maid undress her and, though it was but midday, put her to bed. For a time Vughturoi sat beside her, muttering to himself as he tried to puzzle out the characters of the one letter that she had opened.

Yuan Ti was dead. What would that mean for the Empire's peace with the Hsiung-nu? Silver Snow tried hard to recall the face and opinions of the new Son of Heaven, but failed: he was just another of the parade of capped and richly robed officials who replied to his predecessor practically like a chorus of yeasayers. It was only men like Li Ling and her father who had the courage to speak against what an Emperor wished to hear. Her friend, and her father: they too had written letters, letters that, no doubt, contained advice and sage discussions of court intrigue and policy, letters she had left unread too long. She must rouse herself, must read them to her husband. She tried to sit up, to reach for the letters, but "not now," Vughturoi told her, and made her lie down again.

Willow had sedated her, she thought indignantly. She had time for one reproachful glance at her maid before her eyelids closed and the light vanished.

Subtle drumming at the threshold of Silver Snow's awareness brought her out of deep sleep up into darkness. She tried twice to turn over before her body, still in the thrall of whatever herbs with which Willow had dosed her, obeyed. Her hand, languidly outflung, encountered only furs. What time of night was it? She could not expect Vughturoi to spend the entire night at her side, not when he had been absent from the camp for so long; perhaps he rode now or feasted, holding council with the warriors whom he had left to guard his home, trying to reconcile himself with the old men who saw in his elder brother a hope of return to the violent old days before peace with Ch'in.

The drumming grew louder, pulsing sluggishly as the rhythms in her blood pulsed.

"Willow?" Silver Snow called. She knew that she ought to be shocked at how feeble her voice sounded. "Willow?" This time she had more breath behind the call, but it was so plaintive! That was right; if her husband had spent any part of the night with her, Willow would have taken herself elsewhere. Silver Snow was quite alone, except for that treacherous . . . no, the drumming was not treacherous; why had she ever thought so?

It was soothing, pulsing now as her heart beat, allaying the alarm with which she had waked. If she lay back, perhaps its gentle rhythm would ease her back to sleep: this time a healing, true sleep free of Willow's noisome herbs.

But no, the drum cadence picked up, filling Silver Snow with a febrile energy that, somehow, she sensed came from outside herself. She rose, pulling garments loosely about her in the closeness of the tent, and went outside.

It was the dark of the moon. Faint and far distant, as if it lay across the desert, she could see the *shan-yu*'s great tent glowing from the fires that burnt within. The drumbeat picked up once again, inciting Silver Snow to walk. Perhaps she should go there, she thought. Yes, that would be best. Vughturoi would see that she was ill, would summon Sable and Willow to tend her and remain with her—or he would remain with her himself.

So convinced was she that she was hastening, padding on bare feet, toward her husband and his warriors that she was not fully aware that her path led in a different direction altogether—toward the dark bulk of the shaman's tent, from which the drumming came. She gasped as its flap opened, though by no human hand that she could perceive in the darkness, and tried to stop.

Within sat Strong Tongue, stroking her spirit drum by the fire, bending over it with the same concentration that Silver Snow had always brought to her lute. Her head down, a smile of satisfaction glowing red in the light of the small brazier at her feet, the elder woman did not see her prey approach.

No! Silver Snow cried silently. But the same compulsion that forced her to walk toward Strong Tongue's tent, up to that entrance that gaped and glowed in the firelight, had seized her tongue.

Cold washed over her. If Strong Tongue had indeed summoned her for her sorceries, Silver Snow could very easily die tonight; and who would know? She might have waked alone, abandoned by her faithful women, and—hard as it was to believe—staggered from her tent in search of succor, to be found by Strong Tongue. Who knows? The shaman might even pin the blame for her death upon Willow, who had sought only to give Silver Snow privacy. Let her return to her mistress from Sable's tent (or from a night roving free in the deep grasses), and she would face charges of the blackest sorcery.

She owed Willow better than that, poor Willow who had served her all her life, whose cheerfulness had taught her strength in adversity, and whose quiet mourning after the death of Basich had shown her more of dignity than all of the eunuchs in the Son of Heaven's court. If she had learned to love from anyone, it was from Willow.

As if aware that her victim was hesitating, Strong Tongue stepped up the beat on her spirit drum. It grew harder and harder to resist. *Just let it happen*, thought Silver Snow. She remembered how, that night at a riverside camp before she had ever set foot on the grasslands, Jade Butterfly was lured toward the river, how passively she seemed to consent to her own destruction. Strong Tongue would do anything to protect her son, even risk her own life.

I too have a son to protect, thought Silver Snow. The thought swept over her like a torrent of cold water, and she found herself able to swerve one step, then two in the clutter outside the shaman's tent. Ten more steps, though, and she would be inside. Nine . . . eight . . . sudden pain lanced up Silver Snow's bare foot. The pain broke the spell that had forced her to obey Strong Tongue's summons. With a presence of mind that she had only been able to summon once or twice in her life, she bit her lip against a gasp of pain, and turned her stumble into an opportunity to snatch up whatever it was she had trodden on.

She held an arrow, its head curiously fashioned, its fletching bearing the mark characteristic of Tadiqan. Even as she stared at it, the night wind rose, drawing a faint whistling from the arrow's head. So, it was one of the terrible whistling arrows which, when Tadiqan fired, served as a signal for his loyal warriors to loose their own arrows at his chosen target—which could very well be her or her husband or any other enemy that Tadiqan might choose to kill, if he thought himself powerful enough to do so.

He had been quiescent for too long, he and Strong Tongue. Silver Snow knew that she had been right to regret leaving the two of them alive. She would tell Vughturoi . . .

"Come here, girl."

Strong Tongue stood at the opening of her tent, drum under one arm, silver and bone cup outheld in her free hand. Whatever it held steamed slightly, and Silver Snow no more wished to drink it than she wished to enter that tent.

She had no strength to waste on words, on defiance, or on anything but flight. She whirled to flee, but she felt herself moving so slowly. Warmth trickled from her wounded foot. *Had that arrow been poisoned as well as bespelled?*

"Come, girl." Again the command. Strong Tongue advanced, as arrogant in her power, which was strong now at the dark of the moon, as Silver Snow had ever seen her. "Tadiqan will arrive before dawn. Though I cannot understand why he wants you, he may as well have his pleasure of you before I make an end. Come in and await him."

I too have a son's interests to protect! The thought fired Silver

Snow's blood, gave her the strength to stand her ground just a moment longer while her foot bled into the dust. But it was hopeless, she began to fear. Blood had strength; Strong Tongue would know how to use the blood she shed to call her back.

A large fox . . . a vixen . . . snarled and leapt at the shaman, who staggered back, then recovered in time to kick it strongly. It yelped in pain, and its yelp echoed across the camp. Yet once again it charged Strong Tongue, and this time it was not alone. Two other, larger, foxes joined it in harrying the shaman. The vixen broke its hold on her booted ankle long enough to bark sharply.

Silver Snow did not need to see Willow in her human guise to know that the fox's barks had to mean, "Run, Elder Sister." Grabbing up her skirts, she fled from Strong Tongue's tent, whether toward her own or to the great tent did not matter.

Abruptly she blundered into the solid bulk of someone walking rapidly, and she screamed.

"You, lady! I left you sleeping," Vughturoi accused. "And yet, here you wander . . ."

Bright light shocked her and she stiffened in his grip as the light neared her. Vughturoi squinted to make out its bearer, but as the torch dipped with each step, Silver Snow sighed with relief. It was Willow, limping across the trail of bloody footprints that Silver Snow had left, scattering something with her free hand. Her limp was so painful, so pronounced, that Strong Tongue's kick must surely have left her with broken ribs.

"Blood has power," Willow muttered to herself. "I must prevent Strong Tongue from using that power against my sister."

"Get away from her, witch!" snarled Vughturoi. His face twisted in the sudden, inexplicable fury that made the Hsiung-nu feared wherever they rode. He thrust Silver Snow behind him and drew his knife on her maid.

CHAPTER

= 21 =

Appalled by Vughturoi's rage and the gravity of the charge, Willow recoiled. Her lame leg gave out, and she staggered. Heedless of the pain of her gashed foot, Silver Snow flung herself from behind her husband to catch Willow before she fell: mistress and maid clung together, a tiny island of Ch'in in a sea of grass, eyes wide with shock, pain, and fear.

Vughturoi leaned forward and seized the torch from Willow before it fell from her weakened grasp; there had been no rain for many days, and all of the Hsiung-nu feared fire on the grassland. The flame cast a demon's mask of light and shadow on his harsh features, making him appear doubly fearsome.

What was the punishment for sorcery? One thing the Hsiung-nu had in common with those of Ch'in: a hatred of magic used for their despite. And another: both people had developed highly inventive and painful methods of punishment.

Eyes wild, Willow stared at Silver Snow. Then, even as the maid leaned upon her, she shook her head slightly, as if enjoining silence upon her.

What manner of woman are you, Silver Snow? she demanded of herself. *For all these years, Willow has guarded you, tended you, loved you; and will you abandon her because your new lord calls her a witch?*

Had she boasted to herself just that noon that she had found happiness? What good was it if it came at the price of betraying an old and dear companion's trust?

"You accuse the wrong woman, *husband*." Silver Snow's voice was as sharp as the arrow on which she had stepped. "Bring charges of sorcery against Strong Tongue, if you dare. *She* is the one who bespelled me when I was weak and ill."

"I drugged you," Willow said faintly.

"You gave me herbs to make me sleep—and not for the first time," Silver Snow waved that objection aside. Fury as hot as her husband's flooded her, burning away the cold of her earlier ensorcellment. Even the pain in her foot seemed to have receded. "You are blind, my husband, blind to nourish vipers in your camp yet threaten my oldest friend!"

"Do you deny that she has powers denied to ordinary men or women?"

She had only to say "yes" and be safe, a gentle, cherished creature too innocent to sense the presence of magic in her own household. Yet, she had been asked to repudiate Willow before, and had never done so—and she remembered her father, surrendering to this man's father to preserve the lives of his soldiers.

Her father's surrender had been right and proper; hers would be the blackest treason.

"Nothing Willow does is a secret to me," she snapped. "Who aided me with that foolish girl at the riverbank? And who do you think helped us—*us*, husband—fight the white tiger? I tell you, if you send her away, if you punish her, you must also punish me, the mother of your only heir."

Because Vughturoi had claimed to despise the silent, passive obedience of Han ladies, Silver Snow had shown spirit before. Still, what was that but a form of obedience, of doing his will? For the first time, she sought to oppose him to uphold . . . *not my will, but what is right*, she thought firmly. *This*, not cringing and manipulative trickery, was the obedience and service that wife owed husband, or subject owed ruler: to uphold what was right even in the face of anger in order to protect the best interests of the one who must be served.

"Test me," cried Willow. "Test me to the death. I shall die vowing that I have done nothing, ever, in all my years of service to harm my elder sister!" Her voice was thick with tears and anger, and she spoke directly to the *shan-yu* as might a shaman or a prisoner who had nothing to lose.

Vughturoi watched his angry lady as she eased Willow to the ground, as grateful for its support as her maid. She hated herself for the way the hot, ready tears ran down her face, though these were tears of rage, not of weakness.

"Lady," he spoke softly, but in that moment, his voice was that of the *shan-yu*, not the indulgent lord, "your word is your bond and an honor to our tents, but I must have proof before I move against a shaman and a prince."

"Then take this!" Silver Snow demanded, and thrust the whistling arrow at Vughturoi. "Look at this arrow and tell me that my Willow keeps such for her bow—or that she uses a bow at all!"

"She need not," Vughturoi said. "Not when she is mistress of herbs, spells, yes, and shape-change too."

He gestured both women to rise. Unsteadily, they obeyed.

"Hold this," he ordered Willow, and thrust the torch back at her.

Silver Snow gasped, warmth flowing back into her hands and feet, despite a loss of blood that was turning her giddy.

"One of those vile whistling arrows that Tadiqan has trained his men to obey, like beasts to a command," Vughturoi muttered. "Lady, where got you this?"

"I stepped on it," Silver Snow told him. "Outside Strong Tongue's tent as she stood watching. The pain broke the demon's hold that she had on me, and I could flee."

The night sky and the tents were tilting slightly. She put out a hand and found it enfolded in a familiar grip.

"Then that is the only time that such an arrow has done me service." Again, Silver Snow felt herself falling.

"You cannot even stand!" Vughturoi's voice trailed away into words that Silver Snow was certain must be curses.

"You," he ordered Willow. "Take my little queen back to her tent and tend her well. Check that wound for poison!" Already he was turning to go back to the great tent, his stride long and decisive for a man who had spent most of his life in the saddle. "Yes, and there is this, too. Know that I accused you wrongly and that I will make it up to you."

Silver Snow looked up into Willow's face, which mirrored her own amazement. With just those few words, Vughturoi had accused, tried, and acquitted the maid, and now he thought to make amends. She bit her lip against laughter and saw Willow shake her head. Not for the first time, however, the maid was quicker than she herself.

"Favorite of heaven!" she cried at the *shan-yu*'s retreating back.

Vughturoi spun round, surprised at the tone of command in Willow's voice. She held up the torch to illumine the blood-splotched path of Silver Snow's flight.

"Most noble *shan-yu*." Now that Willow had his attention, she spoke in a less imperious voice. "As the most sacred under heaven doubtless knows, blood holds great power; and that is the blood of your lady and the mother of your son. Grant that I protect her against . . . someone using that power to her despite."

Vughturoi nodded. "Sable!" he called the name of his minor wife, then shouted for his warriors.

"When Sable comes," he told Silver Snow, "let her take you back. You have done enough for tonight. And you—" he spoke directly, "work what magics you deem fit."

"What will you do?" Silver Snow called after him.

Vughturoi shook his head. "What I should have done before, but I feared to shatter the unity of the clan. Now I realize that that unity was simply paint on . . . on wood that has rotted," he sought after and found an image from his days in Ch'ang-an. "Thus, now I shall bring fire to it—if I can. Give me your good wishes, lady, and I shall be the stronger."

Again, the remnant of the courtly speech that he had learned in the Middle Kingdom.

"You have always had that." Silver Snow smiled at him. "As well you know."

Willow held up a free hand, gestured in a sign of blessing that Silver Snow had never seen. To her surprise, Vughturoi nodded thanks. "Shaman," he said, according her Strong Tongue's title.

Willow's magics known now, she did not abase herself before the *shan-yu* any more than Strong Tongue had ordinarily done in the days of her favor. Days which, apparently, were to be ended at this very moment.

Vughturoi glanced down at his hand, which still held Tadiqan's arrow. With an exclamation of loathing, he flung it from him.

Silver Snow shook her head, then regretted both the gesture and her lord's rashness. "Fetch me that," she asked Willow in a voice that was growing hoarse and feeble now. "He may need it for proof. I shall keep it safely hidden among my own arrows."

She shut her eyes wearily and opened them only as Sable cried out in dismay and knelt at her side. All around them now were angry men, stamping and muttering in response to Vughturoi's words. Some held torches, which gleamed on their weapons and their harness in the darkness and streamed out almost horizontally after the men who ran toward their horses or those who hastened toward Strong Tongue's dwelling. From time to time, flickers shed light on the bronze hair and stooped back of Willow as she bent to scoop earth over Silver Snow's bloodstained footprints.

Then Sable was easing her onto her feet and back toward her own tent. Weakened by loss of blood and her own passions, Silver Snow let her awareness drift. How strange, she thought, to find oneself in the midst of what anyone in the Middle Kingdom would have called savages, to know oneself the woman of the chief among them, and to feel more safe and more alive than she had ever hoped to feel.

"I must write to . . ." she murmured.

"Elder Sister?" Sable asked, easing Silver Snow down onto the furs of her bedding. "This will hurt," she warned, pouring wine upon Silver Snow's slashed foot.

It was the worst pain that she had ever felt in her life, but she bit her lips against it. Childbirth, when it came, would be worse; and she must not disgrace herself and her husband.

"Sleep now," Sable urged her after she bandaged the cleansed wound.

Silver Snow shook her head. "I am queen," she said. "He will need me with him. Help me up and robe me as a queen."

The warriors were shouting outside. Silver Snow could feel the beat of many hoofs as horsemen left camp. She nodded. Had she been the ruler, she would have sent her most trusted officers to apprehend Tadiqan.

When Sable offered her a choice of robes, she waved both away. "Before I dress, fetch me silk, brush, and ink," she told her. "No, I am not feverish, but I have thought of a way to help our lord, a way that he himself would not lower himself to take. And find me a man who will bear a message to the garrison."

Lowering himself was what a Hsiung-nu might call it, but Silver Snow, before she did aught else, would write to the garrison commander whose father had served her own and beg him to send troops out on patrol. If they looked like allies massing against rebellious Hsiung-nu, so much the better. Vughturoi would never ask for help where he had meant to bestow it, but she was determined, all the same, that he should benefit from it.

Sable's face, already dark with concern for Silver Snow (who had to be mad, she clearly thought, if, at this moment, she called for writing material), went even more somber. Had her brother lived, he would have been the queen's chosen messenger. Still, there was no time to regret; and it was not the way of the Hsiung-nu.

Silver Snow's hand shook as she picked up the brush. *Did you shake so when you fought the bandits or the white tiger, girl?* she

asked herself. *And is a brush not a weapon, just like bow or blade?*
You are a general's daughter and a warrior's wife. Write, then; and
no more of this frailty!

Despite Silver Snow's impatience, the moon had grown to
a faint, fragile crescent in the sky before Sable, Silver Snow's
thrice-vigilant guard, would permit her to try to rise. Before
she actually was able to walk, however, the moon had grown
more plump, and now assumed the shape of a slice of tempt-
ing, pale melon.

Shaking off Sable's offer of a supporting arm, Silver Snow
leaned on her bow as, robed as befitted a queen, she limped
out of her tent. She met Willow coming toward her and
greeted her warmly. She had not seen the maid much in the
days since her injury. Lacking the services of Strong Tongue,
Vughturoi had pressed Willow into use as a seeress and, incidentally, as a guard for the shaman whom she was replacing.

The two women fell into step and walked haltingly toward
the *shan-yu's* tent. *Why, our gaits match*, thought Silver Snow.
Yet Willow walked without a crutch; while her foot ached
each time she set it to earth.

"It will mend, Elder Sister," Willow, who knew her mind
far too well to need to ask questions, told her. "Soon you will
walk without pain and without a limp. I promise you, you will
chase a little Hsiung-nu prince and not even grow short of
breath."

"How fares my lord today?" Silver Snow asked Willow.

The maid raised level brows in a surprise that she intended
to be humorous. "Does he not tell you?"

Silver Snow shook her head. "He has said very little, preferring—or so he told me—to rest and for me to rest."

What Silver Snow knew and would not tell Willow was
Vughturoi's reaction to her letter to the commander of the
Ch'in garrison. "Once again, lady, you dare what I must not
do! Though I may not ask for help, and do not need it, I shall
be glad to see a troop of Ch'in soldiers, provided they speedily
return to their own place."

At that point, Silver Snow understood that she had interfered as much as she dared and turned her efforts to easing the *shan-yu*'s concerns. That he had been proven wrong had been a blow to his confidence; among the Hsiung-nu, such a blow could turn into a death blow. None of that, however, was something that she could tell Willow.

Perhaps, as a shaman, she sensed it already and, in her own loving way, took steps to heal him too.

Limping in step with her maid, Silver Snow entered the *shan-yu*'s great tent. Heat, noise, colors, and the scent of mare's milk and seething meat struck her like a blow, and she stepped back involuntarily, just as she had the first time she had met Khujanga. Her healing foot came down on a pebble, and she suppressed a desire to flinch or cry out.

She had her reward in the next moment, as Vughturoi's eyes lit at the sight of her, and he gestured for her to approach. He could not seat her in his own place nor rise for her; nor did she expect such immoderate attentions. Still, he saw that she sat beside him, that she was well and speedily served, and that the messengers, both of Vughturoi's own following and from other clans, who rode in and prostrated themselves before him paid her proper homage, too. Just as important, he insisted that the men from the other clans, when they hesitated to disclose their information before a woman of the Han, speak before her.

She sat quietly, eyes downcast in the assumption of modesty that gave her time to deliberate. So. Tadiqan's friends among the Fu Yu had ambushed his guards and allowed him to ride free! In that case, he must be on his way back to the people whom he hoped to make his own.

Hoofbeats rose almost to a frenzy outside the tent, and a horse screamed, then grunted in exhaustion. Vughturoi's guards leapt to watchfulness, weapons drawn, as a single rider staggered in. He was coated with yellow and black dust, and his eyes were red from sleeplessness. For the first time in her time among the Hsiung-nu, Silver Snow saw a man who looked like the picture that fear and ignorance had painted of her adopted people. Yet this man was perhaps the most trusted messenger that Vughturoi had with Basich gone.

He flung himself down, more a collapse than a prostration, before the *shan-yu*, and gasped out news of a column advancing westward from the Ch'in garrison.

"What of the Fu Yu?" demanded Vughturoi. His hand grasped the shaft of a spear and suddenly tensed.

Seeing that, the man went utterly still, and Silver Snow reminded herself of a story of the pale barbarians of the Hu, who dwelt so far to the west. Their ruler, it was said, would execute the bearer of bad news rather than reward him as a source of intelligence.

"It does not matter," Vughturoi mused to those advisors who sat closest to him, "what the Yueh-chih pretender wants. Tadiqan wants this place, these tents; he will not destroy what he seeks to rule. Let us confront them all, however, with what they regard most highly."

He gestured at a servant. "Bring in my father's trophy, the skull of the Yueh-chih's chieftain." Then he turned to his warriors. "Three of you, fetch me Strong Tongue."

Warriors as they were, fearless as they were reputed to be, the men looked uneasy. None of them wanted to confront the imprisoned shaman, the mother of a traitor-prince. Vughturoi had not gained the loyalty of his men by ignoring such signals. He nodded, paused, and, finally, looked down from his cushions at Willow where she knelt slightly behind her mistress. "The tribe's new wise woman shall accompany you—if she will. See that Strong Tongue has what she needs to make a journey."

So it would be exile? thought Silver Snow. Unwise, unwise, to leave the likes of Strong Tongue and her son alive; yet it made sense. Vughturoi, too, feared to slay a shaman.

Strong Tongue glowered as she walked before her guard into the great tent. She folded her arms over her broad bosom and almost contrived to make them appear to be a guard of honor for her, in her robes of hides and rare snakeskins and bits of glinting crystal. By contrast, Willow appeared to be insignificant; but in her hands lay Strong Tongue's spirit drum. Most noticeable about Strong Tongue, however, was that a strip of hide had been tied over her mouth so that she could not use what gave her her name to curse the guards.

"Well done," approved Vughturoi quietly. At a subtle hand gesture, Willow took up a place nearer to him than to Strong Tongue, who flicked one contemptuous gaze about the great tent.

"We shall await your son," Vughturoi told her. "I have not forgotten, however, that he is my father's son as well as your own. Thus, when he rides in, since his oath has proved to be worthless, he shall have two choices: death in battle or exile from the clan he has betrayed. Your choice shall be tied to his."

Strong Tongue's jaws worked and the veins in her temples bulged as she fought the gag.

"Restrain her!" snapped Vughturoi, and her unfortunate watchmen obeyed.

More hoofbeats and a cry from one of the outlying guards told those in the great tent that a troop of Hsiung-nu approached: Tadiqan's men (those whom he had not slain for opposing him), Vughturoi's own guards, who had been sent to fetch him, and even a few of the Yueh-chih.

"I will meet them from horseback," said the *shan-yu*. "Bid the warriors be ready."

Painstakingly Silver Snow levered herself up. How she hated this accursed injury, which made her body a traitor to her will!

"You shall not ride, lady." Vughturoi paused by Silver Snow and gently assisted her to her feet. "This is not a hunt that we await." His eyes turned speculative, and Silver Snow held her breath.

"Do not send me away," she pleaded. "What refuge for me can there be on the grasslands? I am safest with you."

Her husband nodded and, though he was tense before what might turn into a battle, he smiled at her.

Indeed, Silver Snow thought, as she hobbled, leaning on her bow, after the men, there was no refuge for her. More than any other place, this was the death country of which Sun Tzu had written. Yet, for women, all battles were death country, not the games of land and honor that many men thought them. She hazarded a glance at Strong Tongue, who walked with vast disdain among her guards, who had but moderate success in slowing their pace to accommodate Willow. Her limp made her as out of place in that band as Silver Snow herself; but her pale, set face and flaming eyes told her mistress that Willow, for one, was done with hiding, done with meekness. Like a fox whose lair and kits had been menaced, she was enraged, and her rage was all the more lasting for its very quietness. In her hands she still bore Strong Tongue's drum. And that too was proper; whoever had been sacrificed to craft that drum must also be a witness here.

None of the women had illusions that this would be a peaceful meeting. It was only the men who hoped. The women tried to prepare against catastrophe. Many would ride behind Silver Snow, armed with bows or the deadly lances of the Hsiung-nu. The eldest of the Hsiung-nu children would be with them.

"Wait, oh wait!" Silver Snow whispered to Sable. On an impulse that she could not explain, she snatched up the skull cup that she so hated, shrouding it in a square of silk that she pulled from her voluminous sleeve. Then she hastened to join the other women.

Sable it was who brought up Silver Snow's horse; no warrior could be spared. She mounted with relief. On horseback, she was not lame. With a nod of satisfaction, she checked her bowstring, her supply of arrows, and the knife that she kept as a final weapon.

Slowly, without the usual fanfare of shrieks and spectacular riding, the mounted Hsiung-nu warriors assembled outside the camp and waited. Overhead, the sun climbed higher in the sky, straining toward zenith. The wind, as it blew across the drying grasses, tinged now with the colors of autumn, made the land appear to ripple. Silver Snow hoped that it would not run with blood before sundown.

"Sound the drum!" Vughturoi cried.

To Silver Snow's shock, he spoke to Willow. Transformed in that moment from waiting woman or wisewoman to warrior, she struck the spirit drum, and the air seemed to shiver with the drumbeat. That was well, too; the man or boy whom Strong Tongue had slain should have his share of the judgment that Vughturoi hoped to make today. For the first time that Silver Snow had ever heard it, there was no evil in the drumbeat as it summoned the clan's enemies.

As if it indeed had caused them to appear, Tadiqan and his men rode toward the camp slowly. They too rode silently, a menace whose very quietness made it all the more purposeful. Some were familiar to her; she recognized many faces and horses. Others, though, wore the trappings and arms of the Fu Yu or even the Yueh-chih, chief among them a young man whose eyes immediately sought out Vughturoi. Her glance fell at the wrapped bunch she bore on her saddle. She had been right; like the drum, that cup, which had been the source of such pain and such conflict, must be present.

So many opposed Vughturoi! Dismay stabbed at Silver Snow almost as sharply as the arrow on which she had stepped, but she suppressed it, lest her son absorb her fear before his birth.

Vughturoi drew a deep breath. Then his voice rang out over the grasslands.

"Let Tadiqan, who was once my brother, ride forth."

CHAPTER

= 22 =

The discipline of the Hsiung-nu held true, and the lines of horsemen stayed where they were. With a contempt that showed in every leisurely movement of his body, Tadiqan edged his horse closer. So, Silver Snow noted, did the Yueh-chih's lord. Vughturoi rode out to meet them.

"Brother," Tadiqan spoke, without the decency of allowing the *shan-yu* whom he betrayed to speak first. He might as well have spat. One of Vughturoi's men shouted in outrage, but Vughturoi held up his hand for silence.

"You profane the name," Vughturoi told him, "and your oath as well. When I was raised to my father's seat, you bowed yourself before me. Is this how you serve the clan?"

"Yes!" screamed Tadiqan, his face beginning to go crimson with one of his rages. "You will make us into mincing copies of those half men of Ch'in, sell us into slavery for more silks and gems. That whey-faced girl who whispers by night of the splendors of her home will betray us all. Put her aside and ride free! Or, by all that is under heaven, step aside and let a *man* lead!"

"A man?" Vughturoi asked, his own voice rising with a dangerous anger. "A man who hides behind his mother and wars on ladies? I call such a one not *man* but boy and traitor. And to that one, I give a choice. Exile or, here and now, before our men, a final submission. And if you betray that, know that my vengeance may not be swift, but it will be painful and utterly sure."

This time, Tadiqan did spit. "I shall have your place, and my kinsman of the Yueh-chih shall have your head!"

"There is no dealing with a madman," Vughturoi observed. "We shall speak when you are sane once more. You are worse than the people whom you claim to hate." Contemptuously he turned his back on the traitor, and rode toward his own line.

Silver Snow drew a deep breath, fully expecting to see a war begin. Stunned by the audacity of the *shan-yu* in turning his back upon an enemy known to be as deadly as he was treacherous, his men and those of the other side held their places.

Then Tadiqan's hands flashed to his bow, nocking arrow and drawing with the terrible grace that made the Hsiung-nu feared throughout the world. Before she could control herself, Silver Snow screamed, and the first arrow went awry.

Time seemed to slow then. It seemed that Silver Snow sat her horse amid a field of statues in which only three people moved: Tadiqan, Vughturoi, and herself. Vughturoi, who took such care of his mounts, turned his with such speed that it screamed and reared. For that moment, he was so occupied in controlling it that he had no chance to draw weapon.

He could be killed before he could defend himself!

That shall not be! Silver Snow vowed. Though she was no warrior, she was a huntress of no mean prowess. Only it had been so long since she had ridden out with her bow! That made no difference. Even as she lamented her lack of practice, she seized an arrow without looking at it, nocked, and shot.

A terrible whistling shrieked out and the arrow flew—not a deadly shot to throat or belly—but pinning Tadiqan's arm. Silver Snow's eyes widened. By some fortunate chance, she had used the single whistling arrow that she had preserved! Tadiqan screamed, not in pain, but in protest and dreadful fear as, from behind him, that whistling found an answer from the men whom he had trained to shoot upon hearing it.

A hundred shafts whined out in deadly obedience that hurled Tadiqan from his saddle and toppled his horse. Arrows pierced man and horse so many times that some shafts had broken before they could sink into flesh. Blood seeped out from between the shafts and puddled in the trampled grass.

Madly daring, Silver Snow forced her horse forward. "You sought a cup made of a human skull!" her voice rose shrill above the tumult of man and beast as she confronted the Yueh-chih. "Then take this!"

She pulled the cup from its silk wrappings and showed it to the man who had sworn vengeance because that cup existed at all. "As a loyal son," she told him, "take that and bury it after the custom of your kind." She replaced it in its shroud and held it out, offering it to his suddenly reverent hands.

"You do not need another such cup," she added quietly. Her eyes pleaded with him to agree with her even as she hoped that Vughturoi would not race forward and slay him to protect her.

"No," he muttered, turning the wrapped bundle over and over in his hands. "We do not, now that we have my father's honor back. Lady, I have heard of you. They hail you as the queen who brings peace to the Hsiung-nu; and now I see that it is true. I will do homage to *you*," he said, and dismounted.

Even as Vughturoi rode up, his eyes distended, his horse lathered, Tadiqan's former ally went to his knees, then to his belly. Quick to seize the opportunity, Vughturoi beckoned his own men forward to encircle the others.

From behind his own ranks, however, rose a tumult of horses, shrill screams, and finally the deep-throated death shriek of a warrior.

Silver Snow dared to glance behind her.

"It is Strong Tongue!" cried Sable. "Somehow she freed her hands, slew one of her guards, and seized her drum!"

Silver Snow had heard that great grief, or rage, or fear

could make people inhumanly strong. Thus it was with Strong Tongue, who now strode forward, beating the spirit drum to a rhythm more savage and more compelling than any she had ever heard.

Faced with a shaman mad with grief and rage, even the bravest among the Hsiung-nu blanched, and many on both sides hurled themselves from their horses, to cower with their heads to the ground.

"I have it!" screamed the deposed shaman. "And soon I shall have vengeance on you all for my son, I and my demons!"

"Mad," gasped Willow from where she sprawled on the ground. Silver Snow could see white around her eyes, which glared with the terror of madness that haunted human and beast alike.

A howling wind blew up about Strong Tongue. Even as a guard tried to pierce it with his spear, it seized him and tossed him high and far. They could hear bones shattering as he landed. Still the wind intensified until it drowned out all other sounds. Mouths worked on prayers or shouts; horses tossed their heads, whinnying in barely suppressed panic; and all anyone could hear was the whining snarl of the wind, a miniature version of the *kuraburan*, or goblin storms, of the deep desert, a thousand-thousandfold worse than Tadiqan's whistling arrows . . . until the first of the demons laughed.

Shapes worse than any nightmare out of Taoist magical texts half materialized within the whirling vortex of wind, grit, and sand. They danced and gibbered and held out grasping claws. More and more fiercely Strong Tongue beat upon the spirit drum until Silver Snow thought surely that it would shatter, loosing the demons forever upon an unsuspecting world.

"This for my son," she shouted. That much Silver Snow could hear over the roaring of the wind and the giggling of the demons as they headed toward her.

Already she could feel the wind's hot breath. There was no place, she knew, to flee.

"No!" A wail of rejection pierced the sounds of the black storm as Willow forced herself to her feet. Her lame leg buckled, but she caught herself by staggering sideways and steadying herself against a horse.

"Elder Sister, Elder Sister!" she cried and hurled herself, not at Strong Tongue but between Silver Snow and the storm. Her hands fumbled in her bosom and produced her greatest treasure, the silver mirror incised with magical symbols that only she could read. It looked pathetically small, no larger than the disk of the indifferent sun now high overhead, but it flashed with light and in it was reflected, in miniature, all the fury of the storm and, at its heart, Strong Tongue, who summoned it.

The storm seemed to shrink, as if somehow the mirror controlled it. Willow swayed on her feet like the tree for which she had been named. Her head dropped, her whole body sagged, but she held up her hands strongly as though she held a shield against the swordstrokes of a near-invincible opponent.

Slowly the storm reversed the direction around which it spun on its axis. Even more slowly it turned toward Strong Tongue, to engulf her who had summoned it in the first place. Strong Tongue shook her head in rejection and pounded her spirit drum, and the storm edged back toward Willow.

The maid trembled, but forced herself to limp forward, first one step, then another, always holding the mirror between the demon storm and herself, as she stood before her beloved mistress.

"No, Willow," gasped Silver Snow, but the maid shook her head once frantically, rejecting as impossible any help that her mistress or some warrior might offer. Silver Snow herself considered drawing bow and firing into that storm; but who could tell what those winds would do to an arrow? They might send it anywhere, including back upon the archer.

That was what Willow sought to do: deflect the storm upon its sender. Just as clearly, Strong Tongue sought to overpower her enemy and overwhelm first Silver Snow, then the camp. Drum and mirror contended, the storm between them.

And then, as if it had waited all these years for the most auspicious moment in which to turn upon its mistress, the yellowed skin of the drumhead tore, and the wind rushed free, overwhelming Strong Tongue's screams. Even now, they were screams of rage, not fear.

Only an instant later, Willow's mirror broke into two pieces. Strong Tongue fell, lashed by the gale she had summoned; but the maid fell too, a slender tree exposed to a storm too strong for it.

A warrior leapt to Strong Tongue's side, his spear poised for a stabbing thrust at her throat.

"Do not slay her!" Vughturoi shouted, his voice hoarse.

What kind of strength would allow a woman to survive that storm? More, Silver Snow feared, than poor Willow possessed. Silver Snow slid from her saddle, ignoring the pain of her foot to run toward Willow, who lay motionless upon the ground. She arrived just as Sable did, but when the Hsiung-nu woman would have sheltered her, Silver Snow pushed forward.

"Little sister?" she asked in a tiny voice.

Strong Tongue had weathered the storm. Was it asking too much for Willow, whose only thought was to protect, to help, to serve, to have survived it too? After all, lame she might be in human guise, but she had all of the vitality of the fox kind, too. She had taken the entire brunt of the storm upon herself to deflect it; and in doing so, had saved countless lives.

Tenderly Silver Snow turned her maid over. Delicately she brushed dust and grass away from the pale, still face. Willow's lips were blue, and her chest did not seem to rise and fall, even faintly. A mirror . . . where was a mirror? If mist formed on it, then the girl breathed, lived, and might be healed. Never taking her eyes from Willow, Silver Snow scrabbled with one hand in the grass. When a sharp edge nicked her finger, triumphantly she brought forth one of the pieces of Willow's mirror, broken by some fate in the shape of a half-circle that bore a darker splotch at its center. Sable brought up the other half.

Yang and Yin. Neither, when held to Willow's lips, showed any trace of mist. And then both shards of mirror dissolved.

Her own lips trembling, Silver Snow glanced over at Sable, who shook her head and began to straighten Willow's garments, pulling them down decorously to cover her legs, the straight one and the lame. Even as she watched, whatever knot of muscle and sinew had shortened Willow's bad leg seemed to untwist: lame in life, Willow lay whole and straight in death.

That sight broke Silver Snow's fragile grip on self-control. She laid her head on Willow's stilled bosom and wept as a mother would mourn for the death of her first-born.

Vughturoi knelt at her side. "She said that she would endure testing unto death," he said. "I had no idea of subjecting her to such an ordeal, no thought but that she would prove as true as she has." She felt a light touch on her hair, and looked up in time to see Vughturoi rise.

"Take that witch"—he pointed at Strong Tongue's unconscious body, and his voice was chill with loathing—"and bind her. Bind her well, gag her, and guard her until a wild horse can be brought."

In silence, Vughturoi waited while he was obeyed. "Now, tie her to its back."

By this time, Strong Tongue had recovered consciousness, but that terrible vitality of hers showed only in the fires of her eyes.

"I cannot punish you as you deserve," Vughturoi told her. "And being what you are, a wife of my father and, once, before you turned to evil, a mouthpiece for the spirits, I think that I dare not punish you at all. So I shall send you hence, and whatever spirits find you may do with you as they will. *Hei-yahhh!*" he cried, and slapped the horse's hindquarters.

Maddened by the unfamiliar feeling of a burden lashed to its back, the horse reared, plunged, and dashed away.

Faintly Silver Snow heard Vughturoi inviting the Fu Yu and the Yueh-chih—those who had not fled, much to the mirth of their fellows—to dismount and share his hospitality.

She knew that she should rise, should greet them properly, as befitted a queen. She also knew that she had neither strength nor heart to do so, now that Willow was dead.

She shut her eyes and wished that the darkness would overpower her. To her astonishment, warm hands lifted her and held her.

"I cannot have you grieving thus," her husband told her. "What would she say if she saw you?"

Silver Snow gulped down a sob. "She would scold me for endangering my baby, and she would dose . . . dose me with dreadful-tasting herbs."

"Then listen to her memory," Vughturoi ordered. "I . . . we . . . owe her everything. What would you have us do? Just say the word, and we shall give her a funeral finer than any that the grasslands have known before."

Sable gasped. "Oh, but look!"

Two large foxes, totally against the nature of their breed, which hid from humankind whenever possible, emerged from the cover of the long grass and crouched, belly-down, beside Willow's body, nuzzling and prodding it. When Willow did not respond, they yapped shrilly, as if in lamentation, and disappeared once more.

Sorrowfully Silver Snow watched them vanish. "A funeral finer than any that the grasslands have known before?" she repeated her husband's words as a question. "Say, rather, the funeral of a princess. May I ask . . . ?"

"Anything," said Vughturoi.

"Then let my Willow be buried on the border between Ch'in and the lands of the Hsiung-nu, somewhere near green trees and flowing water. Let a mound be heaped up over her, a mound that shall ever be green, even in the depths of winter. No hunter shall come to that place, which shall be as a sanctuary for all living creatures, to honor a maid who was true to Han and Hsiung-nu, to the human and the fox kind."

"Let your women prepare her for burial, and it shall be done," said Vughturoi. "We shall ride before winter. Perhaps some among the garrison will ride with us. Your Willow will rest warm before the snows fall. But you must come now, come and help to seal this new peace. After all, is that not how you are named?"

She let him lead her away toward the great tent where, at least for now, she must greet warriors from the other tribes, who must now be won over as friends and allies. Behind her rose the tribeswomen's lament for Willow, who would be celebrated in death as she never was in life. Silver Snow wondered what she would think of it.

I will say farewell later, she told her friend's memory. *I will never forget you, and, when the time for my own funeral comes, I will join you and we both shall guard these lands, together, for always.*

She blinked away her tears and cocked her head. Abruptly she gasped, her hands going to her belly. Gazing at her, Vughturoi stopped in alarm, his scarred face turning gray under its weathering. He had lost children before to Strong Tongue's spells and poisons, Silver Snow knew.

"Nothing is wrong," she told him. "Our son just kicked me."

"He has his mother's daring," said Vughturoi. "And his mother should sit down."

In that moment and ever afterward, Silver Snow would have sworn that she had heard Willow laugh.

EPILOGUE

Court officials had argued protocol and precedence for months before the heir of the *shan-yu* arrived in Ch'ang-an. He was the subject, too, of much gossip in the Inner Courts. Some even said that his mother had resided there, half a lifetime ago, before being sent into exile upon the plains.

Half barbarian; half Han. Delicious speculation had it that he, like all others of the Hsiung-nu, ate his meat raw or that he was an alchemist, or that a fox-spirit had been his midwife. Rumor ran so wild in the Inner Courts that even the gossip-loving eunuchs had, finally, to suppress it. One thing, though, everyone finally could agree upon. This prince of the Hsiung-nu had come to Ch'ang-an not to argue for a treaty nor to wed a Han princess—at least not yet—but to be educated in the way of his mother's people.

It would be fascinating to see if he could, decided the chief eunuchs, then turned to the more important matter of bribes. These days, ever since the unfortunate Mao Yen-shou had lost his head over the trifling matter of a flawed portrait, one had to be so much more discreet. Perhaps this savage prince would prove to be generous.

The young man who finally arrived in Ch'ang-an, accompanied by a troop of dour and fully armed horsemen, wore silks and furs. A lute hung beside his bow upon his saddle, and he spoke the tongue of Ch'in with elegance and propriety. Even the warriors who rode with him and who had been chosen for patience and steadiness (which meant that there were but a few, far fewer than should have accompanied the *shan-yu*'s heir) muttered at the height and breadth of the city's walls. They had been warned by the *shan-yu* not to think of Ch'ang-an simply as a larger, more permanent winter camp; it seemed more like a huge trap, a . . . the word was *prison*, a fixed abode into which men were hurled and from which they could not escape. *It was my mother's city, my mother's land*, the prince had told them; and, respecting Silver Snow as much as they did her son, they nodded and accepted what they could not change.

For a moment, however, the prince rebelled in thought. He was a free man of the grasslands and desert, used to riding where he would. How could anyone expect him to spend what might be years of his life pent within walls and under roofs? Behind him, his men muttered, and the Ch'in soldiers who accompanied them closed in, looking dour.

Those dour looks steadied him. He flashed his warriors a warning look, knowing that they would feel shame that he must thus reprove them in the presence of men of Ch'in, who wanted only to regard them as savages. If he had not protested, they must not either.

He had not protested when his father had ordered him to Ch'ang-an; the *shan-yu* Vughturoi was the chosen under heaven, and it was unthinkable to oppose him, as even his own brother had learned. Was it not Vughturoi who had consolidated all of the warring clans of the Hsiung-nu?

And just as he dared not present himself to his father as aught but an obedient, loyal son, he certainly could not fail in duty when his mother sat nearby, her thin, fragile fingers holding some piece of stitching, which he could see, and the reins of his father's heart and his, which he could not. It was not just unfilial to disappoint her: it was unthinkable.

So tiny she was, her once-pale skin weathered by half a

lifetime spent among the Hsiung-nu out under the holy sky, her dark, thoughtful eyes webbed in a fine network of wrinkles from staring into vast distances, either of the grasslands themselves or her own thoughts, her incredibly long braids frosted with a silver snow like that of the name that only the *shan-yu* dared to speak.

His journey to her home meant a great deal to her, he knew. He might, warrior to warrior, have protested being sent to what was, for a Hsiung-nu, a luxurious prison; Vughturoi his father had lived among the Han and could sense his unease and distaste. But what of the lady his mother, who had accepted exile from her own people? So tiny she was, and so frail; but so brave withal. Had he not heard the tales, since he was old enough to sit his first horse, of how she thrust herself before the ruler of the Yueh-chih and mended the old quarrel that had abetted treason and nearly brought on another war? His mother was the queen who had brought peace to the Hsiung-nu; a year of his life within walls was a small gift if it pleased her.

With as much courage as he would have faced a battle, he rode through the city, confronted rank upon rank of officials, and, ultimately, was allowed the supreme felicity of hurling himself at the feet of the Son of Heaven. When he rose, he held out a roll of silk, carefully sealed against dust and storm. He cautioned himself that anything he said or did might reflect not just upon the Hsiung-nu but upon the lady who had left these courts to lead them. Drawing a deep breath in lieu of the weapons that would have been far readier to his hand, he prepared to speak.

"This unworthy one who is permitted to style himself as Khujanga, prince among the Hsiung-nu, begs leave to greet the Son of Heaven," he began. Some officials frowned at his audacity; the eldest among them remembered that his mother, too, had had a history of being . . . unconventional might be the most tactful way of expressing it. The lady had taught him the trick of observing such men from the corners of his eyes and of reading the tiny signals of approval or disfavor that they sent to one another; it was a gift for which he was grateful.

"His father, the *shan-yu*, and his mother, she who brings peace to the Hsiung-nu, bow themselves before the Son of Heaven, and beg him to receive this wretched one within his courts to learn the ways of the Middle Kingdom, most illustrious under heaven."

The Son of Heaven nodded and, very faintly, smiled. Although the prince had promised himself that he would not care what such a soft creature—with his silks, his stiff cap, his Dragon Throne, and these oppressive walls—might think of him, he sighed inwardly in relief.

The court relaxed, and the Emperor beckoned the Hsiung-nu prince closer for a brief, precious moment of almost private speech. To Prince Khujanga's surprise, warmth lurked in the Emperor's wise, sly eyes.

"Your mother's letters, all these years, have informed us well. Aye, and told us—allowing for a mother's favor—what manner of young man we now welcome. Be as a son within our walls. We shall try to make your stay pleasant, and not too confining." Then, as if he had delivered the message that he had set himself, he turned to matters of state. "Now, your mother has told me about the barbarians to the west."

It surprised Khujanga that the Son of Heaven included him on the inside of that comment: it was the westerners, not the Hsiung-nu, whom he considered the barbarians. "What can you tell me about them, and what else does she say?"

Khujanga had been primed for that moment, ready with his opinions of the men from beyond the Roof of the World and their horses. Before he spoke of them, however, he owed his mother to deliver one more message and one more gift.

"This one's mother sends her greetings and her observations, contained in her letter. And she begs the Son of Heaven to receive this for her who keeps his tents!"

With a flourish that suited a Hsiung-nu feast better than it did the Bright Court of Ch'ang-an, the young prince beckoned, and two of his men laid a chest before the Dragon Throne. The prince himself knelt to open it.

It held a suit of jade armor, cunningly fastened with delicate gold wire, the mate to the suit that, years ago, the Lady Silver Snow had presented to the Son of Heaven.

We're happy to share with you our fascination with the history and culture of Ch'in, a fascination of which this book is just the latest part.

Imperial Lady, although it is a work of fantasy, is based on an historical incident that has become one of the most beloved of Chinese tales and has served as the inspiration for countless poems and stories: the life of Chao Chun, the concubine who became, first, a princess of the Han dynasty, and, second, the queen of the *shan-yu* of the Hsiung-nu, the fierce, nomadic people who are, to a great extent, the ancestors of the Huns and Mongols.

In a graceful and useful book, *The Purple Wall: The Story of the Great Wall of China* (London: Robert Hale, Ltd., 1960), Peter Lum describes the Chao Chun of Han dynasty history as the daughter of a Hupei official. Like our own Silver Snow, the Chao Chun who actually lived was beautiful and high-spirited, rejected the offer of the corrupt eunuch-artist Mao Yen-shou, and lived for a time in isolation before she was packed off to marry, first, the *shan-yu* Khujanga, and then his heir, Vughturoi.

That much is history. Thereafter, history and legend co-exist. In some rather romantic accounts of Chao Chun, she throws herself into the Yellow River at the pass between the

291

river and the Great Wall because she cannot bear to leave China. Because of her tears, the grass along the river there is greener than it is anyplace else; and the river there is called the River of the Princess. In other accounts, the "real" Chao Chun bore a son to Khujanga, who died in 31 B.C. (a year after the death of the Emperor Yuan Ti, a date that we have simply altered for the purposes of the story). Thereafter, she indeed married Vughturoi, ruled as queen, with, apparently, a good deal of influence on peaceful relations with China, until 20 B.C. when Vughturoi died, leaving Chao Chun a thirty-three-year-old widow with two daughters by her second husband.

At this point in the story, history again fades into myth. No one knows for certain what happened to Chao Chun. Some say that she died within a few years, others that she died of grief when a new *shan-yu* murdered her son, still others that she and her son were both murdered in A.D. 18. Though she never did return to China, legend has it that she asked to be buried on its borders and that she is indeed buried by the Yellow River, beneath a huge artificial mound that is still called the Tomb of the Flower Garden of Chao Chun.

Also a part of history are the suits of jade armor, which are meticulously described and most beautifully photographed in Edmund Capon and William MacQuitty's *Princes of Jade* (London: Thomas Nelson & Sons, Ltd., 1973), which deals with the discovery on June 27, 1968, of the bodies of the Han dynasty Prince Liu Sheng and his consort Princess Tou Wan, which were decked in precisely the type of jade armor that we have given to Silver Snow.

We take much of the rest of the story from the many fine books that Western writers have provided to introduce 5,000 years of an astonishing wealth of culture to Western readers, whose knowledge of one of the most ancient civilizations on Earth is all too often limited to "here be dragons" on the map or "one from column A" on a Chinese menu. In the past thirty years, however, interest in China has flourished, extended far beyond the province of scholars, explorers, and the somewhat eccentric "China hands" of the nineteenth and early twentieth centuries.

For those readers who might be interested in learning more about the poetry and history of Han and Hsiung-nu alike, we would like to suggest Michael Loewe's *Crisis and Conflict in Han China* (London: Allen & Unwin, 1974), which provided the inspiration for the story of Silver Snow's father, as well as Loewe's *Everyday Life in Early Imperial China* (London: B.T. Batsford, 1968).

The fourth- or fifth-century Sun Tzu's *The Art of War*, with a foreword by General Basil Liddell Hart (Oxford University Press, 1963), is undergoing somewhat of a renaissance of its own in the wake of current interest in Eastern martial arts.

Otto J. Maenchen-Helfen's monumental *The World of the Huns* (University of California, 1973) is probably the standard work on the Huns and Hsiung-nu, and is far more readable than it appears.

Finally, the poems in *Imperial Lady* are taken from actual verse from the Han and T'ang Dynasties; they are drawn, primarily, from two volumes and used with permission: *The Orchid Boat: Woman Poets of China*, translated and edited by Kenneth Rexroth and Ling Chung (New York: McGraw Hill, 1972); and *Translations from the Chinese* by Arthur Waley (Knopf, 1941).

We would also like to acknowledge our indebtedness to Dr. Morris Rossabi, director of The China Institute, in New York City.

Whether you actually do travel to China (as we would like to do) or travel no farther than your own bookstore, we wish you a happy and rewarding journey.

Andre Norton,
Winter Park, Florida

Susan Shwartz,
Forest Hills, New York

February 1988

THE BEST IN FANTASY

Buy them at your local bookstore or use this handy coupon:
Clip and mail this page with your order.

Publishers Book and Audio Mailing Service
P.O. Box 120159, Staten Island, NY 10312-0004

Please send me the book(s) I have checked above. I am enclosing $_____
(please add $1.25 for the first book, and $.25 for each additional book to
cover postage and handling. Send check or money order only—no CODs.)

Name _____

Address _____

City _____ State/Zip _____

Please allow six weeks for delivery. Prices subject to change without notice.

ANDRE NORTON

THE BEST IN SCIENCE FICTION

THE TOR DOUBLES

Two complete short science fiction novels in one volume!

BESTSELLING BOOKS FROM TOR